WORDS OF POWER QUEST

WORDS OF
POWER QUEST

COZY

PARTRIDGE

To order additional copies of this book, contact
Toll Free 800 101 2657 (Singapore)
Toll Free 1 800 81 7340 (Malaysia)
orders.singapore@partridgepublishing.com

www.partridgepublishing.com/singapore

PROLOGUE

Kotsuba Musashi.

Hearing that name would instil the image of that one Word of Power hunter. Kotsuba Musashi was that sort of man – A slim, well-built being without any notable scars, wearing a simple tanned leather coat and chitin pants with hair the colour of charcoal. It was easy to distinguish his Ohdean background from other hunters out there.

He paused to behold a place abandoned for the longest of time. With the flooring and walls riddled with soot it was no doubt a strange room. The ceiling had been wiped off by some form of attack revealing the strange inter-dimensional space surrounding the room, a quiet and perpetual swirl of colours too bountiful to describe. Broken debris of the pillars and walls lay on the rotten panels which comprised the floors.

Kotsuba Musashi finally arrived at one of the mythical Sealed Rooms which supposedly housed a Word of Power within. Rumoured to be fragments of castles decades ago, various rooms were ripped from their citadels in entirety and sealed within the strange distorted dimension away from the vile claws of Man. But there he stood, with the resilience and triumphant valour befitting a representative – In defiance of it all.

In the centre of the room was a peculiar pillar with its surface eroded briefly. The pillar was floating above the ground tilted at a forty-five-degree angle with the bottom pointing toward the entry point. Just slightly above the base was a word of Anikan origin radiantly brimming with a golden light.

One ought to have been happy at this sight. To reach the mythical Sealed Room with a Word of Power before oneself, anyone would have gladly accepted the great power with open arms. And yet Musashi's face twisted into a heavy, anguished look of disbelief.

M: "No..."

He was blatantly horrified by what was before him. With his eyes fixated on the golden character, he slowly dragged his feet across the dusty and foul wooden panels. The warning signals in his mind flared and the slight depression of the rotting planks with every step noisily dissuaded him from approaching the Word of Power any further.

Eventually, he stopped short before the column. He recognized that character in his native tongue. But he knew it meant something else in its entirety, something supposed to be spoken in a different language and intonation. That character was 定. It sported many names when read from different perspectives but in its truest, original tongue was pronounced Dìng.

M: "No... No! NO!!"

Kotsuba Musashi collapsed, the life and vigour from before evaporated. He looked up towards his prize while clutching the sides of his head with both hands. From a distance he looked quite insane had what he uttered been left unheard.

M: "This... This wasn't supposed to happen! The most heavily guarded Word of Power should have been 再! Why is it 定!?"

The undeniable fact was almost cackling at his grimace. He shook his head ever so slightly, refusing to believe the reality before his eyes. But there it was – In its greatest glory the golden word was the only thing resting upon the barren and battered pillar.

M: (All the lives lost... All the resources sacrificed. All of that could be rewound if I had 再 to create a 再度 concept. All of it didn't have to go to waste if only it had been 再!!)

He could not even cough. Had that word been something else, it would have been different. Had that word been what he sought he could have saved them all.

M: (There's no bringing them back... I don't have the dignity to walk back alone like this, with them dead. I needed 再, not 定.)

The power to revive the dead and recover the resources expended was certainly valuable enough to risk it that far... Yet it all came to naught over misinformation. His will wavering, his resolve shaken. Musashi looked at the pillar above his head once more.

M: (... I dare not take it.)

He was afraid. Had he taken that word and went back to Rugnud he would be ostracised as a cold-blooded murderer who used others for personal gain; a merciless, dishonourable monster who threw the lives of others away to achieve the end-goal.

He did not want that. In his hands it would be viewed as something obtained through conniving means. The act would be misjudged by the corrupt eyes of the people who sought after it, and those hands of his would be branded by and stained in the blood of the people he didn't kill.

Musashi did not mean for this to happen. His head drooped into a position where it was just dangling on his neck. He looked down at his attire, stained with the blood of those who had given their lives willingly.

He remembered the owners of the stains clearly.

The spattered drops were from the young man Rohat, impaled by a spear wall. A joyful, sprightly child at heart with a loving wife and a great future ahead of himself dead from a moment of folly before an unexpected trap.

The smudge of blood and grime belonged to his childhood friend Dekomura, who gave his life to redirect a swine down a cliff. Unfortunately, the boar's tusk incised a great wound on his left thigh and the persistent Bloodswarm locusts made his wound fester that much faster.

In the end, he too succumbed to fate. And despite that, Dekomura's final words...

He offered Musashi his corpse to disable the traps ahead such that his chances of reaching the Word of Power may heighten, as little as it may be. The moments of their deaths flashed before his eyes in an instant. The valiance and dignity they had in order to ensure that the expedition was a success would be sullied by those greedy hyenas in human skins.

He couldn't accept the Word of Power. Those very lives would have had their sacrifices pinned upon him wrongfully. Those very people who looked up to Musashi as a model would weep and turn in their graves when they learn of their families' spite towards the man they gave their lives willingly for. And yet, he could not let their deaths be in vain.

M: (Everyone... I have let you down. I'm truly sorry. As much as you have put into obtaining this for me, I can't accept it.)

Musashi stared blankly at his body, his head devoid of energy and his eyes losing their brilliance. His focus was, unconsciously, locked onto a specific part of his field of vision.

A vial. A vial dangling from his neck, with a cloudy white liquid within.

It was his lucky charm should he be killed on the job – A bottle of his own semen to carry on his heritage.

M: "...!"

Luster returned to his pupils and he grabbed the vial on his neck gently, but quickly. He sprang up determined. The solution had been under his nose the entire time. He dangled the vial in his hand and slowly tapped it on the pillar. In accordance to his desires the golden character faded away and the vial flared a brilliant, equally radiant glow.

M: (I will never live with myself had I taken this power. I won't be able to answer the dead respectfully. That is why, my precious child, please understand... This is Daddy's only gift to you. Cherish it well, my sweet child.)

He uttered to himself while clasping the vial in his hands. Or perhaps, he was speaking to someone?

M: "Let's go home... Katachi."

He gave the room one last look and exited from whence he came, a door which was not a door, the only entrance and exit of the Sealed Room. And with that, Kotsuba Musashi's days as a Word of Power Hunter ended with his failure.

But what of the 定 he gifted the semen?

CHAPTER 1

A.D. 1569, end of the Month of the Cane.

In his eyes reflected the all-encompassing sky that was no longer blue. It was a sky covered with clouds, an overcast that blanketed the lands. The farmers nearby rejoiced at the gift of rain. Women complained and hurriedly kept their laundry. Children sat by the small windows to await the ritual of Sharyu Zuku to begin, and people hastened their footsteps to avoid getting their clothes wet.

Katachi sat there motionlessly with tired eyes.

K: (The sky is vast...)

His face twisted and expressed a deep longing. Naturally, if dreamers were allowed their desires so easily, they would dream no longer.

K: (Can I fly in it, away from here?)

He stretched his left hand up towards the sky and clasped it gently. A small bird flew past and his eyes followed its petite visage. How he wished he could fly freely, like the bird. If given the opportunity, he would have given everything he had in order to escape town. But what had he to sacrifice, a mere child without a name or anything else to give up on? Alas, what the mind wanted was what the body could never have. He relaxed his left arm and it landed on the soft grass and soil with a thud.

"Katachi! Help me keep the laundry, will you?"

A familiar voice called out to him, a little hasty and rushed, yet with a gentle tone befitting of a nun.

K: "I'm on my way, Mother!"

He slowly shifted his weight between both legs and stood up stretching his arms and stomach. Katachi brushed off a few stalks of grass and dirt attached to his ragged pants and headed towards her.

*** Achievement: Pluviophilia ***

Before he even began to remember things, Katachi was abandoned by his parents.

1

The reason and cause were unknown, and as much as the young man wished to find his real parents he knew he couldn't. What was a nine-year-old supposed to do when nobody was willing to give him the slightest of clue? All he knew was that when he was found, a wooden tablet with "Kotsuba Katachi" carved on it was tied to his ankle. He knew nothing else regarding his parents.

Mother Rinnesfeld, or Mother Rin in short, was a kind soul who found him crying on a soft patch of grass at the outskirts of town. She nursed and raised him as her own against the wishes of the other townsfolk. He was a second mouth to feed at home, but that was not a problem for the formidable nun. The townsfolk however did not take his arrival with equal cordiality.

Adults branded him a bastard child. Children hurled rocks and nasty insults at him because their parents encouraged the behaviour. The abuse he had to endure was, simply put, inhumane. The only ones who hadn't the desire to gouge his eyes or abuse his stature were the elderly whom he had been kind to, and Mother Rinnesfeld herself.

Katachi's childhood was littered with horrible memories, so many he wished for amnesia. He would rather not recall any of them, if it were possible.

His only happy memories were of those he enjoyed with Mother Rin and when he was alone. In the library or open in the fields near where the forests lay, the groves of trees they were warned of; or on the familiar herb ledge where he could admire the carefree children from afar toying and teasing the Plaincoat sheep in morbid silence.

Even when neck-deep in that cruelty and despair, he clung on tightly to hope and isolation in defence. Many would think he'd grow up to become a wretched and cruel person considering the circumstances he was thrown into.

And yet Mother Rin insisted that he should be kind to others.

R: "Listen very carefully, Katachi. It's very important."

The first time he came back crying at the age of four, Mother Rin comforted him.

R: "I'm about to tell you something that will make you sad. I love you a lot, I really do, but I am not actually your mother. Well, that's not quite right... I am not the mother that gave birth to you. You were just outside the town, lying on a patch of grass near a field of medicinal herbs. Your parents may be dead and they may have given their lives to ensure you were safe."

That was bound to crush a child's heart, under normal circumstances. But none could break what was already broken.

R: "But don't worry, Katachi. Mother is here for you. Come."

Katachi remembered the warmth of Mother Rin's bosom and arms clearly when she hugged him. It was that cozy, comforting, accepting warmth which made him relax and feel that he was loved. His urge to cry was suppressed immediately and he reciprocated Mother Rin's motherly snuggle.

R: "That is the first thing you need to know. Mother may not have given birth to you, but Mother wants to be able to love you like how your mother would have wanted to. Is that okay?"

In that sentence, he believed her. He believed in the Mother Rinnesfeld who never saw a reason to lie with the intent to hurt, who always kept that radiant and unfaltering smile regardless of anything in life that impeded progress. She was without a doubt a nun truly worth admiring. Katachi remembered a flashback where one of the adults in town on the pillory accepted all of the bad words and insults from the townsfolk without flinching.

R: "The second thing I want to tell you is also really important. Are you ready?"

With that one adult as his model he mimicked the man with much effort. Katachi took a deep breath and exhaled, gearing himself to accept anything.

R: "You have to treat others with kindness, Katachi. Though they may be in the wrong, though they may hurl rocks and bad words at you, you must never forget to be kind to them. They may be immature right now and might do silly things in a moment of folly, but you have to bear with it and reply with kindness. There will come a day where they will realise their wrongdoings and regret doing those things."

Her words were empowering and it held a wisdom Katachi took to heart.

R: "I don't want you to suffer from the same fate, Katachi dear. Should they do nasty things to you again, I want you to act in my stead and nicely let their insults slide. Okay?"

Mother Rin's love and guidance coupled with the townsfolk's vicious behaviour towards him forced Katachi to warp and mature at an abnormally fast rate; when compared to other children and even the young adults he was perhaps maturing too quickly, forming a rather large anomaly among the children.

R: "So, smile for Mother now, okay? Everything is all right."

Yet, as much as Mother Rin made sense with her insight, he did not run towards her crying because he was bullied. It had been for another reason – One not even she would have expected.

*** ***

K: (This madness... No more shall it plague us. If I must give my life, I shall do so for Mother who has taken such great care of me. Such that the ones to come after me would be free from it... Such that the people after me suffer no more.)

*** ***

In that thought alone he consigned himself to a cruel fate. As he hit the age of ten, he was finally old enough to enrol in a famous institute – the Sage Raufid Magus Academy. Katachi picked up a poster of an event known as the Young Magus Tournament, and he steeled himself to overcome that first hurdle.

He packed his stuff and prepared to set off almost immediately. Being the poor child he was, he had little to carry with him except the clothes on his back and some documents to certify his identity as a new student. Should the worst happen he prepared some herbs with him for the possible myriad of different situations he could end up in.

R: "Be sure to sleep well, eat well and grow up properly, okay, Katachi dear? You can come back any time."

The nun looked back at him with tears in her eyes as she held the wrists of the young boy gently. She was clearly saddened by his departure but it was impossible for change not to transpire. Besides, not all changes were negative in nature.

K: "Of course, Mother. I'll come back and visit every couple of moon cycles."

Katachi straightened the strap to that shoddy and flimsy thing he called a bag and entered the unmanned carriage dispatched by the school. He began his life on a new world stage.

CHAPTER 2

Before the young ten-year-old was a huge facility that gave off a castle-like feel.

It was a plot of land given to an aristocrat and a great sorceror by the name of Raufid, a sage who sought to expand the understanding of magic. To have built an entire academy to service the public and cultivate the potential magi of the world, the place was worshipped as a sacred ground to a couple of notable figures of the world.

He wasn't used to such a classy sight. With much hesitation Katachi entered the building after receiving a leery glare from the gardener. As he set foot into the grandeur hall, his eyes locked onto the first thing he saw – The great interior of the academy.

The elegant, strange design of the place appalled him. The chandeliers were shaped irregularly and some had magic seals on them he would identify if not for the distance between the ceiling and his face. The pillars were not straight ones that normal people used to support buildings, and they twisted and spun in such wayward directions it seemed as if the building was the one supporting them. An orange rug was laid out in the centre almost beckoning 'Right this way, guest of honour'.

At a small corner of the eloquent view was a familiar existence that ruined the entire flavour of that wonder.

"Hah. I didn't think an orphan like you would be allowed to attend this school."

He remembered that voice. That accursed and all-too-familiar voice brought him much suffering. There were three people in Mielfeud that constantly picked on him.

The first was Juval, a big brute who was the raw strength of the three. He would grab Katachi by his ragged cloth shirt and drag him to a dark alley. To the pygmy-like Katachi he was a juggernaut who handled the poor child roughly, although he was never aggressive and abusive as his size suggested. He had been here at the academy once, only to be sent back to Mielfeud as a labour man because he wasn't adept at magic.

The youngest was Zirco, the scheming brains of the group. He wasn't necessarily bad, but his mouth spewed forth the lies and slander that garnered the spite of others. He had probably been here at the Sage Raufid Magus Academy for about a year since he was two years younger than Juval.

And the lone figure before him was the savage one in the group who would hurt him physically and mentally, the one who wrought strength from companionship and took pride in whatever superiority he could eke from the shambling Ohdean figure.

K: "Hello again, Dante."

D: "Don't talk to me in such a friend-like manner! You're just a bastard child unwanted by your parents!"

Katachi clenched his fist tightly and took a few short breaths to calm down before relaxing his grip.

K: "I have no reason to take your humiliation here."

D: "Hah! Are you a coward?"

Katachi remembered Mother Rin's words in his heart – They were still immature, so their acts differ little from a fool's. He saw no reason to be dragged into Dante's pace. With that preceding his baseless insults Katachi walked up the steps towards the second level.

D: "You'll never be able to use magic. You'll be sent back to Mielfeud and live the rest of your days as a lame and dirt-poor priest! You'll always be a coward who's all talk and no action! Get back here, you little shit!"

"Shut up!!"

It seemed as though a teacher felt disturbed by Dante's actions and was now scolding him for misbehaviour. The teacher placed some sort of seal on the magic circle at the top of his arm, most likely for misconduct or something along those lines.

K: (This is new. The adults actually stood up for me.)

He had never received such treatment from a stranger, not even once. To the child it was a shock that he was defended by someone else, much less cared for. It made him shudder that he was denied of such overwhelming protection until mere moments ago.

*** ***

"Good morning, child. What's your name?"

Before him was a strange man who stood out from the other faculty. He wore a crisp green fancy uniform with a white under-shirt and red tie. He had a peculiar hat made out of a strange green jelly-like material shaped into a top hat. From what he could remember those beings were called Slimes.

Soft, brainless and resilient towards physical trauma, it was an obscure animated blob which did not share the anatomy one would expect of a living creature. Why the man before him was wearing one as a hat, though, was beyond any realm of reasoning Katachi could surmise.

But it fascinated him. Such a strange creature told of only in the books of old, from a time where monsters existed, sitting there quietly in its own little world... And yet, the terrors it could induce. It was best to leave it be.

K: "I'm Katachi. Kotsuba Katachi. I... turned ten just a week ago."

"A new student, aren't you?"

In his hand was a strangely-shaped snack that resembled a lizard of sorts roasted over a flame and eaten out from its belly.

K: "Is... Is that a newt on a stick?"

"My, how observant. Most students here don't even know what a newt is."

He licked his lips and took another bite from the abdomen. The right leg of the newt snapped off easily as he pulled the stick away from his face. It made a squishy, chewy sound within his mouth which gave Katachi a good number of goose bumps.

"That astuteness will definitely help you in becoming someone great one day. Right then, your perceptual ability aside. Do you have anything to show me?"

K: "I... I do."

Hearing Katachi stammer was not something people heard often. On the other hand, as he was constantly oppressed since young Katachi lacked social interaction with people except Mother Rin. It was understandable how he panicked speaking to others.

K: "But... Could you get the teacher standing there to go outside first, please?"

Most students upon meeting a stranger would be jittery if they performed poorly on a first impression. However, Katachi was nervous for a different reason.

"Feeling pressured from eyes watching you? I understand. Take your leave, Yorn."

With a grunt the huge teacher with a large upper torso squeezed his way through the small space and left the room.

"What could be so important that no others are allowed their eyes upon?"

Katachi's hands felt cold. He extended his palm and approached the desk with it.

K: (Should I do it? He's suspicious, but he seems pretty broad-minded seeing how he just readily accepts me being observant. It's... It's a gamble. Okay. Here goes.)

With a mere thought, a glowing golden character was formed on it. A small amount of smoke appeared from the book right next to the character.

*** ***

"That was a marvellous display, Mister Kotsuba. That kind of power can get you into the best class easily; in fact, you might not even stay in this school for long if you keep growing at this rate."

Katachi was kind of happy at being called a 'mister' but it was not the time to be elated.

K: "I don't want a 'best class', actually. I want a curriculum that can maximize my own potentials."

He uttered it with flawless replication of Mother Rin's words.

K: "The best is a standard set by the one who has achieved it. I would want something to be set for me, not by someone I could never become."

The man's eyes widened a little as he nodded in agreement.

"Interesting. You truly are interesting, Mister Kotsuba. Most children would blindly go for the 'best class' because it offers the greatest diversity in finding their own affinities in magic, but it seems you have your heart set on what you already own, no?"

K: "Yes."

Katachi felt kind of glad to be around the strange man – He was unusually comfortable to talk to, despite dressing in such an awkward manner.

"I understand. Here is a magic circle indicating your official registration into our school."

The green-attired man snapped a glove snugly over his left hand and placed his palm on top of Katachi's arm. A slight burning sensation was felt and a circle was tattooed onto his skin.

"I really love it when students wear clothes as ragged as these. It may be chilly in the long run, but that beats having to roll up your sleeves to place these magic circles. Convenience is a luxury, as they say."

Katachi shrugged his left shoulder a little bit to get a better look at the newly-added seal.

K: (Maybe he's part of the administrative staff or someone of great authority if he can do something like that.)

"Don't worry. That seal identifies you as an Academy student. It wears off when you leave this area and vice versa."

A simple magic circle with markings he did not recognise. Though he felt some discomfort on his skin, there were no marks or scars from the act. He quietly wondered the nature of the spell before deciding against it.

K: (At least it's not permanent or anything.)

B: "In any case, welcome to the Sage Raufid Magus Academy! I'm your principal and the descendant of Sage Raufid, Bertund. There's magic all over the corridors and walls so you just need to close your eyes, think of your destination and walk forward naturally. It will guide you directly, so there's no need to be afraid of getting lost."

Bertund wagged his finger around as a gesture to represent the magic's assumed omnipresence.

K: (It was kind of obvious that he was the principal, now that I think about it. He asked the teacher to exit the office. That means the office belongs to him since he didn't invite me out to talk.)

B: "The magic is unlocked only during the day and it is fixed at night, which means even if you try to sneak out during curfew you'd be redirected back to your room. Enjoy your stay here, Mister Kotsuba. I'll be heading back to work now, so if you need anything just imagine my attire and you will know how to get to me."

K: "Okay."

The circumstances of his unusual attire began to make sense. If there were ever a dire need for his audience finding the green man would be easy.

B: "One last thing – Take it easy just for today and wander about the school, enjoy the scenery, remember the places if you have to. Walking and admiring without thinking of where you want to go is the secret to countering this magic. You'll receive your time table soon, so enjoy yourself until then."

With a wave he invited Yorn back into the room and closed the wooden door with a gentle click.

CHAPTER 3

The wooden-soled shoes clacked noisily in the hallway.

In cases where most students came from Bellpot or other large cities, their shoes would be fashioned from nicely polished leather with a fresh smell which felt slightly foreign and uncomfortable; a gift from their parents who handed its maintenance to them, a sample of the responsibilities that came with adulthood.

Katachi had no such luxury to get those well-furbished shoes, having grown up with Mother Rinnesfeld who believed that Nature had much to offer those who worked hard. Of course, physical vanity and the like were barely problems for Mother Rinnesfeld and Katachi who used Nature sparingly and expressed their gratitude whenever they did.

Regardless, everyone in the vicinity twenty meters away from where Katachi stood could hear the noisy wooden sabots plopping and clacking on the marble floor.

K: (Bertund wasn't kidding... They all have their heads fixed to their front as they walk. But how do they change the spell's conditions from day and night? It's probably controlled by some kind of ritual circle, but what was it based around? Did they put something to determine when the magic changes in phase?)

A group of girls who were casually chatting with each other noticed the wooden plopping getting louder and clearer. They stopped to stare outside their class at a completely clueless young boy in ragged attire.

"Who is he? Why is he wearing those shoes?"

"Is he a new student?"

"Ugh, he looks so filthy! Look at how worn-out his clothes are!"

His distinctive differences were picked on instantly. Students who went to the Sage Raufid Magus Academy often came from rich and poor families alike but he did not expect the difference in ancestry to be so apparent.

There was a rather large group of those rich children who were talking to each other in a prideful manner, flaunting their riches and such before the others. It was obvious because their uniforms were hemmed with gold and silver which symbolised their wealth. Their bags were of a high-quality shiny leather that reflected the sun's rays similar to their shoes.

They stood with their chests puffed out and arms crossed, trying their best to impress the others in the group with their parents' monetary power and influence. Among the five who stood, one was a female who even flaunted her chest in a prideful stance. She deliberately straightened her back and thrust her sternum forward in plain view.

There was another group who had normal uniforms, classic cloth knapsacks and simple shoes. They were reading the scrolls and books they brought, twiddling their thumbs and discussing something about Axia which Katachi presumed was a subject or chapter they studied. The students grouped like so were obviously those of a lower status or class, a middle-class group who probably ended up in that class by scoring roughly the same as the rich. With that single image one conclusion was made clear.

K: (It appears that the classes here are formed and based on magic compatibility instead of status, hierarchy and ranking. They're centralising and improving the quality of the magically adept by giving them reliable yet relevant competitiveness amongst their classmates. It's still too soon to judge, so I'll keep that as a possibility.)

That was surprisingly accurate had he voiced out that thought for others to hear. In fact, that very notion would creep out most of the other children. How objectively Katachi viewed something as simple as a brief glance into the classroom was by no means a feat for a child.

But that was the very same perceptiveness which allowed him to reach where he was today – Alive.

He wished not to entertain the onlookers now focused on the clear, resonant noise outside the door. Katachi got away as fast as his feet could carry.

*** ***

The entire school and its structures were bewitching and eye-opening to the point where remembering every detail would need one to use those halls repeatedly. Katachi had yet finished admiring one of the more interesting 'attractions' thus far when he had long passed it.

Earlier, he bumped into something while walking backwards with his head turned to face the weeping willow statue. Since turning around to look behind him would set the 'destination' to his rear, the magic continuously forced his body to twist to his left repeatedly and pace back and forth a two-tile wide area.

In turn, that forcibly made Katachi 'dance' to an awkward tune. It wasn't a good thing either since he was causing quite the scene with his already-distracting wooden sabots. Having experienced that once, it was safe to say that turning to look backwards was by no means a good idea under the influence of that magic.

K: (That magic itself is flawed in its own way as well... Ugh. I feel like throwing up.)

The disorientation he felt was overwhelming and Katachi soon found himself in a garden upon regaining his composure without any clue on how he got there. The pavilion to his left was covered in a lot of vines, showing the neglect it suffered. Though it had creeper plants all over the pillars and roof it was perfectly clean in the centre, if anyone put effort into dusting.

Perhaps the seat area was enchanted or made with a certain life-rejecting material blessed by Vithrolu, which would explain why the pavilion was full of nature and yet the centre was devoid of life. To his right-

K: (... ? What is that?)

-was a strange wire attached to a small, well-hidden magic circle on one end and one of the pavilion's pillar on the other.

K: (Why is there thread here? I have never seen spiders spin their webs like that- No, the line is too thick to be spider thread. It's more like a wire based on the reflective surface and texture. What is it doing here?)

Out of curiosity he tapped on the wire expecting it to be strummed or depressed under his finger. The instant he touched the contraption, however-

K: "Wha- !?"

-it burned out into an ethereal realm with a purple tracer leaving nothing behind. The magic circle connected to the tree burned with a sinister vermilion. Tiny bits of what seemed to be fingernails, dead bugs, a beak of a crow and the like floated in mid-air. The tiny pointed pieces were all primed towards Katachi.

K: (Is this... a trap?!)

Within a second of them floating and suspending in mid-air they zipped towards Katachi in a menacing, merciless omnidirectional pincer attack. In that swift instant, the only thing one could do was think. It was a trap made deliberately to assault an opponent without giving them the chance to react. The purpose of its design was to ensure that one could not dodge or cast a spell to shield themselves in time.

Thankfully for the black-haired boy, having time to think was more than enough.

K: (恒定! Constant status – Self!)

A coarse dry whisper exhaled the words out in the back of his head. Two words formed on Katachi's body faster than an instant.

One of the words, 定, radiated with a golden glow. It was placed directly on his stomach region above the shirt which would have made the cast word obvious. The other word, 恒, had a very faint, smoky and grey outline resembling a whiff of a cloud. It was formed the same time as the character 定 but proved to be completely unstable as it had already begun dissipating the very moment it was formed.

The small dart-like objects cleanly landed onto him and dozens of clicks could be heard at that moment. However, 'landing' on him was all it did. The objects were fairly small and did not seem to carry any power in itself. Even if Katachi had not used the Word of Power as a shield he would probably have lived through the trap.

That was only true if the tiny shards did not possess any secrets. For example, had they been coated with poison or some sort of debilitating magic, using the Word of Power for protection was the right choice to nullify its effects. It could have been worth gambling the fact that it did not have secrets, and he could have taken the attack head-on. But Katachi chose not to take the risk since there was no benefit to it. In the first place, setting up a trap that complex seemed too much an effort for it to be a mere prank.

K: (Had I been late I might have died. They may be small, but the speed they were flying at was not to be laughed at. That was a speed meant to maim, not as a harmless prank like those boys who used to dump buckets of sludge on me.)

Katachi brushed the small objects off of his body. He escaped a potentially perilous trap, but he was in greater danger.

K: (...! Oh no! Fade off, fade off quickly!!)

The word melted away from his torso in slightly more than half a second. Katachi took furtive glances around quickly and tried his best to locate anyone who could have spotted him. With only the cries of crickets and cicadas filling the area he finally loosened up and gasped in relief quietly.

It was instantaneous and took no more than a second, but that was still incredibly risky – Had anybody seen that obvious Word of Power he would be busted on the very day he enrolled. That was something he would with all of his power avoid at any cost. Katachi silently thanked Segus for his safety, and continued walking through the garden.

*** ***

The garden was an important piece of history within the Sage Raufid Magus Academy. It was a special place of many flora and fauna isolated in a plane known as Cosmatral Neud. Sage Raufid wanted to preserve as much life as possible during the warring days, so he invested a large amount of gold and sought to make Cosmatral Neud possible by recruiting the aid of many other sorcerors.

Unfortunately, the redirection magic was absent in the garden which also meant that the place was a frequent hiding spot for some of the more flippant students. At least, that was until the arrival of a certain foul-smelling woman. But her presence, unlike Katachi's, was not damaging at all. Rather, her interesting disposition there served to bolster the plants with more fertilizer.

In contrast Katachi may potentially undo whatever efforts the previous custodians achieved in the garden. Of course, so long as he did not enter the place with the intent to destroy everything Katachi was always welcome into Cosmatral Neud. His Word of Power was not something any force of nature could handle, so should it run amok the disturbed wildlife may react unfavourably.

He reached his left hand into his slimy hat and scratched the centre of his head. The slime wriggled excitedly in response to the familiar foreign object tickling it up from the inside.

Y: "Do you really think it's safe for him to be there, Bertund?"

Yorn spoke with a low baritone and an irritated face. The principal took his hand out from his slime hat and interlocked his fingers together.

B: "It's perfectly safe for him to be there, Yorn. He can storm through the entire garden and Bael's traps like a walk in the park. I'm more concerned about some of the animals there acting up."

His paltry and wayward concern was unsettling.

Y: "He just enrolled today! Surely your expectations in this child are too high?!"

Bertund gave a low, sinister chuckle.

B: "You worry too much, Yorn. We both know you're not that foolish to think that all the magic in the world work on the same dimensions. Or have you forgotten how menacing the Words of Power really are, even individually?"

Yorn's face twisted into a deep frown, unhappy at the fact that he was called foolish. But as a subordinate he could only suck it up and tolerate the tactlessness the principal exuded. Moreover, Bertund's words were well founded and there was little room for rebuttal.

B: "You'll see in due time, Yorn. I'm excited to see how things will turn out."

Y: "What do you-..."

Yorn noticed what Bertund was hinting at.

B: "Indeed. He is closing in on her house. Let's see what will become of this, shall we?"

CHAPTER 4

K: (Is that the gardener's house?)

Katachi stumbled upon a small house made from stone. After a three-minute walk from where that trap was set up, a rather exquisitely built house lay before him. Plain and simple – Those words defined the hut perfectly yet the orange roof and beige walls were oddly clean, just like the pavilion.

With a window at the front and the side, and a small wooden door affixed to the granite walls, it strangely resembled a pumpkin pie house of sorts. The Keep Out sign on the door was not enough to deter his sense of adventure. Katachi pushed the door open gently and peeked into the tiny hut.

The interior could be described in one word – Messy. The cream ceiling and orange walls that contrasted its exterior, the milk carpet and pumpkin furniture, the room gave off a strange homely feeling save for the various occult artifacts and apparatus strewn about. There were magic circles etched on some sheets, a cabinet with too many wooden tablets hung onto its mounted hooks, and to his left a study desk with a cork board for securing pin-up paper documents.

K: (Wow! This... This is a gardener's house?)

He was so enthralled by the sight that he had all but forgotten that he was trespassing.

K: (There are so many things here! A blank magic circuit, a weird circle with webbings at the centre, a sword hung on the wall, a portrait of a Sir Phlegmius with a huge knight's sword engraved with a serpent eating a fish on the blade, a weird... Thing with a handle, I don't even know where to begin!)

Katachi failed to notice the groceries dropping onto the floor at the doorway.

"H-Haah?!"

A piercing cry jolted him from his train of thought and made his shoulders tense up involuntarily.

K: (! Someone's there!)

Katachi recovered from his flinch and snapped around to meet a girl slightly taller than him. She had blonde hair tied into four braids and a bust size comparable to Mount. Gigraceldi, stretching the poor slightly-undersized school uniform rather tightly.

"Who are you!?"

It seemed that the lady was the owner, if not a mere resident of the hut.

K: (She's the gardener!? But... That can't be right. She's wearing the same uniform as those girls inside that classroom. Maybe she's a caretaker or student of some sort? Was she punished to stay in this place away from everyone else, or did she choose to stay here?)

Her inquiring gaze and mouth agape expected an answer from the child, so he introduced himself briefly.

K: "I'm... I'm a new student of Sage Raufid's. My- My lesson was supposed to start tomorrow or the day after, so I just- I just... I..."

Katachi was shocked. All his life, he firmly believed that Mother Rin's chest size were the biggest possible. The nun stressed that a girl's chest was sensitive so only their sires were entitled to touching them and he ought not to take advantage of them, no matter how tempted he may be to retaliate against the vulgar girls in vengeance. Having gone through such a limited education, he came to believe that Mother Rin's chests were the largest a woman could achieve.

K: (What in the- Those are huge! They don't fit her body size at all! Not even Mother Rin's were this big! If they could come in this size, I wonder how big they can actually become...)

The blond girl's presence induced the destruction of an established theory.

"You what?"

The lady before him was seething with rage that he was ogling at her chest blankly.

K: "I... I. I just- Just- Wandered around. T- Trap sprung. Al- Almost got killed... Found the hut, en- en- en- entered here. I- I wa- w- wasn't thinking much, but you have cool- Cool- Cool stuff..."

Talking to a girl face-to-face gave rise to an uncomfortable feeling within him even when they were four meters apart. The fact that he was still stammering, and not frozen on the spot completely like a block of ice was pretty remarkable.

"Pfft! What's with you? There's no need to be this tense, it's not like I'm going- ... !"

The girl scornfully mocked his erratic speech but her face changed into a serious frown as she replayed his words in her head.

"... You sprang the trap?"

K: "Y-yes, I uh... I did. I touched that uh, wire thing, and there were lots of shards that flew towards me."

The girl's eyes widened and her jaw dropped in disbelief.

"Impossible...! Those shards were infused with Vithrolu's decay magic! You were supposed to rot at the parts struck and you should have no control over your body!"

K: (Wha-! I knew the trap wasn't that simple! It was a right choice protecting myself after all!) "A trap that decays bodies?! Who are you!?"

The shock incited his natural instincts to defend himself.

K: (I have no idea what she intends to do after turning me into her puppet. But I'm not going down without a fight!)

Katachi bent his legs a little and hunched his back, lowering his centre of gravity. Should there be a surprise attack just like before he would have to be ready to anticipate and intercept them.

*** ***

(This boy barged into my house and now he wants to fight me? He doesn't seem to know who I am, though. I guess I can try to calm him down for now.)

The rational approach was often the correct one.

B: "I'm Bael. I'm an animationist, or, well, reanimator if you rather that. I live here because my room-mates often complain about a rotting smell coming from me, but I can't help it if I want to be proficient in my studies."

The boy wore a dumb look on his face.

K: (Smell? I don't smell anything.) "You're not going to fight me?"

B: "You're in my house. If anything, I should be the one starting the fight against a stranger like you."

K: "Oh."

The boy lowered his arms and blushed at the misjudged situation. He seemed to have noticed that he was the one intruding and should, therefore, expect to be attacked. To have his guard down for even a slight moment showed how long his road to maturity and situational awareness was.

B: (C- Cute!)

Bael started constructing twisted thoughts in her head.

B: (He's so... So stupid, so pure! He's like a clay doll that's still moist! Mmhmm, I want to mould him into a shape that suits me!)

Her face started to contort into a very wide and sinister smile. The boy must have noticed because he took a few steps back in horror when he noticed the shifting eyebrows and lips on Bael's face.

B: "Let's start over. What's your name?"

The boy retracted his neck further and further.

K: "You're... not going to use my name for some curse or something, are you?"

B: "I can't curse you even if I had your name."

The boy finally let his guard down after hearing that response. He reached his hand out slowly for a handshake and muttered softly.

K: "Then... Katachi. Kotsuba Katachi."

The words escaped his lips in a quick hiss, hiding his emotions well.

B: (Kotsuba? That's... familiar. The structure suggests that he might have come from the Far East, or maybe his parents did. Is he an Ohdean?) "I see. It's nice to meet you, Kotsuba Katachi."

She uttered his name in an unusually fast tempo, as though she were exhaling it in an attempt to replicate the speed which he coughed his name out. Katachi's face curled into an irritated frown upon hearing that.

K: "I would rather you omit my surname."

B: (His name... ! Wait, his name! I know it means something in Ohdean! I don't really know what it represents, but I've heard of it before!)

Bael's head brewed with a nasty idea.

B: "I have a better idea. I'll just call you 'Baka'."

K: "..."

It was common knowledge that Ohdean words were strangely designed. Any random combination of syllables gave a different meaning, and among them 'baka' was supposedly a demeaning term. For his name to match with that coincidence was in utter bad taste, much to Katachi's aversion. Bael was going to love teasing the daylights out of him.

*** ***

Katachi walked out of Cosmatral Neud and rested on a bench right outside an archway that led to the halls. His shirt was mended with scraps of varying colours and a small handkerchief dyed beige along with the words 'Micha' cropped by the cloth's edges.

K: (What a difficult woman.)

After mocking his name for a good five minutes, the large lady proceeded to pour some tea for him and they chatted for around three hours with her talking excitedly about the school's history and facilities he wasn't particularly interested in. The only thing he could have done was to tolerate and endure until her mouth ran dry, which was a bad idea in every definition of the term.

She animated her teapots to refill her cup on a regular basis so even before a quarter of the way through Katachi succumbed to torpor. By the time he came to, the rips in his ragged shirt were patched by various pieces of cloth. He was quite shocked to realize that the sun was almost halfway down given that he entered the garden while the sun was still high.

K: (I should head back to my room. Where is it?)

No sooner had he stepped through the archway did he feel the directional magic control his limbs oppressively. Katachi headed left as he entered the doorway but the magic forced his body to spin around and walk to his right. That was certainly disorienting, but thankfully it was short-lived. Had one suffered that effect for long periods one would most likely vomit from dizziness.

K: (So, from the garden to my room I would have to take a right, then a left, up the stairs, walk along the handles of the stairs and loop over it, down the corridor, take a sharp right and go to the third room to the right. My room's not that far from the garden area, it's a good landmark to know.)

The interior was a plain room with a book rack, a bed and some clean uniforms neatly folded on a small dusty desk. The only odd thing about the room was that the rack had been deliberately mounted atop the bed so if he tried to get up normally his head would collide with the rack. On the table was a Dousala wooden screen.

K: (This is probably where the time table will surface.)

He gently lowered his sling cloth onto the table and walked out of his room.

K: (I should bathe soon. I wonder if they have any ash soap catered for the students.)

He started marching towards the boys' bathing space.

CHAPTER 5

He scratched at his beard with an annoyed expression.

"Seven-o clock? Who in their right mind wants to attend a lesson at seven in the morning?"

In the fangled corridor was, wearing a crisp brown jacket with a white undershirt and a green bowtie, a teacher staring at his new schedule. A wooden charm hung out from his chest pocket with 'Rekter' inscribed on it. The schedules for students were carved in Dousala wooden screens for easy reference and the schedules for teachers were placed on a mist screen. Both of those common objects, plain as they appeared to be, were enchanted to update regularly.

Students usually did their homework or research on the table, which meant they could refer to the screen easily. Teachers could see the mist screen whenever they walked in and out of the hundred and thirty-five degree angled corridors to their rooms. Essentially, it was easy for information to be transmitted since the timetables were found on objects that were interacted with on a daily basis.

But most lessons did not start as early as seven. Six was a time for breakfast, and half past six for prayers and piety. Depending on the student and the type of magic they studied, as well as the gods they worshipped, their prayers could vary drastically from a moment-long silent prayer to a large-scale ritual that would require hours. Therefore, lessons usually started at nine to cater to the students in the normal stream curriculum.

Yet he had lessons with a single student at seven on both Wednesdays and Thursdays which invalidated that custom.

R: (You can't be serious. I'll have to consult Bertund about this tomorrow.)

Rekter pondered over his newly-updated schedule.

R: (I really don't want to wake up this early in the morning just to entertain this. It's for a single student, too... I'm used to not eating breakfast, but a schedule like that practically screams that they're forcing me to wake up early for these two days.)

He scratched his head rhythmically, formulating a plan of action for the new conundrum. The student's unique requirements offered various hints – In practice, the students to fill those roles were ones with a very selective range of spells or ones who simply disliked others' company.

R: (Or it could be that this particular student has a tendency to disrupt conducive learning. So it's my turn to take these kinds of problem children, huh? The best idea I can come up with now is to give a crash course for this kid's class. If I can make this kid study at the rate of a few lessons at a time I'd have more time to myself.)

There was nothing saying that the teaching schedule had to be confined to a singular subject or lesson a day. If the students showed promise, they could simply attend and participate in a test immediately to prove their mettle on the spot. Rekter's eyelids sunk and his brows furrowed as he tried to manipulate fact as best as he could.

R: (I should be careful so they don't catch me using 解.)

After reviewing the schedules of the other teachers that may expose the ploy, Rekter headed towards his room and brushed the dust off of his clothes. Unlike the students who shared a singular tank of water to bathe with at the dormitory bathing space, teachers had access to personal bathrooms with water that could be scented to the teacher's preference.

For the most part, hygiene was the main factor to consider. There were also teachers who required the usage of medicinal baths to cleanse their bodies properly. Rekter wasn't one of them, but the Selkpine-scented water was a luxury few could enjoy. He grabbed a towel hanging from a rack on the wardrobe and headed to his bathroom, thoroughly savouring the bliss of being a teacher in the academy.

*** ***

The clicking of hard leather soles on the floor could be heard from outside the classroom. Rekter wanted to set up the room before the lesson began, but when he opened the door he quickly realized someone was already inside.

The boy had dishevelled charcoal black hair covering his head thickly. He was in school uniform and he looked about eleven or twelve years old. He was also clutching a large piece of cloth- Or rather, a makeshift bag in his hands tightly, and his shifty eyes coupled with the scrunched shoulders made him look nervous and edgy.

R: "Who are you? What are you doing here?"

The boy turned his head over to look at Rekter slowly in a very stiff manner.

K: "I... I'm Ka-... Ka-Katachi. Kotsuba Katachi."

R: "And what business do you have here?"

The child quivered a bit, hesitant to reply.

K: "I'm... I'm here for a lesson at seven, but it's... It's kind of dark in here."

The signs indicated that he was foreign to the lighting system, unaware that a symbol had to be drawn on the wall-mounted panel to activate Soltak's magic. That summed up to a definitive conclusion – He's the student Rekter was assigned to teach, and a new student to boot.

R: (I was expecting someone more vulgar. Some mouse-like pipsqueak he turned out to be.) "Look over here. You can draw this symbol on the mounted panel to switch the light on, and this one to switch it off."

Rekter switched the mead to his left hand and demonstrated the actions to the boy. Strangely enough, Katachi seemed to be easily fascinated by the panel on the wall.

R: "Let me introduce myself. I am Rekter Bluo. I specialise in Sha'koth spells and magic related to the trickster legend. As you can see I'm dressed as Yurvik, one of Sha'koth's many impersonators. I will be your teacher for this class. So, since my schedule doesn't say anything about what I'm supposed to teach you, why don't you introduce yourself as well?"

Teacher schedules did not divulge the lessons conducted on the first day to encourage ice-breaking between the teachers and students. Other than that, depending on the nature of the course selected teachers were either to conduct a lecture on a specific topic or assist in study sessions for the children to do their own research. With that said, the arrangement of the lessons was not for them to decide.

The administrative department had the final say regarding the personnel to accommodate the respective students. But from that alone, it was quite easy to gauge the lesson based on various factors like time, the number of students, the location as well as orientation of the classroom which the lesson was held in; to name a few of the many hints. Should one be perceptive enough, everything could be manipulated to one's advantage... At least, to a certain degree.

The boy looked away for a little bit and replied diffidently.

K: "I... I am Kotsuba Katachi, and I'm ten this, this, this year. I, I came to Sage Raufid's to... To... Learn more about the... The 'Curse Words'."

Rekter's face paled.

R: (He already introduced himself earlier. He's meek and cowardly in nature, but how could a child so timid even talk about the Words of Power so openly?) "Did you just say 'Curse Words'?"

The boy nodded briefly and turned his head away immediately after.

R: (Unbelievable. A boy his age actually knows the true name of the Words of Power.)

Rekter gulped his mead down and put the cup aside. His expression turned grave as he quietly cursed the administrative staff for their antics.

R: (Damn it. Teaching a Word of Power is as good as suicide. Don't they know that?) "Okay. But before we begin our lessons, I would like to scope out how much you already know and then we can work from there. Is that all right?"

K: (So he's gauging me from the get-go, huh?) "O- Okay..."

R: (He seems to lack confidence... I should be careful. If he truly knows the Words of Power and he's just feigning his stupidity, then this will turn out really unpleasant. That seems really unlikely though.)

K: (Let's try something generic, like how I used 'Curse Words' on purpose just now.) "Uhm... To- To start with, the Words of Power are originally called 'Curse Words'. But... But during the hunt for them, the name sounded too... too- too ominous, so they changed the name to one more suitable."

The stammering act was docile and convincing at the same time. As expected of a child who lived his life in fear and seclusion, Katachi could pull off the act without a hitch.

K: "But its true name is a Curse Word, but, but-but-but knowing it in... In the mind is enough. Knowing it is called the Curse Words is enough for it to activate its true potential and heighten its precedence levels, or so... Or so the book says."

The boy trailed off, looking down so much his head was almost detachable. Rekter stared at the boy in astonishment.

R: (To even know the term 'precedence levels'... Simple kid 'just learning' about the Words of Power, as if. Are they serious? He could potentially be just as good, if not better than I am.) "Where did you learn of this, boy?"

K: (I don't think he'll buy the story immediately, but just maybe... Let's see how he reacts.) "There... There is a library at the church near... near my house, I often hid there and took it as a secret spot. I stumbled upon the bamboo book by pure accident, honest! But then... But then, there was this yellow glow inside the book and the next thing I knew, this... This thing was on my hand..."

R: (Seriously? He picked one up by sheer chance?)

Rekter considered and weighed the possibilities of his recount.

K: "... Mister Rekter?" (Good. He seems distracted. This is a good chance.)

R: (This boy found a Word of Power inside a bamboo book?... Then, whoever was reading the book probably had that Word of Power on him before he was killed and it must have slipped into the book. But if that's the case, where and when was this person killed? Why did nobody else take the Word of Power inside the book? Was he killed with the intent to take his word, or by other means? How did this boy stumble upon the book?)

Rekter thought long and hard on the subject, furrowing his brows.

R: (Had the bamboo book always laid there on some crate or the floor, just waiting for someone to pick it up? Was that library in the church never used again because someone died there?... But, what if he's lying? What if this kid knows exactly what he's doing and he's trying to eke out my sympathy?)

But the suspicion was short-lived.

R: (No, no. That can't be. He has flitting eyes, his fingers are tense and his lips are apart even though his jaw's closed properly. His actions are quite shy and his hands are unstable, which means he's passive by nature. There's no way he's actually that evil to have murdered the actual owner of the Word of Power and claimed it for his own. How would a kid do that anyway, even if the Scholar were asleep? He must have picked it up or something.)

K: "... Mister Rekter."

R: "Ah, apologies. I'm fine. So, you learnt quite a lot about the Words of Power already, huh."

The boy sheepishly nodded.

R: (One final push. Any sign of animosity, and I'll take him out right here.) "Let's try something more practical. I want you to use that Word of Power on my cup over there. I'm going to try and understand how much you know about this magic in a practical."

The boy silently nodded and looked over at the cup. The words 固定 formed on the cup, and the 固 slowly faded away.

R: (定?... So that's his character. He didn't even hesitate when I told him to reveal his word, so he's clearly on the gullible side. Good. This is a good chance for me to scope out his abilities! 溶解! Dissolve object – Cup!)

A faint whisper echoed in the back of Rekter's head and the words 溶解 formed on top of the cup as well. Both words faded off at the same time in less than a second.

R: (What!?!... His precedence level is equal to my own!?)

Rekter stared at the boy with a dumbfounded look printed upon his face.

*** ***

K: (He didn't notice it. That's good.)

Katachi waved the teacher goodbye. With a few breathless gasps, Rekter dismissed the one-student class.

R: "You already know more than enough... You don't even need to attend any of these lessons. You pass with flying colours. The class is dismissed."

With a determined frown on his face Rekter left the classroom. At the very least, he didn't seem to notice the little trick Katachi pulled. With the only subject he signed up for aborted by the teacher voluntarily he had free time to spare. It was only a quarter after seven, yet to optimise that freedom from henceforth was the real challenge.

K: (I'm surprised it worked as well as it did. He dropped his guard after I placed my 定 immediately, so he was probably worried that I was scheming or something. It's his oversight for not realizing my own interest in scoping out his Precedence Level.)

There was plenty of time to spend in the school, but what was the point of idling in a place where children busied themselves learning something easy? In that sense it was not abnormal to see some of the students about, forsaking lessons and devoting themselves to their personal study of magic instead.

K: (Bael is usually at the library around this time... I guess I should start by tidying the place a little bit.)

Katachi grabbed a tiny duster and found a stepladder in a nearby closet. With only one thought in mind, he walked onward in the magically enchanted halls.

K: (Let's clean the area and learn the school's layout. Take me to a janitor's closet.)

CHAPTER 6

Katachi dipped the dusty cloth into the bucket and twisted it hard, forcing the water out of it. With the cloth at suitable moisture he continued wiping the chandelier in the main atrium.

B: "This is stupid! Don't you have lessons or anything? Surely you didn't come here to be a janitor or a caretaker."

Bael stood idly, reading a book on catalysts and natural remedies used to improve one's efficiency and focus. She was annoyed that the young man atop the stepladder appeared so carefree, and nudged her arm against the wall repeatedly to find a comfortable position.

B: "It's been five days! Five days! You've spent every one of those days cleaning some part or place of the school nobody even visits! And of all days you're cleaning the school when the teachers aren't around so it's not even a punishment! They're not paying you to clean this place or anything, so how could you even enjoy something like that?"

Katachi paid no heed to her and continued cleaning.

B: "I sometimes don't know if, if you're retarded or something! How could anyone stand cleaning the school faculty without pay or any form of benefit?"

K: (I can't let her know I'm trying to map out blind spots and escape routes.) "What do you mean? There is a benefit to cleaning."

Bael was appalled at his sudden rebuttal.

K: (I need to distract her.) "For one thing, cleaning makes the place healthy and habitable. Mother Rin has always emphasized on cleanliness and I don't see why you wouldn't want your surroundings to be clean. Surely you don't appreciate ants and termites eating your documents, do you? Cleaning helps one to keep in touch with their inner self, devoting oneself to the environment much like devoting yourself to the people important to you."

Bael rolled her eyes at the mere mention of Mother Rin.

K: "The exercise allows people to train their temper and attentiveness. Just as how people would not disturb you for passionately studying your field of magic, the practice of hygiene is a form of cleansing for both the area around you and within yourself."

His ramblings were starting to get tedious.

B: (Doesn't this guy give a break or something? For every day I've met him, he's mentioned that name at least once. What is she to him, his lover?) "Uh huh. Yeah, sure."

Katachi put extra strength into the cloth to scrape off a resilient stain which looked like it wasn't getting off any time soon.

K: (She seems annoyed. Is the distraction a success, or have I made my true motive more apparent?) "That's a hidden benefit of cleaning only those who have done it actively would learn of."

B: "I would much rather laze around than waste my energy cleaning then."

Bael continued reading the last few lines of an entry on Surcleus in her book and flipped a page.

K: (That's a relief.) "I have my reasons, but I'll leave it at that... What are you reading?"

Bael looked up at Katachi with much interest, ecstatic that she finally found some form of what could be considered an actual conversation with him.

B: "It's a book about herbs and how certain spices and wild plants can be used to enhance the mental state and the body. Herbs that coagulate blood quickly, herbs that help produce alcohol faster, anything can be used if you look in the right places so knowing them is important."

K: "That sounds interesting. Does it contain the dangerous, poisonous types of plants to avoid?"

B: "Yeah. The book's pretty extensive."

Katachi squeezed and twisted the drenched cloth to adjust its water content.

K: "Are the plants described within all local or is it scattered across the lands?"

B: "This book was made by Irving Daniel. I'm guessing that unless he's a travelling guide or a merchant's tabs keeper, it would most likely contain information about the plants found in Anik."

Katachi frowned a bit upon hearing Anik.

K: (Irving Daniel sounds like a name from Rugnud though.) "Anik? Are you planning to migrate over there or something?"

B: "No, silly. What I meant was, if Anik's market shifts and herbalists start coming over to Yhorfe for the spice trade during Jaanthro season they might be interested in trading their own herbs. I could make unique drugs and medicine that other apothecaries have yet tried, maybe even discover new effects to them."

Katachi nodded slightly in agreement as he continued wiping the glass beads dangling from the chandelier.

K: "I guess that's an interesting idea to have market-wise."

B: "Yes it is, and I'd rather you spend your time doing something more constructive for your future like this instead of wasting all your time cleaning obscure spots in school."

Bael retorted with a spiteful accent but Katachi replied her calmly, having anticipated such a reaction.

K: "I don't really have any lessons to attend for now, not until Tuesday. I might as well spend time meditating like this since I have nothing I need to rush."

Bael's eyes widened.

B: (Tuesday?) "But you said your lessons were on Wednesday and Thursday, didn't you?"

When did he sign up for a different course? Why did he not tell her? Bael felt like she was left in the dark, as though she was not important enough to know. Were they not friends, or was her friendship unrequited?

K: "I asked Bertund yesterday and he helped me sign up for an additional course to discover my affinity."

B: "Wait what? The manpower branch gave you the wrong course?"

It was not normal for a student to attend a magical course when they had no talent for it. It was like telling a fish that could only swim to spontaneously grow two legs and walk on land. So, what exactly did Katachi attend for only one lesson?

B: "Did your previous course end on the first lesson because it wasn't a magic you had an affinity with?"

K: "You could say that, and yet you really can't, but... It's a bit hard to explain, but you can consider it like that."

B: (Katachi's wording it weirdly. He could have just agreed with me but he didn't, so could that mean the lesson on Wednesday was a type of magic that didn't involve affinity?... A Reincarnate Art?)

Certainly, his choice of words narrowed down the possibilities available, yet it was still out-of-reach. Bael felt proud to notice that slight nuance in detail.

B: "Is it a Reincarnate art?"

K: "Ahh-aah-aah-aah-aah! Ahh! Ahh!"

Katachi winced from her response and he gripped onto the chandelier with his free left hand. He desperately tried to regain his balance by holding onto its rings and trying to distribute some of his body weight onto it.

It was quite a miracle since the chandelier did not fall off the ceiling despite being tugged at by the entirety of his body. Yet, would it not be wiser to simply grab the stone stepladder he sat upon? That foolishness easily reflected his clumsiness for anyone to see.

... If one disregarded the sinister brilliance beneath the charcoal hair.

B: (Hoho, that reaction. Perhaps I'm on the right trail?) "I hit a nail, didn't I?"

K: "... I won't answer that question."

Bael's smirk flashed ever so slightly on her face with triumph but her heart was leaping all over the place, barely contained by her façade.

B: (Ha-ha! That reaction is so cute! He's never talked about the magic he's used before but I guess I have a rough idea now! He must be using some form of Reincarnate Art!- ...)

She firmly believed that she was making significant progress by thinking that far, but the answer she derived at only served to raise even more questions. Bael's face stoned into a daze.

B: (... There's quite a handful of Reincarnate Arts to choose from. Which one is he using? Dardicel? Ilpoh? Croxa? Most of these Reincarnate Arts don't require any form of prayer or such, which would fit nicely because of his lesson schedule. In that case, maybe he's attending a different class?)

The rabbit hole only went deeper.

B: (The basic lessons for Dardicel lore began recently in the first days of the Month of the Halberd. What if he's already started on the Intermediate class? That would explain a need to separate him from the normal curriculum... Arrgh, guessing is a pain! Why is he so dodgy about it anyway?!)

Frustrated with half-answers and wild guesses, Bael tried the most standard approach to an otherwise impossible question.

B: "Hey, Katachi, what god do you worship?"

K: "None."

It failed.

B: "Come on, don't be like that! There must be some god or legend you're worshipping!"

But with enough persisten- Or more politely 'perseverance', one was destined to succeed.

K: "Segus."

B: (Segus? Is he serious?! He's not even a Reincarnate!)

Anyone would be taken aback had they heard that he followed the footsteps of a pacifist legend. It was simply not normal for a child to follow someone so passive, not when most bedtime stories she knew of were filled with the honour and glamour of gods, heroes and legends alike.

Unfortunately, Katachi possessed no such fortune. Mother Rinnesfeld had long donated the children's books away, leaving the black-haired child with nothing but reference books, magus research materials and dark histories too cruel to mention.

B: "Are you serious? Segus!? That's not even worth the trouble! He's just a pacifist legend who can't even fight for himself!"

But, exactly who was more unfortunate? Was it the child who faced the cruel and beautiful world alone?

K: "He's reputable because he loves all life. I pray to him at the church back at home. Mother Rin also says that loving all life is important-"

Or were the children cradled so delicately by their parents the unfortunate ones?

B: "-Enough about Mother Rin, sheesh! Also, you're lying, Katachi. Segus lessons are at noon daily, held at the West Atrium to express kindness towards plant life, insects and animals!"

Katachi finally gave up on the stain that appeared to be layered beneath the wax coating. He stopped wiping the chandelier and dropped the cloth into the pail. Bael closed her book gently as Katachi carried it down the stepladder made of floating stones and a magic of Axia's origin that set it in place.

K: "I mentioned that I do indeed worship Segus. However, I said nothing of me attending Segus magic courses. I wasn't aware that those courses existed, but even if I did I wouldn't choose them regardless."

Contrary to Bael's belief Katachi had no need for those lessons. He already understood the very nature of Segus and his spells without the assistance of anyone else since he was raised in a church that worshipped the legend to begin with.

B: "What?! That's not-"

K: "-I have to clean these up at the back, and you don't want that book to get wet, do you? Paper books are expensive."

Katachi gently pushed the core stone upward and the entire stepladder followed suit. He then placed his hand onto a stone step and dragged the stepladder through the air to the back of the school.

B: (Ugh... He's a hard nut to crack, despite being so candid.)

Bael could only pout and frown at Katachi.

B: (... That's not fair. He never answered my question.)

*** ***

Event magic. It was without a shadow of a doubt considered the most unique, and perhaps even the most powerful form of magic currently in existence. It was a type of magic that forced and invoked unnatural events.

Eggs laid moments ago could age until a chick was birthed in a matter of seconds. Ice found on lakes could stay frozen, even in the heat of summer. One could force a person to utter the truth, against his will. Mountains wore down into rubble spontaneously, food that remained fresh forever, people who achieved immortality by taking on a bizarre form that allowed them to constantly rejuvenate lost and withered body parts...

That was the classification of the Words of Power – An absolute magic that would make even the frailest cowards and the weakest beggars triumphant over a king, sigils that perverted the fundamentals of magic.

K: (But that is precisely why this madness must be stopped.)

Katachi could not afford to have his secret divulged. If anyone knew of his Word of Power it would be over. He would be treated as an outcast and leered at by everyone in school for having such a ridiculous and powerful magic. It would be the same scenario in Mielfeud all over again, except this time there won't be adults to obfuscate the truth from their children.

Every waking moment would be spent in paranoia, and every night of sleep restless. Unlike Mielfeud, the academy was filled with students and wielders of magic so the danger of using his Word of Power carelessly would bear heavier consequences. It was, after all, a power with the potential to create 'absolutes'. Should the students find a way to manipulate and force two absolutes to contradict each other, it would be a horrible sight.

The only factor determining which of the 'absolutes' remained was the unique attribute known as precedence levels. But that aside, its wielders were practically invincible as long as their sigil allowed it. It would be no wonder to find one dead the next day as a result of carelessly using the power and giving away its limitations even if for a mere instant.

The madness that swirled in the world was a great, ravenous and cruel hunger that would plunge the unstable into insanity, and the stable into temptation which gradually made them unstable; an endless cycle that fed upon itself, ever-expanding. Something must be done about it.

Katachi picked up a flyer resting on the table.

K: (The Sage Raufid Young Magus Tournament... The winner is allowed three prizes, which can be anything that is within the school's power. There's bound to be competition.)

A child was timid for several reasons. The most widely accepted reason was because a child had seen something he was not familiar with. With the unknown suddenly introduced it was easy for the child to feel a sense of insecurity over what little he knew. With much misfortune, Katachi fell under both categories – It was not uncertainty alone that induced his reticent behaviour.

It was the void of knowing his helplessness against it all. But, he stepped forth to oppose that darkness within himself...

K: (Place the wooden piece on the magic circle, and enter your name into the ballot box. Tournament restriction – sixty-four participants, twenty-one applied...)

Which begged the question; would other children harness that same courage to confront themselves and the world with equal determination? Exactly who was more unfortunate?

Katachi picked up a wooden tablet and placed it on the magic circle attached to his left arm. The magic circle engraved his name 'Kotsuba Katachi' onto the tablet and he dropped it into the participation box.

K: (I'll have to get first place using the most subtle method. The best strategy would be to end every match in the shortest time possible.)

He grimaced at the number of tokens in the box that didn't quite add up to two dozen.

K: (The longer I stay out of battle, the lesser the odds are I'd be discovered. It's wishful thinking, but I hope I don't have to fight any strong opponents until the final rounds.)

CHAPTER 7

"Class, we are going to cover something more practical today. We are going to estimate your orientation."

A lady with a wooden tag labelled 'Lea' stood before the class. She was of a rather small stature with black hair indicating her Ohdean origin, wearing an amber blouse and a long maroon skirt reaching the floor, both obviously made of a high-grade cloth.

Her face, a petite smile which formed on her tiny lips, with widely opened eyes brought out a strangely feminine charm from her. When comparing her attire to the plain and crisp uniforms of the students, it created a strange contrast because the clothes didn't match the atmosphere of a classroom at all.

Katachi's fingers turned cold and numb.

K: (I've never considered it, but if the curriculum happens to have some way of discovering my secret this could turn out pretty ugly, wouldn't it? Why didn't I think this far?)

His face was twitching and his jaw trembled very slightly for anyone attentive or bored enough to notice. Thankfully, the teacher's apparel and charisma created an atmosphere that naturally drew the attention of the students to her. It was appropriate to say her current disposition was the ideal scenario for many novice teachers who faced much difficulty garnering the attention of their students.

K: (I need to avoid those risks at all costs.)

Katachi focused on the teacher's back and imagined her without her blouse, her bare back in view. Though it was a disturbing thought, it had to be done. Had he applied the Word of Power on the blouse itself the purpose of using it despite the risks would be absolutely foolish.

K: (设定! Set thought pattern – Divert from Curse Words!)

Katachi bet on the fact that the teacher's shirt was thick enough to conceal the radiant glow, and his gamble paid off.

K: (I don't see any notable changes at all. I really hope the word works this way.)

L: "As you all know, the most common method of distinguishing a person's orientation as well as scouting for any curse or form of magic afflicted on the body is to use a Lotz crystal, like this one here."

Miss Lea reached into the purse on the table and picked up a translucent crystal.

K: (By the gods!)

The translucent crystal he hoped he would never see. Should he dispel the Word of Power he already placed on her, or should he keep it active? Yet another gamble appeared before him that made him edgy and uncomfortable.

K: (Of all the things she could have fished out of the pocket-... There's no point in panicking. I should weigh the risks and rewards carefully.)

L: "However, Lotz crystals are incredibly expensive and they must be handled with care. Also, Lotz crystals can only glow the colour of the magic applied onto you or present within you. It cannot clearly distinguish what's really going on with the body."

K: (There is the chance that it's already activated the moment she held it in her hand. But there is also the chance that the crystal won't be active once I remove the Word of Power, which means she'll go back to using it assuming the lesson continues. Will the crystal glow dimmer if I remove the Word of Power? Is it noticeable? Will she feel the change in her own behaviour?)

L: "Sad is to say, the legend of Lotz was his desire to see the world as it was through his colour-blind eyes and yet what he perceived as 'colour' was the truth of the world itself. Therefore, although useful for confirming foul play it's not quite as practical at pinpointing your orientation."

While pondering on his next course of action, the teacher's prattle reached his ears and Katachi's brows furrowed slightly.

K: (... So, are we going to use it or not? Do adults get a kick out of speaking in riddles?)

Katachi didn't quite understand where the talk was headed since it jumped to Lotz's history all of a sudden, but there was a more pressing matter at hand. It was hard to see at first but upon closer inspection one could see the Lotz crystal emitting a very faint gold colour.

K: (It's there.)

Thankfully, the weather outside the classroom was sunny with students sitting near the windows squinting to look forward. Maybe the glow camouflaged well with the surroundings, or maybe it was just the surroundings itself reflecting light into the crystal giving Katachi a false impression of its activation. It could even be that the Lotz crystal was working as intended, and it was currently showing the teacher's innate affinity.

It was oddly hard to tell. The way the Lotz crystal worked in the first place was very fishy. If a person had some specific magic affinity and was cursed or blessed at the same time, which of the two would take priority? Perhaps it was never intended to be understood by others, given that its creator was the colour-blind caster Lotz.

Yet having the Lotz crystal glow, regardless of the cause, was something he had to be extremely wary of. Lotz crystals were not supposed to glow naturally without direct contact with magic, yet the one resting on Miss Lea's hand was. The 定 was likely detected by the Lotz crystal, even though their creations were eons apart.

Katachi recalled the books he found in the attic of the church. The Words of Power were created mere decades ago in an event caused by 292 great sorcerors and the Warlock of Wheels. However, Lotz existed at a time far before that around 4000 years ago; quite a few centuries after the Cleansing, according to a biography in the library located at the separate block.

K: (It doesn't look very distinct, I think.)

Technically, since event magic didn't exist during Lotz's time the Lotz crystal should be unable to detect any of the 292 Words of Power. But image power was frightening to behold. Image power could reinforce a branch so it became as durable as a bar of steel. Image power could create tools, objects and even weapons out of thin air. Image power, the Gift of the Father of Sin, was the reason why Reincarnate Arts were so powerful and revered.

In the midst of challenging the gods' reincarnates, their ancestors came to fear the gods' strength and the power worked against them, reinforcing the Reincarnate Arts even further. That was why Reincarnate Arts were horrifying to face as a magus. Image power, the ancient power that it was, was an influential force that rocked the entire course of history into what it was today prior to its discovery.

With image power one could probably reinforce a Lotz crystal so it detected traces of magic even beyond its time. There was a possibility that image power rectified the scope which the Lotz crystal was designed to sense – In said case it was almost certainly true, and the only saving grace rested on the fact that the room was already bathed in radiant light which dulled its brilliance.

K: (It may be wiser to suspend- ? What's she doing?)

The teacher placed the crystal back into the bag.

L: "Therefore, we shall be doing something more fun today! We are going back to the past to how the magi of the old detected orientations and affinities without using the Lotz crystal! Class, form yourselves into pairs of two!"

Half the entire class heaved a sigh in disappointment while the other half of the class turned their heads and chatted excitedly with their friends in the adjacent seats.

K: (... I'm in the clear now, at least.)

Katachi loosened his tense lips in relief and perked his ears up.

K: (I still don't know if that Word of Power took effect. I'd have to try it on something else to get more accurate data. The result from this is too vague... Even though it seems to work well on Rekter.)

"Hey, new kid?"

K: "?"

Katachi turned towards his right to greet a spiky-haired boy looking at him with enthusiasm. Wearing the uniform supposedly gave students a similar identity, but he gave everyone the impression that he was different. He had passion in his eyes that would make anyone retract their heads slightly in a subtle cry for personal space.

He was simply that assertive.

M: "I'm Mafer. You don't seem to know this class very well yet, so I'll help you."

K: "Oh uh, thank you. But I'm afraid that I'd drag you down, Mafer. I... I'm not too used to this class."

The boy widened his eyes a bit and nodded his head slowly as if understanding the scenario.

M: "Don't worry, you won't slow me down. This class has nothing to do with my belief in Croxa."

K: "Oh! A Croxa believer! I... I see." (But, if that were the case, why is he attending this course?)

Katachi didn't feel like befriending the expressive Mafer despite the feeling and intuition that he was trustworthy. But could anyone blame him for being defensive and protective, a child who struggled so much that caution was second nature to him?

K: "Please... Please take care of me."

M: "Oh, pssh, spare the formalities! What's your name, new kid?"

K: "Katachi."

Mafer's head tilted to the side briefly.

M: "That name... It's of an Ohde descent, right? You're awfully polite."

K: "Uhh... Yes?" (He asked if the name was a name of Ohde descent. He didn't ask if I was from Ohde, so it's still the truth... I think.)

Katachi's voice was awfully low and dispirited, so he barely got by without Mafer's realisation of his uncertainty.

M: "I knew it! Did you come here to, oh, you know... Spy on your fiancé or something? Is it Miss Lea?"

Katachi slowly leaned away from him.

K: "I... I- I- I don't know her. I really don't. I just came here for the lessons."

M: "Hoho, I'll leave you to your thing. Right now, we're partners."

Mafer grabbed an empty seat and sat next to Katachi.

L: "Settle down, class. I want one of you to form your fingers into a number 'seven' for both hands, and place them into the shape of the tetear of Axia just like this. Be sure to place your mouth over the medicine- Wait, that's not what it's called in Findeli. Place it over the... Ring fingers and the pinkies. Also, make sure your thumbs are stretched to a right angle or as close to it as possible. Image power will rectify that for you if it's wide enough."

Miss Lea shaped both hands so the thumbs and forefingers extended, leaving the rest retracted. Next, she placed the hands together with the pinky fingers colliding into each other on the side. She then placed her hands on her face and demonstrated the actions necessary by extending the middle finger to indicate the lack of contact between the lips and the middle fingers.

Some discussions on who should do it arose between the groups, but soon enough half the class followed suit.

L: "Next, the student supporting should grab a pencil or a piece of charcoal and place it between the two forefingers, like this. Once you do that you can put it back to its original place."

A piece of charcoal floated in the air and hovered between her forefingers pointed towards the sky. The teacher was well-versed enough in the Marion-Nettie spell and her degree of control easily rivalled Bael's, if not even better.

M: "Just hold still now."

Mafer placed the charcoal between Katachi's forefingers briefly and moved it away.

L: "Excellent. Now, the final part. Exhale through your mouth into the gap between your pinky fingers."

Katachi gently blew onto his fingers and words formed before his face. The dust particles settled and 'Water (Healing)' formed before his eyes.

M: "You're a healer, huh."

Mafer gave him a rather admiring look and patted him on his back.

M: "You know, healers like you often become the nursing staff in this school. If you can learn to heal quickly I bet you'd get a solid job in this place."

But the young visionary did not entertain the idea. A measurement like so was clearly flawed for the tetear to suggest his capacity at healing. Though Katachi held a primarily pacifistic mentality suited for a healer, he could never imagine the serenity and joy that accompanied the restoration of one's well-being.

Certainly not when the child knew perfectly well what it meant to take a life.

K: "I'll take my chances. Thanks, Mafer."

Katachi released his hands and the black dust before him fell onto the table.

*** ***

B: "Hey, Baka~"

Katachi ignored the annoying voice that came from Bael with a fierce frown.

B: "Baka?"

K: "I refuse to engage in a proper conversation should you call me by that name."

B: "You meanie. You're probably my only other form of entertainment around this school besides studying medicine and teasing others, and you're denying me of even that? I'm heartbroken."

K: "Stay heartbroken. It's- ?"

A figure dashed past the corridor. It was fast and hazy, but it looked like a tanned brown-haired female student. It was strange how someone could run in the halls controlled by directional magic, but that person likely used image power or something to overcome its influence.

B: "It's what?"

K: "... It's not like I fancy being teased, even in good humour. I do not think of you as someone close enough to play these in-jokes, and you just want to eke a response from me in the first place."

B: "Meanie."

Bael's eyes turned half-closed at Katachi's reply. It would assuredly be mean, if one ignored the fact that she was the one treating him like some toy to begin with.

K: "Sorry to be a meanie then."

But was she to blame for that behaviour? The child responded in such a stoic manner that Bael was unsure whether his words harboured indifferent intent or entrenched personality.

B: "Meanie! You're always keeping quiet and hiding stuff from me like you're avoiding a plague or something. Speaking of which, I heard you entered the Young Magus Tournament. You didn't even tell me!"

K: "Yes, I did. What of it?"

B: "You've not even enrolled for ten days and you want to join the tournament already? Talk about being overconfident."

That would normally betray Katachi's timid character, both in that he spoke to Bael fluently and in that he took part in the competition. Yet she remained oblivious to the reason he stepped foot in the facility.

He came prepared with a solid plan in mind – Succeed, and he shall boldly claim the prize for his needs. Should he fail, he would sneak about raiding other students' rooms until he collected enough materials and provisions for himself. The outcome did not matter, but the fact stood that winning was a more convenient and morally just alternative.

K: "Judge me as you like it, but I'm going. That's final."

B: "It's useless, you know! You'd probably get wiped out even before the second round!"

K: "I don't mind. I've lost enough."

Katachi walked into his room and closed the door. Since it was a zone only males could enter, Bael was naturally prevented from entering the room in a similar fashion that males were barred from the zones surrounding girls' toilets. He successfully escaped Bael for the day.

K: (She took up a lot of precious time.)

Even now, Katachi could feel her presence behind the door waiting for him to come out when he was tired of sitting about in his room doing nothing constructive. He had already cleaned the room yesterday so there was little left to tidy. At that rate, being dragged along her activities was only a matter of time.

It was a great fortune that Katachi loaned a book from the library ahead of time about the famous folk tales in Auser. He did not need to leave the room to read and that spared him from another round of Bael's teasing.

K: (I can't have her bothering me while I read. It may be against curfew, but I guess I will have to go to the library at night.)

CHAPTER 8

The halls in the Sage Raufid Magus Academy were filled with a special suggestion magic. That inherently meant the students were not allowed to challenge the rules set in place by Bertund.

K: (恒定! Constant status – Self!)

If he were ever caught for this he would be punished dearly. Katachi scurried towards the library as quietly as he could. Since the magic restricted him no longer Katachi could move freely in school, but being liberated from its influence also meant that he had to find the library via his own effort. As luck would not have it, Katachi was not made for memory work.

K: (I sort of remember it being up the stairs or something...? I went up, up, left, down, along the corridor and past the female's toilet-... Wait, where is this?)

It surprised no one that Katachi spent at least twenty minutes walking around the school aimlessly, his feet numbed against the icy floor.

*** ***

Halfway through his blind search, Katachi stumbled upon a rather interesting scene. There was a boy and girl sitting on one of the benches in the halls. They were excessively and unnecessarily conspicuous so he quickly hid behind a pillar, camouflaged by its shadows well.

K: (This shouldn't be possible – The curfew should be in effect! Who are they?)

"This is so exciting! I've never done this before...What if we get found out?"

D: "Shh, hush, we won't get busted. I promise."

He immediately recognized the male's voice.

K: (! Dante! What's he doing out here?)

Katachi peeked around the corner and saw Dante and the girl engrossed in undressing themselves.

K: (They haven't noticed me yet? I'm glad I went barefooted instead of wearing my usual wooden sabots. The chill of the marble floor was worth enduring.)

They were holding some sort of wooden tag that had some Anikan characters shaped like 方針 carved onto it. As they attempted to undress themselves awkwardly they made sure to hold onto their respective tags tight.

K: (I don't know what the words on that tag means, but it must be responsible for letting them stay out here without being affected by the magic. They're clutching it tightly, so does it block the magic or something?)

D: "Show me that beautiful ass, Sherayal. I wanna see it reflect the moonlight into my eyes."

The girl proceeded to hook the panties with her pinkies and slipped her underwear off.

K: (The Sherayal girl is performing that banal act with Dante? Why would they-... Wait, now is not the time to chastise them or worry. If anything, this is a great opportunity.)

Patiently, Katachi waited for the two of them to drop their guard fully. As they primed themselves to conjoin their respective genitals Katachi finally found a window where they were both looking away in the same direction.

K: (... ! Chance! 固定! Fixate position – Sherayal! Fixate position – Dante!)

A golden word formed on the girl's stomach and Dante's bare back.

K: (Good. They can't move at all.)

He was still sceptical about the power working as intended so Katachi waited for a few seconds to affirm that they were properly immobilized. When that was verified Katachi took the long way about and sneaked up behind them.

They were both facing the same direction, so it was a great blessing they chose to act like hounds in heat instead of having the girl hug and mount Dante like a sloth. Forcing the wooden tags to slip from the girl's hands was easy since she held it with three fingers, but Dante's grip was rather strong so a little more effort was needed to retrieve the tag out of his immobilized hand.

Katachi made sure to avoid their lines of sight and left quietly. He shouldn't be careless, considering that both of them were still perfectly capable of hearing their surroundings, as limited as their visions may be.

K: (You two stay there and repent for what you were about to do.)

The normal reaction would have been arousal, but Katachi had only anger for them. How dare they perform the gift of life, pretending they were responsible enough to raise the child? Was his existence itself not a prime example that showed why the gift of life should not be conducted carelessly? And yet the two thoughtless children, though older in physique, showed none of the wisdom he expected.

Katachi retreated back to the same corner and made final preparations.

K: (Anyone can see those words if I just leave them on the stomach and back. I should hide them as well. 固定! Fixate position – Sherayal! Fixate position – Dante!)

The words on both of them faded off and reformed around their ankles where their own garments concealed the sigils. He would handle and dispose of them at a later time during his return from the library.

K: (They can stay there and pose pretty until I'm done. Now, which way is it to the library? It should be somewhere on the second storey, but was it the Intundia or Tinjengel section?)

*** ***

While walking aimlessly, Katachi observed the wooden tags he confiscated.

K: (These strange characters appear to be of an Anikan origin, and I don't understand them at all. If only there was some sort of instructive diction or- Ow!)

Katachi walked right into a wall. Without the suggestion magic to assist him there was no feasible way to avoid any obstacles including the walls. Katachi felt the urge to undo the Word of Power counteracting the magic, but he quickly regained his restraint to do so.

K: "Aaaergh... Huh?"

Perhaps it was a sign, a call for him to observe his surroundings once more.

K: (I found it. What luck.)

Katachi headed inside with haste and checked that no teachers were on patrol before unwinding from the tension.

K: (Great. It's a bit dark since nobody is expected at this hour, but I will have to make do. Where's the R section?)

*** ***

Katachi retraced the exact same route he took to the library and reached the junction where Dante and the Sherayal girl were. But standing there and observing them with a cold glare was a peculiar figure the three of them least expected. As usual, he was in his green suit with the slime hat and white gloves.

K: (! Bertund? But... It's not even five in the morning!)

B: "I received reports from teachers that their tags went missing. I wouldn't find it surprising if you were behind it, Dante, but I certainly didn't expect your accomplice to be Sherayal."

The principal shook his head. While doing so, the funny slime top hat he wore wobbled along with his head's inertia.

B: "It pains my heart to know that even a marvellous student like you can be swayed by your libido. It is another issue if you did it at an inn or in your own homes, but you two should know clearly the consequences for illicit sexual relations on school grounds."

The look on his face was seriously harrowing and even his oft-whimsical grin turned into a hollowed smirk. It was like watching a powerful sorceror trick his opponents into killing their own men, a dark and triumphant chortle void of all mercy.

B: "Thievery, violation of curfew and illicit sexual activity... That's three strikes in one convenient package."

Bertund's right glove glowed yellow and the slime top hat changed its shape to a viscous pointed hat with a crooked crown. What he did next was simple.

The principal gently patted the magic circles on the left arms of both Dante and Sherayal with his glowing right hand. The magic circles on their arms glowed yellow and faded off to nothingness. Despite the severity of the act Dante and Sherayal froze there, still unable to move.

K: (... Oh, right! The words are still on them. But, in that case Bertund already knows about my violation as well, doesn't he?)

The words on their ankles wore off silently.

S: "D-D-Dante, look at what you've done! I'm expelled now! You liar, you had better take responsibility for this!!"

D: "Huh? What... What happened? I couldn't move at all? Was there some time limit to the tokens?"

B: "You two, come with me. Don't lag behind."

Bertund signalled both stude-... Correction, ex-students to his side and stormed off. The two dressed themselves hastily to cover their revealing parts and quickly chased after the principal.

K: (... That was close. But it would be a lie to say I'm in a good position.)

Katachi sighed in relief as the three turned a corner.

K: (That was really cool, though. His hat can actually change its shape like that.)

Perhaps that comeuppance was simply the fates having Dante repent for his misdoings. Katachi rested on a bench and waited for the five-o-clock chime to invalidate his violation. He placed the tags with him on the bench in false pretense that the two left it there accidentally.

CHAPTER 9

Katachi was interrupted by a student with a buzz-cut, holding a box of wooden tablets as he walked across the hallway. He seemed to have something to say because he blocked the passage deliberately.

"Hey, kid. Who're you betting for?"

K: "Huh?"

Katachi stared at the student blankly. The word 'betting' alone held a lot of weight and uttering it in the hallway where passers-by could audibly hear was unbecoming.

K: "W-What do you mean, betting?"

"The tournament has quite a few competitors. You can guess which student would emerge as the champion, and Professor Mint is going to treat the students who manage to guess the winner correctly to a feast."

Katachi stepped back slightly at the otherworldly piece of good news. Mother Rin would normally rebuke at how gambling was prohibited, but the strange thing about it was that Segus mentioned nothing about abstention from gambling. Or perhaps it was more accurate to say Segus believed that life was a gamble in and of itself.

K: (I want to try it, but that seems a bit risky. They even dragged a teacher into this?) "Isn't... Isn't that against the school rules?"

"Well, think of it as a personal bet. If the students manage to guess correctly by luck or chance they would have a nice treat for free. But if the students managed to chart the outcome, then the treat is both a prize and a form of encouragement for them. It doesn't pay to make a bet so why not give it a go?"

Katachi leaned against the wall slightly.

K: (If what he says is true, then it wouldn't be bad for me to participate. I would simply have to guess the winner by random. Although I really want to get the sponsored prize, it may be better to step back a bit and shake attention off myself.)

Katachi pondered over the weight of his options carefully.

K: "Uhm... Who can I choose from?"

"Well, there's last year's champion Deku, there's Cillian, the semi-finalists last year and any of your other dark horse friends you think might stand a chance. If you're feeling lucky, you can try anyone you think will win."

K: (Looks like there are some pre-carved tablets. There are a lot less Deku tablets than there are Cillian ones... Maybe there's a shift in the tournament format that favours Cillian?) "... I'll guess Cillian."

"Cillian, huh? Okay then, place this on your circle."

Katachi picked a tablet from the tray the student was supporting with both arms and held the wooden tablet with the name Cillian engraved onto the magic circle on his left arm. It glowed slightly as Katachi's name formed on a small corner of the tablet in fine print.

"I hope you made the right choice. Good luck!"

The student quickly broke conversation and leapt towards another student eagerly, in a fashion that seemed as though he was getting paid for collecting votes. That enthusiasm served better for the Theories and Articles Fair, but perhaps he had a sibling or relative taking part in the tournament?

K: (To think an event like this is so big that such means are employed... It shouldn't be a surprise though, there are more than two hundred students here so up to a third of the student body are future opponents. He mentioned that they were going to use magic to determine the outcome of the tournament.)

The Young Magus Tournament did not divide the students between grades or age, as a matter of fact the academy encouraged students in different classes to mingle and pool their efforts together. It would be dangerous to face the seniors without adequate preparations, so in a sense the bets were a way to let freshmen engage themselves in the event.

K: (Looks like I'll have to work harder. They're not taking it easy even when they're not competing. I shouldn't expect the actual competitors to relax.)

But first there were more pressing matters to address.

*** ***

"All participants, single file! Queue here to order the weapon you wish to use!"

The various participants queued up in a straight line, taking turns to place their wooden pieces into the order boxes at the waiting area. It was a unique ordering system for the tournament that the students had to participate in should they want weapons to use during their matches.

The tournament strongly promoted the usage of magic, but there were cases where physical weapons were needed be it for channelling a more specific medium or for engaging when magic was no longer an option. Real weapons would defeat the purpose of the magic demonstration so participants had to order their own wooden weapons to use in the tournament.

Each student would use a wooden piece they were given on their magic circle, engrave their name onto it and place the piece into a box tagged with whichever weapon they desired. A variety of weapons were available for selection – a sword, a spear, a pole arm to name a few of the possible choices along with a custom box for unique weapons.

The school would proceed to procure and supply that weapon for use in the tournament. It was a safe method of ensuring that nobody could cheat during the tournament, since everyone would be getting their waster weapons at the same time, devoid of foul play and exploit.

Katachi could feel pricks on his feet after standing in line for half an hour. The quiet and droll wait for his turn was abruptly interrupted by someone in front rousing a rather large commotion; a bald student with a tattoo of Axia's Starlem on his scalp.

"This is ridiculous! There's no option for a blade staff?! How am I supposed to use any of my spells?!"

"Look, you have two choices. You can choose a physical weapon for pitiful self-defence or you can choose a wand or stave to channel better and boost your magic. You don't-"

"But my magic revolves around the legends of the wave cutter! How am I supposed to use my magic without proper equipment?!"

His outburst was quickly met with strong rebuttal.

"Enough!!"

The line of students all froze at the spontaneous outrage as the teacher slammed the table with his palm, performing a spell Katachi didn't recognize. It caused the entire corridor to quake briefly and the children tumbled onto the floor.

K: (Or maybe it's a spell to induce that sensation. Seems like a deliberately misinterpreted version of Dardicel's spell to me.)

Students would often respect and obey the teachers in the academy strictly because every teacher had the power to place a demerit seal onto a student. A teacher could place a maximum of two demerit seals on a student, and the number of demerits a student held affected his or her standing in school.

The principal and some administrative figures like the security staff were possibly able to bypass the limit and oust any student they deemed unbecoming or dangerous. But one defining point stood clear – To rebuke a teacher required either ignorance or a very special brand of bravery tinted with madness.

"There's a customs box here specially made for whiny ass-wipes like yourself who have to use a specific weapon. You can put your chip in and request for a special order. Do you understand?"

The bald student nodded his head in fear.

"Make your choice already. There are at least three dozen others behind you and we don't have all day."

The student put his wooden piece into the custom box and mumbled something to the teacher. He then walked towards the exit, ashamed of his reckless outburst.

"Next!"

That call repeated for a good number of times before it was finally Katachi's turn. As he approached the table Katachi looked at the small wooden boxes once more intently. The small boxes had labels on them to indicate which weapon was to be manufactured. It was a surprisingly simplistic system for the Magus Academy, but it was likely designed to be user-friendly... Or so he believed. Inside the sword and spear boxes were quite a number of wooden pieces already.

K: (A lot of people chose swords and spears, huh... I'm not very good with a sword, and it'd only trouble me if I use both hands for a spear. I wonder which the more viable option is. Sword or spear?)

The others behind him were getting impatient at his indecisiveness and began jeering.

"Hurry up, idiot!"

"Pick up the pace!"

"How much longer do I have to wait?!"

K: (Not good... The people behind me are urging me to hurry. I better choose one fast.)

In a panic Katachi's eyes swivelled all over the table, browsing the other boxes as well. He was even more hesitant as he expanded his choices to the halberd, mace, flail, axe... There were so many options available that it was easy to be confused by the ideal weapon of choice. Finally, one caught his eye as comfortable.

Out of reflex Katachi shifted his hand over the empty box labelled 'Dagger' and let go. The teacher-in-charge stared at Katachi placing his wooden piece into the box nobody had so much as given a second glance to. The boy was unsure whether that stare was in doubt or in disbelief.

"Whatever your choice is, I'll respect your decision. It's very brave of you to emphasize on speed rather than reach."

K: "..."

He didn't even want to look at the people behind him. He didn't wish to show his face to them, and he felt for a brief moment there a slight pang of regret. A diminutive weapon for a diminutive being such as himself was, if nothing else, fitting. Katachi headed back to his room to study the books he borrowed.

*** ***

The next morning a small group gathered at the announcement board. He wasn't really the kind of person that enjoyed crowds, but there was likely something important enough to garner the attention of the other students.

K: (The words on the board... Tournament?)

The strangely-shaped board rested on a peculiar stand, or pillar...? It too confused its observers by deceiving its centre of gravity, a trait shared by a majority of the school's pillars. It had been slightly more than a week since Katachi arrived so he was already used to a spectacle like such, yet he could never quite derive the origin of the spell used for the pillars.

Perhaps its secret lay within the past to a time when sorcerors interpreted tales in different ways, but that required access to Findel's true history. It was an ordeal in itself to politically affiliate oneself to the Findel Magus Association, and even so that was not the objective of his current sojourn. Katachi gradually shifted his gaze from the pillar to the board that looked like the cross section of a tibia bone.

The board showed the tournament participant layout. The participants were divided into four divisions which then reconnected the finalists from each side to determine one final champion. The information about the engagement rules and judging system were also displayed to the right in the form of tablets bundled together by twine. After reading the judging system and the rules in battle, Katachi went down to the main topic at hand – His own placement in the tournament.

K: (I'm in the same preliminary division as Cillian de Vorsche...)

"Hey all you people, look! Cillian and Nea are already in the same preliminary division. We're in for a good show."

K: (Wasn't Cillian the guy I betted for? Looks like I've picked the tough fight... At least the divisions will shuffle after the preliminaries.

... Where's that Mafer person? Is he in here?)

Katachi glanced at the board and found Mafer's name right next to Deku.

K: (! He's going against last year's champion for the preliminaries? That's a surprise.

... Then, is Bael in the tournament?)

Katachi squeezed his way through the crowd and pondered for ten minutes to no avail. Bael's name was not present amidst the sixty-four participants. Though, given that there were slightly more than two hundred students in the Sage Raufid Magus Academy that was already an overwhelming number of opponents to challenge.

K: (Huh. She didn't participate. That trap she laid back then was actually pretty dangerous, she should have signed up for this if she was already a veteran. She might potentially win the tournament with both her experience and seniority. But then again, her absence is also a good sign. That's one less tough competitor to deal with.)

"Hey, new kid."

K: (But for a senior like Bael to take the backseat- ?)

Katachi spun around and saw a student with a buzz cut looking at him.

K: (The guy at the hallway from yesterday...) "Oh, it's you again."

"Who were you looking for? You've been staring and searching the name list since I came, and I've been here for almost five minutes."

K: "Oh, er, nothing. I was looking for the name of a friend."

The student chuckled a bit at Katachi's response.

"Worrying about someone else's safety before your own? You'd be wiped out early with that kind of attitude."

The student left with a scorning look, leaving Katachi bewildered at the insult.

K: (That guy... How rude, yet how very appropriate.)

He wasn't wrong by any means. To look at another and worry for them would be prideful, insinuating that he alone was strong enough to handle himself to the point that he would worry for another. That attitude would indeed make men keel over in shame when bested. Pride like that was poisonous and banal to anyone, and him in particular.

K: (... I should train.)

With a new resolve carved within him, Katachi forced his way out of the crowd and towards the field.

*** ***

Seeing that he had no lessons to attend in particular, Katachi was free to act as he pleased in the academy. That included self-taught training sessions that normal students with jam-packed curricula would not have time for. It wasn't an uncommon occurrence, however.

Some of the richer or lazier students came to the academy in an attempt to escape their responsibilities and their parents' expectations, and rare were the few who willingly delved into the madness that was Image. At the very least, Katachi was using his time effectively. At the moment the lessons had long since begun so the field was empty and available for anyone's perusal.

One would think it strange how an academy for magi would house a field for its students whom were not required to jog or train frequently like the knights of Rugnud, but the open space was useful for understanding Axia lore and practising Territory spells. Katachi sat alone in the field with the sun gently coating everything around the area with its dawning rays.

He meditated calmly on a sandy patch, absorbing the warmth and radiance of the soft sunlight, a nostalgic action that reminded him of the time spent at the herb ledge. He felt a sour pang in his heart reflecting on the memories of being kept to himself without the pestering of the other children or Bael's assertiveness.

K: (... Focus. I won't have to endure once Rekter steps down. I have nothing against the students, but I can't bring myself to trust or rely on them.)

To summarize things briefly, there was not much one could teach about the Words of Power to begin with. They were 293 powerful sigils crafted by 292 great sorcerors and a crestfallen Warlock of Wheels. The secret to their creation was buried and immolated within their graves decades ago since the Words of Power came about. That knowledge had become popular and widely-known, especially given the terrors induced by the rogue sigils.

If there were anything to learn for a Scholar actively wielding a Word of Power, there was an unspoken rule when it came to a duel between two Scholars. The Words of Power, when challenging each other, worked on a special and highly numerical system known as Precedence Levels. Those Precedence Levels allowed the Scholars to quantify the knowledge they possessed of the Word of Power they wielded, thereby determining which sigil's effect would be dominant should they clash.

Perhaps it was becoming for such a term. The more knowledge one amassed about their Word of Power, the stronger its image was to its Scholar. Thus, in accordance, that knowledge was more likely to take precedence before the opposing or conflicting Word of Power. As a result of such a deadpan, inorganic system, it was as good as suicide to teach another Scholar the meanings of their sigils.

K: (Rekter is smart to limit what he taught... Though, revealing his disposition will put him in a tough spot as well. I can imagine the students harassing him night and day over his Word of Power, just like my own.)

Katachi tried to focus on the Word of Power upon Rekter's nape, wherever he may be, but to little effect. It wasn't as though he could magically feel its presence or anything, but he hoped that the trap was still in effect.

K: (... I should limber up.)

Katachi got up and walked under a tree beyond the boundary of the open field. He picked up a twig on the ground and began fiddling and twiddling the stick around his thumb and index finger.

K: (The trump card aside, I have to make sure he doesn't get an advantage over me at all. The books from the library so far aren't as beneficial as I thought in my understanding of 定, but maybe... Just maybe.)

He waved and slashed at the air with the stick in his hand.

K: (I have to beat my opponents as fast as I can to conceal its presence from the students. The first lesson itself is a hairline crack on the mirror just waiting to shatter and ruin it completely. I have to gamble everything at this one junction. Whether I succeed or fail... I'll have to plan for it only after I know the outcome.)

The simple parrying and stabbing techniques from an old book probably fared little use but Katachi practised anyway. He continually stabbed and slashed at the air, his mind and conscious completely separate from his actions.

K: (I might also need Bertund's help on a couple of things... Best not to assume this flimsy plan might actually work. I need to raise my precedence level as quickly as possible. That's my safest option right now since it's the only real way I'm going to stand a chance against Rekter.

... I'll go ask him after I finish practising this.)

CHAPTER 10

Friday morning.

Under the overcast sky, a circular plot of land with obelisks erected at various points was trodden on by countless students new and old. They waited impatiently for the start of the Young Magus Tournament held next to the open atrium. The tradition for such a competition was that a particularly renowned official, Minister Lein, from the Findel Magus Association would visit the Sage Raufid Magus Academy in search of those who would benefit the country.

If the student was an intelligent strategist, Lein would gift the student a chance to lead as an officer that commanded a platoon in Findel's army. If the student was discreet or savvy he would be hired as a spy and assigned to the field. If the student was good at aggression and combat he would be enlisted in the military as a war magus.

Whatever the country lacked, Lein would replenish by picking the potential candidates that would fulfil the jobs with the utmost proficiency as aspirants and protégés of their greatest. His recommendations were highly revered by many, a mere reflection of his great influence. And as luck would have it, that important figure in the Duvel made a habit to revisit his home town upon the blossoming of the first daffodil in the new year as the world welcomed the Month of the Halberd.

The academy held an exquisite annual event as such to provide an official reason for his return. The stirring darkness of corruption overshadowed by confetti and fanfare marred the bright visage of the country for those who dabbled deep in its society. But that was for another tale, for he who acted without malice shall know none such. The students, mere flowers drifting along the streamside, knew naught the erosion of the riverbed.

As badly as the students wanted to watch the tournament, it was not allowed to start. Commencing the event without the guest-of-honour's presence would be disrespectful and, more bluntly, pointless. So with bated excitement the students chattered amongst themselves excitedly.

Some would talk about how charming or attractive the competitors looked. Others talked about how hard-working or diligent they were. Some chose to observe their spells and fighting styles, deciphering the lore and construing a counter for every participant where possible. From the nosiest gossipers to the reluctant loafers dragged along by their friends, there was always something to talk about.

It didn't take long before murmurs could be heard about his arrival. The guest-of-honour draped in a purple-and-white garb obscuring everything but his face stood at the ledge prepared for him specifically and raised his right hand with elegance. With a crazed wave the crowd roared in excitement.

"Students of Sage Raufid, I am Minister Lein. Sorry to keep all of you waiting! I would like to take this time to thank the champion from the previous tournament for being my escort. If not for him, we would have been held up by the congestion and delayed the event further."

The previous champion gave a slight bow as a show of courtesy.

K: (So that's Deku. He looks a little older than the portrait of him on the poster.)

L: "Now that we are behind schedule, I shall conduct the opening speech later after a short recess. Without further delay, let the tournament begin!"

The official named Lein picked up his goblet filled with wine and emptied it towards the bird resting on a perch. The wine caught fire mid-flight, soaked the bird and the miserable creature transformed into a flaming beast flying off into the sky with an ear-piercing screech. With the commencement of the tournament complete, the students' cries frenzied.

Katachi never quite understood why the Academy chose to conflagrate and murder a Woodtail every year. It might have some symbolic meaning he was unaware of, but if given the choice he would let the poor bird fly free.

K: (Woodtails aren't considered pests... Are they?)

*** ***

"Alright, form up. 'Tis time for the preliminary match. I'll only go over the rules once."

The teacher instructed all the competitors to gather. However, the limited size of the small hallway was too constrained and the students ended up bumping into each other shoulder to shoulder.

"Don't bother about lines, fools! I don't expect uniform queues so just listen up. You lot are from the second division and we're running late. Each division is given only eight tokens suspended on a rope ten meters off the ground. There are sixteen of you this batch so only half you lot will make it to the actual match. Each person is only entitled to take one token. No hoarding."

The enthusiasm of the fidgeting crowd was abated due to the stuffy and unventilated corridor.

"When the token is taken the person receives an immunity spell for two minutes. So once you grab it, don't let go and walk out calmly. Anyone who attempts to take two tokens will be electrocuted by completing the Uzab rune on them so don't test it. You may use any method you wish to obtain the token, but remember that the rules always will apply regardless."

The rules were designed such that a capable person was unable to take a second token for a friend. If one blindly charged forward he could be beaten down or used as a stepping stone while their backs were exposed. However, to be engrossed in fighting meant that the tokens may be snatched while one was fending off another meaninglessly. It truly was a rowdy test of skill, power, speed and manipulation of one's enemies. Katachi thought carefully about his engagement strategy.

K: (I don't know any competent magic for movement in particular... I can think of multiple ways to grab the token using 定, but blowing my cover in the preliminaries is stupid. Should I immobilize everyone? Should I make some kind of impregnable wall that traps everyone briefly?)

He quickly shot the idea down since using 定 on many people at once increased the risk of its disclosure. Using it in a wide area was bad as well in the same regard.

K: (Or maybe displace the token into my hand directly- No, that's too suspicious. Maybe I should minimise all interactions with the other students and head straight for the tokens instead? Which would be the best solution?)

"If you don't have any more questions you may go to the armoury at the back there. Grab the weapon you ordered and ready yourselves. Dismissed!"

The students broke formation and quietly walked to the cabinet filled with dozens of wooden weapons. A green-haired guy grabbed a spear, a familiar-looking bald student grabbed a blade staff and a girl reached for a wooden stave. They were busy arming themselves with the ordered equipment, prominently emphasizing the fact that one needed to get used to the weapon they ordered quickly.

The atmosphere about was solemn and tense since everyone around them was an enemy somewhere down the line. While the other fifteen students geared themselves and practised their wooden weaponry, Katachi squeezed through the lot of them and finally reached the rack. What remained was a tiny, wooden waster dagger.

It was finely-crafted with a solid hilt and an elegant simple design. The handle was secured with a different type of wood, trading the toughness of the dagger in overall for a tighter grip. The wooden blade portion was a fine twenty centimetres long.

Alas, since it was wooden it held no offensive power; not to mention its only viable use was probably for shielding enemy attacks or for hitting someone with a surprise attack. At worst it served as a distraction by throwing it at the enemy.

K: (The grip is decent.)

It seemed suicidal to carry such a tiny dagger with almost no reach into a tournament.

K: (It's light enough to carry, it seems solid enough to hurt a bit and the thickness of the wood is comfortable. Not to mention, it's light... It's anything but cumbersome, but that's more or less the point.)

The merciful path was the renowned path. Katachi swung the tiny dagger on his right wrist a few times to get a feel for its weight. It fit naturally onto his arm and was pretty easy to get used to; as expected of a waster dagger meant for training.

It could be flicked around his hand quickly with just enough momentum and timing to match his own rhythm. The jarring weakness of its reach was a real problem but Katachi didn't have much time to think about that for the moment. The teacher signalled the beginning of the preliminaries with a pair of wood clackers.

"Line up at the gate! Get ready!"

The other contestants were feeling restless as inferred from their hushed mumbles.

"Go!!"

*** ***

The iron gates lifted. A hanging rope on the squarish scaffolding had eight red coloured tokens tied onto it with some strange mixture of what seemed to be bakeflour and water. The participants all charged fervently towards the scaffolding.

K: (Let's go with that then! 恒定! Constant velocity – Self!)

The golden coloured 定 formed on Katachi's chest, his uniform hiding the word well. He kicked off to an explosive start and overtook the others struggling in the sand. It surprised everyone else who were using their feet to push against the sand that they were already lagging behind. Their unified movement was likely a collective strategy to get onto solid ground so they could cast their spells with greater success.

"What the-!!"

The other contestants merely reached the stairs to climb the scaffolding after twenty metres of running, but Katachi was almost at the rope already without worrying about having to squeeze and compete for the cleanest beeline. He grabbed the rope with his hands and began climbing it as fast as his hands and feet allowed. With the Word of Power erased in sync, it made the entire act appear as if he had naturally floated towards the rope.

The act was a bit flawed because had Katachi truly been able to float there was no need to grab the rope to begin with. In contrast, it was impeccable because someone below was already beginning to attack him. Incidentally, he was climbing at a speed faster than he did while floating so the transition was natural enough for the suspicion to be minimal.

"I won't let you! O, great and mighty Kafki, silence this insolent man!"

A purple cloud that appeared miasmic in nature sprouted forth from beneath, gushing towards him like raging rapids. His diminutive figure helped in his ascent tremendously. Katachi's fingers barely gripped onto a red token, and his body was instantly coated with a white membrane just before the purple cloud engulfed him – Yet he was fine.

Katachi loosened his grip on the rope in a panic and fell. Down and down he went until he was diving headfirst into the sand.

K: (Not good! 恒定! Constant status – Self!)

The Word of Power formed on his chest again as he fell and buried the dome of his head.

K: "Auegh!!!"

The participants paused to look at the black-haired child. Because Katachi still had 'Constant status' on him, he was strangely still 'falling' down despite being already on the ground. His arms and legs were still upright in the air in a falling motion that instilled an almost tranquil state of being.

It looked as though he was standing on the roof of his head in some form of bizarre and highly dangerous dance move, as though he were about to break from his neck supporting his full body weight. It was only when Katachi removed the word on his chest did his body and feet drop forward naturally and land on the hard ground in an almost-comical fashion.

It appeared amusing and all at first, but when the other students saw Katachi getting up in slight pain even after the suicidal fall they regained their senses and rushed toward the rope. They concluded that the immunity spell would protect them from falling off the scaffolding, although he achieved that by a completely different method which eluded their attention.

Some would knock others off, who in turn dragged their attackers down with them. Others just wanted to blast spells of earth and fire at everyone, turning the token capture competition into a battle royale. Though his head was dizzy and he could not see the chaos about, they were loud enough for Katachi to briefly understand his surroundings.

Those on the scaffolding reached out for the rope in desperation while those below fought intensely with each other, trying to knock out their opponent. It was a large-scale scuffle with no holds barred but the ensuing battle was his concern no longer.

K: (Ugh... That still sort-of hurt, even with 'Constant status'. Well, I guess my 'status' is constant but I can still feel external forces and attacks even though my status doesn't change... I'll have to use that more carefully from now on.)

The tag that coated him with a white membrane was clasped just barely between his middle and ring fingers. He couldn't begin to imagine what would happen had he loosened his scrunched fingers for even a bit – He would either be dead from his Word of Power not working as intended or he would be alive with his 定 exposed.

Both were horrible in their own right, and he wasn't keen on learning either outcome. Katachi staggered out of the arena clutching his neck in great pain.

*** ***

Four tokens were taken since Katachi's departure. Right now seven students remained, still competing for the remaining tokens with the others knocked out cold.

"Cestia! I didn't think I'd be fighting you like this!"

The boy with the green hair and wooden spear faced the blue-haired girl holding the staff.

C: "Why are we enemies in this, Loar?!"

L: "I have to talk to Minister Lein, Cestia. I have to get that tag and win the tournament so I can return to my village!"

C: "But what about me?! I need that tag too! I must have the funds for my sister's medicine money, and now you're going to deny me of this chance?! You said that I could trust you! Is that promise so cheap to be cast aside just like that?!"

The girl pointed her staff at Loar and chanted with the fiery tempo of her wrath.

C: "O saintly Kafki, grace me with this savage's silence!"

As though it were a punishment, her weakness was pronounced from the way she cast her spell. Rather than visualizing herself as the legend Kafki she envisioned a devout follower who cast the same spell. It was already made clear and decisive where her limits were, to derive a spell from watching someone else rather than believing in the legend herself.

Coupled with her motives Cestia's reason for being there in the gigantic sandbox was justified enough for Loar to feel a slight sting in his heart. He knew with every fibre of his being that he wished to fight her the least. With the wooden staff channelling the magic as a conduit Cestia sprayed a purple mist towards him.

He used his spear as a vault and jumped to her left evasively, clearing the way and causing the huge cloud of poisonous gas to miss completely. Loar regained his composure and thrust the spear towards her, but she sidestepped it and knocked the tip into the earth beneath their feet. Cestia slid the wooden staff over the spear's body and pointed the stave at him.

C: "Give up. I know your tricks all too well- ?!"

Loar dug into the sand with the spear tip hastily and drew a small rune on the sand right beneath Cestia. The scraping sound of the spear's tip was clearly heard amid the ambient noise due to its proximity. Despite being at point blank range of her 'enemy', Cestia gambled a peek at the ground beneath.

C: "!!"

She leapt away as quickly as she could. She recognized that rune – It was a simple Etims rune prepared with her in mind. Had she stayed in that position for long she would have crumbled under his mental suggestion and eliminated from combat effectively.

L: "You're too naive, Cestia! Why did you think I picked a spear over a sword? It's because I know your techniques involve cornering and disarming!"

She readied her staff again and steeled her stance, but her vision was a blur. That was odd – Blurring of eyesight was not an effect the Etims rune inflicted.

C: "Gh!?"

Cestia had to close her eyes in pain. It felt like the water in her eyes were evaporating rapidly which caused extreme discomfort. She cringed and held her hands to her eyes in pain.

L: "How do you like my Scura-"

"You stupid Kafki believer!"

A bald student with a blade staff landed behind Loar. To converse so openly either meant his opponent abandoned fighting him, or that the poor sap was knocked out cold. But that was far from normal; why would a student stop a battle going on between his competitors instead of snatching the tokens himself? The bald student also appeared incredibly angry for some reason.

"Enough with your pointless squabble! The scaffolding's been weakened by both miasmas you shot!"

The two turned to face the scaffolding and ascertained the pandemonium with their own eyes. Cestia couldn't see anything, but Loar could easily commentate for her if he weren't as shocked as he was. The central pillars and base of the wooden scaffolding were corroding, its durability compromised by the toxic cloud Cestia unleashed at the charcoal-haired child earlier. There were still three students battling on the scaffolding and some kind of leopard ascending the sides, but only three tokens remained.

L: (Not good! If the scaffolding falls, someone likely won't make it out alive!) "Cestia! I won't pursue this matter with you for now. We have to help them first!"

Loar started running towards the scaffolding and dug his spear into the sand, scribbling many simple patterns that circled the base of the structure. Cestia was still in great pain lying on the floor with both hands clutching her eyes.

Her sight didn't seem like it would recover soon since moisture in the eyes was not as easy to regain as one's sense of balance. She was as good as being knocked out for most of the round, so the bald head dragged her to a side under a shadow at the rim of the sandbox. He used the opportunity to gain some distance and observed the situation from afar.

(To hell with the tokens! Their lives should come first. But their positioning is a little bit high which limits my options a lot. If I want a shot at getting them out safely I have to time it right.)

The base let out a creaking sound. The corrosion did significant damage to the wood, and the scaffolding's core and legs didn't seem like they would hold out for much longer. Loar was busy drawing the repulsion runes on the sand and soil with his spear but that was at best a flimsy safety net as it was not founded on something solid like stone or wood.

(Wier runes on the soft ground? Such poor handiwork. It wouldn't hold if the debris falls onto the runes and destroys them! What is this guy thinking, wasting his energy like that?)

The bald student tightened his grip on the wooden blade staff.

(Still, that speed... He's got some talent for them. An aspiring runesmith? Either way, with his aide hopefully this spell will go a lot better.)

The platforms wobbled and resounded with a mind-scraping creak. The three students on it were still in danger and among the confusion a sixth competitor was already leaving the scene with a token in hand, a tanned brown-haired female student with her uniform befouled by sand. One of them, a girl who wielded a spear fell toward the rope, grabbed it and sliced the rope with her bile gauntlet.

The two tokens attached to it fell along with her and she grabbed one of the tokens quickly. As she was surrounded by a white membrane, the girl landed on her posterior uninjured and proceeded to run towards the exit without looking back. Without the last token on the scaffolding both students were in danger. It rapidly snowballed into twice the amount of collateral damage applicable.

"Spearman with the green hair!"

Loar paused to address the bald student calling out to him.

"I need a Tespi symbol on the ground! Make it deep so it can't be removed by the falling debris! Carve one at the clearing over there!"

Loar did not understand what he had in mind, but he did know that drawing a Tespi symbol would help the baldie's plan succeed. Without doubt in his mind Loar quickly dug a Tespi symbol on the ground and continued making runes around the scaffolding. The bald student ran towards the prepared rune and positioned himself so the rune and the students were properly aligned.

(Good. Now, then. The waves spread out from disturbances and inequilibriums in the sea, from the tiniest fish to the largest sharks. The Tespi symbol is Axia's method of reading the waves from the stars. Tying his fabled hammer onto the end of a sail, Axia made a dowsing to divine the right course for the ships to sail past the thunderstorm. If I misinterpret his tale and change the students into raindrops...)

He reinforced the image of that legend he read of countless times.

"May the rain upon these sails chart our path to success! Novadis Graté!"

The students atop the scaffolding were tugged by a mystical force unwillingly towards the Tespi symbol. The scaffolding had yet to fall but it was better to pull them out as quickly as possible. It would have been much harder to deal with them had the debris obstructed the path.

(Not yet... Not yet... They're not close enough... ! Now!!!) "HAAA!!!"

With a swift movement, the bladestaff's blade emitted a faint silver-blue glow at its tip and the bald student swept the blade at the area above the Tespi symbol. A rather strong shockwave before him forced the bald student himself to guard his face and vitals, and the two who fell towards the Tespi were thrust upwards for a very brief moment before sliding across the sand safely for about five metres.

The two were rescued unscathed. The bald student gave a sigh of relief, a symbol of triumph over an ordeal most challenging. However, the external force from the wave cutter did not disperse harmlessly, causing the scaffolding to immediately give way and collapse onto the ground. The last token was unfortunately buried under the huge mass of broken wood and rope. Some of the debris were caught by the Wier runes, but most of it had been pointless as he deduced earlier.

L: "The last token's under that scrap!"

Loar quickly ran towards the heap, and wrote in saliva a Tespi rune on his spear. With a strong stab, the wooden debris quickly stuck to the tip of his spear like a magnet, clearing the lot and revealing the rope with the last token wedged between splinters of wood.

L: "There it is-"

Before Loar could exclaim in joy a swift shadow swooped down and grabbed the rope with the token.

C: "I'll take that!"

The person grabbing the rope with the token was the girl from earlier with blue hair. Her eyes were still slightly red, dried and twitching from the Scura rune earlier, but she could ignore that flesh wound if it were for her little sister's medicine.

L: "Cestia!?"

C: "It's mine now, Loar. You lose."

Cestia waved the rope around her hand in a proud manner, but-

-the token on the rope was snatched away. A white membrane coated a student with orange... Brown?... Rustic brown hair.

"I... I did it! I managed to get a token! YES!!"

... Nobody could blame him. Those were the rules of the match, after all. Loar, Cestia and the bald student could only sigh in misery at the anti-climactic conclusion.

C: "It should have been mine..."

L: "The unsung heroes never win."

"... For what it's worth, at least I can sleep well tonight."

The three sung their grievances in unison as they watched the timid Pitin walk away with a radiant smile on his face.

CHAPTER 11

With the preliminaries settled, it was currently a recess for the next match. The participants were given access to a tonic in exchange for confiscating and restoring their wooden weapons. The gel-like drink was copper-like, viscous and truthfully quite disgusting, too mucous to even attempt chewing, but it revitalized the students for the next round.

The students were supposed to perform this trade so they may not infuse their wooden weapons with any magic during the breaks between the matches. But that was not quite true. It was a choice – To keep one's wooden weapon enchanted and coated with their magic or to recover their stamina and have the wooden weapon restored to its original intended form.

There were indeed competitors that were strong enough to last through the whole tournament without recovering or resting even once, namely the veterans like Deku. There were also other competitors that relied heavily on the enchantments inscribed upon their weapons, the unfortunate ones who were forced to play defensively and gave up on the healing syrup in order to sustain the magic on their weapon.

Katachi struggled to drink the thick, gooey copper syrup, unaware of the option to forgo its ingestion. It was wriggling and wobbling between his mouth and throat, like a pouch of water that was well-preserved and unbroken, a concise-enough description of how thick and cohesive the syrup was. The sensation easily plagued nightmares in one's sleep but the after-taste was mildly sweet.

He felt like he would choke if he didn't drink it down quick yet it was difficult to swallow the liquid because of its very nature. He felt his throat obstructed by the liquid, unable to retract after widening for its initial entry. He forcibly tilted his head upwards, compelling the jelly-like goo down his mouth and throat before it finally yielded.

M: "Hahahaha! Disgusting, isn't it?"

A spiky-haired boy walked up behind him, patted him on the shoulder and sat down on the wooden stool in front of him.

K: "Mafer? You're here... You got a token as well?"

M: "Yeah, I did. It's not as hard as I thought. I'd think that Deku would wipe the floor but nobody even tried to hold him back. That guy just strolled towards the rope in a carefree manner and grabbed a token like he was buying groceries. That's next-level respect scarier than anything I've ever seen. Did you see it?"

K: "I... I didn't. The preliminaries were held at roughly the same time, weren't they?"

M: "Huh. Good point. But seriously, he's a real toughie. I have never seen anyone so intimidating that the rest of the competitors view the mere thought of challenging him as silly. There were loads of murmurs and the like among the crowds but I heard you did pretty well yourself, snatching the first token with a trick like that."

Mafer seemed to have noticed from the audience chattering about that Katachi used some kind of unknown magic during the preliminaries.

M: "How did you do it, Mister healer?"

It came down to a challenging decision.

Katachi could directly tell Mafer that he possessed a Word of Power on him, but the problem was whether the secret would leak. If the news got out Katachi will never be able to relax, not even in his own room. The students would glare at him for being a cheater. The teachers would likely plan to kill him and claim the Word of Power for their own. Bertund promised that he would do his utmost to assist Katachi in that aspect but his word left much room for doubt.

The safest solution was to lie. Segus once cited that 'One ought tattle only lies of white when need be.' So, if Katachi was lying about his power to protect everyone from the madness and power lust it was acceptable behaviour. But even so, he had to come up with something convincing to lie about.

He couldn't just say 'Oh, I can partially float' because he would be questioned on the type of magic used. He needed a convincing argument that could cover up the Word of Power's true potential, a foreign magic or something powerful enough to rival it.

K: "... I'm..."

Katachi revised through all the knowledge of gods, magic and reincarnate arts he could think of. It was better to use the tales of gods instead of the tales of legends so the authenticity of his deceit could be masked. Finally, he found one that was suitable.

K: "I'm a believer of Soltak."

M: "Wha- Seriously? A Soltak believer? That's really rare."

Mafer seemed to have bought the argument.

K: (Good. Very good. He seems convinced.)

M: "So, you're only that powerful so long as you're in direct sunlight?"

K: "There was no need for direct sunlight. It's been overcast since this morning, Mafer. I can also use regular sunlight about, though the Reincarnate Art would be weakened."

M: "Huh. So, even without direct sunlight you can still use Soltak's Reincarnate Art?"

K: "Yes, but to a lesser degree."

Soltak's Reincarnate Art used sunlight in favour of one's mental image to evoke the unnatural. It implicitly meant that Soltak followers were indomitable by day but became much weaker at night, especially on a new moon where they would become enfeebled and their efforts in bolstering their fortitude undone.

It was a convenient lie because nobody would be able to notice any significant difference at night. Katachi had yet to show his Word of Power at all, and since the students only saw each other in the day for the most part it was easy to pull the bluff.

M: "That's cool. Well, I'll be off now. The first official match begins really soon and I'm first up. See you around."

*** ***

Katachi squeezed through the students to reach an empty seat on the huge stone stairs. He found a comfortable spot in a corner that distanced him from the other students and peered into the ring of the coliseum-like stage for the first battle. It was an empty, barren platform with a projection of a match between two students in Cosmatral Tlod through an Eye of Jedivh.

But that alone was exciting enough to eke the interest of the crowd. Mafer was holding a wooden staff in his left hand and a small unlit candle in his right. He was consistently dodging and swatting down the opponent's attacks the entire match. His opponent was throwing strange tablets of what seemed to be wooden card pieces.

K: (A Feister-61 deck? So he's using Sha'koth as a base for his spells?)

"What a joker! Vikarr's striking a cool pose again!"

One of the male students sitting behind him was scoffing the behaviour of the student named Vikarr.

K: (That looks pretty tough. That Vikarr guy is not giving him time to catch his breath or formulate a plan at all, pinching and cornering him aggressively. Are they all like this?)

*** ***

M: (This guy's bound to run out of these wooden pieces sooner or later.)

Mafer continued avoiding the wooden pieces as best as he could. Some would hit him on the arm or his sides, which felt like a hard rigid pebble had been thrown at him. But thankfully none of them hurt to the point of flinching. Just as he believed to have survived the worst of it, the opponent began the trick up his sleeve.

V: "Okay, I have now exhausted all of my cards."

His opponent openly declared that he ran out of cards to throw.

M: (Is this a trap?)

V: "Now then, don't be shy. Look at this card."

Vikarr picked up a wooden tablet on the ground and showed Mafer one of its faces. On the card was a simplistic pattern on it. From the way he phrased his words one could assume that every card had a broad-headed V on it.

V: "Do you think this card is a V for 'Victory'? Or do you think it is V for 'Vicious'?"

Mafer raised his guard even more. There was no reason why a student would reveal his magic's pattern and trick to give the opponent a second wind. Not unless...

V: "Make your choice."

... Not unless the winner was already decided.

M: "I go with V for 'Vicious'. Is that fine?"

Mafer raised the candle on his right hand he clutched onto dearly and aimed his spell towards Vikarr.

V: "Sorry. Wrong answer."

Vikarr snapped his fingers and the cards scattered about his feet started to rattle. The bright V's on every card radiated a sinister blood red, and they started to fly in the direction the V's bottom tip was pointing at. Mafer realized it the moment the cards started rattling, but it was far too late.

M: (Sha'koth, the trickster legend said to have become a god by impersonating one, had a story where he was able to make a duck walk backwards in a bet. He did it by attaching fishing lines onto the duck's legs and someone from the bushes tugged the duck's legs step by step to make it look like it walked backwards. But the highlight was that he painted the duck's feet with a reverse arrow underneath, and claimed that the arrows made the duck walk backwards. Converting it into an attack spell with Image Power...)

The wooden tablets flew in the air like swallows and bats, beating up, bruising and even incising Mafer with a flurry of attacks from all directions. In the pain Mafer tried to kneel down, but the knee that became exposed was struck by a card immediately as though capitalizing on every opening he revealed. In utter agony Mafer could only clench and wrap his body in a foetal position with his back against the ground to protect his vitals.

V: "Game over. They are not letter Vs – They are arrowheads."

Vikarr placed the one wooden card he held flatly on his hand and raised it above his head. The rest of the cards, still fluttering about and ravaging Mafer, responded to it and flew out in every direction in a coordinated manner before heading towards Vikarr. The cards flew behind him and neatly stacked themselves above the one card in his hand.

"And that, my friends, is how you use a Feister-61 deck properly. This is for my juniors Samuel and Ginevette!"

*** ***

K: (Beaten completely in the first round like meat to the tenderiser.)

Katachi wore a grim expression on his face. Mafer was demolished by a foe who didn't even break a sweat, denied any chance to retaliate. No matter how impressive Croxa's Reincarnate Art was, if it could not be used it was as pointless as teaching a pet dog to swim in lava. The first official match took less than two minutes, and it could barely be called a match – A one-sided beat down was more appropriate.

K: (I should expect this level of difficulty against my own opponents... No, even greater. I can't expect everything to sail smooth. If a participant fared this well against Mafer, I wonder what the champion could do.)

*** ***

The previous champion couldn't have come at a more opportune time.

D: "Hello, everyone!"

Deku exclaimed in a pep and energy nobody could resist. The crowd went absolutely nuts over his simple greeting.

D: "Let's start raising the stakes immediately! Alright, what will it be... Hmm, well, let's see... What would be a good punishment for my incompetence?"

The crowd hushed down quickly, awaiting Deku's words like orphans who couldn't afford education peering into a classroom to learn new things from the teacher.

D: "I know! If I lose this match, I'll drink that disgusting healing syrup as water for a whole week!"

The crowd roared with laughter over that ludicrous declaration. Of course, that moxie radiating from Deku was not without base. He had been the champion of the tournament for thrice in a row already, and to be bested by someone he defeated thrice would be an utter disgrace.

It could also be proof of said individual's improvement should the worst occur, but healthy competition was difficult to come by for Deku. That aside, the crowd did not take his bets seriously since he was likely going to win the match.

Z: "Hello again, Deku. You ready for this?"

D: "Of course! Same rules as always, then? Though, I doubt you'd have enough time to even cast your spells."

And so, with the ready signal present from both sides, the two began their match.

*** ***

That was the fastest match yet.

In two seconds, Deku punched the floor with his glowing fist and the land beneath him glowed yellow before being 'absorbed' into his right arm. In the next two seconds, Deku simply punched toward the general area where Zul was and the yellow liquid-like attack lashed out like a whip from his still-glowing arm. The yellow tassel expanded into a strange shape before losing its yellow lustre. The huge chunk of land that was once beneath Deku's feet was thrown toward Zul at a ridiculous pace.

With nowhere to run, Zul could only hold his arms forward in a defensive stance and ram into the huge mound of sand and grit head-on. The land broke apart into many fine pieces because it was mostly made of sand, but Zul received the full brunt of the blow. In five seconds, the second match ended with the poor student partially buried in the barren field.

K: (Vikarr and his Feister-61, Deku with Conduit Imbue... These people are all power freaks. I remember Bael mentioning something like her not having enough time to set up her traps in the arena, but this is ridiculous.)

That may be so, yet the child was not shocked to say the least.

K: (At least they don't look like the type to counter spells. Even if they're mostly older than I am, they're just students after all. Most of them have likely never seen Minister Lein or an actual sorceror in action before.)

He felt a harrowing disposition as he recalled a most displeasing scene of a man arrested and humiliated by a certain renowned sorceror years ago, a darkness to Image far more severe than the magic the children now perform. In comparison to their mere enactment of tales, to forcibly construe a spell of malice by trapping a man in his own history was far more cruel.

K: (Not that I'm in any position to speak. I feel like I will utterly die without my Word of Power as protection. Muscle is just muscle and they treat magic as some tool to better themselves, but spells that can't be prepared for ahead of time are the most fearsome. It's not all bad, though. At least they are using magic.)

Katachi squeezed his way past the spectator zone and to the armoury.

K: (It's my turn next... But it's against Cillian de Vorsche, a knight. Of all the opponents I could be paired against, it had to be a warrior who favours might over magic. Gods help me, I feel my throat choking up.)

CHAPTER 12

Something rumbled within him. It was an uncomfortable anxiety of being watched by hundreds of strangers. The audience wasn't technically around him since Cosmatral Tlod was a separate plane from Cosmatral Naturale as proven from the stone steps earlier. Yet, Katachi tensed up a little bit at the thought of being observed by at least a hundred pairs of eyes.

C: "So, I heard that you're the student that flew through the sky and snatched the token."

He remembered that name. Sporting dark blue hair and a uniform far classier than his, with white fingerless gloves on his hands and a standard wooden sword of 80cm provided by the academy, Katachi remembered that student's name clearly. He remembered it so lucidly that he hoped to avoid fighting him if possible – He was the finalist in last year's tournament, after all.

K: "You're Cillian de Vorsche, are you not?"

C: "Yes. I am. It's great that the divisional shuffling put us against each other this early on."

The cold affirmation of his status only served to increase Katachi's guard and nervousness. Katachi subconsciously despised his decision to nominate him as the winner for the bet with that strange student from the other division, a possible omen to the event today.

K: (I have no idea what techniques he uses, or how he attacks. The best solution would be running around and dodging his attacks until I get a good feel for them.) "You're quite the opponent to have for my first match."

C: "So it must seem to you. Am I really that renowned? I didn't think my name would reach the new students this soon."

Someone was certainly ecstatic.

K: "It's an honour fighting you."

C: "The pleasure is mine, but will your skills sustain it?"

Cillian raised his wooden duelling sword and ran the blade across his free left palm. With legs spread wide apart he stood firm in a stance Katachi didn't recognise. The child drew his wooden dagger and entered a more suitable stance as well.

*** ***

C: (A dagger?)

Cillian was honestly surprised. A dagger in a competition between magi was strange indeed. In most legends and tales which involved a dagger there were often cosmetics and additional parts on the dagger that made it ceremonial.

Since the daggers in the competition were pitifully plain waster daggers with a simplistic hilt and blade it could only mean that the weapon was to be used as it was originally intended. Even so, that was a strange choice for a magus. Why would he use a weapon that required him to get into a range where he could be killed off easily?

Not to mention, most magi were physically frail unless they were trained hybrids like Cillian so they shouldn't be able to execute tricky or advanced attacks like the knights or champions would. Even if that were the case, the child looked unusually frail. So, perhaps it was to be used as a spellblade that increased the range of his attacks deceptively?

C: (Maybe it's best not to brood over it. Worse comes to worst I'd be hit hard by a surprise attack or something. The more on guard I am, the stronger I reinforce the image of a frightening foe. Focus.)

Without hesitation, Cillian readied his guard and stepped forward.

*** ***

The match proceeded for a full minute fruitlessly. There was no real development between the Ohdean constantly retreating along with the Rugnud warrior pursuing the talentless child around.

Naturally, since the tournament was supposed to focus around the individual students' understanding of magic that skirmish was starting to become a yawn. It certainly didn't help that both Cillian de Vorsche who did little even with his magic, and Katachi who was not fast enough to cast any spells of sorts were incredibly boring to watch.

C: "... I don't like this. You're not doing anything besides dodging."

He deliberately threw off his footwork at times to prevent the unnoticed casting of potential spells, but that only allowed Katachi to run further to stall the match that should have ended as soon as it began. Cillian leapt back after dashing in for yet another fruitless strike against the ever-defensive foe.

C: (He's just retracting like a turtle of sorts. Maybe he's not as good as I gave him credit for.) "I want you to fight me at your fullest, but you're holding back. Are you so naive to think that you could beat me without using magic at all? Or are you trying to disrespect me by deliberately doing it?"

With that, Cillian held his free left hand over the blade portion of his sword.

C: "Or perhaps you are the type to go all-out only after your opponent has?"

With a simple motion of running his hand along its fuller, the blade portion of his sword released an uncomfortable light. It was a magic Katachi recognized, but knowledge was only half the battle won.

K: (The Vorsche family is known for a transcendent magic known as Bringer of Dawn. It began with Tarren de Vorsche using magic to lead the lost sheep back to him in the darkness of night. The light was so lucent and glaring that the villagers were roused so he was heavily criticized for it.)

Unfortunately for Katachi, the very nature of supportive spells gave him little room to act on its potential weaknesses.

K: (One of the descendants, Bryne de Vorsche used it in actual combat to blind his opponent, and since then it's been revered as a situational support magic. There's nothing for me to pry apart, though. It's not like I can make him believe that he is incapable of using the magic, especially considering his heritage. I can't do anything about this.)

The light was glaring enough for people to shield their eyes from the source and still be partially blinded. It was emanating with such intensity that merely looking at an object reflecting its light would hurt one's eyes much like the sun itself. Cillian himself did not seem to be affected by the magic at all, but he was either immune to its effects or accustomed to the glare from the swords being pointed at him by his own family.

The knight was never really liked for that form of magic. Stunning as it may be, the spectators barely if at all got the chance to see Cillian fighting his opponent because of the blinding brilliance. As a result of the magic's nature it was quite a mockery to the other students who saw little potential in its utility.

K: (I wish he would teach me how to use Bringer of Dawn, but that does not seem likely. Utility magic is harder to counter compared to offensive magic so I would like to learn it if he's keen on teaching.)

With his opponent blinded Cillian walked towards Katachi slowly, raising the sword above his head primed and ready to cut it down. Yet the child did not frown.

K: (But that is exactly why it will be undone.) "... Perfect."

The first word he spoke in two minutes and he was completely unfazed.

*** ***

K: (恒定. Constant status – Wooden sword. 固定. Fixate object in space – Wooden sword.)

Two golden sigils that formed 定 surfaced on the blade of the tool. Katachi took advantage of its radiance to disguise his 定 so that nobody could see them placed on the waster sword.

He blindly rushed forward and swung his dagger wildly. The dazzling light placed him at a disadvantage, but if he couldn't determine where the enemy was or at least get the light behind him without showing his back it was going to end much worse.

In response to his sudden aggression, Cillian tried to jump away to distance himself safely. But he realized the trick a moment too late; his sword could not be moved at all. Cillian loosened his grip and leaped back to see the sword hanging in mid-air. By then, Katachi had already reached a position where the sword was behind him.

The brilliance meant little to something he wasn't looking at directly... Even though the eye-searing radiance was the linchpin to the success in his strategy. Katachi opened his eyes and assessed the scene before him with care.

The senior's uniform seemed so much cleaner compared to his own – Katachi tumbled over and rolled across the sand repeatedly to avoid some of the knight's riskier attacks so his uniform was stained with countless grains of beige on his sleeves and back.

Cillian merely needed to advance and retreat on his two feet as a proper knight ought to. When comparing their uniforms his was definitely much dirtier and sandier. But was it really the time to concern himself with something so trivial? Cillian's sword was behind him, and Katachi now strategically stood between him and his weapon. This was a great opportunity to counter-attack.

Yet there were still risks present. Winning the battle meant little if the war was lost. For example, if the weapon was not meant to glow when it left Cillian's hand then the foul play would be obvious from the moment Katachi removed the weapon from his grasp. He didn't know enough about Bryne de Vorsche's history to determine if he had once dropped or thrown his sword to blind his opponent from a distance.

There was also the issue with positioning. If Cillian could circumvent his strikes and make Katachi turn around to face the glowing sword, the advantage would be lost. To that end Katachi considered going for horizontal and diagonal slashes that promoted Cillian to duck sideways, limiting his ability to reposition.

C: "... Not bad."

Cillian's face didn't show an expression of shock, but rather one of admiration and respect that he was ensnared in his enemy's trap. From his expression it seemed as though the sword was able to glow even when there was no body contact, which brought him slight relief.

Yet there's bound to be a time limit as to how long it remained glowing, and every second ticking away brought his Word of Power closer and closer to being revealed. Every moment he spared was every moment Cillian came closer to realizing the flaws in the hasty plan.

K: (It can't go on any longer than this. I have to end it now.)

Katachi gripped his dagger tight and slashed at Cillian aggressively. Swipe. Swipe. Swipe. Stab. Swipe. Swipe. Backhand. Swipe. Katachi unleashed a torrent of blows against the defenceless Cillian who could only dodge backwards without his weapon by his side.

Despite being superior in close combat Cillian had yet to recover from the shock enough to take the initiative and overcome Katachi's ploy. His short opponent may be wet behind his ears in close-quarters combat, but confronting Nistier's Style was no joke even when performed by an amateur.

Under the mêlée fighting rules, should the wooden blade touch the opponent enough times indicating an amount of damage the magus could not withstand the round would be over. It could be many repeated slashes on the arms, or a direct stab at the heart. So long as the 'cumulative damage' was substantial it could be anyone's victory.

It was the job of a magus to avoid such situations both on him and his comrades in the first place, so if that could not be avoided or if a magus could force his enemy into a situation like this it was as good as declaring the victory of the battle. Finally, *pa!* with an aggressive lunge that forced Cillian to jerk back and lose his footing for a brief moment, his swing finally connected.

C: "Huurk!!"

Katachi's wooden dagger cleaved towards Cillian's throat, pushing the knight back and forcing him to stumble.

*** ***

C: "... I'll be honest here, I never expected an opponent like you."

K: "It's a pleasure fighting you too, Cillian de Vorsche."

C: "I guess I'm too used to having a blade by my side that my body has rusted. This will be a good lesson for me to train my body along with my swordsmanship. Thanks, Katachi."

Cillian walked towards the obelisk to his right and left Cosmatral Tlod with dignity and satisfaction.

*** ***

S1: "Mister Jiel!"

J: "Hello, students. I don't see you in study groups often. What are you doing?"

S1: "We're discussing about the type of magic that new kid uses."

J: "New kid?"

S2: "Yeah. The one that beat Cillian!"

S1: "Oh, Mister Jiel! Do you know any magic that could recreate the third round just now?"

J: "I'm sorry, but I don't have time to watch those competitions. Not with my children-"

L: "You lot sure are energetic. Have you figured out how he disarmed Cillian?"

S1 & S2: "Mister Lamale! You know the magic he's using?"

L: "I won't spoil too much, but you should think about it carefully. That student didn't use any chants or items to invoke his spells. From there, you can guess that he used some form of Reincarnate Art in that match." (Well, assuming he's below a Meister's level, at least. It's possible to treat Cillian's weapon as an idol of worship 'not meant for human hands' if he finds the right story for it.)

S2: "Reincarnate Art?"

L: (But, if that were the case... To do so without any preparation prior, he is a terrifying one. The Magus Association could use an assassin like that who can cast magic discreetly without the target noticing.) "What do you think, Jiel? You're better at Reincarnate Arts than I am."

J: "I'm sorry, Mister Lamale. I haven't watched the match so I really don't know what happened. You know how playful Totta is, and it's hard to keep Seiene from being teased."

S1: "Aww, you should have! You should have seen how awesome that was! Cillian's sword was floating in mid-air, and only when that new kid struck the fatal blow did the sword fall onto the ground."

J: "Floating in mid-air...? Would the field happen to be sunny while they were fighting?"

S1 & S2: "Yeah."

J: "Well, if nothing else I'm guessing it's Child of Sun."

S1: "Child of Sun?"

S2: "Is that Soltak?"

L: "I suppose he could very well be a Soltak believer. The Vorsche family's magic was, after all, based around light. You would use light itself to counter something that uses light."

J: "You shouldn't jump to conclusions so quickly. This is just a guess, so don't go crazy over-"

S3: "What's this about the new student being a Soltak believer?"

S4: "Is he really using the Child of Sun Reincarnate Art?"

S5: "Hey everyone! The dark horse's a Soltak follower!!"

J: "Hold it right there, hasty decisions are the bane of-"

L: "Well that's just great. Why do the students always do this?"

*** ***

A mass of voices came from behind him as he headed towards the tournament participant layout. Katachi felt compelled to spin around hearing his name briefly in the conglomerate of sounds to see at least eight students with empty wooden tablets in their hands.

"Follower of Soltak, could you give us an autograph or something?"

Katachi was speechless. He witnessed first-hand the terrifying power of what rumours could do once more. It began as a simple white lie to Mafer, but to think that there were students already addressing him as a follower of Soltak. Was it wrong to trust Mafer? But at the same time, any possible suspicions over his Word of Power were thoroughly erased. Katachi felt a great relief that he avoided what could potentially spell his downfall.

K: "Uhm... I-"

Before Katachi could even begin to answer, eight wooden tablets were shoved into his hand.

K: "..."

It would normally be easier just to raise the tablets to the magic circle on his left arm, but that word grafting method gave power to the tokens. Giving those away was the equivalent of selling his identity which, as an obvious violation of the school rules, was prohibited.

K: "... Can I borrow that, then?"

"Take it! Consider it a gift to you."

Their smiles friendly, but their thoughts sinister. Katachi had the suspecting feeling that they planned on using the carvings for something unethical. They were likely cussing under their breaths for him to fail and die, and his signatures sold as mementos. It was not uncommon for the novices to be given tall seats only for the chair to be yanked from them, as was the poison of pride. It applied to offices, brothels, chandleries and banks, so what would dispel that malice from academies?

K: (They would wish harm upon others while hoping for mercy, always doing things they come to regret. I wonder when they may reach the maturity Mother spoke of.)

If the children ever knew how warped Katachi's interpretation of their presence was, they would click their tongues in disgust and walk away. But none would refute his otherwise accurate claim. Katachi could only sigh as he graciously accepted a carving pick from one of the students and proceeded to scrape his name onto the tablets.

CHAPTER 13

The wooden door was knocked on loudly in a rhythmic 11-knock pattern.

B: "Come in!"

The figure at the wooden door was Katachi holding a carving pick in hand. With a tired expression looming over his face he dragged his feet across the carpet and sat down on a comfortable orange couch before looking up at her. That was certainly unusual. Katachi wasn't the proactive child to approach another so openly... Or perhaps he warmed up to her enough to do so? That notion excited Bael briefly.

K: "Bael..."

B: "Katachi?"

Bael placed her notes down and manipulated a couple of teapots to begin serving her guest immediately.

B: "What- What brings you here? It's not like you to visit me. Usually I'd go to you instead."

K: "N-nothing much. I just wanted to uh... Ask you something."

B: "Something? What do you need?"

K: "Do you happen to have a map of the world?"

B: "What do you plan to do with one?"

K: "I've never had an actual map of the world to refer to when I was back in Mielfeud, and since you collect a lot of data and meaningful stuff, I... I was just thinking, you know... If you'd have a map of the world."

B: "I do have a map, but it doesn't show the whole world. Western Anik isn't mapped out."

Since Western Anik was a massive jungle ridden with plague and dangerous swamps which only the toughest animals survive it made sense that the area would barely be mapped, if at all. The most they could actually do with Western Anik was map out the border between the forest, Findel and Eastern Anik, a simple outline skirting along the borders of safety. No towns were marked nor recorded down even if they did exist in the past.

K: "That- That's good! That's good enough! Can I take it to my room to trace it?"

B: "Sure, as long as you don't wrinkle it."

K: "Thank you Bael! That's a great help to me!"

Katachi sauntered from his seat to the map on the messy table and picked it up delicately with a grateful look on his face.

B: (Heeheehee, he's so lively when he's happy, just like a pet.)

As Katachi stored the map into his bag delicately an itching sensation could be felt from the magic circle at the top of his left arm.

(Contestant Katachi, your match begins in thirty minutes. Please assemble at the entrance to Cosmatral Tlod.)

K: (Huh. That weird voice again... She sounds rather familiar, for some reason.) "Bael, I'm afraid I have to go."

B: "What, already? It hasn't even been five minutes!" (He hasn't even explained to me why he cooped up in his room the other time! Am I really that displeasing to him?!)

The sudden departure was unannounced and unruly of him, but Katachi could only excuse himself politely from the room-

K: (... ?)

-but that action was quickly rejected by the locked door.

K: "Uhm... Bael, the door's locked."

B: "I know."

Despite the unsettling answer, Bael smiled at him with a cheerful demeanour. It was quite unnerving to affirm and acknowledge the door being locked as 'normal'. Her face was starting to take a creepy turn in all the wrong ways.

K: "Bael?"

B: "You think I'd let you leave that easily? You owe me an explanation to the other time you left me hanging, Katachi! I won't let you weasel out of this one like you did the other day!"

The situation was turning sour real quick.

K: "Bael, I'm serious here, the magic circle told me to assemble at the field before everyone else for the next match so I really have to go. Where's the key to the door?"

But the senior was clearly not entertaining the idea. Bael accosted Katachi with a wicked smile, one which sent shivers down his spine and made him subconsciously retreat to another part of her house. If anyone was asked to describe the scene with a suitable metaphor, it was akin to an injured pigeon running away from a child keen on holding the poor frightened animal.

B: "Why are you running away, Katachi? Am I that scary?"

K: "Unfortunately, yes! You're freaking me out right now! I don't have the courage to approach you!"

B: "Come now, I won't bite! You know that, don't you?"

Bael's attempts to approach Katachi at the couch section were futile as he pulled back to her workbench.

B: "Katachi, be a good boy and let me pet you!"

K: "Stay away! Stay away! I don't want any!"

B: "Don't be like that, it's my turn to tease you!"

K: "When have I ever teased you? That was never a competition!"

Katachi was starting to feel like his life itself was at stake. He had the vague feeling that he would, once more, relive the experience of being stuck in her house for five hours on his first day at the academy. An animationist like herself was at her strongest when surrounded by her tools, and her house was essentially a giant tool used to keep all her smaller tools, hand-sized or otherwise.

He tried to topple a life-sized model of Byrh to his right so it could serve as a blockade impeding her advance but the model ominously resisted his efforts. Even after he leaned its head on the table slanted at a perilous angle that threatened to damage and destroy the model should it slip and fall, it miraculously levitated for a brief moment and assumed its original upright position. He was wasting time with that fruitless attempt.

B: "Are you kidding me, Katachi? I'm an animationist! Everything in this room is under my control!"

K: (What do I do?! Everything in this room is controlled by her! There's no real way to impede her progress, and I don't think I can outlast her in terms of stamina!)

Katachi retreated further back to a water purification model and shoved at it towards the region between the workbench and walkway, but that was quickly rendered futile with the model resisting his push deliberately.

B: "How else did I lock the door without using my key? It's obvious, silly!"

K: (Even the model!? What's next, the carpet will swallow me up like some kind of man-eating plant?! I need to get out quick!!)

He made yet another round back to the workbench in what appeared to be a ceaseless game of cat and mouse. Unfortunately, time was running short for Katachi both in his deadline to reach the field and in his stamina to outrun Bael. He grabbed a hat stand to blockade the path once more, but something unexpected happened.

The grooves situated at the top of the creepy duck-head lacquered hat stand knocked one of the apparatus off the workbench, and that was an act so horrifying he could see Bael's eyes and mouth widen in slow motion. The apparatus hit the ground with a solid thunk and it explosively released the catch at its base, revealing a magic circle he didn't recognize. Suddenly, the room shuddered and everything came to life at the same time.

B: "Oh no! My project! It's taken priority over my control!"

K: (What in the good woods-)

Her papers and documents, the various artefacts and objects on the workbench, the couch and sofa and rug and fire stoker, everything began to float and circle the room in an idyllic fashion. Interestingly enough, the furniture were knocking and clapping against each other and making music out of the mess.

B: "By the gods, all that research I did for Uncle Dinpill's new business! Stop! Stop right this instant!"

Bael was utterly flustered and overwhelmed by the sheer mess, but Katachi took advantage of that chaos. He grabbed his bag and headed for a blank wall in a part of the room.

K: (If the door won't budge then I'll make my own door. It's fine every once in a while, isn't it?)

Katachi jabbed his left elbow into the wall and performed a series of complex actions with his hands. He rotated the arm so the palm faced the floor, pulled the middle and ring fingers out and shoved them back into his fist with his right hand over the left.

He then twisted the left hand so the palm faced him, pulled his index and middle fingers out and used his right hand to grab and direct both fingers to face the ground. After that, he twisted his hands again so the palm faced the floor once more with the right hand still on the index and middle fingers like a door hinge being lifted.

Finally, he loosened his right hand while swinging at the door with his left hand still shaped like a hinge. The wall gave way to his spell and opened a rectangular hole in the wall. Katachi quickly escaped the house and uttered his partings.

K: (I feel bad, both for reanimating the furniture and staining her nice clean wall with my sandy sleeves. But that can come another time.) "I'll leave the mess to you, Bael! I'm really sorry!"

He didn't give Bael any time to rebuke and closed the wall on her gently.

B: "Don't say it like it's that easy, Katachi! I made the trap difficult on purpose so there won't be any gatecrashers that would disrupt the- He's gone already?! Damn it!"

*** ***

K: (That was exhausting.)

The incident drained him thoroughly, both in escaping from Bael and in racing to the opposite end of the academy to reach the coliseum in time. By then it was about an hour after noon.

The first round to decide the sixteen remaining ended off at roughly noon before shuffling the initial divisions together. The students who returned early from an hour lunch were waiting for the next event in anticipation.

"... You there, with the black hair."

Katachi spun around to see a boisterous lady with brown wild hair accompanying a tanned and slim figure, her bare feet with her uniform tattered, worn off and torn in some places – It was unkempt just like his own but it was damaged and torn rather than sandy and stained. Or perhaps she rolled only on her back instead of rolling towards the side, which caused her back to be dirtied; in which case Katachi could not tell because she was leaning her back against a wall with folded arms.

Katachi didn't have the time to change out of his tattered uniform from when he fought Cillian. What he originally planned for was to head towards Bael for a world map before heading to his room to change and sketch. But he was interrupted by a few students who wanted his carving autograph for defeating Cillian. Along with the shenanigans that Bael pulled, a majority of the free time he was allowed had been consumed involuntarily.

"Heh, you rolled a lot too, didn't you?"

K: "Y-yeah... My opponent was pretty tough. I had to wait for a good opening before I could hit back."

"That's cool. I just go on the offensive from the start."

The girl brushed her wild hair hanging by her left collarbone to the back and ruffled it up. She now looked like a wild, primitive cave woman with disheveled hair frizzy like an afro.

K: "May I know your name?"

N: "Chotil Nea, from Casa del Chotil. Everyone calls me Chopstick Nea, though."

K: "Oh, er... That's very... Creative, I guess." (A chopstick?... A pair? With whom?)

N: "Thanks. I managed to beat up poor Aldia, the gods have mercy on the first year. The only ones stopping me now are Deku and that kid who beat Cillian... What was his name?"

K: (It's better if she doesn't recognize me. In fact, the less she knows about me the better. It makes me wish I was paired with less competent fighters.) "Uhh... I think it's Katachi."

N: "Right, Katachi, that fly-boy they were talking about-"

"Contestants, please stand by. The next match will begin shortly."

The crowd cheered excitedly for the next match. Katachi didn't actually remember the tournament lineup, nor did he take note of who the remaining contestants were. He wanted to see the tournament bracket but he was cropped up by the incredulous events bordering along atrocity that transpired. Despite that, the free carving pick was a reward in and of itself. Katachi made a mental note to view it sometime after the match with Nea.

N: "That's my call. See you around, kid."

K: "Actually, that's my call too."

N: "!? Wait... You're Katachi!?"

K: "... Yes. Yes I am."

She gave a brief pout that was rather cutesy, but as someone younger than her he felt weird watching the act performed.

N: "Aww, what a pity. I wanted to save you as some kind of dessert after the main dish, you know? Oh well. We can't all have nice things, can we? See you inside."

Nea walked towards the obelisk with a sharp crystal at its top, and with a touch she was sent towards Cosmatral Tlod.

K: "... Best of luck to you too."

A bitter look flashed on his face briefly.

K: (That's what I wished for as well, but I ended up fighting Cillian for the first round.)

Katachi could only sigh. Even the best laid plans go awry, but such was the cruel and beautiful world. It was as though the tournament deliberately altered the contestant allocations for its own amusement. In what appeared to be mischief manifested it defied Katachi's wishes of fighting weak opponents. It also appeared to have gone against the wishes of other competitors as well.

Mafer had his hands full fighting the Vikarr guy, Nea had to prematurely accelerate her own plans and fight Katachi immediately, and he already had his first two rounds sparring off with tough opponents like a finalist and a senior. Katachi wondered if the other contestants faced similar problems.

*** ***

Nea and Katachi stood in Cosmatral Tlod quietly looking at each other from a distance. One was a semi-finalist of last year's tournament – A monstrous brown-haired student whom evenly challenged many of the older opponents, only to fall before Cillian in the semi-finals. With a fiery passion to win she stood proud and tall once again, prepared to face the adversaries before her.

The other was a kid nobody knew.

Both were about to begin the match for eliminating contestants. At least, that's what the students roaring on the coliseum benches were waiting for. It wasn't that those students were poor at magic, but that some of the students did not specialize in magic as a form of combat. Magic's potential in support was, after all, much more frightful than magic as a means of offence.

N: "Let's enjoy ourselves."

Had he spent time watching the matches he would have at least seen what Nea was capable of, but it was far too late to regret now.

N: "And so his hands grew, and his nails sharpened into those of a beast's."

Her hands grew into paws with sharp claws. Nea stared into Katachi's eyes and gave a cheeky smile.

N: "I hope you're ready!"

K: (A transformation? I would like that as well, but my reflexes are poor so agile ones are out of the question. There's been multiples tales of people transforming into monsters, but paws probably mean a predatory animal.)

Katachi took his dagger out from his back and readied his stance. He bent his legs down and held his hands up to protect his front. Nea looked carefully at him and his posture before determining the best means of attack.

N: "And his legs burst forth, a new, unbound strength."

Her leg muscles rippled and grew, and her bare feet changed into paws. With a celerity befitting her slim figure, she leapt towards Katachi and-

N: (Foolish little man! You can't beat a cougar.)

K: (A head-on charge?!)

-changed her direction right before hitting him, and got behind him before he could react and spin around. The lethargy from the commotion and ring-around-the-rosie earlier persisted, rendering Katachi too sluggish to respond. Nea proceeded to pounce on him from the back. With his rear exposed, striking him down was a feat too easy-

N: (He won't go down?!)

K: "... Hehehehehehehe."

-except that the boy stood stalwart and unyielding, contrary to his demeanour.

N: "!? What!?" (Why is he chuckling? Did he figure out the spell I used?!)

Nea leapt back to put distance between them and quickly transformed back to normal.

K: "I'm surprised you fell for my trap."

N: "What?! What trap?!"

*** ***

Katachi executed a clutch move in that moment. By using 恒定 – Constant status on himself, he set his status of 'standing up, unmoving' as constant. He managed to pull it off right before Nea hurled her body weight at him.

K: (Her magic is derived from the tale of Qin Tsung Yao, an Anikan hunter who travelled into Western Anik and transformed into a cougar. Its obvious weakness would be how Qin Tsung Yao died – Impalement from a thrown spear by a hunter. In that form her stab wounds won't recover.)

It was often dangerous for magi to engage each other in close-quarter combat. Placing one in a range where the other could kill you easily was something suicidal, especially if one did not know what forms of sorcery and magic the other knew.

For example, there was a tale of an Auseri pope cursed by the reincarnate of a Findeli god in that he had bone spurs growing on his entire spine. The spurs, as a mockery of his indolence, grew to monstrous sizes half of his body and gave him a proper reason to resume his indulgent lifestyle.

Using the tale as an attack spell one could simulate the curse and create a fan of bone spears on their back, which would have spelled a fatal blow for Nea... Provided the caster was prepared for the attack. He rhythmically exhaled on purpose so he could take advantage of her paranoia and force Nea to cancel the transformation.

K: (固定! Fixate position – Nea!)

A 定 word was placed on her back without her knowledge, and Nea was rendered completely immobile just like Cillian's sword. Her transformation back into human form was crucial because the cougar's fur would not suffice in concealing the 定 in the slightest, should she opt for the full transformation.

N: "What... !?"

It was therefore imperative to deceive and manipulate her train of thought to discourage the cougar form immediately. Katachi walked towards her with dagger in hand and pressed it against her throat.

K: "I'm sorry. I don't know what history you have, and I don't know why you need to win. But I need the champion's prize. Once I win, I won't need to stay in this academy or pretend to be someone I'm not any longer."

With an unexpected, abrupt ending, the divisional best of eight concluded.

ADDENDUM 1

She alone held the title of "Princess". She alone stood before the masses of people under her father's gaze and guidance.

King Matalpalhallafaelladrapahamo Fastiel's daughter, Matalpalhallafaelladrapahamo Roberia Slingeneyer.

She hated that name a lot. She hated it with a passion enough for people to flinch at its ferocity. For one, it was troublesome to pronounce. She had seen many people stutter while declaring the king's name or give up after a certain point. Yet, because it was 'a meaningful and symbolic title' it was continued as a heritage. Even if she hated it, she could not change tradition.

For another, it was a name that never gave her peace.

Roberia, being a young lady and the only princess of Rugnud, did not live a life of extravagance other princesses had. Where they had to wake early for their corsets and make-up, Roberia was forced awake to train with her father and the knights at five in the morning before the sun rose. Where princesses had the time and luxury to enjoy confectionery during tea-time while on diplomatic visits, she was often hunting for animals under the sweltering sun, all to mould her hunter's instinct.

At night, the princesses might have a curfew where they were expected to rest after a day of lessons and tending to court matters. Some might have guards to reinforce that they should not stay up later than a certain time. Roberia was instead assigned to guard duty at night, watching and ambushing anyone disrupting its peace and engaging actively in its patrols.

She had slightly more than two hours of sleep every single day because of that. Image power, a necessity for magi to perform spells, manifested differently for the knights and became a passive power that made the most ludicrous of claims not just possible, but commonplace. For the knights who honed themselves tirelessly a generous sleep was only four hours long.

She had been raised as a warrior princess, one which knew naught of grace or delicacy. The only actual breaks she had were during huge events, celebrations or parades of the like. Only then was she given the chance to step outside the castle not in battle wear but in extravagant robes and dresses which were, still, armour-clad.

But, even when she was graced with such opportunities, that name would never give her peace. Rugnud was a country where the strongest was hailed king, and her father the model example. Naturally, the king's son ought to have become king, for a male was a symbol of power and initiative.

Matalpalhallafaelladrapahamo Michael Slingeneyer, Roberia's half brother, was supposed to be king. He was an excellent strategist and an able fighter favoured greatly in his prime. His weakness in raw brute strength was offset by his empathy for his people, the knowledge of his enemies and the combination of his brain with brawn.

However, he was ambushed by the very creature he stalked one afternoon. It tore his tendons and crippled his right leg before he could slay it. When Michael returned from the expedition wounded he was criticized as an incompetent knight.

Michael's materialistic fiancée left him. His supporters turned their backs on him and he was deemed a failure even in the king's eyes. But none could blame him; it was his first prominent failure, and his only failure. No longer did he stand as a powerful leader and thus receded to the only position he still held – The King's Tactician.

So it was Roberia's turn to be groomed as the next monarch of Rugnud – At the young age of six. Of course, females were not particularly favoured when it came to candidacy. The ministers agreed that Rugnud should be ruled by a man without periods of weakness and so they sought many candidates across the country. Countless men from all walks of life and occupations met her to take her hand in marriage.

Roberia resented that. Since the age of six Roberia had been hounded by lecherous, conniving men whom demanded her as their spouse not for mutual love, but for the fame, wealth and glory of being king of Rugnud.

Those men went far to become king – Sowing discord amongst the ministers whom took care of Roberia, boosting their reputation by making others commit fake crimes that they themselves 'resolved', harassing Roberia countless times whenever and wherever possible and even going so far as to hold a blade against the princess herself.

Boys above the age of thirteen tried their luck with her to no avail. Men as old as fifty-five wished to wed her. She became a target for every greedy man and every jealous woman. She hated the name she was given. She hated the men who were after her because of that accursed title. She hated the plentiful number of gifts she received every single time she returned to her bed room. She hated her daily life itself.

The only things she didn't hate were the servants and maids whom she shared her troubles with, attendants who witnessed and understood her plight firsthand. Even so, there was little they could do for her. Roberia started becoming defensive and cynical towards the people she once genuinely cared for.

Then, she realized – There was no use.

As long as she stayed within Rugnud, as long as she was still a widely-known public figure she would be hounded by those bastards. She was harassed and bothered on countless occasions, she did not have as many successful expeditions, skirmishes and patrols. Those people, that name, all of the miscellaneous events ate into her warrior lifestyle. Her skills slowly deteriorated because of them.

She may very well become a mere tool used by others to obtain the throne, and nothing else. She started imagining the future of Rugnud, led under a foolish person whom merely desired to become king. She pained and cried her heart out one night, at her home being turned into a festering cesspool of depravity.

She was frightened by the idea of having her beloved Rugnud weakened so badly that other countries like Auser and Anik could easily invade and pillage everything. Not to mention that Findel might take advantage of the confusion and betray the peace pact. She just wanted her home to be safe and strong – So her people may live a life of peace.

And thus Roberia took up arms. She ordered a sword with a weight of seven and a half kilograms, prepared a medium pouch of gold with a small number of coins, and set off on a journey. The sixteen year old travelled West towards Findel.

Matalpalhallafaelladrapahamo Roberia's journey had begun.

CHAPTER 14

Katachi had some time to himself again until the next match. He chanced the opportunity and decided to understand more about the tournament's structure.

In a normal scenario he could openly walk towards the tournament board, but from the past experience of being hounded by students wanting his autograph Katachi considered a more subtle route. He walked past the teacher's lounge, down the stairs to the neglected toilets before going a huge loop around the academy.

K: (It looks clear enough.)

Katachi carefully studied the chart before marking out the eliminated students. Sure enough, he slowly got a rough idea of the opponents he would face.

K: (I just beat that girl... What was her name, Chopstick Nea? I can cancel her out. So that leaves me with a bunch of potential challengers for the divisional best of four. Pitin, Djinnje, Iven, Vikarr or Deku- !)

Deku. He made his stand clear as a powerful magus that plucked out a chunk of land and threw it at Zul. He showcased one of the more severe and violent aspects of magic and his charisma was incredible. The name that was so far away in the chart on the preliminaries suddenly became so close to him. That was truly frightening to have all sense of security evaporate away in that mere realization.

K: (If given a choice I would personally prefer Vikarr over Deku since that guy uses Sha'koth based spells, but the chances of him winning seems grim against a counter magus. Also, I might eventually face Deku since he will likely crush whoever he fights.)

But ruling him out immediately was unwise.

K: (I'll note him down just in case, though... I've seen his technique after all, so every little bit helps if he has some sort of reversal or trick up his sleeves. I can't say much for the others since I have yet to witness them, but I should work with what I have.)

As he eyed through the foreign names, Katachi finally stopped his eyes at something familiar.

K: (... He's in the tournament as well? How did I not notice him before?)

*** ***

87

C: "Loar."

Loar snapped back at her with a pissed tone.

L: "... What do you want from me, Cestia?"

C: "I'm, ah... I'm sorry. I-... Your parents, friends and your whole village... I know how important they are to you. And yet, I... I selfishly entered the tournament to get the school-sponsored medicine for my sister."

That was certainly not the time for him to be unreasonable. The child felt ashamed that a stubborn girl like herself would take the initiative to apologize first.

L: "! Oh, that, uhm... It's okay, Cestia. Your sister is way more important to you than my village is to me – You're blood-related, after all. I have my faults for attacking you seriously as well."

C: "Aren't your parents blood-related too? I know you want to make me feel better, but at least make your argument sound first, you idiot!"

Loar's face blushed into a blooming peach.

L: "..."

C: "..."

Since that match, the atmosphere between them became awkward. They were both wrong in their own ways and they simply wished to forget and move on. But the damage had already been done. They were inches away from maiming each other for their own ideals back at the preliminaries.

L: "... I hope we can still be friends."

C: "J-... Just friends, huh."

L: "Uh... Hey, did you hear about that bald guy at the preliminaries?"

With any amount of luck changing the topic would alleviate the discomfiture.

C: "The guy with the blade staff?"

L: "Yeah. Apparently Minister Lein visited him personally to recruit him."

C: "Wow, really?"

L: "Yeah. 'I was chosen because my leadership skills and situational assessment during the preliminaries was something they were looking for', or so he says. He sure is lucky – He went straight to the Findel Magus Association even though he didn't pass the preliminaries."

C: "The FMA? That's amazing!- Wait, does that mean he would be getting full payment since he's officially working for Findel now?"

L: "Yeah, he did say that."

Unbeknownst to the young boy, that revelation was punishing for the young girl.

C: "..."

L: "W- what's wrong, Cestia?"

C: "I wanted a job to earn enough money for my sister to get better..."

Cestia's voice croaked and her eyes grew red hot with regret.

C: "... But I ended up becoming a stepping stone for someone else."

It could have been her. It could have been a blessing in disguise, but her inelegant performance broke down the stray chance of immediately landing a job that would generate income necessary for her sister's medicine. And of all the people she lost it to, it had to be that one student with a shine on his scalp that was undoubtedly bad for his health. Cestia's head hung downwards in melancholy.

L: "Ah- ..."

C: "..."

There was little Loar could do except change the topic once more and divert her attention.

L: "... Let's not focus on that any longer – Look, Deku and Vikarr's fight is about to begin! Maybe we can learn a bit from those two. We still have next years' tournaments to come, and we might even beat him next time!"

C: "How could you stay so carefree, Loar?! I'm not in the mood to watch them!!"

His positivity was baffling to her. It made her wonder how he could afford to be so enthusiastic. Did her dilemma not matter to him? Was her problem so trivial that a match between two seniors was more important than her?

L: "Why not?"

C: (Am I just a bother to him? Mother did say that my indelicacy would cost me, but for the one guy I really like to find me displeasing?) "How could you just look away from the problem?! Can't you consider my troubles seriously for once?"

She began to question the boy before her. Perhaps he regarded her presence as though she was some kind of furniture in his room, and her problems trivial. Or perhaps he was secretly cursing her sister and hoping for her death, to treat the talk of helping her with neglect.

L: "It's not like I don't want to talk about your problems, but there's really nothing we can do at this point, is there? I mean, no matter what happens I'll always be there for you! It doesn't matter if you succeed or fail. Your family is my own, and I promise to take care of you, your parents and your sister even when you lose all power to move, speak or see. I might be unconvincing saying this without any immediate action, but I want you to rely on me!"

His words surprised her in unexpected ways. She could feel the conviction in his voice, the presence of an oath established without her knowledge of it. For the first time since they took to liking each other Cestia felt the security and certainty that went beyond mere companionship.

L: "So, it's just that, well... It just can't be helped. It happens, so we need only move along and not dwell on what we could have done, but rather what we can still do. I... I just don't want to see you sad because I... Because I love you so much. Can we not talk about something this depressing? Let's just watch the- !?"

Without any warning at all, Cestia rested her head on Loar's shoulder. Her blissful face and swoon said it all – She had fallen in love with the boy named Loar all over again.

C: "I'll abuse you, you know."

He recognized that gentle and tired voice, the adorable pout and the soft warmth on his left he loved. Loar slowly rested his head on Cestia's and wrapped his arm around her shoulders in consolation. The two were closer than ever before.

L: "I wouldn't have it any other way."

*** Achievement: The True Symbol Of Peacetime ***

D: "For those of you who recognise this catchphrase, here's something for you. 'I told you to keep the classroom clean!!' He-hey, how did you like my impersonation of Mister Lamale?"

Deku's extravagant entrance received just as much fanfare as before, if not more.

V: "Hey, Deku. I've improved from last time-"

D: "Let's add on to the previous bet, guys! If I lose this match, I'll drink the healing syrup for two weeks straight!"

Once again Deku seemed to hold no regard for his opponent. This tensed a temple muscle of Vikarr's as he tried his best to receive the respect he deserved.

V: "Looks like you really are going to drink that syrup for two weeks straight after all. Unless, of course, you're not man enough to take it."

It was only with attempted provocation did Deku spin around and actually address poor Vikarr properly.

D: "You'd make me eat my words? You're pretty confident to answer me this boldly! Let's go, little man!"

V: "You don't look so tough. All you did last year was fling sand about!"

Vikarr took his cards out and stood in a battle stance that made him look like a professional killer – Left leg out, right leg in, cards in his hand, and a glare at the champion which signalled that he was ready. One could only wonder how nervous he actually was to dissuade his fear with confident postures.

*** ***

Vikarr expended everything he had. A flutter of wooden cards flocked and circled around him like a hurricane, ready to attack anything close-range like a barrier with many gaps. He was more than prepared to take on the mound of sand Deku hurled at Zul in the previous match. As expected, Deku's left fist glowed yellow and he smashed the ground with it.

The chunk of land converted beneath him was much larger than the chunk before in his first match. He absorbed the 'thing' into his left hand and the yellow liquid-like substance crept onto his torso from his left hand. It coated his entire body spare the head and his size grew significantly. When the yellow substance faded, in its place was a sort of beige, sand-coloured armour.

V: (What the- He's not going to throw the sand?!)

More accurately it was sand reconstructed into a form of armour.

D: "Vikarr. I'm going to go all out. Don't hold back, all right?"

Deku's stern voice echoed through the entire coliseum. The students were excited to see Deku fighting seriously, and Vikarr too was taken aback by Deku's declaration. The sand gauntlet on his hand glowed yellow and he punched the sand on the floor once more. This time the chunk of land taken was on a colossal scale, leaving a crater about one-third the field.

The chunk of land was simply absorbed into his body, and he expanded into a humongous golem made completely out of sand towering at twenty-five metres. Vikarr's eyes were wide open and his gaze failed to avert from the giant before him.

V: "Wait, isn't this-... The Gatherer's Golem?!"

He looked like he was recovering from a practical joke. From the looks of it Vikarr was probably expecting the same handicap Zul received, so it was a shocker to have things go amiss.

With a change in his hand gesture the cards flew towards the huge golem. It clashed and clattered noisily against the sturdy exterior of the golem to little effect. Some sand came out when the cards struck hard enough but the sand spewing out merely glowed yellow into tiny orbs and flowed back, or more appropriately 'reabsorbed' back into the golem. It was a good effort, but the result was already obvious.

The magic was on a scale that Vikarr couldn't defeat. He did not plan for the fact that Deku could simply choose to protect himself with the sand instead of throwing the bulk at him, which he planned to unleash his trick as some kind of dramatic reveal that would make his juniors admire him. Deku had already won. The golem's right fist was raised and it punched the sand with a powerful blow.

It caused a huge quake that made most students cry out in appal and awe at the Eye of Jedivh conveying the sand projection of the battlefield distorting with its impact. The sand beneath Vikarr flew at his face, obstructing his nose, eyes and ears and most of his other senses. Vikarr couldn't even keep his balance from its sheer magnitude and landed on his posterior.

D: "I could punch you instead of the earth, but that would be unnecessary murder. Wouldn't it?"

With both his face and butt hurt, Vikarr clutched his posterior in agony as he struggled to stand up, rubbing his eyes and blowing sandy air from his nose strongly.

V: "You win. Okay? You win."

Deku smiled briefly at the surrender and the crowd cheered at the amazing display of magic. With the entire golem glowing yellow he alighted from it and slammed the liquid at the floor, covering the crater perfectly. The third match of the second round ended with Vikarr feeling a complicated sense of defeat.

CHAPTER 15

Katachi recalled the ridiculous power Deku used at the coliseum – He collected the sand and created a giant golem with it, and the golem seemed capable of repairing itself. That was a tricky magic to deal with – Simplistic, without any intricacies or interactions and completely plain. That would mean the magic was one that couldn't be abused or exploited easily.

Had Katachi simply used the Words of Power, a Reincarnate Art like that was nothing compared to what he could do; but that would present the risk of blowing everything he did to keep it concealed. In an attempt to prevent that in the future matches Katachi resorted to one final safeguard, Principal Bertund's office. Katachi raised his hand to knock on-

"Come in!"

Even before Katachi could knock on the door, a familiar feminine voice instructed him to enter.

K: (Who is that behind the door? Is that a woman? It's almost as if she can see me through the wall or something.)

Katachi closed the door behind him and seated himself on the creaking wooden chair. Before him sat a woman with blonde hair tied up into a bun at the top. A ponytail extended from the bundle of hair mooning down to her left shoulder. Her clothes indicated that she was most likely a teacher in the academy, and given how she was boldly sitting at Bertund's seat she must be of high authority. Either that, or her ego was incredibly inflated. But she had an air about her which suggested otherwise. After all, she wore attire highly similar to Bertund's – A green-themed attire with a crisp jacket and a white shirt. Her legs were dark... Or were those stockings? Her pencil skirt was also green and it covered up to just before her knees.

She wore a green-coloured minuscule top hat much like the green slime top hat Bertund had. What made her attire differ from Bertund's was that it had a gold lace hanging out from the chest- or rather, breast pocket of the green jacket, and she wore a diamond-shaped ruby locket on her neck.

K: "What... Where's Principal Bertund? Who are you?"

S: "I am Bertund's wife, Shelly. I'm not of Raufid's blood, but you can say that I'm the acting principal while Bertund's entertaining Minister Lein."

K: "I see- Wait a minute, you're the announcer!"

The voice that came from her lips clicked in sync with the voice he heard not too long ago.

S: "Yes, yes I am, but surely you didn't walk all the way here just to tell me that, did you? Let's get down to business. So, what brings you here, Mister Kotsuba? Here to look for another course to add to your curriculum? Invite me for tea? ...

... Or have you finally realized that you can't solely rely on your Word of Power alone for the entirety of the tournament?"

Shelly's words were spot-on. Katachi couldn't deny it – Thus far, he relied upon the Word of Power he had far too much. Leaping towards the tokens, disabling Cillian's blade and stopping Nea's movements without being detected was impressive, but it could very well end in disaster if he weren't as lucky. There was the possibility that his clothes might become damaged or ripped, revealing the Word of Power unintentionally.

Of course, since Katachi didn't possess any actual knowledge on the Child of Sun it was not possible to feign the Word of Power as body paint or something along those lines. Besides, their distinctive glow was a dead give-away since glowing paint tattooed onto skin was as credible as a herbivorous Sludgewenge.

There was also the threat of Rekter catching on to his strategy. Even if he succeeded in fooling everyone, Rekter wasn't a person who could be deceived by a trick like this, not especially since he was consciously aware of his 定 itself – A proof strong enough to override all of his lies.

He could expose Katachi's act and blow all his hard work away with a simple huff of his breath. And, because their precedence levels tied, they would surely be put into a fervent duel between who raised their precedence level faster. The one with more knowledge won decisively but there was no certainty as to who would break the deadlock.

In the event that he was to be exposed, Katachi would have to use his Word of Power to escape. But, at the same time he needed something else – An alternate source of power. One he could freely use without being discovered and one that was risk-free. One he could apply to the tournament that people could see and recognize so as to divert their attention.

K: "Yes. I have come to learn two things."

S: "What will they be?"

K: "First, I want to increase the precedence level of my Word of Power."

S: "You don't have a need for that, do you? There's pretty much nothing in this school that can rival a stupidly powerful magic like that."

K: "There is. Mister Rekter's precedence level ties with mine."

The revelation caused her brow to raise.

S: "A tie in precedence levels? That's really rare."

K: "Yes it is. I've... I've pulled a trick to stop his precedence levels from rising too quickly, so I must take advantage of this window to... To... To increase my own as much as possible."

Shelly nodded her head briefly and responded.

S: "Consider it done. I'll give you lectures on the Words of Power that's sure to raise your levels. What of the second topic at hand?"

K: "Oh, er, yes... The sec- The second thing is, well, my affinity with water."

S: "What about it?"

K: "I would like to learn spells and stories related to water."

S: "Don't look for me regarding that. I've always hated water magic – Their tales are too sappy for my liking. You'd have to ask Bertund to prepare a course application for you when he comes back."

K: "... I was hoping for direct tutelage from Bertund, but... Okay."

With the problems addressed, Shelly's shoulders raised a little bit as she leaned forward onto the desk, eyeing Katachi down carefully.

S: (I could arrange that.) "And here I thought you were going to discuss with him about something more important, like how you're going to start collecting all of the Words of Power."

K: (This woman... Her eyes pierced right through my mind... !)

His jaw dropped so wide it was almost comical.

K: "!! YOU-..."

Katachi accidentally leaked a scream and he glanced around nervously to see if anyone was listening in on their conversation. As though he forgot that he was inside the principal's office, Katachi gasped deeply to remain calm, and spoke in a soft voice.

K: "... you already know?"

Shelly leaned back onto the comfortable looking leather seat.

S: "Why wouldn't I? Look at you, acting all shifty and timid. You probably want the school-sponsored prizes to provide you with the travelling equipment needed, didn't you?"

K: "! Yes... But, but... But, how did you know?"

S: "Simple – You're poor. Nobody would expect a mere child that comes from a Segus church in some dusty corner of Mielfeud to be wealthy without even working for coin. Those with great power would strive to use that power to improve themselves in some way, wouldn't they?"

Shelly pinned down and summarized all of Katachi's plans with mere words. Katachi was once again forced to recognize his weak and hapless self who must get his act together to survive the cruel and beautiful world.

K: (Of course that much was obvious to her, wasn't it? But this is a valuable lesson for me. If Shelly can derive my current circumstances so easily, others would have just as easy a time if they willed themselves to. I should mentally prepare for people who might know and exploit my shortcomings.)

The weak do not stand a chance against the strong in a direct confrontation. He must work to remedy the gaping flaw in his mask.

S: "So, Mister Kotsuba, have you any plans on how you should start looking for the other 290 Words of Power?"

K: "... Not really."

Shelly's shoulders dropped slightly and she leaned her head against her fingers with her right elbow on the table.

S: "Wow, seriously? I expected you to be more far-sighted than that, Mister Kotsuba, especially since you're the one with the crazy dream."

K: "... Sorry if I don't meet your expectations."

S: "Well, whatever. Let's begin with the lecture. Tell me everything you know about your Word of Power and we'll work from there."

Katachi paused when he realized the potential disruption of her work with his selfishness.

K: "Uhm, okay- No, wait! Don't you have to announce for the tournament rounds and the like?"

S: "Don't worry about it! It's all pre-recorded. That announcement hasn't changed since I started working here."

The two stayed in Bertund's office for Katachi's first actual lecture on the Words of Power.

*** ***

S: "That should be quite enough to raise your precedence levels. Okay, one final recap. Repeat to me everything you've learnt thus far."

K: "Okay... Uh, the Words of Power can be used in tandem, or rather chained with one another, thereby raising their precedence levels even higher. However, that restricts the meaning it can assume so... So it only works under some circumstances. Secondly, two Words of Power can- can... can affect the same object, but they cannot affect the same property."

S: "Good. Go on?"

K: "Uhm, uh... Third... Thirdly, Divine Beasts are also empowered by image power, so they have some... some level of resistance towards the Words of Power. And lastly, three new terms for 定 I've learnt are 定居, 定睛, and 定婚. 定居 means to s-settle down, like having someone that has moved to another village settle down. 定睛 would- would be forcing someone to stare at a certain area, location, or object, and finally, 定婚 would mean for others to be... To be... To be betrothed."

His pronunciation of the Anikan words could use some polishing, but for now the knowledge of it sufficed.

K: "However, 定婚 cannot be used carelessly at just-... Just anyone, because the gods' blessings are powerful enough to cancel out the effects of making two strangers, uhm... betrothed."

Shelly collapsed the fan in her hands, unfolded her crossed legs and stood up from the desk.

S: "Very good! That should put you in quite the lead. Unless of course, Rekter has been busy researching the Words of Power and raising his own levels as well. It's about time to end it off for today."

K: "For... For today? There's more?"

S: "Of course there's more! Why do you sound so tired? If you really want to beat Rekter and collect every Word of Power out there you're going to need every little bit you can get, right? Surely you don't expect your enemies to stop learning just because they have an edge over everyone else! So why should you take it easy?"

K: "Oh, uh, no, it's not that, but uh... I... I was just wondering... Wondering, you know, why would you, the principal's w-wuh-... wuh- wife, want me to beat Rekter so badly?"

Shelly's head depressed slightly and her spirited expression turned sour as she gazed outside the window.

K: (... ? There's the itch again.)

(Contestant Katachi, your match begins in 30 minutes. Please assemble at the entrance to Cosmatral Tlod.)

Shelly's voice resounded through his head, overlapping her explanation.

S: "I hate that man's guts. He thinks he's all mighty and powerful with him being the only Scholar in the school. He knows exactly how absurd and broken that sigil is, and yet he flaunts it at every opportunity he gets. But now, he's not the only Scholar in this academy."

Shelly spun around to face Katachi with a serious expression.

S: "You're just the person we need. You can punish him for being arrogant. Go show that bastard Rekter what it takes to anger me and bully Bertund."

That was a shocker to hear.

K: "Bertund? Bullied?"

S: "Yes. Rekter would often set up pranks to make Bertund look silly, but he doesn't mind – He's too soft. Far too soft and kind to actually retaliate..."

Shelly's face twisted into one of sorrow. Her eyes softened and she looked away to her left into the distance.

K: (Bertund, soft?) "... Er... My, my next match is uh, going to begin soon. So I guess... I guess I'll be going."

S: "Oh, right, you're fighting Deku. Good luck out there, Mister Kotsuba."

Katachi left the wooden chair and headed for the door-

S: "Oh, one last advice, Mister Kotsuba! Just... Don't mind Deku too much. He's mostly joking around, so don't treat his taunts and follies as something serious. After all, he wouldn't want to deal with students that are too serious when he comes to work here."

Was she rooting for his victory, or was she trying to teach her future employee a lesson?

K: "His- His taunts don't look joking, though."

S: "Yeah, well, that's always been a problem with him. But he still insists on acting like this because he wants to enjoy what little youth he has left – He's working here after his graduation, don't you know. So don't worry – Think of it as him experimenting with a wild, crazy style of interacting with the students."

K: "... Uh, okay. I... I'll be sure to ignore his uh, provocations."

S: "They're not provocations, actually. But you are right – It might come off as a little aggressive, and the younger students may have doubts approaching him with how he handled Vikarr. If you can, try to talk to him nicely and tell him what's wrong with his methods. That would help him the most."

K: "I- I don't think I would, but... I'll do my best."

S: "Good luck! And be sure to kick all of their asses for me!"

Katachi left the office of the wacky principal and his wacky wife. But it felt as though every step away from the atrium and closer to the field made his limbs grow colder.

CHAPTER 16

On the coliseum seats was a senior with a chest size comparable to Mount. Gigraceldi, an attractive feature for a lady. However, she reeked of foreign herbs and decay so the other students weren't too fond of sitting next to her. She impatiently awaited two familiar figures to enter the ring while fiddling with her fingers.

B: (I can't believe Katachi is actually going to fight Deku.)

The light in her eyes reflected a great worry and she held her hands in prayer.

B: (... This, I have to see.)

Deku was facing off against Katachi for the divisional best of four seating. To others they were mere students in the academy, but Bael had a special connection to both of them. Having attained the pride of being the last man standing for the past three years Deku was held in high regards by many – His wish to become a teacher greatly bolstered his resolve to improve himself, making him one of the rare few students in the academy's history to match a teacher toe-to-toe.

As his childhood friend Bael was rooting for him to succeed. He was smart, bright and thoughtful, often using the tournament prizes to reform the neighbouring towns, helping with the construction and reparation of the older buildings.

Katachi managed to take down the semi-finalist Nea and the finalist Cillian, which meant that he would be competing with Deku for the next round. He was just a quiet kid nobody really knew, but Bael was the first student he got along with. He gave off a mysterious and eccentric feeling akin to a cat that she wished to unravel for herself.

The thrill of seeing two contrasting sides matched against each other was enough to make anyone interested. People chattered and discussed what little they knew, and there were even students who started illegal bets to rake in the stakes.

C: "Hey Bael, what are you doing sitting all alone here?"

Interrupting Bael was a young maiden in love.

B: "Good afternoon, Cestia. I was just... Well, I'm waiting for the next match."

C: "Isn't that obvious? You're sitting on the bench. How do you even tolerate this heat?"

B: "I... I just do. Ahaha, hahaha."

Bael looked down in embarrassment when she realized that her clothes were accumulating a good amount of sweat. She was baking herself in the smouldering heat without realizing how fatigued or thirsty she was. Cestia sat down next to the depressed beauty and unwrapped a piece of cloth she placed on her lap. Beneath the wraps hid a small fish, roasted finely and its heat preserved with an unusual rune she didn't recognise.

C: "I was about to ask why you were sitting all alone, but I guess the smell on you has been driving people away huh..."

Cestia easily noticed the odour on Bael's body and hair. It was obvious to the point where the flies that normally favoured the rancid smells of decay steered clear from her.

B: "Yeah, I guess they're afraid of getting their noses burnt out."

C: "So, do you want some of this Moontwine mudskipper? It's from Anik, you know."

Bael looked over at Cestia's morsel in disgust upon hearing the name mudskipper.

B: "Mudskipper? Is that edible?"

C: "Don't worry about it."

Cestia pinched a small piece between her fingers and raised it towards Bael's face, tempting her to taste the exotic food.

C: "The fishmonger called it a mudskipper but it didn't have any mud when I bought it. It's really tasty! Try it, I guarantee its taste. I made Loar roast this for me."

Bael stared hard at the small piece of roasted fish between her fingers. Reluctantly, she reached her lips out and enveloped the meat with her mouth with a slow chew. The lasting flavour and briefly slimy texture of mudskipper filled her mouth with a tinge of mild nutmeg, honey and ginger chicken.

B: "... Mmmm. Delicious."

C: "I wouldn't lie to you about stuff like that, Bael. Of course it's tasty. Apparently you keep the mudskipper alive for more than a week in clean water to wash out the muddy taste. It's nice to try fresh game once in a while, isn't it?"

Cestia spoke with mudskipper chunks escaping her mouth in a manner most uncouth. How the teenager known as Loar fell in love with the zany girl was, however, not for anybody to judge.

B: "Interesting. It's pretty good."

C: "So, I heard this next match is a highlight, isn't it?"

B: "Yeah. Deku and Katachi are going to fight it out."

Cestia licked and sucked her fingers in an unwomanly fashion.

C: "Katachi, huh. Do you think the new guy would win?"

B: "..."

Bael didn't want to choose between them. Katachi showed some strange promise but against someone thoroughly experienced like Deku it would probably require a miracle. Unless... Katachi was concealing something even greater, a trick to turn the odds just like what Vikarr prepared.

B: (Katachi's always behaved in this shady, obscure manner. It's almost as though he is capable of something much more, like how a proper magus conceals his strength to fool and lull his opponents into a false sense of security. It's the opposite of the Champion-like approach that Deku opts for to relish in immediate brute strength.)

As she was absorbed in her own thoughts, Bael was left unaware of the screams and shouts the students around her chanted as the competitors gathered for the next match.

*** ***

Andarmasi Dekuruvischelon was unusually quiet.

Normally, he would have screamed and confidently entertained the audience but he was silent this time in an unusual turn of events. It wasn't really that unusual, though – Deku used his voice so much in the past two rounds that his throat hurt a good bit. Though the healing syrup recovered many wounds, a sore throat was not amongst what it was brewed to heal.

K: "Nice to meet you, Mister... Uhm... What- What was your name?"

The sounds within Cosmatral Tlod were projected at the coliseum seats with a slight distortion, and interaction with the audience was possible to some degree. That was clearly evidenced by Deku's bets made in Cosmatral Tlod which were audible to the other students. Yet by the same process, upon hearing Katachi's voice even Minister Lein himself had a hard time stifling the astonishment.

It was shocking to be unaware of the poster boy's presence. Deku was renowned as the model student for three years straight. His face was prominently displayed in fine print across the towns, on the posters, the news articles and the like. To round things off, Minister Lein specifically introduced him at the official start of the event so if the child was present he would certainly remember Deku.

That very Deku had his existence forgotten as though he were unimportant. He felt like a doll in the provisions shop that parents would dissuade their children to buy due to its impracticality. It was laughable, unthinkable, unbelievable that a student enrolled into the academy without even seeing Deku's face at least once.

D: (No way... This guy hasn't see my face before? He didn't recognize me at all, not even during the first two rounds!? There's no way a magus would be overconfident to the level that he won't observe the matches unless he doesn't know how to go to the spectators' area!)

Deku reached a startling conclusion.

D: (Then, he's a... A- A bona fide country bumpkin who's completely unfamiliar with the school?!)

K: "Wait, you're... Mister Andar- uh, Andarmasi Dekuru-something?"

Katachi tried to stay level-headed and composed by opting for brief comedy. The crowd chuckled a little at the awkwardness of the situation as they caught onto his joke. Deku sighed in response to the redundant wave of panic from before.

D: "I was about to say, if you didn't recognize me I would have been truly shocked. I'd have screamed till I was hoarse for nothing! Hahah!"

The crowd laughed with Deku and whatever tension that draped about diminished.

K: "It's quite the hurdle to fight you this early, Mister Andarmasi, but... Are you ready?"

D: "Wha- Are you serious? I'm always ready for a fight!"

K: (From that response he seems really confident about his abilities. I wouldn't be surprised, he could make golems and he can hurl mounds of sand at me. That means he's best at mid-range combat whereas I'm better at close-range combat. He has a wooden sword while I have a wooden dagger so his reach is farther in close combat. I'd have to work around the range of his sword and consider a Melias strap to bind-)

Just as Katachi began to formulate a plan in his head a dull sound was heard. The wooden sword in his hand fell, its muffled sound against the sand heard clearly. Katachi's eyes widened. Normal enemies would not let go of a weapon and put themselves at a disadvantage on purpose. This was a handicap that only those who were certain of their ability would do.

D: "I feel so energized right now, I think I won't need a weapon to deal with the likes of you. Consider that a handicap of sorts, yes?"

The crowd went wild hearing a cool and stylish response like that. It would be one thing if it were against Cillian de Vorsche, but Katachi's reliance on his dagger for the previous matches painted the importance of having some form of close-range defence. To display such bravado despite Katachi's general approach towards the fights thus far was nothing short of firm confidence.

D: "In fact, I don't think using my golem is necessary either. I'll beat you with Conduit Imbue alone. How about it, kid? Wanna try fighting the champion with that handicap?"

K: "Take it back."

D: "... Huh?"

Deku was bewildered at the response which surprised the audience. Logically speaking, for Katachi to survive the match with the handicap, let alone win it at Deku's full power was enough of an ordeal to make others cringe in fear. Deku brought up a great offer, one that could potentially threaten his winning streak; and the strange child rejected it flatly. Why would he want Deku to revoke the handicap?

K: "Take it back. I wouldn't want my opponent to get hurt without fighting seriously."

The concern and kindness behind those words were clear and it was admirable how a pipsqueak would show such chivalry, if that were the true objective behind his words.

D: "Very well. I'll start it off easy and go all out when you've proven yourself worthy. I'll play by the same rules as the previous matches, this time with increased stakes – If you win, I'll drink the brown syrup for a whole month. If you lose there will be no penalties. Would that make you happy?"

That was not unlike the methodology of Dardicel, one of the most revered gods in Auser.

K: "... Pray you don't regret your choice." (设定. Set Eye of Jedivh position – Southwest of my relative north, fifty centimetres away from my back.)

Deku kicked the wooden sword next to his feet across the sand and lowered his stance, fully prepared to slam the ground with his fist.

K: (He discarded it anyway...)

D: "Don't worry, kid. I'm a professional."

They both gave a brief nod to signify that they were ready.

*** ***

Deku's right fist glowed a strange, entrancing yellow. With great force he slammed it into the earth and the mound of land beneath his feet was absorbed, causing him to sink into the crater smoothly. With a jab, he released the yellow fluid from his arm which solidified and reformed into the chunk of land beneath his feet just seconds ago.

K: (设定! Set land's durability – A million fold! Set land's weight – A millionth fold!)

Two tiny 定s surfaced on the top of the land which Katachi caught in his extended right hand with ease. Because the words were tiny and the object was moving very fast it was hard to see the golden words on the sand. Also, the Eye of Jedivh obelisk receiver displaying the projection to the spectators was behind him and nearing his knee level so it didn't have an overhead view of the mound of land that risked exposing the sigils.

D: "!! What-!"

Deku had never seen anyone properly catch a mound of land like that. The sand was maintained in its original shape and he managed to cushion that landmass perfectly in his palm. With a simple push, the sand expelled outward. It was sent flying back towards Deku which he punched with his glowing left fist in response.

The sand mound glowed yellow immediately, broke apart and liquefied into the substance that was absorbed back into his body once again. It didn't make sense at all. When Katachi caught the sand, it didn't change in shape and remained the way he threw it. But when Deku tried to reabsorb the sand it behaved naturally and broke apart like a mound of sand ought to. What was the determinant?

D: (This guy... I've heard the students praise him as a Soltak follower, so he probably uses sunlight instead of the usual array of magic objects or symbols. Is he using the light prism technique to keep the mound of sand intact? That's pretty impressive, since this place isn't even sunny to begin with.)

The surprise was pleasing for his opponent who had a habit of ending his matches in less than twenty seconds prior.

D: "Hahahahahaha! How interesting. It seems I cannot beat you with Conduit Imbue alone."

Katachi's stance lowered and he drew the wooden dagger, gripping it tightly with his right hand.

D: (Soltak's Reincarnate Art relies upon sunlight, so if there's none for him to use this match will be one-sided.) "Did you tell me to take my words back knowing that you could use Soltak's Light Prism even in Cosmatral Tlod?"

K: (Light Prism?)

Deku began forming sand armour with the mound he reabsorbed. Katachi remained silent and maintained an alert, defensive posture ready to intercept any attacks Deku might dish out.

D: (If I design it in a mushroom shape, the amount of light will be filtered down tremendously. This will end soon.) "Very well. But how will you fare against the Gatherer's Golem?"

With a punch, Deku drew up even more sand and created a gargantuan made completely of sand and wind. The golem now manifested in a form even more menacing than it was when he fought Vikarr – Winds twirling around its right elbow joint and flowing down to the hand, raging violently around its centre and head, and the harsh gales comprising most of its lower torso that repelled Katachi's approach.

It was smaller than the one Vikarr faced, but the behemoth was at least fifteen times Katachi's size with a broad torso like an umbrella cage. He looked up at the monstrosity and acted immediately.

D: (!! He's... He's unaffected?!)

*** ***

The Gatherer's Golem was a name given to a combination of two techniques – Dardicel's Reincarnate Art Golem and the Conduit Imbue technique. Normally, to perform the Reincarnate Art alone was a very tough ordeal. Dardicel was the god of Trials who was bestowed a title known as Lord of the Earth for being the first to collect a piece of every terrain and by extension, the first to travel the world.

His Reincarnate Art required his followers to unite themselves with the Earth itself as a trial to attune oneself to the world and unite as one, so they may call upon a mighty sentient being at will wherever they may be. However, not many people understood what he meant so their attempts at recreating his Art of Trials often ended up shoddy and weak.

Conduit Imbue was a technique used by miners in Rugnud – It was a magic where the miners melded the excessive soil and rocks into their own bodies so they may release them when they reached the surface. It worked effectively as a transportation system because of the relative ease of the technique.

The only drawback was that when objects were absorbed into the body the objects themselves added to the weight of the person – That meant users of the technique needed to be physically resilient if they wished to move about with items stored within the Conduit Imbue. It was only useful in limited situations which led to its gradual decline outside of Rugnud.

Conduit Imbue's peculiarity was its favourable side effect – It softened up the element absorbed into the body and imbued a circuit into the object that allowed the body to absorb the material without rejecting it. In a sense, it was 'uniting' with the material because one imbued circuits into them before they were assimilated for ease of absorption.

Should the two techniques be used in tandem, an equally potent form of Dardicel's Reincarnate Art could be produced at a much lower difficulty. The elements comprising the golem were already accepted into the body so it was much easier to create and control the golem since the material was already magically charged. That was the birth of the technique known as Gatherer's Golem.

*** ***

K: (固定! Fixate position – Magic Circuits!)

The golem raised its foot and came close to stomping Katachi when it stopped moving altogether. As Deku tried to move the golem's legs to force Katachi out from beneath him, the champion realized the trick one step too late.

D: (! What- I can't move!! Is his Soltak's light prism so powerful that it can lock my whole golem in place!? Even though the mushroom cap design is blocking the sunlight!?)

There was a 定 behind the golem's foot and hidden from sight, a strategy Katachi also exercised on the Eye of Jedivh. The observer was still following his relative north which allowed him to limit the feedback to an over-the-hip view point which made spotting the sigil nigh impossible.

K: (恒定! Constant velocity – Self!)

With a leap Katachi set his velocity to 'Constant' and travelled through the air in a straight beeline right towards Deku.

D: (How did he manage to immobilise the golem?! There's not that much sunlight in here, is there!? No, wait! What if he used light to lock and pinch at the joints alone?)

Katachi held his wooden dagger by Deku's neck and offered him sound advice as Shelly requested.

D: (Its fundamental design is no different from the suits of armour the Rugnudi use! If he tackled me at the joints, then using a golem was a mistake after all- !!)

K: (The flashier their techniques, the less attention my Words draw. All according to plan.) "Don't throw your sword away next time."

With a motion imitating a beheading Katachi won the divisional best of four through the mysterious 'flying' technique nobody could quite understand.

*** ***

Deku patted Katachi on his shoulder with a smile on his face.

D: "Good work! You caught me off-guard. I guess I'll have to uphold my bet and drink that syrup for a month."

K: "You don't need to. I didn't want to bet anyway."

D: "Really? That's doing me a huge favour! But I have the students, the audience to answer. If I fail to uphold my promises now I will not be able to promise anything when I work."

K: (That's honourable.) "I recommend against it, but I can't stop you."

Deku breathed deeply and eyed Katachi with newfound respect.

D: "Come to think of it, I don't think I've caught on to your name."

K: "Kotsuba Katachi."

D: "Kotsuba, huh... Sounds like you're from Ohde. That would explain your black hair."

K: "Many people say that, but I'm from Mielfeud though."

It was surprising to say the least. Only people from Ohde would have their hair black; everywhere else, hairs were usually blond or brown or dyed in funky colours to connect the magus to the legends of the past.

D: "Are you, now... Hmm. Well, whoever you are, you've changed my view on Soltak completely. I thought if I made a golem with a larger upper torso that blocks sunlight your Reincarnate Art would be less effective, but it didn't work at all. I guess I underestimated the limitations of your Light Prism."

K: "? Uhm, yeah, I... I guess. I was a bit surprised as well."

But the discrepancy was too large to ignore.

D: (He's uncertain of his own power? That's odd. Most Reincarnate Art users speak plainly without holding back because of their faith in the god they worship. To doubt his own ability is to doubt the god's ability. He can't possibly be a Reincarnate Art user.)

It took one to know one.

D: "You're not really a Soltak believer, are you?"

K: "No. It's just a rumour that someone else started."

D: (... He can't be serious.)

The answer was so swift and plain it was shocking. Deku didn't expect the idea that what Katachi used earlier wasn't a Reincarnate Art. Or rather, he didn't want to believe that normal magic could compete with the Reincarnate Arts on an equal level. Yet Katachi was a living proof of that, standing right before him. If someone was truly capable of magic that rivalled even the Reincarnate Arts...

D: "... Exactly what magic did you use, Katachi?"

Katachi didn't stop to answer, and left the waiting area as fast as he could holding a wooden cup filled with brown syrup.

D: (He's definitely hiding something.)

CHAPTER 17

K: "Ugh. Gross."

As a child of Segus faith such words were heresy. The amount of suffering Segus had to endure was incomparable to a mere moment's drink of the foul-coloured sludge, but Katachi had only complaints about its taste. Katachi worried for Deku whom promised the students that he would drink the brown syrup for a whole month. It was quite pitiful that he would have to gorge down the jelly-like substance, but to be fair he brought it upon himself.

He placed the wooden cup into the bin and headed towards the exit, but he was interrupted halfway by a familiar figure. A senior with four blonde braids and a dynamic body impeded his path.

Ba: "Ahh, Katachi, you were resting here?"

K: "Bael?"

Ba: "Nice work defeating Deku back there, Katachi! I didn't know that you were, uhm..."

K: "... 'were' what?"

Bael's face flushed a bright pomelo red and she turned away in embarrassment.

Ba: "... Were... Pretty good. You were pretty good out there. You just beat Deku!"

Her eyes shone with a strange light, one Katachi couldn't quite describe... Yet it was a familiar one, a stare he felt before. Her eyes reflected the distrust and distance that he felt from the glares of the Mielfeud townsfolk. But, it might just be over-thinking on his part. She probably didn't expect Katachi to triumph over Deku, certainly not when he was much larger and more experienced compared to the scrawny figure. Yet the threat of exposure made him wary and particularly sensitive.

K: "Ah, so I did..."

His faltering confidence was not very reassuring.

Ba: "You know, I don't think you've told me the magic you've been using. Isn't it about time you explained yourself?"

Her suspicions were starting to feel suffocating. That was only natural given how the unknown magic was capable of taking down the champion of three years. Even without Bael asking there would definitely be other students curious to hear the secret from him.

K: (Did they see it? Did they notice the two golden words glowing at the top of the mound of sand? They didn't catch on to it during Deku's first attack, did they?) "Ex- explain myself?"

His anxiety welled as he mentally prepared himself to silence everyone.

Ba: "What were you using back there?"

That sentence was almost a relief in and of itself. The fact that she questioned him meant that she did not understand, so the possibility of the Word of Power was not as prominent. Katachi had to think fast and come up with yet another convincing argument.

K: (Deku mentioned something called the Light Prism back at Cosmatral Tlod. If he hasn't told anyone else, the excuse just might hold.) "... It's called Light Prism. It's... It's using sunlight to seal off the movements of the golem."

Bael's eyes widened slightly, since she had yet heard of Soltak's Reincarnate Art being capable of that before. It was a precarious gamble which anchored solely upon the opposing party's trust, but thankfully the risk was negated.

Ba: (I thought he said he was a Segus follower... I guess he's starting to become more honest now, what with everyone calling him a Soltak follower and all. May as well follow a god instead of following that incestuous legend.) "That sounds cool."

She knew the criticism people gave to Segus followers from how her cousins were shunned and imprisoned. Unions between siblings were never encouraged by the other legends and various gods, so naturally the pacifist legend who permitted such relations was viewed with snide.

She believed that Katachi was only using the legend in name so as to avoid excessive interactions with others... Or perhaps she was giving herself an excuse, a chance to talk with the boy more. Had he followed after that depraved legend with the intent to marry a kin she wouldn't know what to think of him.

K: (I think she bought into it. That's a relief.) "Uhm, Bael, listen. I... I need to sketch out the map you lent to me, so I'm in a... uh... kind of in a rush."

Ba: (He's worried about that?) "Oh, that? You don't need to rush that. You can return me the map any time."

K: "Yes, but- but I would feel like I'd be... imposing on you."

Ba: (Imposing on me? How cute. He's like a little puppy, wanting to love me in the only way it knows how! He's so adorable!)

K: "... Bael?"

Ba: (Haa~ I'm imagining him with puppy ears, barking in a high-pitched 'arf'! I can't calm down!)

Her devotion to Image was admirable enough to visualise Katachi in obscure apparel, if not repulsive.

K: (She's in a daze again, looking at me all funny.) "Bael? Bael!"

Katachi clapped lightly before her face, pulling her conscious back from a trance.

Ba: "Huh, what- Yes?"

K: "Let's go. Your room is still a mess, right? I can clean your room and sketch at the same time."

Katachi was wholly prepared to help her tidy the house after all that chaos earlier.

Ba: "Oh, it's not messy any more. I got it covered already."

But the need was uncalled for.

K: "Really?"

Ba: "Yeah. All I needed to do was recite two whole chapters of Lotz's meeting with Fuegil and arrest control back over my furniture. They're very obedient, I'll have you know."

K: "... If you say so." (That's kind of incredible.)

Yet he couldn't help but find the magic peculiar. For a moment there, he thought Bael was addressing her own furniture in a manner similar to pets.

K: (Is that even normal, talking to furniture like that? Or is it just something animationists do?)

Fretting over the matter was pointless. At the very least, his schedule was free for the rest of the day so Katachi decided to visit Bertund's office once more.

*** ***

Be: "Come in Mister Kotsuba, come in."

Without even knocking on the door, Katachi was invited into the room by the creepy smiling green-attired principal with the slime hat on his head. The other lady, Shelly, was absent from the neat office.

K: "How do you two even know I'm outside the office in the first place? Is there some sort of see-through magic on the door?"

Be: "Nothing of the sort. It's quite simple, really. When someone steps on the carpet outside this flap unclips itself and drops down."

Bertund pointed at a flap on the wall and demonstrated its function by pulling the flap out before closing it back in. The hinges squeaked and a solid tense sound of a strummed belt was heard when the leather strips were stretched to its fullest allowed. It was easy to see how the two sounds were clearly distinguishable from the ambient noises.

Be: "It's pretty easy to tell if someone is outside the door loitering around or has just arrived. We automatically close it and call people in whenever it opens."

K: (It's one thing to know if someone's at the door, but how did he know it was me? It could have just as easily been another teacher. He's hiding more than he reveals... As expected of a sorceror.) "It's an interesting construct."

Be: "I agree. Apparently this was implemented since Sage Raufid's era. So, I've heard this from Shelly earlier – You wanted to discuss something with me? Is it about adding yet another course to your curriculum?"

K: "Yes. I- I mean, no! No. Uhm... Missus Shelly couldn't teach me any water magic at all because she isn't good with it. So, I was... I was hoping you'd teach me water magic."

Bertund maintained his creepy smile as he assessed the situation at hand. He got up from his seat and walked towards the bookshelf in the room, picked up a book and began flipping through its contents.

Be: "That is an interesting offer, Mister Kotsuba. But the thing is, I don't teach magic for free. If you were to request for a normal teacher to assist you in basic spells and the like it would be fine and we can have it arranged. But as the principal of this school and a head figure for aspiring magi I cannot simply teach someone a spell."

K: "Why not?"

Bertund paused the flipping and looked at Katachi with a slightly wider smile on his face.

Be: "Because, Mister Kotsuba, when I teach magic that is a guarantee that you will not just learn, but master it."

The brilliance of the principal shone through for that brief moment, and beneath that eerie smile was a schemer far creepier than the façade suggested.

Be: "I can teach anything and everything about whatever magic I've managed to learn myself. And that is the reason why I am the principal, not a teacher – If I simply allowed anyone to study under my supervision, they will quite literally become a second version of myself, a replica if you will."

That would defeat the purpose of having an academy without question.

B: "The elemental affinities, the limitations of astrology, details and lore and even the most advanced of spells, all of the tough reading, deciphering and researching, the construction of mediums and weapons, all of that can be mitigated and even negated under my proficient teachings. That wouldn't be nice if everyone became as powerful as the principal now, would it?"

K: (From the way he phrases that I'm guessing that anyone who studies under him will learn everything as though the experience was inherited... Does he have a kind of magic to transfer his knowledge to others, allowing them to master the spells as well as he does? I wonder which legend that's derived from?) "... That sounds amazing."

Be: "That is why I cannot afford to teach a student for free unlike the normal education the other teachers here provide. This academy is a place to nurture, ripen and foster the power of potential magi. It is not a factory for producing sorceror-class soldiers. If you wish to learn spells from me you will have to pay."

K: (I suppose great power comes at a great price. But, what do I pay with?) "Pay in what terms?"

Be: "As you probably have guessed, my favourite food is roasted newt. My favourite pet is slime, and my favourite colour is green. If you wish to learn a basic spell, offer me something green. If you wish to learn an intermediate spell, fetch me something slimy, or a slime-related by-product. If you wish to learn an advanced spell you would have to catch and roast a newt for me by yourself. Those are my terms."

Even his demands seem to defy common sense. Or, did it? Bertund was always dressed in his green prominent attire, he was always seen with his slime hat and he was likely enjoying newts every once in a while. Perhaps that in itself was a ritual of sorts he derived at to maintain some spell after studying the Path of Image for so long. Katachi could not resist the urge to ask.

K: "... What's with the funky currency?"

Bertund's smile receded a little and he began reading the book he was holding.

Be: "There are children around who rely on their parents' money in order to obtain fame, fortune, status and power. I despise those who would use others' gold for their own advantage – And you may have noticed, but about a third of the students here are rich."

Katachi recalled some of the students he saw around the school and their uniforms hemmed in gold and silver.

Be: "Some of our students here have families rich enough to purchase this entire academy. That would distort the fair, balanced learning environment this place is supposed to be, would it not? Is that not defying the wishes of Sage Raufid himself?"

K: "I guess you're right."

Be: "So, Mister Kotsuba. You now know what you need to do. What have you to offer me?"

K: (I should go get a newt then.) "I'll be right back."

Katachi exited the room silently with a determined look in his eyes.

*** ***

Two and a half hours later, Katachi arrived at the principal's office once again.

Be: "Come in, Mister Kotsuba."

As he stepped through the doorway Katachi was greeted by Bertund and another teacher in the room. This particular teacher looked familiar, to say the least – His upper torso was bigger than his lower torso and he looked like a gorilla human.

Be: "Yorn, let us discuss this some other time. I need you to tell Shelly that the mess hall has refreshments prepared for Minister Lein. It will be cleared at six in the evening so alternate to route C after the last two rounds conclude."

The man resembling an inverted pear grimaced slightly when he saw Katachi holding a cage in his hand.

Y: "If you would excuse me."

Yorn slowly shuffled his way out of the room, avoiding collision with the furniture to the best of his ability. With the door closed behind him Katachi could openly discuss with Bertund on his issues again without as much restraint.

Be: "I was expecting a roasted newt, but you actually went and caught a live one?"

K: "Segus forbids killing."

Be: "Fair enough. I believe Mother Rinnesfeld mentioned something along those lines in her letter."

K: "Yeah. Specifically, though, she... She mentioned that the church which, well, we lived in served Segus, so it wasn't very clear."

His stuttering was quite amusing to the sorceror.

Be: "It's fine, the message got through."

He pulled at the glove strongly, and his fingers clawed inward, almost threatening to fuse with the cloth itself. Bertund took a good look at the small lizard in the muddy cage and paid careful attention to its tail and underside.

Be: "This newt... Smells of the moss in the Langstrade river, healthy scales, no injuries... Yes, yes, this is good. Not quite an adult yet, but it will be one very soon."

Bertund nodded slowly in approval at the offering presented before him.

Be: "So, you wanted to learn an advanced spell?"

Katachi placed the cage on the desk and sat on the chair opposite the principal's seat.

K: "A-and I'd like to learn one that can accustom to me and my needs properly."

Be: "Mister Kotsuba, I've watched your performance today from the observation deck. But are you sure you want an advanced spell? It might not be of great use to you in the tournament."

It almost made him cry. All that effort of setting up a sun bowl and waiting for a newt to stop by before trapping it in the cage... The amount of work invested into it, unrewarded.

K: "It... It won't?"

Be: "Not in the slightest. The Young Magus tournament has rather specific limitations where you are only allowed the wooden weapon you have with you as well as any magic you are able to cast with your tools or by yourself. Even if I do teach you one that does not use any additional materials it would require a rather large magic circle made entirely from sand, for example."

But that was a scenario only applicable should the foe give him the liberty to.

Be: "You would have to draw the circle in the sand while avoiding the attacks from the other magi and stopping the opponent from disrupting the circle. That's unless, of course, the spell requires your opponent to be in a specific position where you activate a spell while they try to move in and disrupt you. That's not an easy manoeuvre to perform neither, especially without practice."

Bertund's advice was disheartening but enlightening at the same time.

Be: "Not to mention, pulling tricks like that are often to force the opponent to move and counter before you can pull it off or to lure them into a bigger trap. It's not out of the question but if you'd like to learn a bigger trap to go along with it that would require another newt."

K: "..."

Katachi's head drooped a little at the news.

Be: (Well, that's only true if his capacity for Image is weak. But for someone like him, saying that is like calling a sloth the most active thing anyone has ever seen. If I were to teach him anything serious he could easily strangle and overpower everyone. Best to put him in check.) "Don't worry. You've presented me a newt anyway, so I shall teach magic of value equivalent to this offer. How about a couple of useful fast-casting basic spells and some advice?"

K: (The greatest of magi make the most of the least.) "... I guess that's not too bad."

Be: "Very well. Let's begin with the advice then – Every little bit helps, does it not?"

He began scribbling a familiar yet foreign character on a piece of papyrus as he continued to convince the child. He raised the papyrus to reveal two characters: 锁定.

Be: "Did you know that your 定 is actually capable of a term known as 锁定, which means 'to lock'?"

The abrupt and random trivia was uncalled for.

K: (It can mean 'Lock'?) "... I thought we were learning water magic!"

Be: "Ahh, but I said 'some advice', did I not? I did not specify what advice I would give. Besides, an advice on your own Word of Power is far greater than any advice I can give on magic you don't even know yet."

K: (That makes sense, kind of. 锁定, huh... That sounds really good.) "That is nice to know, but how would I use it? Does it directly mean 'lock' or does it prevent opening?"

Be: "It's as simple as it suggests. 定 in this sense means to 'secure' and 锁 is the Anikan word directly responsible for locking it. You can use it to lock other objects, like chests, doors, gates... Well, that's a hint big enough for you. You can figure out what you want to do with that knowledge."

K: (That's really good to know. Locking, huh... So basically, by using 定 in that way I can lock anything that is below the word's raw precedence level.) "So, can we touch on water magic now?"

Be: "Yes. Relax yourself, Mister Kotsuba. To be at peace, to reach a tranquillity the same as water is an important facet of using water magic."

Katachi leaned back against the chair's backrest comfortably.

Be: "Just one last thing before we begin. Let's review your strategy for battling – You like to head in for close-range combat and clash against the magi in that uncomfortable zone. That's a good strategy against them, if I may say so myself. Did you learn that somewhere beforehand?"

K: "Yes. There were these bamboo books laying outside one of the Mielfeud townsfolk's house, so I picked them up and carried them to the library to read. One of these... One of these books was about how people have generic fighting styles and how each could be countered by exploiting their shortcomings. Like how warriors have a habit of using their dominant arm as their sword arm and striking them from that side forces them into a defensive to protect their means of retaliation."

Be: "From your description, I'm guessing the book's name was Gnote's Guide to Paganism Survival?"

As expected of a literary man, Bertund was quick to catch onto the topic discussed.

K: "Yes, that's the one."

Be: "So you already know that much. But the book isn't dedicated to magi or champions or anybody besides travellers and pagans like Gnote himself. Adversaries who specialize themselves open up new options that Gnote did not have access to. It won't help a whole lot, but it certainly did improve your strategic thinking. Hmm..."

Katachi took a piece of charcoal and papyrus out of his sandy blazer and set it down on the table.

Be: "Very well! I'll start teaching you water magic now. You're going to be thankful you learned these – I guarantee it."

*** ***

A long day of competitions finally simmered down into a peaceful night. Katachi put down the chalk and charcoal in his hands. He folded the two maps and placed them neatly on the side of the small desk.

K: (There we go. I'm finally finished.)

As he gazed upon the night sky, a half-moon shone across the scenery outside his window.

K: (Tomorrow's going to be a big day, huh... The semi-finals and the finals together on the same day. I sure pray I don't have to fight him at all.)

He immersed himself in his own thoughts, entranced by the dark blanket of stars.

K: (If all else fails I'll rely on the Word of Power then, but that should only be a last resort. If I can, I want to settle the matches with the rest of them as soon as possible with these new spells. But what will they think? If they truly believe that I am using Child of Sun, won't it be strange to diverge and suddenly use Image spells?)

Or perhaps it was not as unusual as he believed.

K: (Then again, over-using a spell brings a big risk as well. The weaknesses and limitations are exposed and counter-plays become possible, just as how so many students try to find ways to circumvent the Gatherer's Golem. Changing to a new angle of attack they're not prepared for has its merits.)

The smell of sand, soil and the uncomfortable itch and stickiness across his body broke him out of his trance – He had yet bathed. Earlier that day he ran around rolling, tumbling and fighting on the sandy dunes of Cosmatral Tlod, dug around Cosmatral Neud and hunted for a newt, skipped his dinner so he could finish the map... By the time he noticed the dirty uniform he was still wearing, twilight had long past.

K: (It's almost nine... The curfew begins in a short while. I should use this time to bathe quickly.)

Katachi grabbed a towel and headed towards the bathroom.

*** ***

The huge bathing space was eerily empty and quiet.

K: (I'm surprised how nobody's here at this hour! Maybe it was because there are no actual lessons today that the students can bathe at their own time, so they chose to do it early?... Huh. I guess not all students want to bathe late in the night.)

Or it could be the unbearable heat in the day which strongly encouraged baths early on to wash off their sweat. Katachi didn't sit at the field area for long enough to tell so he couldn't judge impartially. He undressed his uniform, neatly unfolded his towel and hung them on the racks.

K: (For the uniform, well... I'll probably have to wash it another day because I won't have enough time to bathe if I don't. Or I could simply use the cleaning spell, but it's costly.)

Katachi leered at his immediate surroundings and focused on his hearing for any footsteps or human activity.

K: (There's no one around... I guess I'll use magic to clean it this time.)

Katachi took advantage of the fact that he was the only one in the bathing space.

K: (恒定! Constant status – Gold!)

A tiny 定 was placed over a small piece of gold. Katachi placed that piece of gold in the centre of the magic circle and the shirt began to move on its own. Though the gold piece was unaffected still, the magic circle gleamed with a gold brilliance and the sand and stains were all expunged outward forcefully, cleansing it in an instant. He repeated the process for all of his other garments while scrubbing his body thoroughly. When it was all done he removed the Word of Power on the gold and placed it into his pouch.

K: (That should save on some of the gold... Excellent. Nobody's around to see it.)

Katachi was suddenly forced to walk out of the bathroom with all of his items. He barely managed to pull his undergarments up in time before he exited the bathing area. It was good practice to place his items near the entrance of the bathing space so he could simply collect them on his way out.

K: (It must be time for curfew now... Well, at least I got the clothes clean.)

Katachi walked back to his own room obediently and grabbed the mug by the side for a sip. He folded the clean clothes properly before placing them aside. After the apparel were put away neatly he prepared the bed for the night.

K: (Mother Rin... I don't know what will happen tomorrow, so I don't think I can keep the promise of visiting you every few lunar cycles. Please stay safe.)

The exhaustion finally caught on and the young child dozed off to sleep.

CHAPTER 18

Deep in the night, five tiny lights flickered in the academy. The first light was from the principal's office – Bertund and Shelly were still busy with administrative tasks and so they burned the night doing what they did not have time for in the day.

Be: "... Hmm. Strange."

S: "What is?"

Be: "According to the cafeteria's reports, we seem to be running low on rock salt."

S: "So we are. The princess of Rugnud disappeared recently so the markets are suffering from wide-scale economic panic. It's throwing all sorts of things out of order – The trades are delayed and border checks all around Rugnud are being reinforced. At this rate Findel might run out of resources besides rock salt like building materials. The price of jewels and crystals might quickly appreciate too."

Be: "We need to look into this matter more after this event. The tournament comes first."

S: "We should plan and prioritize a day for it though."

Be: "Should we do it right after the tournament ends?"

S: "And leave the academy unattended? Squeezing our own matters into the curriculum is too selfish."

Be: "Okay. Let me see, the next available days we have are... the third and fourth week after the tournament. We can check it out while tomb-sweeping."

S: "Schedule that."

Be: "Okay. I'll reserve it now."

And so the couple continued working the night away. The second light was the small light at an emergency station, one that was always lit and operationally ready should any emergencies occur. The last three lights came from the semi-finalists of the tournament. They stayed up late, they revised and planned their opponent's movements, and they expended sleep for victory.

Well, at least, two of them were – One of the students, Pitin, was chewing his nails rigorously in a state of panic. Arguably, that could have been precious recovery time had he followed a certain someone's example. It wasn't uncommon for the child to stay up at night and collect flowers that bloomed in the moon, however a day full of events drained Katachi of his energy. And so a peaceful night passed.

*** ***

An itch formed on his left shoulder.

(Contestant Katachi, your match begins in 30 minutes. Please assemble at the entrance to Cosmatral Tlod.)

K: (... Already? I want to sleep more...)

As he opened his eyes, Katachi was greeted by the mounted rack right before his face.

K: (That was close. I almost tried to get up normally.)

He took great care not to hit his head and folded up the table rack before an accident could occur. Katachi climbed off his bed and changed into the uniform he folded yesterday. He secured the pants onto his waist with a belt, put on a white under-shirt, and stuck his arm into the blazer's sleeve. As he did the sound of a hinge creaking was heard. His door was being opened by someone.

"Yeah, it won't take long. I'll just change my socks- ..."

Another student entered his room without knocking on his door. The student was dumbfounded at Katachi being in the room, with eyes wide open and attire half done. He looked at the door plate again before apologizing earnestly.

"... Sorry about that. I thought this was the first floor."

The student closed the door gently and left. As benign as it was, the astonishment caused Katachi to flinch severely. The anxiety of the idea that he had two more rounds to go was a powerful vice. He forcefully convinced himself that it was going to be okay.

K: (... I feel so restless.)

*** ***

Katachi took his seat on a nearby bench awaiting his match patiently.

P: "... You..."

K: (? Is someone calling me?)

Katachi glanced at the student next to him – A rustic brown bowl-cut adolescent slightly older than he was holding a wooden Vanaelis rune carving in his hands.

P: "Are you Kotsuba Katachi?" (By the gods, look at him! He's so young! He's the guy that beat Nea, Cillian and even Deku!)

K: "... Yes? Yes I am." (What does he want from me? Is he trying to figure out my weakness?)

P: (The only feasible magic I know is the Curse of Rhetsis, but that won't work on knights who can stab and attack like Cillian does! How am I supposed to beat someone who beat Cillian in close combat?!) "I have to fight you!? But, but- but, you're the guy that beat the champion! You beat Cillian too! I can't- I can't possibly defeat a guy who's beaten both Deku and Cillian!"

Pitin, the pitiful child, shook in fright and terror at Katachi's demeanour. He seemed the sort who would break under a certain level of stress.

K: (He looks a lot more unnerved than I am. Somehow that makes me edgier.) "... Are you okay?"

P: "No. No! I am not okay. I've seen what you did in Cosmatral Tlod. The way you savagely attacked Cillian... You're going to smack my rune out of my hands and hurt me a lot, aren't you?! I... I forfeit! I give up!"

By now, the student's face paled and his teeth clattered nervously.

K: (... Is he afraid of pain or something? How did he get this far then?)

Katachi witnessed with his own eyes what was possibly the reason he had to face difficult opponents for his earlier rounds. Perhaps the child siphoned the good fortune with his presence, usurping many of the opponents that were relatively easy. He could have been paired against the novices while Katachi was the unlucky student tossed into the half filled with the veterans and seniors.

Fate was a cruel, relentless prankster whom would mock and scorn Man time and again, as though he were its very idea of entertainment. Though it could have all been in his head, a concept born of paranoia and madness...

K: (If there ever were a spell meant to control a person's fortune, I would be very upset and intrigued at the same time.)

... but Katachi had long forgone that unfounded ideal.

*** ***

Shelly's voice projected over the whole coliseum.

S: "Your attention please. Due to the semi-finalist Pitin requesting for a forfeit, contestant Kotsuba Katachi has won the match by default. As such, we shall only have one match for the divisional best of two, Djinnje against Zirco."

D: "It's 'the amazing' Djinnje! You forgot to put 'the amazing' before my name! Hey-"

The voice of a student was projected throughout the school before the announcement was abruptly cut off. With an unexpected turn of events Katachi was allowed to partake in the finals.

K: (That was projection magic... Wasn't it?)

Two minutes later, Bael beamed a bright smile as she walked in.

Ba: "I'm impressed. You just won the divisional best of two without lifting a finger. Literally!"

K: "It's not really... Not really my fault. He wanted to forfeit when he realized that I was his opponent."

Ba: "Why did he just give up, though? He came all the way to the semi-finals, be it by luck or skill, so he should have at least aimed for the champion's seat."

K: "I don't know. Maybe he was afraid of pain? He looked like he was in agony from remembering how I beat Cillian."

Ba: (Oh, the one time where Katachi fanatically struck Cillian.) "Yeah. The way you fought Cillian was pretty aggressive, actually."

The child was painfully unaware of just how dangerous Nistier's style appeared to others. But it should surprise none of its viability, praised enough for a book to be made detailing it in the first place.

K: "It... It is?"

Ba: "Yeah. I mean, I haven't met a magus who would attack like that. You're like a hybrid similar to Cillian or something, wielding a dagger like that."

K: "You're exaggerating."

As they chatted away a sudden roar could be heard from the other students observing the semi-finals match. From what they could make of their cries the ongoing match was intense.

K: (Sounds like they're heating up in the other divisional top match. Whoever wins will promise a tough and unrelenting match regardless, but I haven't really checked either of them out. So much for taking it easy.)

Ba: (He's just standing there, pondering ceaselessly as he always does. What is he thinking about?... Is he worried about the championship match?) "Hey, Katachi?"

K: "Ah, yes?"

Ba: "If you need me, I'll always be here. In fact, I feel great when you say that you need me, so be sure to rely on this senior more, ahahahahaha!"

It was at that moment Bael's eyes widened and she turned away immediately to hide her shame. Her face reddened uncontrollably and her lips straightened to form a curious mixture of joy and fear at the same time.

Ba: (Wait, what am I saying?! That has got to be the most embarrassing thing I could have ever said! It's as good as a confession!!)

K: (She must see seniority over me because of our age differences, but I wish she would not treat me like her own son. Still, it's a form of goodwill, and it's the thought that counts. I guess I'll thank her for the blessing.) "... Uhm... Thank you."

Ba: ('Thank you'? Is... Is that a yes? Or a sympathetic no? Which is it? Why does he talk like that?)

The two sat there while the crowd roared a second time. Immediately after, their awkward silence was interrupted by an announcement.

S: "Your attention please, remaining contestants, please stand by. The finals will begin shortly."

The recording sounded awkward. It was definitely Shelly's voice, but it was far too energetic compared to how she taught Katachi during the lecture. Still, because proper communication magic was far too expensive this was one of the better alternatives the school looked to.

K: (There's no break between the semi-finals and the next?)

Ba: (Wha- The semi-finals are over already? We've only been talking for a few minutes! That was fast! I guess that's why the crowd went wild earlier, the victor was probably aching to bring out the next match. Or maybe it was a flawless victory.) "You should prepare yourse- Katachi?"

Katachi's face turned serious and his head quivered slightly.

K: "... I don't want to fight this final round."

Ba: (He looks really intense... I understand his concern over facing someone who finished the semi-finals flawlessly, but why wouldn't he want to fight the last round? Is it because the semi-final match was settled this quickly?) "Why not? You came this far already, you should go all the way!"

"You still have time for senseless banter?"

A voice Katachi hoped never to hear echoed through the corridor to their ears.

Ba: "Who's the rude one who declared that? Show yourself!"

"Shut up, woman."

Zirco. He was another one of many children in Mielfeud who gave Katachi a hellish childhood. He was the brains of a trio of delinquents in town that picked on him deliberately. Compared to Juval and Dante, Zirco did not harass Katachi physically. But he deceived the adults and set up the bullying to reverse their roles – Katachi was made to look like the bad child everyone thought he was.

His actions promoted Dante's bullying and glorified the act to the other kids. To worsen the situation, he was enrolled for about a year compared to Dante and Juval so it wasn't an understatement to say that he was considerably the most dangerous of the three given his seniority. Zirco likely knew a great many things about the school, about the lore that Katachi himself probably didn't.

Z: "Don't look at me, scum."

Of course, his intellect was the source, if not the equivalent of his egoism.

K: "... Zirco."

Z: "A sinner like yourself does not deserve to address me. Your feats of defeating Deku and Cillian are commendable, but I'm not some goof who screams and swears stupid promises around. Nor am I a fool who splits time between learning magic and swordplay. I am a pure magus."

That haughtiness was new, though. Zirco was usually a more reserved person who favoured silence. What changed him?

K: "Chotil Nea's a pure magus too if you put it that way."

Z: "She doesn't count. She transforms into a cougar using Qin Tsung Yao's tale, and transformation magic can't be considered proper magic. To have her up on the semi-finals last year was a blunder. I should have just beat Cillian so I could defeat her too."

K: "... So you were in the tournament last year."

Z: "Of course. And now thanks to you, I can't test my new spells and strategy."

Zirco's eyes gradually filled with hatred and spite as he complained about the absence of the already-established opponents. It was in and of itself a mere shout down – Zirco had long concluded that Katachi wasn't strong enough to be a worthy opponent, as though his victory was already decided.

K: (Perhaps this was a result of his days in school? Hubris is a dangerous trait for magi. I should be careful not to become like that.)

Z: "... No matter. I'll take this chance to show everyone the monster beneath your skin."

Zirco walked towards the obelisk that was the entrance to Cosmatral Tlod and transported himself to the plane of plain sand. As he did, Shelly spoke up to remind him of something important.

Ba: (Monster beneath his skin?)

S: "Mister Zirco? The finals this year aren't held in Cosmatral Tlod."

The crowd laughed at the fool Zirco made of himself as he rebutted as hard as he could. Since the voices and sounds inside Cosmatral Tlod were broadcast to the coliseum everyone could hear the bashful dialogue clearly.

Z: "What do you mean, it's not in Cosmatral Tlod? It was the same last year!"

S: "Mister Zirco, the tradition for the final round of the Young Magus tournament is to determine the field for next year's tournament. Last year, the roll was just a coincidence that the field happened to be Cosmatral Tlod again."

K: (Projection magic... Huh. That's kind of cheap. How did she set it up to project her voice into a different plane?)

As a poor child himself he deeply understood the means the odd couple took to preserve their funds and resources for the long term. Yet the secrets to unravel remained ever bountiful.

S: "This year, the final round is to be held at Cosmatral Silo according to the raffle conducted last evening. Please exit Cosmatral Tlod now, Mister Zirco."

Zirco quietly left the plane and headed to the obelisk for Cosmatral Silo instead. The crowd was laughing at Zirco for his mistake at first but the revelation of 'Cosmatral Silo' caused many of the students to sigh, moan and lament at the news.

Ba: "Ooo-hoo-hoo! Cosmatral Silo! That's my field!"

S: "Don't look so down! Cosmatral Silo might be a bad place for cardinal element users but that means Dardicel magi are going to be weakened as well! This should be your chance to beat Deku while he's weakened!"

K: (Deku? Weakened?)

Katachi's ears perked up straight away.

K: "Bael, what's Cosmatral Silo?"

Ba: "Cosmatral Silo? It's another plane, like Tlod and Neud."

K: "What are the differences?"

Ba: "Well, Neud has a lot of soil and trees which allows other plants and animals to live there. Tlod's a sandy plain with a bunch of rocks about."

Two diversely different planes with contrasting alignments that benefited magi who handled the earth, plants and the cardinal elements. Deku's dominance was rather pronounced.

Ba: "Silo is completely metallic – If you dent the floor it becomes an obstacle people have to look out for. If it's utilized correctly, the entire battlefield can be made to one's advantage. Because it lacks nature the spells centred around cardinal elements are crippled, but fields like that which emphasize on the space available to manoeuvre makes an animationist like me shine."

K: (I wonder how many planes there are out there.) "You sound like you have a plan ready already."

Ba: "Of course! I can force the metal to crumble and make a lot of material to reanimate while the others are left hanging dry!"

K: (She looks like she's done it before.) "... You're really far-sighted, aren't you?"

Ba: "Oh, don't look at me like that. I've been here for six years and I've joined this tournament twice already, don't you know! Besides, the Young Magus Tournament is just a small event. What I really look forward to is the Theories and Articles Fair coming next year."

K: (She really is a lot older than the students here. She's sixteen years old, but I didn't think she came here since she was ten years old as well- Wait, that's stupid. I'm ten too and I'm here, why wouldn't she?) "I suppose I should head to Silo then."

Ba: "Good luck! Have fun! And be careful – Don't get impaled!"

The words sent shivers down his spine as though someone yanked his entire backbone out and threw it back perfectly intact within a flash.

K: (Impaled? Impaled by what?)

CHAPTER 19

Z: "So this is Cosmatral Silo."

Katachi appeared from the warped space and entered Cosmatral Silo.

K: "... Oh."

Cosmatral Silo was a stark contrast from the other planes. Everything looked metallic. The air was full of dust and it stained the presumably blue sky's azure into something between a sickly green and brown. The platform they were brought to had already been damaged and reduced into abstract art.

There were dents and cave-ins all over the floor, there were broken parts of the footing here and there, there were even shards of crystals littered over the ground acting as a hazard. Strangely enough there were no 'sharp objects' to 'impale' them with, so Bael's meaning was unclear.

Z: "Remnants of the previous battles?... Don't they ever take care of this place?"

K: (Floating islands of steel... A retelling of the Grave of Segus? This is the battlefield that Bael prefers?)

The place literally reeked of death and would offset anyone that relied upon the natural elements to battle efficiently. Large mounds of metal floated peacefully in the background, equally scarred and worn out by the previous students whom set foot upon the plane. The air was stagnant and reeked of rust, both from the pieces of corroded metal and from the bloodstains on the ground.

It was completely stale – Cosmatral Silo was a battlefield that imposed the restrictions of one's mobility by the obstacles on the plane as well as the deprivation of fresh air available to the competitors. It truly befitted a battlefield for testing the power of magi who properly honed their image power, not those that relied on finesse, affinity, brute strength or anything of the sort.

To Katachi, that did not affect him as much given his passive nature. He used the dagger to deliver the dangerous blows that decided his victory, so given his almost-negligible capacity at offence the drawback mattered little. He needed only to create an opening and strike from there.

*** ***

126

Katachi faced his opponent who was seven meters away, dagger in hand poised to strike. Zirco reached for his wooden sword's rough position to ensure that he had a way to fight Katachi at mêlée range should he decide to close the gap like in the previous rounds.

Z: (He struck down Cillian, Nea and Deku with his dagger so I should assume the same will happen again. Once he reaches anywhere closer than four metres I should be ready to draw and retaliate.) "I originally planned to use the sandy plains of Cosmatral Tlod to my advantage. This just means that my spell will lose out in its efficiency, but that can be recovered with a little image power."

Zirco clapped his hands together twice and began reciting his spell.

Z: "Hear me, students of Sage Raufid Magus Academy. Hear the cries of I the man, and Katachi the fool."

K: (He's marking me with a specific name, of the 'Fool'... From what I can recall right off the bat there are dozens of tales that use 'man' and 'fool'. It's a pity I didn't get to see his semi-final match. I need more clues if I want to know what tale he's deriving his spells from. He's also using the image power of the students to offset the lack of an advantage... Like sand, perhaps?)

Many clues could be derived from his simple actions, but filtering them to find the right answer was the real problem.

K: (Maybe it's an elemental spell which suggests his eagerness to compete in Cosmatral Tlod? There are nine stories I know related to sand with 'man' and 'fool' within... That's only if he's actually using the sand, and not some additional component from Cosmatral Tlod. Dust, thirst, dry wind... They all seem a bit too specific, nothing really comes to mind.)

Zirco held his hands up towards the green sky and continued his chant.

Z: "The man treads lightly, and is thus protected."

K: (There are three stories I know heavily relevant to sand, man and fool. Aleksei and the Wiseman, Braver of the Dharan and Tholneus forsaking his village. At least that narrows down the scope I have to guard against. I have to prepare for whatever he's doing and derive the tale's origin appropriately before I properly strike him.)

Z: "While the fool stomps and leaps, happy-go-lucky as he ever will be."

The metal beneath Katachi's feet began to shake.

K: ('Protect', 'Stomp'-! Caution and bravado, contrasting movements! Aleksei and the Wiseman! If that's what he's using as a spell base, then I have to move right now!-)

Z: "And so the flames spewed forth from beneath the fool's feet!"

Katachi leapt away quickly to a clearing on the platform. Where he once stood the metal tented upwards and exploded like a pie with too thin a crust, fire erupting erratically from that spot. The air above cleared for a moment before it was consumed by the faint green miasma-like gas once again. Zirco carefully observed the effects of his actions while Katachi took the time to reorganize the new information from his spell.

Z: (The metal isn't soft like earth, so it takes longer to crack open for the flames to spew. The place where the fire gushed out from is still hot and I'm not going anywhere near the eruption zone so that's going to be to my advantage. My attacks are going to be delayed in here, though... The fire seems to be equally strong even when the air isn't fresh.)

Even after the effort he invested into the storytelling, it did not produce the result he desired.

Z: (Perhaps the image power received from the students only intensified the flames, not the spell's speed. Maybe the inflection on 'flames' was too heavy compared to the emphasis on 'spewed'. I wanted this to be a swift victory, but the unexpected turn of events screwed it all up. Setting up the Peony Flame Ritual will be difficult if the flames are this delayed.)

The consequence of preparing himself for Cosmatral Tlod's atmosphere bared its ugly face far too soon.

Z: (If only I knew the battlefield's going to be comprised of metal instead I would simply have settled with another spell... No point in regretting what's done. I'll just use this spell as I just had.)

K: (The tale of Aleksei and the Wiseman... Aleksei, a happy-go-lucky Auser fool who travelled onto a mountain where he met a Wiseman crossing a volcano as well. They landed into deep trouble because of Aleksei's foolishness, but the Wiseman helped Aleksei move about without disturbing the volcano's delicate peak.)

There was a very useful application of the spell that could be derived.

K: (If he's the Wiseman, then he needs to shout 'Tread with care, young fool!' or his spell will affect me. It's often used as a generic spell for training magi to dodge attacks from the ground, and the safe sentence protects the trainee from being damaged by rising columns of flame.)

But Zirco's variant of the spell was contorted.

K: (He's using it offensively where the Wiseman would never need to scream that line... I can't use the Vapour Domain spell Bertund recommended – He can probably surround himself with flames intense enough to disperse the mist before it even reaches him. I guess the only other option I have is Croxa's spell. That's assuming he doesn't have any other spells up his sleeve.)

Katachi tucked his dagger back into his clothes to free up his hands for evading Zirco's spell. Zirco saw that as a window of opportunity and quickly took to the offensive. Clapping his hands even tighter than before, he began his incantation.

Z: "And lo, the fool leapt out of the pennsic and into the flames."

K: (! It's not specifying anything, so it must be a continuous spell-!! Not good, I better move!-)

Katachi began running around the battlefield quickly in large circles, hoping to outrun and avoid the attacks erupting from the floor. The flames were gushing out in a tracing ripple – Wherever Katachi stepped on the fire would spew from that piece of metal a moment later for a few seconds. It formed many, many medium columns of flame and it pursued him relentlessly, the only saving grace being how short-lived the attacks were.

Round and round he went, forming lots of cracks on the ground and dividing the battlefield's border between him and Zirco. But a defensive play like that was subpar at best and he exerted no pressure on his opponent with the passive strategy. He was only giving Zirco the time he needed to set up a bigger spell.

Z: (One stagger or one stumble is all I need. The moment he shows any instability, I can use the Peony Flame Ritual immediately.)

K: "Gh!" (He's going to make me waste my stamina, a main weakness of most magi. Fine then! Let's see how you'd handle this!)

As he ran and dodged the flames, Katachi began reciting his own spell.

K: "From beneath her feet, an unending stream flowed."

Water started pouring out of Katachi's hands and eyes. They flowed and covered the metal field with water all over. The flames were still spewing regardless, but the water made the metal platform cool rapidly so Katachi wouldn't feel the residual heat on his soles.

Additionally, the heat dried and reduced the water puddles fast enough for Katachi to re-run over the surface without feeling the slippery texture and eliminating the risk of skidding and losing balance. It was a calculated decision that allowed him to last longer while frightening his opponent with the possibility of a counter-attack.

Z: (! What the-!! Urdythari's unending tears!? That requires her rune to cast, but he's invoking it without any form of guidance? Did he tattoo her rune onto his skin or something!? Or did he cheat and bring in a rune prepared beforehand?!) "Are you cheating!?"

It was either that, or the rather unlikely possibility that Katachi truly understood what it meant for Urdythari's tears to flow for her beloved. But surely, that could not be! To lose one's beloved, and to weep at that which could have been was a sadness that he couldn't possibly have experienced. From the start, a sinner such as himself had nothing of the sort to lose... Or did he?

Zirco lost his focus upon unearthing the seemingly impossible trick. His hands which were clapped together tightly loosened, and in accordance the pillars of flame stopped. But Katachi's palms and eyes were still releasing water like a busted tap and it was now dressing and blanketing the metallic floor in multiple puddles.

The water poured from his hands like a ceaseless fountain and changed the floor into a mirror-like surface. It flowed into the dents made by the previous students. It flowed into the cracks made from Zirco's spell and it seeped towards wherever he was swinging his arms at. Katachi calmly walked around the battlefield, coating the water all over as though it were icing.

Z: (He wants to wet the entire field so the spell becomes ineffective? That won't work because the flames burst through the metal-...)

It took a while for Zirco to work out his ploy. The visage was vague, but Katachi was indeed drawing the water on the ground in a defined shape.

Z: (! Sharyu Zuku's rain call!! He wants to douse my spell completely by wetting the entire field in a rainstorm! I'll just increase the sun's intensity to- !!)

Zirco finally realized what Katachi was planning, and acted to dispel the potential disaster. With his hands held close Zirco recited a spell quickly in a desperate attempt to stop, or at least impede the process.

Z: "Flames born unto his palms, and took the form of a ball. With a rampant intensity it expanded!"

A ball of fire was created in the gap between his hands, and it grew larger and larger until it was about a quarter of his body size. Zirco held it high above his head-

K: (Vesja's Will of the Flame? What a disappointing sight. As if a real magus would give you the time to set up properly!) "Her tears poured forth, and paved into rivers!"

Katachi side-stepped to an area outside of the circle and swung his arms wildly at Zirco from four meters away. The arbitrary streams of water whipped out towards his opponent in a turbulent bloom. It doused his spell while soaking his clothes and face with water – It was merely extinguishing his spell by flailing about randomly in his general direction without any precision training of the sort, but it was enough to interrupt his spell thoroughly.

Z: (That was an unglamorous move for a magus, but... Shit. He planned for this! He's going to turn the field into one where fire spells are unfavourable. If I let him use the rain call as he pleases, I won't be able to use Aleksei's spell properly. That's the safest spell I have since the flames erupt from the floor. If he smothers it with rain it will weaken a lot, and I won't be able to cast other flame spells easily because of the rain obstructing the other spells.)

It was Zirco's turn to be in a pinch, even though Katachi had yet mustered any real offence.

Z: (Not to mention, he's soaked my clothes so my movements will be sluggish and both my magic and sword will be impeded. But if I strengthen the sun, it will strengthen his Child of Sun's powers.)

Zirco, though raised in Mielfeud as well, heard and knew so little of Katachi that he would blindly believe the child's faith in Soltak. What bitter irony it was, that alienating him was perhaps the greatest boon Katachi had.

He was tempted to use the free-spirited Mother Rinnesfeld as a form of blackmail and intimidation against him, but that would disrespect the nun who took care of his family during a period of distress. Also, their voices were projected back to the students watching and Minister Lein himself; the unbecoming act would likely destroy any of his chances to be viewed in a favourable light.

Z: (Is he betting on Soltak's Reincarnate Art to guard himself from the flames? I don't have much choice. I would rather fight him at full power than risk being weakened!)

Zirco recited the exaltations of a Soltak worshipper and began a Clear Sky spell.

*** ***

K: (... is probably what he's thinking. If I guessed it right, then it should play out perfectly.)

*** ***

Z: "Oh, great mighty Soltak, you who embody the holy sun,"

K: (He's begun reciting... I need to play along as well.) "Sharyu Zuku, spare us pain. Heed our call, Goddess of Rain."

Katachi began counter-reciting with his hands cupped together in prayer while the water soaked his uniform and pants thoroughly. Zirco raised his hands above his head in reverence to the sky imitating a Soltak follower as closely as he could.

Z: (He's pouring the water onto himself so he doesn't draw anything excessive... Smart move, but you should have kept refreshing the water on the circle.) "Grace us with the glory of the bringer of hope! Let the sun purge the foes of the darkness which we fear!"

K: (Will he shorten his spell before I finish mine to evaporate the magic circle? Or will he finish later to replace the weather? I'll keep playing along. Either will be strenuous for him.) "Bless the fields and grant us hay, grace us water, everyday!"

Z: (Faster! Before he can complete his ritual!) "Clear the skies, so we may observe your magnanimous love toward us all!"

A strange light radiated from beneath the platform they stood upon and poured through from beneath the battlefield, leaking through the cracks along the floor. The light emanating from the base of the mound of steel they stood upon was one so pure that it blanketed the floor in a giant shadow.

That lasted for a few seconds. When the light faded it blew away and evaporated all the water on the platform and the green, unhealthy air cleared out revealing Cosmatral Silo's true appearance – A vast, beautiful space with glittery clouds of shredded metal high above their heads that reflected the light back down to them, surrounded by a sky of the purest azure. It was a beauty that captivated even Sage Raufid himself when he was still alive.

Z: (Beautiful.)

K: (He's not paying attention to me even when the match isn't over? Looks like he's nearing the end.) "As he touched the river they first met at, the water crept upwards."

Zirco turned to face Katachi who was now coated with undulating blobs of water.

Z: (!? First the Poetic Eddum of Diehl Und Urdythari, now the Prose Eddum? Did he focus his studies on the excerpts instead of the whole tale?)

K: "It enveloped his limp dead body like living armour, the same way his love embraced him."

The water took the form of a full set of body armour spare the helmet and Katachi finally withdrew his dagger when it enveloped him and settled down.

Z: (A protective spell of Diehl Und Urdythari... It's well-remembered because it was one of their most dramatic tragedy scenes, but its usefulness is rather limited. It's good against the flame spells, but if I use the wooden sword I should be able to swing right through the water. Is he trying to make this a close-range battle again? My sword has a much longer reach, so he's at a severe disadvantage if he attempts it.)

K: "I was just joking, Zirco." (Confuse and disorient. Don't give him the liberty to recover.)

Z: (Joking?) "I do not understand this joke you speak of, scum."

K: "I didn't actually learn Sharyu Zuku's Rain Ritual."

Z: "! You... Didn't know the spell." (Shit! He made me tire myself out. He simply made a fool out of me by setting up the scene without actually casting anything!)

It was like placing tomato-smeared clothes on the floor and pretending that a murder took place. Zirco over-reacted to the possibility of the threat and focused his attention on the Clear Sky spell when there was never the need to.

K: "I didn't. Besides, even if I did, haven't you noticed it in the skies above? There are no clouds I could have used. The 'clouds' above us aren't made of water."

Zirco felt like he had been slapped on his cheek so hard that the sting would tattoo upon his skin and linger for life. While he was made to believe that he was countering the opponent's play, he boosted his opponent's power exponentially and fell right into his trap while exhausting himself with Aleksei's and Soltak's spells.

Z: (He's bloody right. Those aren't normal clouds at all.) "... So, all that-"

K: "-Was just to throw your breathing off so you couldn't use Aleksei's spell."

Zirco consciously checked his breathing – It became erratic from reciting the spell before Katachi finished his, in an attempt to limit his moves as much as possible. Moreover, to cast a spell specifically meant for Soltak followers without their stamina or physique was debilitating for him, especially when the amount of energy the impersonator had to exert must be equal to the object of imitation.

Z: "... I figured as much." (He distorted my breathing on purpose while maintaining his own stamina, forcing my body to tire out... Shit. I predicted this scum playing underhanded tricks, but something this elaborate? It's almost scary how well-planned it actually is.)

In a duel between magi, it was the better evil to be over-prepared than otherwise... Lest that ignorance became an opening to thwart one's efforts. Zirco could feel his victory slipping from his fingers over the strategy Katachi prepared. It truly was unthinkable and frightening for a plan to resemble the modus operandi of an agent from the Findel Magus Association, to the point that Zirco felt more comfortable believing that Katachi's scheme was not his own.

K: "Seeing as how you're tired right now, how about a story of Croxa's reincarnate, Sigurd?" (This should give him no time to relax and rethink his strategy at all.)

Zirco was once again pelted with another problem – Should he listen to Katachi's story? Usually, listening to a story was a bad idea because the image power of that story only served to empower the opponent's tale further. That made the image produced more effective which empowered the magic, just as how Zirco used the same trick when their match started by declaring Katachi the fool to fuel his Aleksei's spell.

But, not listening to the story would mean not knowing what the spell was capable of, and not knowing what to expect nor how to counter it. It would be a different scenario if and when fighting a stranger with no witnesses or bystanders, but this was not the case.

Since everything said in Cosmatral Silo was projected onto the coliseum, it was certain to gain strength through the image power from the audience anyway unless he knew of some mass silencing spell he could cast on the spot. If there were 217 students at the coliseum, listening in would empower the story's spell with the thoughts of 218 people; whereas not listening would empower it by the beliefs of 217 others while he knew absolutely nothing about it.

Yet another gamble. Katachi cornered Zirco with all of his traps well in place.

Z: "Speak then, you bloody sinner. For this shall be the last time you'll ever step into the finals."

K: "... Okay then. Croxa's third reincarnate, Sigurd, was one of his lesser-known reincarnates. He didn't fight an epic battle with Sha'koth's impersonators, but rather he died being kicked in the head by a horse in an accident. His technique was also considerably the weakest among Croxa's reincarnates. But, he did perform something interesting while he was alive."

As Katachi continued his story Zirco tried to regulate his breathing and regain his stamina and rhythm. He could feel small bursts of energy returning to his fatigued body, more than enough to squeeze words out of his lungs.

Z: "What 'something' did he do?"

K: "Sigurd had a pastime which was dabbing his finger onto one drop of water in a cistern and pulling it to another drop. These two drops then fused to create a bigger drop of water. It was a base for one of his most offensive attacks of surrounding himself with electrified water and charging at the opponent with frenzy, but this discovery also led to the creation of the water-powered systems we see today."

Katachi could see the piqued interest in Zirco's eyes and continued his explanation.

K: "Our bathing area does use Urdythari's unending tears as a water supply, but what makes the water flow out is actually Sigurd's discovery – The showering hole has a small pocket of water right before the pipe leading to the wall. That pocket can merge with water from the tank to 'pull' the water from the large tank towards the shower hole."

Z: (I see. I always wondered how the water system at the bathing spaces worked, since there were no water towers about.) "You may be a bastard child, but you research well. For that and that alone I give you credit."

K: "Yes, and thank you. But, you see, Zirco-"

Without warning, he leapt forward and travelled towards him. Fast. He was still listening attentively to the conversation but Katachi had already appeared at point-blank range, right before Zirco. Within half a second he covered the five metre gap between the two contestants at an astonishing speed almost invisible to the eye. Katachi punched his throat with his right hand clasping the wooden dagger tightly before Zirco could even flinch from the coiled snake strike.

Z: "Khaahgh-!"

Zirco clutched his neck as he fell backwards. He coughed twice before Katachi placed the wooden blade against his throat and performed a swiping motion with the dagger. That day, a standing ovation was conducted for the child who thoroughly played his opponent like a fiddle.

*** Achievement: The First Taste Of Magic ***

Z: "Damn it. I should have blown away the water on my clothes."

K: "It would have been useless anyway. Even if your clothes weren't wet, even if I wasn't wearing water armour, the spell would have worked regardless. People drink water, after all. Everyone has water within them."

Z: "! You don't mean- !"

The devilry of his plan finally bore its portentous form in the most unsettling light imaginable.

K: "Yeah. I could have used Sigurd's Water Linkage at any time. The only thing I was concerned with was that you would have defensive measures against such a straightforward attack, so I considered lowering your stamina first."

Z: "But, that speed... I could never catch up to that level! That is way too fast even for my fastest-casting spell-!"

K: "Then, I suppose you've already lost this battle the moment you stepped in here. You keep focusing on what you can see, and not on what eluded your eyes. In the end you worry yourself over the effects of my attacks, not the cause. Is that your extent as a magus?"

But what was perhaps the most frustrating fact of it all was that Katachi could have opted to conceal that truth from him. Zirco could have spent his whole life thinking that Katachi's success was a fluke, continuing his supercilious attitude without ever realizing the true genius behind his strategy.

He didn't need to pretend that he was executing the rain call spell. He didn't need Zirco to exhaust himself first. He didn't even need a set-up as obvious as coating Zirco or himself with water.

It was horrifying to imagine meeting an untimely end out of nowhere without even knowing how one died, had the weapons they used been real. In a sense, Katachi unveiling the technique instead of keeping him in the dark was another form of his kindness to help him mature and grow. But Zirco did not have the temper of a saint.

Z: "Kh-!"

Slamming his right fist into the ground, Zirco expended a good bit of his remaining energy.

Z: (Losing, to the likes of this bastard child? Losing, to this inferior?!)

K: "... I hope this changes your attitude. Please stop calling me scum or bastard child, or cry-baby pisspants. I will tolerate your abuse no more."

Katachi started walking out of Cosmatral Silo-

Z: (Losing, to this heretic?! This, this despicable little runt defeated me!?!? ... You... YOU ACCURSED BAAASTAAARRD!!!) "And lo, the lava spewed FORTH from beneath the fool!!"

Zirco expended most of his remaining energy to enact a spell – One that was cast when the tournament match was over. That was a direct means to an expulsion, but it didn't matter. If Katachi could die, it didn't matter. If he could get rid of that eyesore permanently, it didn't matter.

Lava gurgled and burst out in Katachi's place. Everyone in the coliseum saw the scene through the receiver as the molten globs of heated, liquid earth eroded and disintegrated anything it touched. Katachi melted.

CHAPTER 20

Zirco lay on the ground and panted heavily. His entire body was sluggish and it felt like his muscles were torn. He reserved the lava-spewing trick throughout the entire tournament in the event that he was going to fight a tough enemy that was resistant to simple flames like Deku's resilient sand armour. He saved it as a last resort should all else fail, and that was as good an opening as he could get.

Even if the round was over, it didn't matter. Even if he didn't get the prize, it didn't matter. All that mattered was that Katachi was dead. All that mattered was a stage where he could be seen performing a spell as powerful as that. Surely his strength would be recognized regardless of the skirmish's outcome. Zirco took deep breaths and readjusted his blood pressure. He felt the slight bursts of energy returning to his body with every inhale.

Z: "..."

Zirco stared silently at the azure sky of Cosmatral Silo, a beauty that couldn't normally be seen over the skies of Mielfeud. It was not a scene common to anywhere in the world, perhaps – The only place with such scenic visuals was probably Auser with their mountains and wide, open plains. But travelling to Auser for the view wasn't really worth the effort-

Z: (!?)

A sound. A loud sonorous sound that was not made from the bubbling lava. A sound of wood dropping onto metal which was not made by Zirco's wooden sword echoed throughout Cosmatral Silo.

Z: (That's probably from Katachi's dagger.)

Zirco reassured himself a little bit with the information, and slowly closed his eyes to recover a little more stami-

K: "Quite the surprise attack."

Z: "!?" (What?)

Zirco widened his eyes in shock. Did his attack miss? No, it couldn't have. Lava provided an immense burst of heat over tenfold of a stove, one that surpassed the flames he used in the tournament. Even if he barely dodged the lava, its heat should be strong enough to make him scream in pain from the burn, or grate and drag himself over the metal floor. It should have at least produced some form of sound even if he survived the process.

136

But it didn't make sense. Those noises were absent and the delay the wooden dagger took to drop was far too long. Something beyond his expectations must have happened. With the tiny bit of regained energy, Zirco forced his body up to see what happened.

... Amidst the lava was a naked boy with numerous bruises and scars across his back and limbs. The sight of raw flesh was rather repulsive, but considering the pile of fabric that resembled the school uniform burning next to his feet it was clear the get-up was unintentional.

It was the bastard child he looked down upon so, but something was truly unusual. The child stood within lava naturally and he bent down to pick up a dagger. How was he not dead yet? Could anyone actually walk in lava? Were there ever records of legends who withstood the molten earth? As he stood up straight, something even more baffling caught his eye.

Z: (! A golden word... 定!? That thing on his chest is a Word of Power!)

Much to his disbelief.

Z: (Where... Where did he get that from? Did he ask for that Word of Power from one of the teachers? Was it Mister Rekter? That's cheating!)

K: "Are you happy now, Zirco? Does foiling a plan bring you joy? You have no idea how hard I've worked to hide this power from everyone."

Yet the answer was not as innocent as he imagined.

Z: (Hide... The power?)

With a snap of his fingers, Zirco suddenly experienced an immense pressure. The air around him became heavy. It weighed his body down, and he couldn't get up at all. Was the energy he regained that minuscule? No. That wasn't it. It felt like something was pulling and chaining him down.

Zirco tried as he may, but the force was too strong – He gave up after a few seconds of meaningless struggle and was pinned onto the floor by an unknown force belly up. As he forced himself to turn his head Zirco saw the huge, golden 定 on the floor he was sprawled on.

Z: (!! There's one here, too... So he didn't borrow the power – He has the Word of Power itself! When did he get his hands on one?!)

K: "... All the effort I've put into learning water spells..."

Katachi pinched the dagger by its handle with only three fingers and positioned it above Zirco's immobilized left hand. He simply released his grip and let the dagger plummet into the ground at a shocking force.

Z: "GAAAAAAAHHH- AHAHH!?!" (The dagger just went straight through my hand!? It's made of wood! How is that even possible!?)

The searing pain coursed through his arm. Blood was coming out of the hole in his left hand. The middle and ring fingers slowly grew cold, limp and numb. As he clenched his left hand to relieve the pain with pressure, he felt the sticky, crimson liquid over his index and little fingers. It smelled of liquid iron and it stained the wooden blade.

His middle and ring fingers didn't move at all. They were dead – Their nerves were severed cleanly with that attack. Katachi stepped on his left wrist and pulled the dagger out from his hand. The scene before his eyes was so surreal that Zirco didn't even notice that the word on the floor was gone. He grabbed his left hand with his right to clamp the parted flesh and ease the pain as much as he could, but then...

K: "All this time, I had to use my Word of Power in discretion so nobody would see it." (设定. Set dagger weight – seven hundred fold.)

The dagger was sent pile-driving downwards at him once again – This time, on the right hand clutching the left. Both hands were impaled like meat on a şiş kebap with no bell peppers or onions.

Z: "AAAAAAAAAAAAAAA!!!!!!!"

His screams were projected over the coliseum, intensifying the feelings of fear amid the audience. They were all staring at Katachi in horror at the misuse of his Word of Power brutally hurting Zirco over and over again. The child plucked the dagger out once more before wiping and spreading the blood off on Zirco's sleeve like it was butter.

Zirco's breathing turned erratic as he tried to relieve the pain on both hands. They were both bleeding – One with a horizontal wound and the other with two intersecting lines across the palm that formed a wayward cross. The dagger punctured cleanly through his hands and there was no way to apply pressure on the both of them effectively to stop or lessen the bleeding.

K: "All of it, ruined by you and your stupidly large ego."

Katachi grabbed Zirco by his left arm, wrapped it around his neck and hoisted him up. He was about to sheathe the dagger before he remembered that his clothes were gone, so instead he slotted the wooden dagger into Zirco's coat pocket and began walking. Though he could have left Zirco to himself, though he could have returned the abuse even more.

He could have just outright killed him, for all it was worth. But he didn't. Mother Rin told him that the teachings of Segus were sacred, and ought to be treated with the highest respect. If Segus forbade killing, he shall not kill. If Segus encouraged him to feed his body to the needy, he would gladly follow. If Segus insisted to resolve situations with the least damage, he would oblige.

If it were to honour and respect the mother that raised him Katachi would willingly follow a figure like so. He slowly staggered with the dazed, hyperventilating Zirco to the obelisk in Cosmatral Silo. A light touch on the obelisk crystal was all it took to transport them out.

*** ***

Ba: "... Katachi."

Katachi slowly rested Zirco on the bench and caught the dagger before it slipped out of the pocket. He grabbed a cup by the side and scooped a bit of the brown remedy from a barrel in the centre of the room.

Ba: "Katachi!"

Katachi moved the dagger to a side so he could sit.

K: (The bench is hot... Then again, I don't have clothes on so I'm feeling the full brunt of its heat raw. Just stomach it down for now.)

He shored Zirco against the wall in an upright position and fed the viscous murk into his mouth.

Ba: "Katachi!! Don't ignore me!"

K: "Just say what's on your mind. I don't care if it's an insult."

Ba: "You had a Word of Power with you? All this time?"

Katachi placed the empty cup down on the bench and glared at Bael with cold eyes. His reluctance to divulge the information finally made sense.

Ba: "Why were you trying to hide it?"

Katachi looked away to the side, afraid of meeting Bael in her eyes again.

K: "... Because it wouldn't be fair using such an absurd magic in the tournament."

A 定 formed on Katachi's right palm and he looked at it, lips curling down with a bitter light. He raised his hand and displayed the sigil to Bael clearly.

K: "Because having this meant being ostracised."

Ba: "Why would I ever judge you for it?"

K: "I've read it in bamboo books. I've noticed how the one person who's the oddity is always looked down upon, who's always the target of others. People will always push their misgivings on others to make themselves feel better. I've had enough of that in Mielfeud. That's why... That's why I wanted to zip past everything in life, to just move along without making friends. Then you showed up."

Ba: "Nobody would blame you for having a magic like that."

In response, Katachi leered at Bael with a fierce expression. His eyebrows loosened and he closed his eyes while taking a deep breath. He walked towards a pile of damaged uniforms, and dressed himself in the clothes he found the most intact and fitting. When he was properly attired, he picked up the dagger and shoved it in his coat.

K: "I think not."

Katachi headed towards the door to the coliseum's spectator area and opened it casually. The students all peered at him with doubtful looks. Hundreds of eyes pierced the doorway, many mumbles and background chatter were heard, and they all stared at Katachi like he was some sort of rare animal.

K: "Isn't this proof enough?"

It wasn't doing any good trying to confront Katachi in the first place. She too knew deep down that the odd one out was always isolated. When she experimented with Vithrolu's spells for her traps, she constantly touched the decayed and rotting objects. She began producing a similar odour as a result of her overexposure. It stung the noses of other students who didn't understand her, and in response they all complained and suggested that Bertund should move her away.

Wherever she went, she was shunned – As much as Katachi was the target of gossip right now. She knew those feelings well. Yet in a desperation to stop someone else from experiencing the same, she hypocritically spoke up. But if speaking up was all it took to resolve the problem, then Bael would not be suffering from her current situation.

Her role was redundant. She couldn't do anything to help Katachi be honest or relieved. She couldn't be the 'big sister' role she wanted to be for him to confide in. She didn't even know why she spoke up, apart from the faint notion that she felt something was wrong.

D: "I figured your trick wasn't so simple."

Deku walked towards them from the corridor.

Ba: "Deku?"

K: "I'm surprised you figured it out."

D: "Of course I'd notice – Powerful Reincarnate Art users have great faith in the god they borrow power from. Defeating me despite your lack of faith in Soltak was a dead give-away."

K: "... I suppose I can't hide anything from the informed."

D: "No. You can't."

The two sat quietly in the silence, simmering in their own shortcomings. Deku clicked his tongue and pointed behind him towards the doorway.

D: "Bertund wants to see you. He's waiting at the atrium."

K: "Okay. Tell him I'll be there shortly."

Katachi walked out of the doorway and towards the atrium, ignoring the spectators and the gathering crowd.

*** ***

Be: "Ahh, you're here-... With a majority of the school's cohort, I see."

Katachi walked into the atrium with the huge group of students fearfully following behind him.

K: "They followed me here. I don't know why, but they did."

Be: "The Words of Power are a rare and powerful magic after all. It's been mere decades since its emergence and everyone is afraid of it because they know that they're staring at death itself. They would clearly be afraid and curious at the same time as to what you'll do with it."

K: "... Okay, but how do I get them to stop?"

Be: "Explain it to them."

A solution was often simple, but that did not mean it was easy.

K: (And risk Rekter overhearing?!) "I- Ex- Explain?!"

Be: "Yes. Explain."

Bertund used a stick that surfaced from nowhere and 'drew' on one of the curvy pillars the word 解. The stone pillar eroded where the stick came in contact and formed the word on that section of the pillar immediately.

Be: "Right, then, Mister Kotsuba, tell me something you know about this word to me. Clearly."

A lot of chatter appeared behind Katachi.

"What's that symbol up there?"

"Did you see the principal draw that effortlessly?"

"What kind of magic is that?"

"Is that in Ohde or Anik?"

"It's probably Ohde, since that guy has black hair."

Katachi ignored the noisy students behind who knew little about what was going on. He faced Bertund and spoke softly, but clearly, reassuring the green man that he was mentally prepared to face Rekter.

K: "The word up there is 解. In Ohde it's read as Kai, but in Anik it's read as Jiě. The meaning it has in Ohde usually refers to a solution to a problem, and it also means an unlocking or unsealing power. In Anik it can have different meanings besides solution and unsealing. For..."

Katachi nervously looked around himself at the students who were now attentively listening to him. He didn't want Rekter to be around, just in case.

K: "For example, 了解 means 'understand', and 松解 means to release or loosen and free, which is contextually different from unsealing. The word can have many different meanings depending on how it is used. That's... That's pretty much all I know for this word though."

"That word's different from the one on his chest earlier..."

"Does that mean he has two? But, that can't be possible! Nobody's ever had two!"

"Do all Words of Power glow? And what colour do they glow in?"

"So that's a Word of Power..."

"That's real, huh..."

Be: (You sneaky little devil. Coming up with common terms in fear of raising Rekter's precedence level by accident? Smart, commendable, but unnecessary.) "... Good. You've done your research. Now then... Mister Rekter, your attendance is required."

Bertund took off his glove and held his hand to his opposite shoulder. The recall spell activated and a familiar teacher in brown appeared from thin air.

R: "Yeah?"

Be: "I'm afraid you're going to be humiliated, Rekter. The child's already won."

R: "What? Him?"

His chuckle was innocuous and plain – It made Katachi a little worried, but if everything went according to plan it was the ideal outcome he sought.

R: "Ahahahahaha, no, no, a mere student can't possibly beat a teacher."

K: "Is that so, Mister Rekter?"

Rekter's face turned serious when Katachi spoke up.

R: "What do you want, a test?"

K: "Yes."

R: (I figured it'd boil down to this sooner or later, but this early? It doesn't matter. I can beat him. I've improved my precedence level so I'm not the Rekter from before!) "Very well. But, if you're so insistent on a test, you're going to have to take into account the responsibility of failure!"

That declaration was immediately followed by a despicable act.

R: (解开! Unfasten hook – Chandelier!)

A golden word formed on the chain attached to the ceiling. The hook on the chandelier unfastened and the chandelier on the ceiling fell. The students in the atrium were completely unprepared and most could only widen their eyes in horror at the imminent crash.

K: (Not good! 固定! Fixate object – Chandelier!)

The chandelier froze midfall with a 定 on its rim and the students finally recovered from their daze upon hearing the jingling of the chandelier's ornaments.

R: "I got you!" (解除! Remove external effects – Chandelier!)

Rekter's 解 was stapled over Katachi's 定 and the true battle began.

R: (The chandelier shall fall, and the students beneath crushed by his failure- !?)

解 faded away. Not 定, but 解. The result of the absolutes clashing was made completely clear; Katachi's precedence level at the moment was now higher than Rekter's.

R: "What?! How?! When!? Mine should have dissolved yours! How did you raise your precedence level so quickly?!"

Katachi pushed the students beneath the chandelier away first, before undoing his 定 to let the chandelier crash into the floor without casualties.

R: "What did you do?!"

Katachi glared at the irresponsible teacher with seething eyes.

K: "Are you insane!? Why didn't you pull the students away first?! What would have happened if they died by your hand!?"

Katachi's hands were trembling in cold sweat and his eyes burned vibrantly, reflecting his inner rage. The fact that other innocent lives were mere moments from being injured overshadowed the pacified outcome like a giant maw devouring a shed feather.

K: "I can't believe such an irresponsible teacher even existed! Shelly was right – You really are mad with power. You are so delusional that you neglect the most important and basic of things like respect, or ensuring everyone's safety!"

A child's anger would be chided as immature to throw illogical tantrums. But Katachi's rage burned a new history in his resolve. For the very first time, Katachi cussed in a manner most uncouth.

K: "You... You asshole!"

CHAPTER 21

R: "Impossible! I researched and prepared for this day, knowing you would come after me! How did your precedence level exceed my own?!"

Rekter stared at Katachi in disbelief. He should not have lost! He learnt two new terms, 解悟 and 解愁, which should have been enough in the event that Katachi tried to learn one to boost his own Word of Power. So why didn't it work? Rekter's precedence level ought to have surpassed Katachi's by now!

K: "If you would take off your shirt right now, Mister Rekter... That would explain everything."

Take off his shirt, Katachi said. But, why take off his shirt? Rekter followed his instructions blindly and-

"By the gods!"

"There's a word on his back!"

"That's the word on his chest from before!"

"He used magic on a teacher?!"

"Isn't that against school regulations?!"

"He used non-healing magic on a teacher!"

R: "Wha- What is the meaning of this?!"

Surely it should have been enough to learn two new terms to raise his precedence level! And why was there a word on his back? Katachi wriggled his finger, and in an instant the word on his back faded off. Rekter finally turned back to normal after suffering the influence of the Word of Power for more than a week.

R: "-! You... You conniving manwhore...!! What did you do to me?!"

Katachi glared at Rekter in the eyes sternly, his victory decisive.

R: "Answer me! What did you do?!"

K: "If you're that compelled to know... I set your thought patterns to gullible." (恒定! Constant status – Self!)

It all became clear to the teacher only now. Katachi used his Word of Power to make Rekter think in a gullible fashion. By mentally steering him away from shrewd thoughts and logical strategies, Katachi was able to limit Rekter's ability to raise his own knowledge on his Word of Power and gain a huge lead in terms of their precedence levels.

While he believed that Katachi was a foolish child who thought that raising his Word of Power by one would have been enough, Rekter imagined himself outplaying the 'foolish' child by raising his own with two terms. Katachi had it all planned out – The trap was sprung without giving Rekter a chance to retaliate.

R: "When did you pull this off?"

K: "To be honest, I was sceptical when I tried it. I thought that my plan would never work."

Katachi used his right hand to feel the wooden dagger from the tournament on his chest, under the pretence that he was dramatically pressing his fingers against his chest in a bold declaration.

K: "Then, I noticed it – I have yet to see a single teacher at the public bathing space. That's when I realized that teachers used their own bathrooms because the Teacher's Bathing Space didn't exist on the academy map."

Would anyone have the courage to call him 'unfortunate' after a showcase of his exemplary manipulation? Katachi didn't know. He certainly didn't view his disposition as a weakness, so he figured that nobody ought to.

K: "So I was betting on the fact that you would never be able to counter my trap because there is no one around you when you bathe to check your back for you, and that your room would always be brightly lit so you won't be able to see it. It may be good luck on my part that you don't wear clothes in the dark or you would have noticed it immediately."

Just as the lions and tigers demonstrated their strength through direct means, so too do the snakes and raccoons exude their worth in subterfuge, cunning and ensnarement of their prey; All things in nature their part to play, and Katachi filled his role with frightening precision.

R: (He figured out a trick like that from plain observation? Then it was a mistake on my part after all! Have I become so accustomed to the luxury of this academy that I can't even notice something glowing bright gold?!) "You made me stupid and gullible...!"

His rage was barely contained and he lashed out recklessly at the child.

R: (溶解! Dissolve object – Katachi!)

A 解 formed on Katachi's chest. Normally, that would have been fatal. Katachi ought to have melted like an ice cube in scorching heat, but the golden 解 word fading off reinforced Katachi's current dominance over him.

K: "Frankly, part of my good luck may have been the Word of Power itself for making you gullible and easily fooled to the point that you're not as perceptive. Well, no matter what you do it's useless now. Your words are no longer on par with mine."

Rekter clenched his fist in fury. He had been too late in stopping Katachi's ploy. If only he trusted his instincts from before and took precautions against Katachi from the very beginning, before he even stepped into the classroom... The humiliating fate could have been avoided. But Katachi used non-healing magic on a teacher, so he still had chances at a reversal.

R: "It's fine. I've caught you red-handed anyway. Kotsuba Katachi, for disobeying the rules of using non-healing magic on a teacher, my authority as-"

K: "I figured you would use something like that as a shield." (固定! Fixate position – Rekter!)

A golden 定 formed on Rekter's shirt and he was left frozen on that spot. Rekter's opinions and feeble rebuttals were now inconsequential.

K: "... Bertund."

Be: "Yes, Mister Kotsuba?"

K: "I may be expelled now, but am I still the champion of the tournament?"

The students caught on to his plan and began their rebellious uproar.

"No, Principal Bertund, you must not give him the prize!"

"He's a cheater, he used a Word of Power!"

"You should give it to Zirco instead, he's the real magus here!"

"Give it to Deku instead! He always uses it for charity!"

"He may have saved that group of five, but he doesn't deserve the school's sponsorship!"

Be: "Mister Kotsuba, you- Sorry, let me repeat myse- I am trying to say tha- Stop blocking my vision- Calm down, students. There are two flaws to your complaints."

It's astonishing how Bertund kept that straight, smiling face while speaking to the aggravated mob. The astute students hung back when they caught wind of the underlying meaning while the foolish ones simmered their rage demanding an explanation.

Be: "First of all, the Words of Power are indeed a form of magic – It's considered event magic. It may be strongly discouraged in the tournament because of its very nature, but it is magic nonetheless. It is merely discouraged, not prohibited. None of you may say that he's cheating. Second point, did you not watch the finals? Mister Kotsuba didn't use his Word of Power at all for that match. It was purely a magus-on-magus competition where Zirco used Aleksei's spell while Katachi used Urdythari's."

"How can you be so confident that he's not cheating?"

"Yeah, how do you know he's not using his Word of Power to imitate water magic?"

"How would you know? You barely do your job, Bertund!"

"You wouldn't be able to know, would you?"

"How would we know he's not cheating with his Word of Power?"

Be: "It's because I- Hey, I'll have you know I do my job- Stop pushing and squeezing- You wouldn't want me to- Relax! Let me explain!"

It was strange how Bertund maintained his cheeky, smiling face as the students retreated a little bit. With the slime on his head bubbling and snarling at them, the children knew better than to contest it.

Be: "Do you all want to know how I know he didn't cheat during the finals? Simple – I personally taught Mister Kotsuba water magic myself."

Everyone was shocked at the answer. Nobody in the school believed their ears spare the ones who knew about Bertund's conditional requirements. Few believed that he had the time to teach a student considering his position, but the unlearned were not creative enough to decipher Bertund's almost-heretical teaching methods.

Ba: "Is... Is that true?"

"You're lying-!"

"I've never seen you teach us before!"

"That can't be-!"

Be: "Yes, I taught him those spells. What need has he to learn from me if he could simply force his way through the tournament with his Word of Power?"

"But how would you explain Cillian's sword floating?"

"What about the time Chotil Nea pounced on him?"

"What about Deku being defeated?"

"How is he pardonable for the tournament up to the finals?"

"He didn't use water magic at all when he fought the other competitors!"

Be: "Yes, yes, he probably did use the Word of Power for the rest of the tournament. But still, it is his victory even if you claim otherwise. He at least has the mind to end the tournament off with proper magic, did he not? Look at it this way – He was more than sufficient in taking out Zirco, and the fights before that are simply means to conceal the magic he knew."

"Why do you keep defending him?!"

"You should have just expelled him the moment he stepped in here!"

"This is so unfair! He should have used water magic against Deku!"

"I demand equal treatment!"

"Principal Bertund, you're a biased person!"

He waited patiently as the insults of the students were hurled towards him... And ignored them coldly. Bertund closed his eyes and waited for the commotion to die down. The students eventually gave up and stayed silent after their attempts at his attention were made futile.

Be: "... To be truthful, if I were to make a judgement myself Katachi has always been unstoppable. Even if you tell me to deny or expel him, is there a point? Would I rather risk him going berserk, tearing the entire academy down just to accept him as a student here? Would I risk fighting a battle like that with him, knowing the outcome was already pre-determined with his Word of Power? No. I would not."

K: (... Way to make me look like a villain, Bertund.)

Be: "That would most probably be what most of you think I would think. But should I think like that as the principal of this school? Should I, as a head figure of the academy and the direct descendant of Sage Raufid, reject a potential magus out of fear? I think not."

The principal had his own reasons that required Katachi to be reimbursed for his efforts against Rekter, beyond the student body's knowledge. The desperate defence was disguised by a chance opportunity for them to learn a life lesson.

Be: "If I were afraid of every single person out there, I would not be able to raise my head against such honour I've been bestowed. If I held fear towards strangers, I might as well not enrol any of you at all. Would it be fair if I didn't allow you into the academy simply because I heard other people say that you shouldn't become a magus? Would you like that?"

Bertund now controlled the entire ambience – None of the students rebuked or spoke against his intentions. For the first time, Katachi witnessed a different form of persuasive prowess even he was swayed by.

K: (... What a sudden change. It's as if he read my thoughts.)

Be: "I know you wouldn't like that. Thinking like that is unlike me. Rather, encouraging students to uncover their aptitudes, embodying the vision of the school, ensuring that every student gets a fair chance at magic – That is my role as a principal. And it doesn't matter if their magic is powerful, potent, or forbidden – My role is simply to offer you a chance at mastering the fundamentals of magic. If you can grasp that, then surely you can one day become as powerful as he is right now, and maybe even more!"

K: (I somehow feel grateful for this speech, considering that it's actually aimed at me... I think Bertund really does have some form of mind-reading magic or something. But if that were true, why can't I feel it?)

Be: "And so, I say – Mister Kotsuba is allowed to partake in this chance as much as you all do. He will be expelled and never to return as an alumni for breaking the rules. But he shall be awarded with the three school-sponsored items for his service in the tournament. And let this incident be a note for you all – Never, and I mean never underestimate your opponent."

It wasn't hard to take it seriously despite his perpetually smiling face, since Bertund's voice and tone were solemn enough to puncture their doubts.

K: (That... That played out in my favour, I think.)

Be: "Mister Kotsuba."

K: "Ah, yes?"

Be: "As a congratulatory form of encouragement for your outstanding performance, I hereby officially declare you the champion of our 17th annual Sage Raufid Young Magus Tournament."

Katachi's face warped at the sight of everyone else. The students around him looked like growling hunting hounds, ready to silently pounce upon and gnaw at him.

Be: "You may request for 3 items or services that the school deems affordable, and receive them free-of-charge. But, be warned – Should your request be invalid that would be a chance wasted."

K: "It's fine. I know what I would want for a first item. I would like a really, really big paper book full of blank pages."

The students were confused. Why would he want a blank paper book when he could have the school prepare a paper-making machine for his personal use? An opportunity enough to purchase the most expensive medicine, the fanciest of supplies and even personal space in the academy, and he chose a blank book made of paper? Why would anyone want that much paper?

Be: "Understood. Shelly?"

The lady in similar attire walked towards Katachi and handed him a really thick book with a leathery hard cover.

Be: "There you are. A thousand blank pages bound into a book."

K: (A thousand!? I... I didn't think I'd need a thousand... I thought five hundred would have sufficed.) "Th-... Thank you."

Be: "What's next?"

K: (Right, the next issue would be Mister Rekter.) "I would like to request for permission, uh... For my second item."

Be: "Permission, Mister Kotsuba?"

K: "Permission to claim Mister Rekter's Word of Power as my own."

"What!?"

"Did he just say 'take his Word of Power'?"

"As if having one wasn't enough, he wants two!?"

"Hah. That's not possible! No person can possess two Words of Power at any one time!"

"What a greedy coxcomb!"

Be: "I don't think you would need the school's power nor authority to do that. What you do to him is for you to decide. You have wasted your second request, Mister Kotsuba."

The students laughed at him for asking the impossible, but Katachi simply gazed at the stagnant Rekter.

K: "I don't mind. I just thought I would say that to be polite."

He walked towards the statue with the book in hand and his mind set on one thing only: 解. Katachi placed his hand over Rekter and silently invoked the new power learnt from Bertund.

K: (锁定! Lock within book – 解!)

When Katachi opened the book to see if it worked, the golden 解 formed on the first page. The students who were jeering at his stupid request a moment ago turned pale white. A fatal oversight on their part caused their blood to chill rapidly as they doubled over their memories to revise their claims earlier.

He briefly paused to wonder if the children never considered how a lone Hunter would collect multiple Curse Words. The ignorant students were frightened at how it was possible while the perceptive ones were petrified at how fast it took for Katachi to become that much more powerful, now that he possessed a second Word of Power.

They finally understood the purpose for the first item. Every two blank pages could be considered a single sheet bound with many others by adhesive or thread. In that case every page could contain a Word of Power since the pages were considered singular objects. Theoretically, Katachi could contain all the Words of Power in one neat book and not have to use something like pebbles as their vessel.

K: "That's two of 292... Bertund?"

His soft voice held weight far greater than the energetic hollering displayed during the matches. The mere hint of his goal made the other students lose all will to retaliate. The career path as a Word of Power Hunter was, after much preparation, finally ready and set in stone. Katachi was going to collect that monstrous power repeatedly until he obtained them all.

Be: "Yes, Mister Kotsuba?"

Their simplistic goals of joining the Findel Magus Association or becoming reputable meisters and sorcerors, were thoroughly diminished before a desire as deranged as his own.

K: "For my third request... I would like a complete basic traveller's kit."

Katachi's destination wasn't the school. It wasn't to pass his time enjoying an idyllic life with established bonds between friends, or to evade the expectations others set for him, accrue knowledge, earn recommendations, best others at competitions, bring honour to his family, any of those mundane ideas a child might have... He was devoid of them all.

Be: "A basic traveller's kit?"

It was at a destination so far away, beyond the expectations of the students that only his journey itself could tell where and when the endpoint lies. Life itself was short and fleeting, so why spend that precious time on trivialities that failed to improve the real problem at hand?

K: "Yes. I need a basic kit that can help me hold this book and some clothes, a water bag and, and... A ground sheet. Probably with a side pouch for me to store some coin as well."

That's why he didn't mind being ousted – Rather, expulsion on the contrary hastened his process of leaving the school which worked in his favour.

Be: "Inclusive of new clothes and a blanket?"

It was a maddening, reckless rush towards evanescent life which left the bystanders wondering the most poignant fact of it all – Was that truly a life well lived?

K: "Ah- Uhm... Yeah, that will suffice."

Alas, they never did behold the pain and burden he shouldered. For Katachi whom embodied a madness that innately understood the cruelty of the mortal coil, calling him a child would be unfair.

Be: "Very well. All right, students, you don't have to stay here the whole day. Go and enjoy yourselves! Today's events have concluded – The lessons start tomorrow! Come on now! Move along!"

And yet, calling him a child was the only fairness permitted to the young one.

*** Achievement: Heretic ***

Bertund shooed the students away like a grocer scaring crows from his crops, and the atrium was empty once again – With only two people within. Katachi, the despised and expelled student along with the still-immobile Mister Rekter.

K: (I'm not sure if it actually managed to strip Rekter of 解 entirely and lock the Word of Power inside the book. I can probably use the Word of Power within the book, too... Hopefully.)

Katachi tried to open the door, but it was locked.

K: (I wonder if ownership of the book is sufficient enough for anyone to use the words within... This is a nice opportunity to try it out.)

Katachi held the thick thousand-page book in his hands tightly and focused on the door's lock.

K: (解锁! Unlock object – Door!)

A golden word was applied onto the door and it clicked open.

K: (Interesting. Does it stay unlocked when I remove it?)

Upon the removal of the Word of Power the lock snapped shut once again. But, the door was left ajar so Katachi could see the locking mechanism as well as the interior of the guest room. It was a lavishing beautiful mixture of beige and caramel brown, and within housed a bed, three comfortable seats with cotton padding, a coffee table and a small desk with a stool. The bed was made nicely with red velvet of the highest quality and a faint tint of Brosenveide filled the air.

K: (It's so pretty. This room's almost a direct upgrade from my place.)

Katachi entered the room for three steps and admired the interior of the guest room before getting back to the Word of Power that worked on the lock.

K: (It's just like 定 then – Its effects are persistent only when the sigil is applied.)

Katachi left the guest room with a satisfied expression. The magical hallway guided him on a familiar path as Rekter was left alone in the atrium, frozen on that very spot. Nobody tried to free him because it was futile to begin with.

*** ***

The dormitory room's door was knocked on.

S: "Mister Kotsuba? Are you there?"

Outside the room were Shelly and Bael with a bag, some nice-looking clothes, a rope, a groundsheet and a blanket among other sundries.

K: "Good... Good afternoon."

Ba: "Katachi... You're going to leave?"

Katachi looked away from the now-depressed Bael while patting her shoulder.

K: "... Yeah. I am."

Ba: "You're not even going to deny the fact that you're being expelled?"

K: "I'm fine with it. My goal-"

S: "I'm sure you two have a lot to say but could you please take these into your room first, Mister Kotsuba? They are quite heavy so do it fast."

K: "Oh. Right. Sorry, Missus Shelly."

Katachi carried it all into his room in three trips while the two ladies rested the items against the handrails of the stairs.

K: "Thanks for the help, you two- Hey, why isn't Principal Bertund the one bringing these to me?"

S: "Bertund? He's busy with seeing off Minister Lein."

That much should have been obvious.

S: "Right then, I have my own things to do, so you two have a nice chat. It will probably be your last in a while unless you leave with him, Bael."

Bael quickly changed from a stoic to flustered expression and snapped back quickly.

Ba: "Wha- What's that supposed to mean?!"

In an attempt to hide her embarrassment Bael quickly left the area.

S: "Katachi, be sure to come to the principal office at four in the afternoon sharp. You have about three hours – It should be enough to pack everything. I'll be off doing administrative work if you need me."

K: "Okay."

*** ***

K: (Let's see... I really don't need these tiny runes in the pouch, do I? I'll keep the Urdythari pebble as a memento, it could be practical to make others think I cannot invoke the rune myself. I should also make room for the map. These clothes are brand new... They're light traveller's clothes that fit my body well, but I'd like to wear them only when my original clothing is damaged beyond repair or when I outgrow my old clothes.)

One must be far-sighted to prepare for the journey ahead.

K: (There. It's all set.)

Katachi walked towards the principal's office with the bag saddled tightly. The students whom he passed by leered at him with hateful glares, lambasting him in harsh whispers.

K: (How nostalgic.)

In his mind, a memory of a certain man surfaced. He was sentenced to be humiliated on the pillory and he had three young girls hugging his legs while he stood there. They were begging him to give up and return the burden of the sins to them.

But he insisted on shaming and flagellating himself for their misdeeds. Katachi remembered that man; he came to Mother Rin's church often and performed silent prayers for his children while mourning his wife. He was a silent and passionate man of few words, one whom Katachi looked up to as an idol.

K: (I must strive to be like him.)

With that back on the pillory in his mind, Katachi ignored the stares and continued walking towards Bertund's office.

CHAPTER 22

Be: "Come in, come in!"

Katachi walked into the principal's office without bothering to knock on the door. On his hasty entry he noticed that Bertund closed a flap to his left – The flap which dropped down whenever people stepped on the carpet outside.

K: "Good afternoon."

Bertund was busy doing paperwork, his quill dancing and scribbling on paper upon paper while dabbing on an ink fountain occasionally.

Be: "Ahh, Mister Kotsuba. Are you prepared to leave?"

K: "Is it fine if I walk around the school one last time? I'd like to bid my farewells."

Be: "Go ahead. But surely you don't intend to carry that large bag with you around the academy? Leave it there in the corner – I'll keep watch until you're done."

Katachi left the bag in the corner of the room while the principal used his left hand to scoop the slime from his head before tossing the lump at his bag. The scene was quite confusing to him, but nevertheless Bertund's safekeeping was trustworthy enough. He had the decency to permit Katachi's victory in the tournament, so any unwarranted doubt would be unbecoming. He left the room while the principal continued with his work.

*** ***

S: "Mister Kotsuba!"

Katachi encountered someone familiar after leaving the Principal's office for a few steps. Though, the frequency of her presence ought to be expected given that the office belonged to the couple.

K: "Good afternoon, Missus Shelly."

S: "You're pretty early today, aren't you?"

K: (The clock in the room is ten minutes faster than the actual time... I think. A personal timepiece would be nice, but that's a luxury too much for me.) "Yeah, I guess the clock in my old room is responsible."

156

S: "Calling it old already? You sure adapt fast, Mister Kotsuba. That's a splendid trait. Right then, let's begin your next lecture. It'll be your last."

K: "... Right. If you please- Ah, can I move Rekter out of here? I don't want him to hear any of it."

It was a new level of humiliation for a child to address oneself as though he were merely an object. However, Rekter was clearly in no position to object or rebuke his mistreatment.

S: "Certainly."

The child walked down the winding stairs of the atrium and looked at the immobile teacher briefly. He could only wonder what it felt like to be fixated in the poor sap's place for more than a few hours already. Katachi dragged him into a janitor's closet before sealing him in the dark completely.

S: "Right. Follow me into the guest room, Mister Kotsuba. I'm not keen on standing for long periods."

The two walked into the guest room and closed the door gently with no concern for Rekter's depleting sanity.

*** ***

S: "Let us conclude for the day. Summarize the lecture, Mister Kotsuba."

K: "When using the Words of Power, I have to be specific about what I want to happen or it will be very vague and give the Word a chance to produce an undesired effect. Also... Also, I have to be careful using 了解 because of its potential to grant and reveal any kind of knowledge – If I ask questions with a complex or vague answer like 'What will I become in the future', I might faint and even die from having too much in my head at a time."

S: "Good. That much should suffice."

Shelly switched her folded legs around out of discomfort.

S: "Mister Kotsuba, have you no plans as to how you would begin the search for the other 290 Words of Power?"

Katachi nodded briefly.

S: "You may have it easier now that you have Rekter's sigil but using that to find other Words of Power can be tricky. As I've taught just now, you need to use specific commands or the answer will always be undesirable – You still have your original Word of Power so you won't be leaving the detection range any time soon."

K: "I understand."

S: "It's good that you do. I can offer guidance, but you will have to find the means yourself."

Shelly walked up to Katachi and placed her hand on his shoulder.

S: "Finally, I would like to thank you for helping Bertund. As you know, there are some matters which adults cannot intervene in no matter how unjust Rekter may be. Your interloping has overturned what was otherwise an impossible feat."

But was it really ethical using a child to achieve that which an adult could not, to usurp and invalidate another's rights with a war underlying another's scuffle, regardless of how despicable Rekter might be?

K: "You're welcome...?" (I don't feel that happy about it, though.)

The darkness within those words was never meant to be fully understood, not with any amount of time or progress. It was a dilemma even their descendants would have difficulty answering. But that very darkness was also responsible for the gracious funding that went into the travel gear, so there was no room for argument.

Shelly walked out of the guest room, and as though in cue Bael entered a few seconds later. She appeared rather fidgety and agitated for reasons unknown to him.

Ba: "Katachi."

Bael quietly sat down on one of the comfortable, velvet seats adjacent to Shelly's warm seat. The two remained silent in the room, suffocated by its awkward atmosphere and unable to break the ice.

K: (What would be a good topic to talk about? She has six years of experience on me regarding the things in the academy. But it's not like I'm particularly interested in the stuff related to this facility. It would be useless to talk about them when I'm leaving.)

Ba: (I want him to have the best, but I also don't want to limit or hold him back... I want to plead him not to go, but he's been expelled so it's not like anything I say will change the outcome. I want to go with him if he really does leave, but I'm under a contract. Besides, this academy is important to me as well.)

The topics they could discuss were minimal.

K: (Ah!) "Bael, you mentioned to be careful in Cosmatral Silo about me not getting impaled. What did you mean by that?"

Ba: "Oh, that? You got a different platform. Yours was covered with greenish gas, right?"

K: "Yeah?"

Ba: "That one was affected by a previous student casting a metal decaying spell. I remember that on the platform I competed in I used a Rhodan's trap while the enemy used some sort of spell to make half the arena filled with spiky metal spokes."

K: "Spiky... Metal?"

Ba: "Yeah. The metal bits on the floor were all drawn out like tiny needles. I didn't step on any of them nor did I destroy them, so they might still be there even now. If you were to face that hazard, it would have been very dangerous especially since you often run through the field to hurt the enemy."

Katachi shuddered at the idea of his new shoes getting perforated by the terrain filled with needles.

K: (Scary...) "So that was just wishing me good luck, if I ever got that platform?"

Ba: "Yeah."

K: "I see. Thanks."

On the topic of wishing him good luck, Bael mustered her courage to confront him.

Ba: (He's not coming back... If I don't ask him now I don't think I'll ever get the chance to.) "Hey, Katachi?"

K: "Hmm?"

Ba: (But what should I say? 'Do you like me?' What am I, ten? Well, he should be at least ten years old, so that makes me a big sister figure?) "Do you think I'm a good big sister?"

K: (Big sister?... I've never had a big sister, so I don't know for sure. She's more like a mother, like Mother. She has been pretty helpful like a friendly aide.) "Well, not really. I can't tell for sure, because I've never had a big sister. You're helpful and really friendly though... More so than I'd imagine a big sister would be."

Ba: (More so than a big sister would- !? Is that... Is that implying that we're already beyond that?!)

Bael blossomed blissfully on the velvet chair with a big grin on her reddened face.

Ba: (That settles it! He really does see me in a romantic light.)

K: (Speaking of 'big', there's the oversized uniform in my room. I have to return the uniform I borrowed from the pile.) "I still have some matters to attend to, so if you need me I-"

Ba: (He's running away already?!) "T- This doesn't excuse you from ignoring and leaving me here all alone, Katachi! I want to know the reason behind your recent attempts to avoid me!"

In an aggressive fit Bael challenged his introverted nature. The child was unsure what the best way to convey his true thoughts was.

K: "Do I really have to say it?"

Bael nodded her head violently, hell-bent on hearing the answer.

K: (If she insists, then I suppose...)

Katachi took a deep breath and gave a slight sigh.

K: "... Because the departure becomes that much more painful otherwise."

He wasn't wrong to think that way. People were inherently social, after all. The desire for someone who understands. The want of company and acknowledgement. The necessitation of events and festivals. If there was one thing he knew with certainty, it was that when the time to part with Mother Rinnesfeld came... Katachi felt an overwhelming sadness from leaving her along with the fear of the uncertain future.

Departures hurt more when bonds were stronger, and one might even feel compelled to stay and avoid getting hurt. But, having a second Word of Power early on was significant progress in his journey and the hampering cowardice meant that more of the children to come would suffer the cruel world's malice. He was compelled to keep the momentum going when it had such a strong start.

Ba: "... Oh..."

As she began to understand the wisdom behind his actions, Katachi left the guest room for her to ponder over it alone.

*** ***

After apologizing to Mister Lamale for borrowing the perforated uniform without permission, Katachi walked up the stairs to Bertund's office while Zirco walked down towards the exit. They glanced at each other briefly and continued to walk on. They were both getting expelled for violation of the school rules – Yet the atmosphere between the two was a stark contrast.

He thought that Zirco would at least thank him for healing his hands and carrying him out, but he appeared too prideful to apologize or admit it. Katachi didn't mind; it would take too much effort to succour or appease him. Furthermore, there was no obligation to befriend everyone he met, certainly not when they caused him much grief and suffering in the first place.

K: (... The more I think about it, the less I want to.)

Friends were great to have, but for the child accused of heresy that was a luxury he could never afford. Katachi affirmed himself and walked towards the principal's office.

*** ***

Be: "Come in!"

Bertund greeted the sullen child with a slight grin, closing the book in his hands.

Be: "I presume that your presence here means that you are finished?"

K: "Yeah."

Be: "Good. Let's get this over with then."

Bertund's palm glowed yellow and he approached Katachi slowly. With a gentle pat the magic circle on Katachi's shoulder was gone.

Be: "Mister Kotsuba, in accordance with the following terms violated, you are hereby expelled for usage of magic devoid of supervision or authorisation, attempted assault on our staff and casting non-healing magic on the academy faculty."

It would be mortifying for anyone else to hear those words had they not known the story behind the breach in conduct. But since that was all as planned it wasn't a very emotional event in particular.

Be: "Okay then, now that this is settled I suggest you begin setting up camp immediately. It is getting dark and the night can be quite unforgiving, even in spring. You can stay the night if you want-"

K: "I don't need to."

Be: "Are you sure?"

K: "... To be honest, this academy is great. It's a wonderful place, a peaceful and conducive environment to perform studies and learn about the world. But, how should I say it?"

Katachi gave Bertund a look he wasn't expecting; a maddened glint in his eyes, the desperate and unstable vibe of a forlorn victim in the tides of fate.

K: "The teachers, the other students, the school itself... It unnerves me. I'm not used to being protected."

His distrust and paranoia was a horror most wished their children never had to face until the latter part of the latter part in their lives, when the hairs on their heads turned white.

Be: (How many times has he been derided for him to doubt another so much? Maybe his desire for the Words of Power isn't as ludicrous as people want to believe.) "... I understand. There's your bag."

The slime grew in size behind Katachi and held up the bag in an extended state, ready to hand him the object. Katachi slipped his arm around the strap and situated the bag next to his hip for stability.

Be: "May the gods guide you. I have faith that you will excel in your future endeavours."

With a brave step, he walked towards a new road. The second piece, Kotsuba Katachi's turn had begun.

ADDENDUM 2

Agnes stared at the molweds waving back and forth in the field.

A: (Why?... Why here? And why are there so many of them!?)

Molweds were peculiar flora – Spongy flowers of a vibrant yellow that released a scream-like sound when the plant felt threatened. Even when removed from the soil, the flowers and stem could continually release screams which made handling molweds an advanced trial for florists and herbalists alike.

The frequency of the screech was affected by the quality of the soil it grew upon, the air's humidity and many other factors yet researched upon. Progress on them was difficult enough as things stood due to the tricky nature of the molweds themselves. When molweds grew in large areas like the field in said example, merely crossing the vegetation caused multiple molweds to go off, resulting in splitting headaches and the like.

This feature had time and again been exploited to emulate the effects of an excited cheering crowd, but strictly speaking they were not to be trifled with. Deforesters would quickly realise that fire was ineffective against its spongy and damp flowers so burning fields of them failed. As a defensive mechanism it was particularly meddlesome and the only people who could openly interact with them without discomfort were the deaf, which made removing molweds a big problem.

Agnes was tasked with tutoring amateur magechanics on repairing a broken bridge. However, on his journey towards Rulid he came across the startlingly large field that consisted almost purely of molweds which stood in his path, determined to bar his progress. It would be hard traversing around such a large and troublesome area, yet cutting and destroying the plants would only worsen the current situation.

It would be appropriate to say that it was no small obstacle.

A: (Do I take care of this immediately so nobody else would have to handle this field in the future? That would be best, but it would take too long. Or do I just try my best to waddle through this place? I have never seen such a large number of molweds in my life... If I make a wrong move, I might faint in the middle of the field and never wake again.)

Agnes twiddled his fingers and debated over using his tool to cross the field or to simply walk around it.

A: (Forming a snuffler is probably the most efficient solution but it's going to cost me a few of the Uzab runes, and they probably don't sell any of the high-powered runes there... If I make a glider here, I can probably smooth my way over this field but that's going to deplete the runes quickly too. If I form a bridge it's going to be a while before I can cross the field, not to mention if I build it too low it's going to trigger the molweds anyway. Or maybe I should just walk around these and save my runes?)

Agnes looked around for a better solution, hoping to receive at least some form of inspiration or guidance on what he should choose. Finally, with nothing else but the barren rocks and the trees Agnes hit an ultimatum.

A: (I'm going to stick with crossing it directly since I don't have that much time. But should I use the snuffler or the bridge? The glider is going to cost the most so that's not viable. The snuffler drains the runes continuously since the construction is dynamic and I would need to run as fast as I can before they deplete. I'm going to have to save at least three Uzab runes for Rulid to execute the demonstration, so my speed decides how much I use. The bridge is slow and useless if it's too low, but if I do it right I only need to burn a single rune with its static nature.)

Agnes looked at his surroundings once more.

A: (Gods, Dardicel knows how much I hate choosing. I guess I'll spin around with my eyes closed until I no longer know which way is which. The next time I open my eyes, if I see the trees I'll build a snuffler. If I see the rocks I'll build a bridge.)

Agnes put his luggage down, closed his eyes and began to spin. He balanced his weight on his right leg and kicked his left foot against the ground, forming a circular momentum. He spun and spun until he no longer knew which direction he was facing, until his ability to balance went awry and he finally collapsed onto the floor.

*** ***

Agnes laid down his tools and placed a Uzab rune written on a wooden tablet in the centre of the circle. With a simple hand sign the pile of rocks in the surrounding region floated and came together to form a straight row of stones. Connecting them to each other was an occasional spark of electricity to align the stones should they drift too far apart.

On his left hand seated a symmetrical magic circle comprised of tiny, blue transparent stones and a single piece of ruby. It seemed as though it were a small-scale model of the bridge itself with the ruby being where Agnes was.

A: (Okay. The bridge is stabilized.)

Slowly, Agnes stepped onto the small floating stones one by one. As he walked further and further onto the bridge he shifted the pieces at the far end of his hand toward the front. The pieces at the beginning of the bridge disjointed towards the half-complete end. It slowly formed a bridge suspended purely by the floating rocks.

A: (Steady... Slowly now.)

Agnes made his way through the field when something sped past his face abruptly.

A: "!?" (What... Was that?... It's not safe. Rearrange the stones to form a circle around myself first...)

Agnes shifted the stones on his left hand around and formed a fanning, circular shape around the ruby. The rocks at his feet floated about and formed the same circle around Agnes. He glanced around and tried to grasp what was happening to find only the rocks, trees, molweds and the wind about.

A: (... Nothing at all? That was so fast I could barely see the blur. Was that a galerider? I haven't seen one live before. What a pity – I've only seen illustrations of them, so missing one that flew right by me is kind of depressing.)

With that in mind he reassessed the severity of the variance.

A: (I guess that's why they're called galeriders. Still, if they are dancing about it's not going to be safe forming a cheap bridge. I've already come this far, so I should go the extra mile and use another rune.)

Agnes felt up another wooden tablet and expended the second Uzab rune. He picked up the ruby with his left hand, which caused all the blue stones to float off his hand and in the general position they were before, now suspended around the ruby. With the ruby pinched between his fingers, Agnes mentally arranged a few of the stones such that they formed little platforms before him.

The stones automatically shifted and adjusted themselves to his front, hell-bent on adhering to the formation of the blue stones in his hand as closely as possible. The troublesome process of moving each individual piece forward was no longer necessary.

A: (I've already used a second rune, I may as well use it efficiently.)

He raised a few stones to around his chest level so he could grip onto them should the galerider return and throw him off-balance by surprise. With his safety nets in place, Agnes finally had the peace of mind to continue walking.

*** ***

Agnes eventually made it to the end of the field intact. He looked around for an effigy and found a thorny vine growing on a rather large rock. Agnes slowly set the ruby on the rock and cleared the area of immediate danger.

With a snap, the blue stones clumped together around the ruby. With that same snap the stones floating about attracted and melded themselves onto the large rock, forming an interesting sculpture of sorts. The ruby on the rocks popped loose and he caught the precious gem in his hand.

A: (It was a bit of a waste because that galerider never came back... Oh well. Can't be too careful about these things.)

Agnes crashed his butt onto the ground for a brief moment of recovery and took the chance to admire his sculpture while recovering his stamina.

A: (I'm not sure what to make of the shape... It kind-of looks like a little girl with twin tails and really stiff hair- Who's that?!)

Behind his sculpture was a red-haired young lady of about sixteen years wielding a large grey great sword. With a slash she broke the sculpture cleanly in half and proved the handiwork of the blade.

A: (Whoa!! All the way through three inches of rock with a weapon made for flesh?! I better get back!)

Agnes rolled backwards and planted his feet onto the ground before springing up and backwards, away from the warrior and her ridiculous strength.

A: (That sword... It has a blunt and thickened tip, the kind Rugnudi smiths always use. I see, that's how she crushed through the rock without getting her blade stuck, it's a hybrid bludgeon of sorts. Was she waiting for me?) "Who are you?"

Without giving him the time to react the young lady ran forth and smacked Agnes on his left side with the sword's fuller. It may be an act of mercy to spare the weapon's bladed edges, but the strength of the swing was tremendous even for her size. In a single blow Agnes was knocked out cold from the numbing pain.

*** ***

Crackling sounds filled his ears. Agnes woke up to a camp fire with the brief scent of roasted boar meat wafting about. There was a red-haired girl on a rotting log nearby enjoying the warmth of the flames.

A: "... Ugh. My side..."

Agnes clutched his left and felt up the swell on his side.

"You're awake."

A: "And you are very rude to attack me like that. If you weren't going to kill me, at least knock me out with less pain or something!"

"I see. I'll keep that in mind for my next target."

A: (Next target?) "What do you mean, next target?"

The red-haired girl looked away from the boar kebab and locked eyes with Agnes. Her greenish irises reflected the light from the camp fire which gave the illusion of a monster with glowing eyes.

R: "Don't mind what I said. I am Roberia, Matalpalhallafaelladrapahamo Roberia. Remember that name, will you?"

A: (She dodged my question. By Dardicel's rump, my side hurts so much I can still recall the moment she smacked me. What is with that ludicrous name?) "... Okay?"

Roberia watched the meat intently so the boar kebab would not be overcooked.

A: (Why does she even want me to remember her name? Is she trying to build a reputation for herself in these parts or something?... Well, a girl of her physique landing such a blow really is worthy of praise, I suppose. But she said that her name was Matal... Matalpal-something. That's way too troublesome to remember! Is this supposed to be a joke?)

R: "... Hey, stranger."

A: (What does she want now?) "What?"

R: "You don't mind if I take everything inside, do you?"

A: (What?! She's taking all of my stuff!? That's brutal!) "What?!"

R: "Well, you see, stranger, I don't travel with a lot of things. My goal is to practice and train my stamina by running to the next town and sleeping at the inn there. But, see, you weren't strong enough and fainted on the first hit. I just wanted to immobilise you, see? I wanted to knock you onto the floor, take my fill as usual and run to Rulid immediately. But you fainted, so I had to set up for the night here using your stuff, see? So... I'll be taking it all."

Her explanations left much to be desired, seeing how poor Agnes got the wrong idea.

A: (Unbelievable... She's running from town to town as a form of training? Hastily making her way around, fighting and beating up any travellers on her routes, and carrying their belongings on her back as training weights before selling them as goods for coin...)

R: "I'm not comfortable with people looking at my sleeping face. So I'm going to have to ask you to leave, see?"

A: (Ask me to leave while using my stuff?! That's as good as telling me to drop everything and starve!!) "You take and use my stuff without permission, and you expect me to leave in the middle of the freezing night?! Who do you think you are!?"

R: "... Uhh..."

A: "I mean, come on! I have had the worst luck these few days! Sneaking past an Earthtiger with all my stuff clinking and clanking and almost getting killed, dealing with thieves at night, crossing a field full of molweds nobody bothered to clear, and all my efforts of trying to cope with time wasted by you?! Give me a break, Dardicel!! Stop throwing all these trials at me when I'm actually busy!! Why does it have to be me anyway?!"

His outrage caused the girl to shrivel back slightly.

A: "... Sorry. I overreacted a little. Just so you know, I really had it bad these past few days."

R: "If it makes you happy, I've only taken your gold and borrowed your groundsheet. I haven't touched any of those other things in your backpack. I only have a problem sleeping when someone else is nearby, see?"

A: (She... She's not going to take all my stuff?... Oh, she was referring to the coin in my pouch. I was going to be really upset if she tripped while carrying the sensitive equipment in my baggage.)

Agnes gave his belongings a quick glance.

A: (The equipment looks untouched. That's a relief.) "Leave those as they are please. I need them to teach others how to reconstruct and repair a bridge properly."

R: "... And, well, if you come back tomorrow morning you'll find your groundsheet to be intact. If you come back early enough and not have it snatched away by wildlife, I mean."

A: (At least she seems civilized enough to return my belongings. A warrior... Rugnud?) "Are you from Rugnud by any chance?"

R: "Yes. I am. Please leave soon and allow me to sleep, stranger. I need the energy for tomorrow, see? I haven't slept well for a long time since I left Rugnud, see?"

A: (She means no harm. Her eyes aren't wide open – She simply just wants to rest. A Wanderer, perhaps? She does give off the air of being one, kind of.) "Okay. Consider this... Consider this as a thank-you, for sparing my life."

Agnes staggered away from the camp site slowly, clutching his side still throbbing in pain.

*** ***

Less than an hour elapsed. The sun had already risen in such a short time.

A: ('Tomorrow' sure came quickly... I wonder if she's still asleep.)

Agnes caressed the swell in a circular motion and slowly trudged back to the camp. What little remained was the groundsheet next to the glowing embers of a fire.

A: (Did she seriously sleep for less than an hour? That's not very healthy, is it? I wouldn't mind if she rested a little bit longer since she did spare my life. Then again, as a warrior she's probably afraid of being attacked in her moments of weakness like when she is sleeping. Even as a victor it seems she doesn't trust that I can't overpower her. A cautious type, is she?)

He walked toward his backpack and reached for a bottle of medicated oil. He applied and gently massaged the swollen wound with the heat rub.

A: (It's going to be hard managing without my pouch... I might need to work a little at Rulid before I go back for some gold to hire a coach.)

Agnes checked his inventory once more.

A: (She wasn't lying about it – Everything except the gold and the groundsheet's been left untouched. Such blatant honesty... Matalpal-something Roberia, huh?)

Agnes put away his equipment and continued his journey towards Rulid.

CHAPTER 23

It had been three days since Katachi set off from the Sage Raufid Magus Academy. He arrived at his first destination after walking for a couple of hours on foot.

Bellpot, the City of Hardauten, was a marketplace famous for commerce. As it was located near a sea rich with Nemhea and moss, it was famous for its wide variety of exotic salts. Salt from Oceandrift moss that preserved food, salts from Jjtungi fruits that enhanced flavour, aromatic salts believed to be good for the body, salts that mended injuries when applied on wounds.

Many varieties of salts could be found here – And that was no wonder why many traders and merchants hailed from far and wide to exchange resources like lumber, ores, food and information. They were primarily meant to be combined with different foods, others with medicine; then there were magi who use the salts themselves as a medium for magic, usually to create aroma effigies or divine a person's fate using Axia spells.

Regardless of what they do, it wasn't hard for one to earn a sum in a place as lucrative as Bellpot. Commerce was bountiful, but so were the gambles; it should surprise none to see a once-magus beggar on the streets, offering to enchant salts for a small fee to get by for a living after trading away everything they had. It was also not alarming to find those very magi curse the salts of rude customers, so there was rarely if any disarray where one might think otherwise.

Katachi did not wish for his brand new leather shoes to be dirtied or worn out just yet so he continued to use the sabots. He recalled being tipped by Bertund to search out 'strange' areas around the vicinity. Those 'strange' or 'unnatural' places that affected the world were often a clear indication of a force like the Words of Power at work so with any amount of luck he would find one.

Bertund's hint was a crucial one. The Sealed Rooms once belonged to citadels, castles and forts decades past which were forcibly robbed by 292 mighty, great sorcerors – The very ones whom created the Words of Power. The Words were ripped and placed into an unnamed dimension, yet strange in that the spaces did not exist in the same region.

Each entrance led to a separate space and each 'zone' was unique. The rooms were made prisons, both to contain the Words of Power and to keep people out for the sake of Mankind. But though a measly few decades elapsed since their confinement, the influence proved too much even for the grand plan that was meant to suspend the problem to the generations beyond. It was not possible to seal the magic completely.

The magic leaked out and seeped through the dimensions, sometimes into Cosmatral Naturale, sometimes into other dimensions; and that alone was enough to induce a magical change. The space and general vicinity of these affected areas often held a certain characteristic to it usually relating back to the Word of Power itself.

Katachi remembered one of the worst tragedies the residual power caused, overheard from the rumours whispered among adults in Mielfeud. It was the most severe amongst them all, where one of the Words of Power turned rampant on an entire village. That uncontrolled power turned residents and visitors alike faceless.

The very thought trepidated just about anyone from deep within – The entire incident was finally resolved when one faceless little boy, after climbing past countless bodies of the dead that were unfortunate enough to fall victim to the Sealed Room's traps, arrived at the Sealed Room itself and used the Word of Power within to undo the faceless phenomena.

The official who visited the village quickly rescued the poor child and there were burial expeditions conducted across Findel for the victims. Though the villagers regained their faces, the dead did not regain their lives. That was an event most gruesome which sparked an immediate need for Words of Power hunters.

*** ***

Katachi walked towards the fountain in the town square of Bellpot. He set his backpack down to a side and fished out the wooden dagger he received- Or, more appropriately, took without permission from the Sage Raufid Young Magus Tournament. On the waster dagger's fuller were signs of carvings that anyone could tell vaguely resembled the character 定.

There were a few known methods for raising the precedence level of one's Word of Power. The first was the most direct method – To understand and know more about the character itself. To know the Word of Power meant to understand the sigil before oneself, thus to master the Word meant to understand everything about the word. The applications, its different forms and meanings, each of them reflected a different aspect of the sigil.

Yet there can only be so many possible combinations for some of them, thus the sigils had varying grades. How many terms and meanings the word could ultimately possess decided how valuable the sigil was. Katachi didn't know where 定 stood in that aspect but it was likely one from a lower tier. Still, this was a problem of concern in the future and mulling over it now was pointless.

The second was to reduce the amount of cloud words used – If a word created a phrase of a specific meaning, then most likely it was possible to rephrase it such that the number of cloud words could be reduced while retaining the same meaning. Such was the marvel of language, to shorten a moisturising herb oil mix into a salve.

Another method of increasing the precedence levels was to create a place for the Word of Power to reside within – A chamber, a carving or some housing for the Word of Power to fit snugly. By believing that the Word of Power itself was not an extension of an object but rather a part that made an object complete, the precedence level can be increased through the owner's subconscious belief and image power.

There were likely other methods he was unaware of, but Katachi wanted to focus on just one for now. With the free pick gifted by one of the students he continued to scrape out a slot for the Word of Power. He quietly carved and scratched the wood out while listening to the conversations around the marketplace for twenty minutes...

... By the poorest strokes of luck, a little boy chased by an older couple came from around the corner rapidly. The boy ran forward with his head facing back at the couple and he tackled Katachi into the fountain without paying attention to where he ran. They both formed a large splash in the fountain that thoroughly soaked Katachi, his pick and dagger, the child and everything around the fountain's rim.

"Tonquat! Let go of him this instant!"

He was a rather brash man with hairy muscular arms protruding from a collared check shirt, rough trousers and a gruff face. The lumberjack lookalike barked at the child still atop Katachi in the fountain. The frail lady next to him in a plain brown dress was clutching his left arm and panting.

T: "I don't wanna! You'll just spank me again, and again, and again!"

"Come home with us now, child! If I don't fix you today, I will-"

"Sire, please, spare the child! He has had enough!"

"Not yet, Froile! This child needs it beaten into him before he learns not to steal from our neighbours!"

F: "Sire, no!-"

He held Tonquat by his torso and picked up the young boy.

T: "No! No no no no! Let me go, Papa!"

K: "... Ah. My clothes." (At least they're my old clothes.)

The lady affirmed Tonquat's safety and heaved a sigh of relief. Evidently, she had yet to notice the Ohdean in the fountain since the lumberjack was obstructing her view. He pulled the mischievous Tonquat squirming and struggling away from the fountain rim so he would not hurt himself from hitting his head against the stone.

F: "-?! Oh my! I'm so sorry! Are you okay?"

The lady hurriedly walked towards the fountain and bowed with sincerity. She apologized to Katachi in a panicky manner and offered to clean his clothes for him. The child wanted to refuse at first but on his second observation the water splashed past the fountain's rim and dampened his nice, clean groundsheet. Without the time to establish a makeshift clothes line, Katachi was left with little choice and took up the kind offer.

With the man pulling Tonquat's ears throughout the entire walk.

*** ***

K: "Th- Thank you for the hospitality."

F: "Please, don't mention it. It is the least we can do for having him drench your belongings."

"We would also like to thank you for helping us catch that child before he hurt himself."

The two parents sat on the wooden dining table with Katachi on the opposite side quietly chewing on some bread and cheese.

K: "It's a bit much to even provide dinner for me..."

F: "Young man, you don't look too old yourself. Are you, uh..."

The couple looked at each other. The man was staring with fierce eyes while the woman flashed a worried expression.

F: "... Travelling, perhaps?"

The man's eyes drooped a little upon hearing her continuation of the sentence. Katachi could feel the uncertainty and tension from the way they sat and spoke with their unwarranted wary towards sensitive subjects.

K: "Yes ma'am. I am indeed travelling."

The lady relaxed a little and leaned against the chair's backrest comfortably. The man was twiddling his thumbs with impatience.

"What's your name?"

K: "I... I'm Katachi. Kotsuba Katachi."

F: "That name... Oh dear, are you Ohdean? Ohde is far from here, young man. Are you okay?"

K: "Yes, I am perfectly fine, ma'am. Uhm... Would it be okay if I addressed you two by your names as well, uh... ?"

F: "Most certainly."

"Sure."

The man sat up from his seat briefly and cracked his neck.

N: "I am the head of this household, Nicholas Demant. You may call me Mister Demant."

F: "And I am his wife, Froile Demant. You may call me Missus Demant."

K: "… I have a question, Mister Demant."

The man was most likely used to a lifestyle of action, which explained his twitchy and fretful compulsion to shake his leg and toy with his fingers.

N: "Speak."

K: (Nicholas feels like the name of a Rugnudi.) "Are you from Rugnud, by any chance?"

The man looked away for a bit as though confirming his suspicions.

N: "... Yes. Yes I am."

K: "Ah. That would explain your name. Nicholas is a common name in Rugnud, is it not?"

N: "Yeah. You're smart for your age."

However, that was detrimental to Katachi's plan. A foreign background also meant that his familiarity with the town was limited.

K: "I see... But, you're from Rugnud so you wouldn't know too much about this town-"

F: "If you need an aide or a guide through Bellpot's markets, you can consult me instead. My sire mostly provides for the family while I supplement him in chores, childcare and information."

K: (Froile... It's an ambiguous name, but definitely of Findeli origin.) "Okay then. I would like to ask the both of you a very serious question."

Katachi glanced toward Tonquat's bedroom door. While it was possible to control the damage of information leaks through observing the connections adults have and blackmailing them, children were free to befriend anyone since they were at the age where establishing relations was crucial for healthy growth. Adults were easy to silence and coerce, but not children. It was imperative that Tonquat remained unaware of Katachi's 定.

K: "Before that, though... Is the boy asleep?"

F: (He's not that much older, is he? Why call him a boy?) "Yes. He should be... A four-year-old shouldn't stay up this late."

K: "... Can we close his door? If possible, I do not wish for him to see or know this."

N: "I do not mind, but what could be so important that requires such privacy?"

Nicholas walked towards Tonquat's door and closed it gently before returning to his seat. Katachi withdrew his wooden dagger, the one with the incomplete carving of an Anikan character. A golden 定 manifested on the dagger.

K: "Do you know what the Words of Power are?"

*** ***

N: "So you're on a pilgrimage for the Words of Power?"

K: "Yes."

Nicholas frowned a bit and tapped his feet impatiently.

N: "I don't get it. Why not just trace the words out themselves if you already know what they look like?"

F: "It's not that simple, dear."

K: "It's not as simple as that, Mister Demant."

N: "It's not?"

K: "No. Think of it as two soil patches. The Word of Power would be a mushroom patch filled full of mushrooms while the other patch that merely looks like the Word of Power has no mushrooms within – It's just barren land. It is useless without the mushrooms within. I need not a simple tracing of the Word of Power, but rather the Word itself."

Froile, on the other hand, was a lot more receptive to the situation.

F: "How can we help, then?"

K: "Are there... Are there any interesting, weird or unique places around here? Is there anywhere around this town that has something funny or unusual, a topic of rumours?"

The couple looked at each other and dived into their memories to answer such a bizarre, uncommon question.

F: "There is indeed one such location."

K: "There is?"

F: "Well, it's not much, but there is supposedly a famous place around here where parents bring their children and serenade them to sleep, both mischievous and otherwise. At the

Serene Alcove, the children are mysteriously pacified. I'm not sure if it's what you're looking for, but you can take a gander at it if nothing else."

K: (Sounds like it, but something more conclusive would be nice.) "Does it apply exclusively to children?"

N: "It's not just children who are calmed."

Nicholas gazed into the distance with a longing look in his eyes.

N: "That place used to be a secret sleeping spot of mine. I came to Bellpot when I was of seventeen years, and it was my favourite haunt. The moss... It was nice and comfortable, the place was overflowing with a strange tranquillity. I can't quite explain it but it's not just a rumour."

His gaze wandered from outside the window to a part of the homogeneous ceiling.

K: (Favourite 'haunt'? I've never used that word before. Hmm.)

N: "I could birdwatch openly since there were many forms of wildlife about as well. I would nap there during lunch break alone for months until some couple brought their child there and sung her to sleep. Since then, the spot gained some odd nickname and I haven't found the time to sleep there by myself peacefully."

K: (Even the animals are affected? It could be a Word of Power at work. Bertund may be alluding to this.) "An alcove where everything is serene... It sounds suspicious enough."

F: "I hope that was enough assistance for you, Mister Katachi."

K: "That is indeed something interesting enough to investigate for myself. Thank you, the both of you. I shall set forth tomorrow at daybreak to this Serene Alcove."

N: "Fancy a map to the area?"

K: (了解! Understand information – Location of aforementioned 'Serene Alcove'!... It's northwest of the town following the small pebble trail and to the right of the Sharyu Zuku statue... Okay.) "That won't be necessary – I roughly know where it is. Even if I don't I'll just ask around for the place, and if all else fails I can ask you two again- Er, if... If it's not too much to ask."

Katachi retracted slightly at his own lack of tact. The mere thought of chancing upon another Word of Power made him reckless and assertive, qualities that he knew would spell the end of him.

F: "You're welcome to do that, Mister Katachi. I would aid you to the best of my abilities."

N: "If you insist that you can do it alone, I trust that you can. No shame in asking for help."

He quietly swore to rectify his impatience should it ever show.

K: "Thank you... It is late now. I ought to sleep for tomorrow."

N: "You can use that wooden rocking chair. It's not much, but that should be plenty."

F: "That rocking chair belonged to my late grandmother. I'm sorry we couldn't provide a proper bed with how small our house is, but if you're fine with that chair-"

K: "-It's okay. I wouldn't want to get too comfortable."

Katachi walked towards the rocking chair in the Demant's living room. He sat on it, laid back, and the creaking of the wooden chair resounded through the house ever so slightly.

N: "Have a good rest."

F: "Good night, Mister Katachi."

K: "Segus bless you."

The couple went to their room after hushing the lights. The slow rocking of the chair and the creaking lulled the child to sleep.

*** ***

Nicholas and Froile crawled on the bed in their nightwear.

F: "... Poor child."

N: "He's so serious he could compete with my foreman. I certainly didn't expect a child like him to exist. It's a miracle he's still alive."

F: "I don't understand, sire. Aren't children supposed to be innocent angels like our beloved Tonquat? I find it hard to believe that a person like him is younger than us."

N: "It might be his heritage. His hair was a signature trait of the Ohdeans but the Findeli he spoke was even more fluent than my own. Maybe he's been bullied in a nearby town."

F: "Do you think his father was Ohdean?"

N: "Most likely. If the two loved each other, then taking up his surname would make sense. If, however, the mother was horribly violated and left to die, she would probably have the child be named after her instead. Either way, that boy- ..."

Froile tugged at his left sleeve slightly.

F: "... Promise me you wouldn't abandon me like that, sire?"

Nicholas locked eyes with Froile.

N: "Of course, my love. I wouldn't want a tragedy like him to occur again."

Froile snuggled her head against Nicholas's chest and felt the warmth of her husband.

F: "I'll take your word for it."

The couple slowly drifted off to slumber in their embrace.

CHAPTER 24

Sunrise. The birds merrily flew about hunting for prey. The villagers were getting up while the variety of shopkeepers in Bellpot prepared themselves for another day of commerce. Katachi began following the pebble trail winding up the cliff and stopped at a small shrine just as the morning rays gently shone into his eyes. The clouds drifting between him and the sun filtered the light and made it relatively tolerable.

In the shrine, some food and bread were respectfully placed into several wooden bowls and a pair of chopsticks lay on the stone tiles. On the side of a shrine hung a rabbit's foot on one of its tiny pillars, and a sign that spelled 紗竜.

K: ('Sharyu'... What a strange place for a shrine.)

Katachi prayed once at the tiny shrine and turned right towards the wilderness.

*** ***

K: (... I'm tired already.)

Katachi had not taken a dozen steps from the shrine before he was persuaded by his muscles to rest on the soft, mossy roots. He sat down to regain his strength and slowly absorbed his surroundings. A sound of water flowing could be heard somewhere but the source was unknown. The cicadas nearby created a merry, pleasant ambience and contributed to the serene atmosphere.

K: (This is a nice place. The morning is rather cool and fresh.)

The birds on the trees chirped, signalling to each other the locations of twigs and branches. A lazy looking Oilskin snake rested upon a branch waiting patiently for the sun to warm its poikilothermic body. The little Flowermane bees began drawing nectar and pollinating the flowers that were to become fruit. The trees rustled at a gentle pace, moving in tandem to the slow, soothing breeze flowing inland from the sea.

K: (I feel weird, like I'm forgetting something... I wonder what this feeling is.)

Katachi slowly rested his head against the moss and adjusted himself to a comfortable position.

K: (Is it because I woke up too early?... That probably isn't it. I'm used to waking up at this time. But why do I feel so tired? Maybe the rocking chair last night wasn't as comfortable as I thought it was?)

The moss, ever inviting, was of a warm and briefly damp texture to the extent of it being almost surreal. Something felt awry. There was nothing dangerous around, the surroundings showed no signs of peril and it felt serene enough for anyone's guard to drop.

It gave the same feeling he experienced in the academy, as though he was within someone's vigilant gaze. It felt as if the entire area had been attuned by something or someone to create this place and he was inclined to believe that everything in the region was shaped deliberately, from the smallest sprouts to the largest rocks.

K: (Maybe I'm over-thinking things... Still, I can't shake this suspicion off. I wish I knew what it was- ! Oh! Right, I can do just that, can't I?)

Katachi felt his left hand over the thick, heavy book strapped onto his waist and reassured its presence.

K: (Okay. It's here. If this Word of Power is truly as powerful as I believe... Then I should be able to know exactly what's wrong. 了解! Understand reason for discomfort – Self!)

(There are birds and oilskin snakes about. Why aren't they eating the bees and cicadas?)

A soft 解 was heard in the back of his head before that unfamiliar voice spoke to him. He could see clearly that the animals stared at their prey unmoving yet none acted to consume the idle insects. Even if they were full and lacked the appetite to consume any of the critters, remnants of consumption like dung should have been about the area. Yet the zone he lay within was free of such signs.

K: (That behaviour is definitely unnatural. If I pair it with the Demant's claim, there is definitely something acting up. This means... The Word of Power, or the Sealed Room hinted by Bertund should be nearby.)

Katachi quickly stood up and glanced around the area, trying to look for the location of the dimensional rift or at least for something that looked out-of-place.

K: (... Nothing, huh.)

The naiveté of that decision quickly hammered him back into place. If it were that easy to locate the space where the Sealed Room was, there wouldn't be a need to warrant actual Hunters for the job. The danger of the act itself, let alone the difficulty, was usually enough to deter most from the mercenary-like job. Only the truly powerful or desperate would attempt to seek strength that made great men even if they broke in the process.

K: (Now that I think about it, this new Word of Power... It's amazing. I've never even noticed that the cicadas around the area were left alone by these animals, but... It felt like I knew the answer all the long, except it surfaced only with the aid of this Word of Power.)

Was it not the folly of Man to misjudge themselves above all else? Or perhaps the phrase 'Darkest under the lamp' suggested a wisdom deeper than he gave credit for?

K: (I would guess that the power works more like a guide, a shepherd pointing me in the right direction... But I can't be too sure. It could be putting thoughts into my head. Shelly did warn me about being specific when using this Word of Power, lest I kill myself with it.)

He paused to recollect the events that transpired.

K: (Rekter had access to all this power before I took it, and he misused them. So many people in the world abuse power for their own benefit. Is the appeal of power that intoxicating? If that stands true, then I fear the day I become a monster like them.)

He grew weary of the many things he was powerless against.

K: (I wish I could just put an end to all of this without facing much resistance. People have suffered and conflicted enough over these Words of Power...)

His fists clenched hard – Had he not cut his nails, he would have bled from self-inflicted injury.

K: (... It must end. Even if all I have done here is wasted and I die halfway through this journey to someone else who is also collecting these Words of Power, all of this insanity... It must end, one way or another.)

With his will to search for the Words of Power rekindled, Katachi took assertive action.

K: (了解! Understand location of Word of Power in the closest proximity – Self!)

(The Word of Power within your body, 定.)

Shelly would be disappointed in him to have committed the mistake she specifically instructed him to avoid.

K: (That surprised me... I probably need to change the context. 了解. Understand location of Sealed Room in the closest proximity – Self.)

(To your right, walk towards the tree with a branch that splits to three. Stand to the left of the rock, stick the dagger completely into the earth above the blade of grass and apply Fixate Dimension on the dagger. An entry to a sealed room is located there – Rip the dagger out of the earth and enter the dimension.)

K: (What-!! I didn't know it could give such specific instructions!)

Katachi was shocked by the outcome.

K: (I didn't even know I could tether a dimension onto another object and completely omit using Roadless Path to weaken dimensions. This magic... The same applies to the 290 Words of Power I do not possess, don't they?)

The cruel truth was suffocating for him.

K: (If anyone got their hands on 解, merely knowing the term 'Understand' will allow one to become whatever he wishes. If it were a sigil far worse, then they would put themselves and others at peril.)

Katachi stared at the thousand-paged book strapped to his waist.

K: (A mere modicum of its power could allow anybody to dramatically increase his intelligence and precedence level at the same time... This is able to benefit the righteous and raise a fine duke to rule the land. But it is equally capable of plunging the greedy into a mad thirst for power and knowledge, until they eventually destroy themselves in their own avarice.)

He tapped the book with his left hand to reassure its presence.

K: (I am really tempted to use Understand on the Word of Power itself... But the information overload might kill me on the spot. At this point I'm not even surprised how Rekter succumbed to depravity. This cannot go on.)

Katachi stood up and walked towards the rock behind the tree with a three-joint branch. Behind it was a Caciabear sleeping soundly to the right of the rock.

K: (... Even predatory beasts like this bear can be soothed to rest?)

*** ***

When he pulled the dagger up from the floor a strange rip across the space was observed. Katachi peered at the slight, colourless distortion of space. It made the world seen through that tear appear black-and-white. When he reached his hand into it the space seemed to devour his fingers – It was still present, but it could not be seen at all.

K: (Nothing ventured, nothing gained. Here goes.)

Without any form of preparation at all, he slipped into the dimensional tear.

*** ***

Katachi was greeted by a rather long corridor made entirely out of some sort of faintly glowing stone. The passage appeared plain at first sight but the stone blocks that comprised the floor were strangely uneven in a peculiar and jutting pattern. They seemed strangely inviting and ominous at the same time. It wasn't possible to tell which rocks would be safe, which rocks would trigger a trap or anything of that sort.

K: (恒定! Constant status – Self!)

With a safeguard present he felt slightly safer and more assured about proceeding. Katachi traversed the corridor cautiously, taking slow steps and testing his footing carefully. He tried to step on the rocks that were already depressed because they seemed the safest should they really be a trigger for some horrid trap.

After taking a good number of steps on the sunken tiles he safely made it to the second section of the long corridor marked only by the unlit torches covered in growth and fungus. He took his first step on a part of the section joint that looked indifferent to the other adjacent tiles, but-

K: (-!!)

-the first stone he stepped on sunk downward.

K: (Not good...)

A rumbling sound of sorts was heard. It originated from the space above him, then it passed his head and rumbled from beneath him. It was like a serpent or badger or some horrifyingly large burrower was released, digging about the corridor before him.

Katachi tried the second depressed stone block and that sunk even more than the first – It fell through and made a square hole on the ground. Of course, since the full weight of his body was transferred onto the leg, he simply dropped and sat on the stone blocks around the square hole with his left leg dangling precariously.

K: (!! I have to get out!)

Katachi pressed his arms against the floor trying to free his leg fruitlessly. The rumbling sound cascaded along the walls and right underneath him. Something hit his leg which wedged the limb between the stone blocks and itself, rattling the entire corridor slightly.

The stone blocks were shaken slightly and some shifted out of their lodged positions – If one paid attention they would have known which stone blocks to avoid and crossed the corridor safely. Unfortunately, he had a leg through a hole so he could only see the immediate blocks before him.

K: (Something hit my leg?)

There was little time to notice, let alone respond to the second set of tremors. The second 'thing' too hit his leg, and once again the entire corridor was shaken up. The second collision caused the blocks to loosen even further, and even more stone blocks fell through the floor. While there were still trap blocks attached to the corridor, those were so obviously misplaced that avoiding them was impossible only for the clumsy or blind. Katachi didn't understand what was going on.

K: (I should free myself from this first. 恒定! Constant status – Dagger!)

Katachi drew his wooden dagger and hacked away at the blocks trapping his left thigh. Since the dagger could not be damaged with its status set as Constant the act was akin to piercing paper pulp with a chisel. He managed to break one of the blocks loose from the corridor's construct and freed his left thigh. There was a whole group of blocks that fell and created a pitfall-like trap ahead, so he proceeded onward to examine the situation.

It might have been dangerous to hop down, but the stone blocks below looked just fine. It was probably not that deep a fall so he lowered himself slowly. He landed solidly on the ground, his two feet planting into the strange space with little problem. However, it hurt his eyes a little looking at his feet and the Word of Power he wielded did little to mitigate the distortion effect he experienced.

The swirling colours that surrounded the space made everything appear as though it were in motion, yet his feet were perfectly stationary. He made a note not to stay in the region for too long.

Katachi looked towards the earlier section of the corridor and realized what hit his left leg. Two boulders that were broken down into pieces were stuck in a track winding along the corridor for them to roll on perpetually. Katachi's left leg, with its status set as 'Constant', was not crushed or affected in any way – It simply bumped into the boulders and caused them to go awry.

K: (So these were the things rumbling in the walls. It looks like the track was designed to pursue the people in the corridors so that when they get a leg trapped in the hole it would be crushed by the rolling boulders. Praise Segus that I'm all right.)

There were familiar jagged carvings on it that gave him a slight chill down the spine. He had a vague feeling they were related to an incredibly dangerous story he wasn't really sure would qualify as its source, yet would be mortifying if true.

K: (Yggn ad noasam, the depiction of Man's inherent nature? Or maybe it's some other spell that looks similar?)

In any case, the worst was over. He got back up to the corridor by setting his velocity to 'Constant' and thinned his body as neatly as he could while navigating through the pitfall. The trap's effectiveness had, by then, plummeted to pose a negligible threat.

*** ***

The end of the corridor was a strange swirl of chromatic colours similar to a marble cake of sorts. Something unsettling about its mere design gave Katachi a sense of apprehension. He briefly glanced at his chest to affirm himself that he was protected by the 定 to some degree. He peered his head through the portal and saw an amazing sight.

The most prominent furniture was a large bed appropriate for royalty. There were many little butterflies in the area hovering over flowers in a vase by the window, the floor rendered spotless and well-polished, the ceiling and walls enamoured in wonderful art of families reconciling.

A miniature counter with elegant chairs by the side sat in a small corner of the room, and on it were two exquisite royalty-class glasses of some blue-coloured liquid. A couple lay asleep peacefully on the huge bed and the area was scented with the ever-faint hint of Tinjengel.

K: (This is a Sealed Room? Bertund mentioned that they were parts of citadels and castles decades ago, but I didn't expect one to be this grand. Why are there people here? Are they guardians or something? They look like they are sleeping, so maybe I should leave them be.)

In the centre of the room was a white bird with a yellow plume resting on a bird stand with the golden coloured word 安 placed on it.

K: (There it is!- Wait. I have to be careful about this. I don't know what might happen.)

He shifted his focus on the golden 安 word and raised a query.

K: (了解! Understand active sigil phenomena!)

The hoarse and raspy voice echoed in the back of his head once more.

(The word 定 is filtered for selective effect and the property applied is 'Constant'. The word 安 is leaking power due to extended neglect and the property applied is 'Contentment'.)

K: (Contentment... That means the affected are content with something, doesn't it? I thought it was a little bit weird how 'Calm' could stop a Caciabear, but if it's content with simply sleeping away that would make a lot more sense.)

Katachi slowly approached the stand while the creature eyed the young boy.

"What do you want? What do you want?"

The bird crowed with a curious tone. Was it normal for birds to be capable of speech? He didn't know.

K: "I... I want to absorb the Word of Power on your stand into this book."

"Okay!"

The bird flew off and landed onto the table in the room next to the two glasses. Katachi stared hard at the bird stand, held his book out and opened to a new page.

K: (Here goes nothing then. 锁定. Lock within book – 安.)

The rogue 安 slowly faded off and surfaced on his book.

K: (There we go-)

"RRRRAAAAAAAARRRR!!!"

It let loose a frenzied caw all of a sudden and morphed in cue to the cry of anguish. Its feathers dyed black, its wings outstretched, the glasses next to the bird were sent crashing onto the floor. With a few caws many other black apparitions flew in from the broken window, and crows swarmed the room in a torrential storm.

K: (!? What- What is this?!)

The crows flew about destroying everything around them. Katachi still had his 'Constant' status held up so he was fine and unharmed, but bearing witness to the utter destruction of everything while one remained unharmed was a terrifying phenomenon even for the most trained magi and champions alike. The most accurate likeness to describe the mess would be a black and ominous twister of death. There were so many things happening in the room at the same time that he didn't even know where to look at.

It swallowed everything in the room. The walls were scratched and defecated upon. The couple in bed were reduced to their skeletons, their blanket torn up so badly if anyone asked it was comparable to a scrap used for patchwork. The butterflies were absent – Presumably chased away, or even devoured by the monstrous avians. Feathers and scraps and remnants of the objects in the room scattered all over the floor in an unkempt twisted mess.

The destruction ended as quickly as it came. The murder of crows dispersed into black clouds and soot, a mere illusion that took a most impossible form. It was as though the room's grace from before a mere lie construed by his own mind to convince himself that his actions were of the lesser evil. Clawed, pecked at, rammed against, smudged, everything was defaced from a suite of the nobility class to one even the vagrants would steer clear from.

K: (Segus have mercy.)

Though he remained unscathed, the damage was irreparable.

K: (This... This is the consequence of my selfishness. Had I not taken the Word of Power, the talking bird would never have transformed and nothing would be ruined.)

Yet for some reason, his facial expression betrayed what one might expect.

K: (But there's nothing wrong with that. A talking bird is certainly not normal, not by any means. Had I left it unattended the possibility of the influence expanding may have increased, and soon the people in Bellpot would have contentment with sleeping like that couple on the bed, or... Worse. The dead may have risen to content themselves.)

But it wasn't as though that justification made the act any less in humane than it already was.

K: (Contentment... It differs for everyone. For the couple, company in each other's arms may be their ideal. But for me, I will only be content knowing the ones to come after myself can live in the peace I seek.)

With mixed feelings, Katachi exited through the swirling portal he came in from. He slowly walked through and balanced himself across the stone blocks. He phased through the dimensional space at the start of the corridor and returned to the outskirts of Bellpot – It was all changed as well.

The Caciabear sleeping next to the rock disappeared and the cicadas stopped crying. The Oilskin snake resting on the branch lay limp, unmoving, and the birds were gone. The trees were the only things that appeared immutable and stalwart, but they probably were affected in some other way just like everything else.

He knew that the animals, no longer under the influence of Contentment, had long scattered into their respective roles in Nature once more. He also knew that the act removed a potential resting spot in Bellpot for the commoners to enjoy. Though he now wielded the Word of Power itself he did not know the correct characters to replicate the Contentment effect, let alone its pronunciation.

But that may be the greatest blessing one could ask for, to be incapable of using a power with such allure.

With his eyes affixed to the floor Katachi continued the trudge back to the Demant's hut.

CHAPTER 25

K: "Thank you very much for letting me stay the night."

Katachi bowed respectfully at the Demant couple.

F: "It's the least we can do for Tonquat's mischief. Please, don't mention it."

Katachi looked at the two and felt up the book strapped to his waist. It had not changed at all in weight, but somehow the book felt heavier than before.

F: "I pray for your success."

N: "Take care."

K: "Before I leave, I would like to know if there's anywhere else similar to the Serene Alcove."

The Demant couple glanced at each other and gave a negative.

N: "I don't recall other places like that."

F: "Me neither. I'm sorry, this is as far as we can aide you."

K: "It's fine, actually. I wouldn't expect myself to be able to find all the Words of Power bundled together in a single town. The world doesn't work like that, does it?"

N: "I suppose not."

K: "Segus bless the both of you."

Katachi rubbed his feet against the soft and comfortable rug on the floor and slipped into his sabots after thirty seconds of enjoying a luxury he could never afford.

*** ***

K: (It's nearing noon.)

He rested his items on the right of a small bench under the shade. He sat at the edge of the bench on the left so the wood chips and shavings would land on the floor in a neat pile. As he worked, his ears were to the street and focused on the gossip about town.

187

Katachi couldn't make up his mind on where to go. It was a choice between heading South and toward Findel's capital; or going further up North-East and reach Rulid first before heading back to Mielfeud. Therefore, he reached a conclusion – Sit around the busy markets of Bellpot and eavesdrop on the conversations and rumours about.

Hopefully, by doing that Katachi would be able to pick up topics of interest and get a general idea of where he would head next... Or so he planned. It was already noon and Katachi was more-or-less finished with the carving on the wooden dagger. He leaned against the backrest on the bench, closed his eyes and relaxed himself under the comfortable shade of the tree.

K: (It's no use. I haven't heard anything interesting yet. They mainly discuss things like Flamgellite purity over price, or Greengut Salmon freshness over size… But then again, why would merchants talk about anything else?)

Katachi's eyes glazed the area, searching for something of interest. He looked up at the clear sky and at the leaves that filtered the sun's rays ever so gently.

K: (I still can't believe the Word of Power I took was actually this... Overwhelming. I had to take the Word of Power before anyone bad misuses it, but I've also destroyed the Sealed Room by taking it. I'm not even sure whether taking the Words of Power can be considered a good thing. I'm kind of scared of using any of the other Words of Power now.)

Katachi thought back to the moment he used 解, the threatening amount of potential it held gnawing at him.

K: (I need to be very, very careful using Rekter's 解. It's similar to 定 in that they are both powerful, but their strengths come in very different forms.)

Katachi let his gaze wander for a good bit at the ringing of the bell tower that signified mid-day, and looked over in the direction of a little girl about six years of age with brown shoulder-length wavy hair playing cheerfully on a swing. She was wearing a shoddy bodice that seemed too big for her with a skirt that had a few strands of thread loose. And, in the corner of his eye...

K: (That girl has a Word of Power placed on her?!)

Katachi caught a glimpse of the girl's shoulder when the bodice slumped, which revealed a golden word beneath.

K: (A Word of Power, right in plain sight... I only managed to catch a glimpse of it. It was for a brief moment, but I definitely saw a 亻 just below her collarbone. There's probably more to it.)

Katachi planted his feet upright and swung himself forward with momentum.

K: "Excuse me?"

The girl glanced in Katachi's direction wearing a big grin on her face.

K: "What is that thing on your shoulder?"

"Oh, this?"

The little girl gently pulled and stretched the neck hole down to reveal her shoulder and pit. Where the arm was connected to the body lay a barren, golden word – 信.

K: (She has a Word of Power! No, she has a Word of Power placed on her. But if I'm not mistaken, 信 means trust. Why would anyone need to put that kind of Word of Power on a little girl? Maybe she's dishonest or something? Or... Maybe they're manipulating her for some ulterior motive?) "That- that thing on your shoulder..."

"It's a friendship mark!"

K: (She's been made to believe it's a friendship mark? I ought to be careful. Whoever is wielding this Word of Power might be using it as a form of brainwashing.) "Where did you get that friendship mark?"

"I got it from Igtana! He gave it to me!"

K: (Igtana? A man? I should locate him as soon as possible and take his Word of Power before the situation goes out of control. In fact, odds are I'm already in his trap.) "Please take me to where Igtana is! I need to speak to him at the shortest notice!"

"Hmm? Why's that?"

K: (I need to come up with a convincing reason for her? This could be tricky considering that she's younger than me... But the Word of Power should come first. I have to ensure it lands in safe hands, at least.) "Uhm, be- because... That is not a mere friendship mark!"

"It's not?"

K: (No, wait- It's too late. I can't pull back the words I spoke. May as well go with it.) "No. It's not. In fact, that symbol there may prove to be very, very dangerous."

"How so?"

K: (Do I really have to demonstrate this? I suppose this is what I get for saying that it's not a mere friendship mark. I locked myself out of an easy solution, when I could have easily said I wanted one myself. I would be able to locate the Scholar immediately if I just feigned interest.) "Let me give an example."

Katachi raised his left arm a little bit, showing his back hand to the girl.

K: (恒定. Constant status – Self.)

As he willed, a 定 surfaced on his hand.

"Wow! You can do that too?"

K: "Yes. Yes I can. But it's really dangerous."

Katachi drew his wooden dagger from its strap sheathe and forced the wooden dagger onto his chest. Naturally it would seem ridiculous, pointless and ineffective, but Katachi felt the full strength of his arms forcing the object onto his chest from the dagger's trembling... Though it did not hurt in the slightest.

"How is that dangerous? It's wooden, not metal."

K: "! Good... Good point." (What was I thinking just now? Of course this wouldn't be convincing! Assuming that she knows the danger beforehand is a mistake. I need to try something more obvious.)

The example would need to be flashy to draw her attention, much like how an infant was attracted to loud noises. At the same time, it had to be simple and void of intricacies to prevent error in judgement. For the black-haired child who over-complicated many of his thoughts, this was a change in gear that troubled him considerably.

K: (Maybe Rhuibat's tale would suffice.) "Do you believe that wooden axes can chop trees faster than metal axes can?"

"That's impossible. Metal is cold, hard and more painful than wood."

K: (Good, let's go with that.) "But have you seen a wooden axe cut a tree faster than a metal axe?"

"I've heard about a story of the young Rhuibat who moved a goddess and he was given a metal axe to replace his wooden one. I think metal would be better at cutting a tree since he cut the tree much faster than when he did with the wooden axe."

K: "That may be. But, what if I use this wooden dagger not meant for cutting trees to chop faster than a metal axe?"

"You can try, but Rhuibat took a few hours to cut a tree as thick as that one."

K: "I can prove otherwise."

"Show me then."

K: (Good. I've got her attention.)

Katachi set the status of his wooden dagger to Constant as well and walked towards the tree calmly. He then proceeded to hack and slash at the tree with a flurry of attacks. It was quite messily cleaved into sideways, but the tree was felled in less than a few moments after being struck at the same wedge repeatedly. That in itself was a feat to behold – Trees were not easily felled, not even with the proper cutting tools.

K: "Does Rhuibat cut trees this quickly, then?"

When Katachi turned his head to look at the girl, she was gawking in awe.

"Wow! The... The tree...! You must be some sort of super berserker or something!"

*** ***

And so the little girl brought Katachi to the unknown scholar.

"Igtana!"

I: "Femmi!"

A young boy about eight years of age with really funky and curly hair greeted the little girl next to Katachi. They held each other's wrists and spun round and round, dancing in circles and laughing merrily.

K: (This boy is the owner of the Word of Power? His hair's all messed up. But why would he need to apply 信 on a little girl?) "Hello, Igtana."

I: "Femmi, who's that?"

F: "This is the super berserker! He cut down a whole tree with that wooden dagger there!"

K: (... 'Super berserker'? What kind of name is that supposed to be?)

Katachi winced at the little girl who was twirling and playing with Igtana's hair. The mystery was solved before the question was even presented.

I: "Really? But he looks so weak! That dagger of his can't be made of wood!"

Igtana walked to Katachi's back and withdrew the wooden dagger from the waist sash. He felt and tested the weight of the dagger himself, he clipped the wooden blade with his teeth and knocked his knuckles on the dagger, and even inhaled deeply at the dagger's blade for any signs of 'metal rust' before being fully convinced that it was a wooden dagger.

K: (He's not planting anything suspicious on the dagger... Or is he? I don't see anything that resembles sabotage, though.)

I: "That's awesome! It's a real wooden dagger! Did you really cut a tree in half? How thick was the tree? Did you use a spell? Can you cut one right now?"

His excitement was easy for anyone to see. Thankfully, the Scholar possessing 信 was not as malicious as he imagined. Katachi was wholly prepared for a fight with some middle-aged crook, not a friendly conversation with children younger than him.

K: "This may be a bit much of me to ask, Igtana... Do you have something similar to this?"

Katachi showed the 定 still glowing on his left hand to Igtana.

I: "Yeah, I do! Here."

Igtana copied him and placed a 信 on his right hand.

K: (That's a relief. He's not a procurator of the mastermind.) "... Igtana, do you mind if I-"

F: "Igtana! Igtana!"

Femmi happily ran over to them and handed him half a piece of bread.

F: "Igtana, here! Today's bread!"

Igtana's face quickly changed into one of gratitude and repose upon seeing the bread. He wiped his smudged hands on his plaid shirt and happily chowed it down with Femmi.

K: (Half a bread- ! Wait... Half?)

Something struck him as a vivid idea. It was such a good idea that should he pull it off, it could very well mean a new world of possibilities.

K: (Half... If bread can be halved, can Words of Power be halved as well? It should be able to, I think. Maybe I can try that right now?) "Igtana, can I have half of that?"

I: "Are you hungry too?"

K: (It's called a friendship mark for them, so I guess I'd play along.) "No, no, your friendship mark! Can I have half of it?"

I: "This? You don't need half, I can just place it on you-"

K: "Igtana, I... Uhm, this is pretty complicated. What I meant was, I would like the ability to use your friendship mark as well."

Katachi wouldn't know what to do if it failed. Perhaps he would have the boy take on a near-death state, forcing the Word of Power out? Or would he simply kill the boy by accident in the process? What if the child had a higher precedence level than he did? Either way one more Word of Power early on in his journey was bound to be helpful, but had he the heart to deny someone younger than himself the right to live?

I: "Why?"

K: "Because, well, yours looks cooler than mine? Yours has three straight lines and it probably means good fortune or something like that. If it doesn't bother you, can I have it?"

I: "Hah? Oh... Okay then, but is that even possible?"

K: "Is it okay?"

I: "Well, yeah, I guess. I'm okay with it if you can do it."

K: (I've tried 锁定 before, but never 半锁定... Would it work, I wonder?)

Katachi touched the book strapped to his waist with his left hand and focused on Igtana's hand.

K: (半锁定! Lock half within book – 信!)

The 信 on Igtana's right hand faded off on one half, leaving a simple イ behind. Katachi opened the thick book and flipped to where the Word of Power would naturally be – A 言 was found in the page.

K: (Nice! It really did cut into half as I envisioned it... That makes the whole concept possible!)

The resplendent answer to his previous dilemma made the road ahead brighten that much more.

I: "Whoa! Is this... Is this supposed to happen?"

Yet it was folly to believe the solution was universal. To dilute the Word of Power so with two cloud words instead of one, it was a miracle the technique even worked to begin with.

K: "Don't worry, let me see..."

Katachi picked up a small branch on the floor and gently scraped the paper of the book at its very surface. Slowly, the Word of Power filled up the scratched regions and formed a perfect 信.

K: (It works! Segus, I praise thee!) "It works just fine."

I: "Cool! Do it for my side too!"

K: "Hold still now..."

Katachi dabbed the twig into a small puddle of water next to them and drew 言 on Igtana's hand. Naturally, the Word of Power he once held was restored to its former glory.

I: "Cool! My friendship mark's back!"

K: (I wonder if it will dispel the sigil... Well, I only know one term for 信, but I can try. 相信! Trust Igtana – Femmi!)

The Word of Power surfaced on Femmi's forehead and the two children smiled brilliantly.

I: "Wow! You can place the friendship marks too! That's so cool!"

F: "He can? He can! That's amazing!"

But the outcome was more than confusing for Katachi.

K: (What the-... That shouldn't have worked! I- I... I think? Two Words of Power can affect the same object but they cannot affect the same property. Which means the 信 placed on her isn't 'trust'?)

Then, what explained the sigil on Femmi? On one hand, it wasn't as malicious as he believed it to be since she wasn't forced to trust him. Yet it also meant that there was some possibility he missed. On the basis that Igtana harboured absolutely no ill intentions against Femmi only one conclusion made sense.

K: (Maybe it's actually a beneficial trait?)

I: "Hey, can I place yours?"

Katachi recovered from his trance only to face a question he wasn't prepared for. That query sent him soaking in cold sweat.

K: (I didn't think that far! Uhm...) "Well, Igtana... The thing is, it's not possible."

I: "Hah? Why not?"

K: (Maybe, I can explain it to him in a way he could understand?) "Because... Because my friendship mark is like a brush. I can draw other friendship marks, but I can't use the drawing of a brush to draw."

Igtana stared at the 定 on Katachi's left hand for a while.

I: "Cool, so in the end it's just a drawing huh?"

K: "Yeah."

I: "Neat! That's-"

The racket disrupted their conversation and the two children turned their heads towards one of the stalls in public with wide grins on their faces. An old lady hammered a ladle against the soup cauldron and the starved, poor children with ruined rags for clothes ran forth to grab at the charitable foods that were likely facing perishability issues.

F: "Let's go, Igtana! I'm confident that we'll get a couple of bowls this time!"

I: "See you around, super berserker! Nice knowing you!"

They took off quickly, and Femmi was moving in an almost unwomanly fashion. She ran with such recklessness and disregard for safety that it was almost as if...

K: (As if...)

... As if her courage had been forced out of her body, transformed into a destructive, reckless form.

K: (... I seem to recall that 信 has a term related to confidence. Could that be it? But, what is it? I can't recall the symbol at all for some reason.)

He gazed at the children running towards the daily charity event held in Bellpot to feed the homeless with a strange and sullen feeling lurking in his heart.

*** ***

K: (That is incredible. The ability to separate and lock half of a Word of Power into the book opens up so many opportunities.)

Katachi rested beneath a tree in Bellpot, set up his groundsheet and covered himself with a comfortable blanket out at night.

K: ('The symbolism of the Word of Power holds its strength.' Interpreted another way, so long as the symbolism is correct the power will naturally flow and expand. If a mushroom patch was divided into half and left to regrow to the original patch's size, it becomes possible to obtain two mushroom patches much like two copies of the same Word of Power.)

Katachi rested his head against the bag in a snug position.

K: (But whether I can use this to my advantage will be up to me. Still, this is really helpful. I won't have to threaten the lives of those willing to give up their Words of Power!)

Katachi recalled the dilemma this morning after having read the map.

K: (I guess I'll go to Rulid, then Mielfeud after all. I did promise Mother Rin that I would be visiting every so often.)

Katachi gently placed his left hand over the thick book, feeling the ridges of the pages with his middle finger.

K: (The reason Igtana's 信 didn't fade off was because he used Confidence, not Trust. At the very least I now know that 信 can mean either Confidence or Trust, depending on its application. I'll need to keep an eye out for them.)

He stared at the book in his hand. What if his whole journey had been fruitless? What if Katachi's efforts were to be wasted should he be killed along his journey, and the book full of Words of Power hoarded and taken from him? What if others riddled with malice sought the book and used it for their personal means? Would that not defeat the purpose of collecting the Words of Power, expediting the acts of depravity he sought to prevent?

K: (That kid, Igtana... He's a good kid to give Femmi confidence. May the gods grace the blessed child.)

Brooding over it wasn't going to get him anywhere. Katachi needed to survive. He knew that he had to live, to keep the book safe from harm before the destruction of it in proper could take place. The harsh coldness of the night could not permeate Katachi's cover and he dozed off to a light sleep. But, for some reason a restless and pervasive feeling kept him from deep slumber.

He felt that he would come to regret leaving the Word of Power with a vulnerable child instead of killing him outright.

CHAPTER 26

Roberia sat in a relaxed position with her knees tucked towards her chest.

R: (It doesn't sound like a cart, more like... Stilts?)

Her green irises matched the slightly-mouldy rock she was leaning against. Her brilliant red hair was tied into a ponytail behind her and tucked into her shirt so that it would not be grabbed easily. Roberia waited patiently for her next target, her huge sword firmly clasped in her hands.

There was little for merchants and sightseers to stop by for. Rulid was better known as a pit stop, a place to spend the night for travellers who wished to transit between Bellpot and Eliasbury. The mountainous regions in Findel made it hard for people to travel about so the forked roads were necessary for transporting goods safely. One would have to decide between taking a left or right at a specific crossroad from Dermesten, the town next to Yhorfe to reach Eliasbury or Bellpot.

While the direct route from Dermesten to Bellpot was guarded and secure, Rulid was in a difficult spot with forests to a side and the mountain another. Travellers or merchants whom stocked up enough for both Eliasbury and Bellpot would use the Rulid route to avoid congestions or paying tolls. Thus, the goods they harboured would be essential for crossing the winding trail with her diminishing supplies. Roberia waited on that route with that in mind.

*** ***

Katachi stopped in front of a small straw doll left on the roadside. On the out-of-place toy was a rather peculiar marking tagged onto it.

K: (A straw doll... Where did this one come from?)

Katachi couldn't understand the symbol at all. It was simply in a language he could not understand, if that mess of scribbles could be considered a word. Without the knowledge of foreign languages Katachi could only scratch his head at the confusing squiggle.

K: (Some kind of good-luck charm? Best not to worry about it. I still have quite a way to go before I reach Rulid... I should hurry.)

Katachi put the doll to a side of the road and resumed the hike.

*** ***

R: (That's it... Keep walking. Almost there.)

Roberia picked up a small pebble on the ground and poised to toss it over the road to the bush on the other side. She held it between two fingers and her thumb, anchored her foot on the ground firmly while closing an eye to aim her shot with more precision. The loud clacking footsteps slowly and gradually got closer and closer.

R: (Now!)

Roberia sent the pebble zipping across the road but it didn't hit the bush on the other side. Instead, the legs of the traveller intercepted its trajectory.

K: "Ow! What-"

R: (Oh-! That's not good! I didn't think the person was still there!)

*** ***

K: "Ow! What-"

Someone in hiding flung a pebble at his legs. It wasn't a light throw either – The pebble slammed its entirety against Katachi's calf forcefully, sending goose bumps up his legs and right half of his body. Katachi placed his hands on his shin and applied pressure over the injured area to numb the stinging pain. He glanced at the ground only to find a small pebble that wasn't there at first.

K: (What the- A pebble? Who threw this?) "Who's there?"

Katachi turned to look at the huge rock to his right and withdrew his wooden dagger out of instinct.

R: (That voice... A child? Of course he wouldn't have a cart or anything. I attacked a poor, beggar-like traveller... Well, it's better than waiting around pointlessly. I'll take the chance to refine my skills while I'm at it.) "I guess I have days where I misguide my throws."

From behind the rock emerged a red haired lady with a slender figure holding a giant sword in her hands. Her eyes reflected the discipline of a knight, a chevalier of great respect. Her walking stance painted in her a calm warrior prepared to intercept any tricks that may be employed against her.

K: (She looks quite slender, but she has this faintly muscular outline about her at the same time. She concealed herself behind the rock? Maybe she was hoping for a surprise attack, so she was trying to toss the pebble to distract me instead of actually hitting me. A diversion tactic?)

If not for her ominous presence she would simply be viewed as a lady with an average face. The lady walked towards Katachi slowly, paced herself and tightened her grip on the pommel.

R: (Bony and short, tattered clothes and black hair. A battered Ohdean with an unscathed bag. Quite the jarring sight.) "I wonder how much coin you have on you."

With tremendous power she swung the blade down on Katachi hard.

K: (Direct attack when she fails a sneak attack? 恒定! Constant status – Self! Constant status – Dagger!)

A golden 定 formed underneath Katachi's tattered shirt and on the dagger's engraving. Using the dagger Katachi withstood the full impact of the blow with his body.

R: (Blocking it head-on?! That strategy should only be for people who can withstand a blow like this! Is he an esquire or retainer? For some reason, his wooden dagger feels a bit weird, like it's way tougher than it appears to be. Who is this child?) "Are you from Ohde?"

The lady pulled back her sword and distanced herself from Katachi. But the hostility had yet to fade – She held the sword upward, in a hybrid striking and stabbing stance. Katachi stepped back to distance himself, dropped his belongings spare the 1000-page book, raised his arms to cover his vitals and stood in a defensive stance.

He briefly saw the prints on the sandy path beneath his sabots and immediately understood the sheer amount of force from that singular swing. If she were to spear him with the sword despite its rather rounded tip he would be out cold like being hit in the gut with a gigantic hammer.

K: (That strength is inhumane! Is she a knight or a warrior or something?) "... No, I'm from Mielfeud. I'm Findeli."

R: (Findeli? He's from this country?! That's probably a lie to throw me off, isn't it?! I've never seen a Findeli warrior, let alone one that blocks my blow like this! It's more believable if he were from Ohde or Auser no matter how you look at it!) "That can't be right, you have black hair! That's exclusively from Ohde, isn't it?"

K: "I can't tell if I'm really from Ohde or not. All I know is that I grew up in Mielfeud."

R: "In that case, state your name!"

K: (My name? How would knowing my name help anything?... I better say it before she blindly attacks me again out of suspicion.) "Kotsuba Katachi."

His decisive answer was a bit too convincing.

R: (! His eyes didn't waver at all, his shoulders didn't shake. It's either the truth or a severely gambled lie. But it doesn't make sense!) "If you really are from Mielfeud, why is your name of Ohdean descent?!"

K: "How am I supposed to explain that?! I didn't choose my name!"

R: "I won't stand tomfoolery! If you refuse to answer me honestly, then fall by my sword!"

Roberia increased the grip strength on the blade and primed the tip of the great sword at the scrawny child in a purely stabbing stance. With celerity she kicked off the ground and plunged the sword downwards, vaulting over the pole-like sword-

K: "Wha- !?"

-and in turn letting the sword vault over her in an overhead cleave, carrying a momentum far more powerful than her first swing. The possible array of movements granted by the dull edge made her a fearsome foe even among warriors. Yet the boy took it head-on without a flinch. He grated the wooden blade of his tiny dagger against the great sword's blunt fuller, its durability betraying its wooden appearance.

R: (He definitely blinked a bit there, but he blocked it effortlessly. Strange... He can block my attacks head-on without having to move or compromise any excessive strength at all. How is he afraid of taking a hit like that? Is this his way of mocking me?)

Roberia's motivation fuelled from her anger and dignity, and right now both of them were at their highest peak from being physically challenged by the black-haired boy.

R: (So be it then!) "Rraaaarrgh!!"

The lady wound the great sword back slightly, dug her shoes into the sandy path and threw her body's weight with the sword in a twist. She sent a huge horizontal arc swing towards Katachi. Even when the sword's blunt sides was swung, even with the great air resistance similar to swiping a huge fan it was done quickly – Fast enough for the boy to not react in time. The sword's fuller clapped into Katachi's side and he was sent flying and tumbling toward a tree along the roadside.

R: (That should do it- !!)

As though rendering her efforts futile Katachi got back up after a few seconds.

R: "Incredible." (He's still standing even with a force that threw his whole body to a side. Did he jump in time with the swing? I didn't really see his feet move though. A magic of sorts, perhaps?)

K: "Please. I don't want to fight you."

R: "Don't want to fight me?! Have you no honour left in you?!"

Roberia, angered even further by his words, poised herself and vaulted over her sword again before swinging it overhead to cleave him once more. The swing this time was for cleaving so the bladed edge was used instead of the sword's fuller.

R: (His stance is broken! He will not be able to absorb the attack properly even if he manages to block the attack. I doubt he can defend against this swing I've trained years for!)

Katachi unintentionally cushioned and caught the blade with his bare left hand.

R: "!!" (He... Caught my blade?!)

*** ***

K: "Why are you attacking me?!"

The lady withdrew herself and held the sword in a different, lowered position this time – Bending her body down a little, slinging the huge hunk of metal behind her right and holding it with both hands as if to horizontally cut the person in half with the next attack.

K: (Her physique is slender but her attacks are ferocious. Even with Constant Status applied on me I felt its true, hammering impact from the way my sabots dug into the earth. She's not using strength to wield that sword – Rather, she's using the momentum of both her body and the sword to swing it about.)

That explained why she could wield that large cumbersome sword without using much strength. It was an ingenious strategy for saving stamina by utilising more than just her arms to manipulate its position.

K: (But knowing that won't stop her attacks.)

Katachi changed his stance to one that was more assertive. His arms were more relaxed and further apart, his field of vision widened – The stance was more focused and reflexive, one more suitable for intercepting attacks instead of simply blocking and cushioning blows.

R: "HAAAH!!!!"

She struck with the pommel first as Katachi raised his left arm to block it. In response the red-haired lady quickly pulled the weapon back, planted the tip of her great sword into the road and vaulted backwards.

K: (!? She's retreating?)

But this time, her grip wasn't as strong on her sword and her positioning as well as the way she vaulted over changed – Deliberately causing the blunt tip to claw and dig into the path, sliding its bladed portion through the area between Katachi's legs.

With an immense strength that betrayed her slender figure Roberia forcefully lifted the sword off the ground, hoping to throw her opponent off balance at least. Katachi took opportunity of that perfect window. As the sword guard was lowered to ground level, right before she raised the sword pommel to strike his nether regions, he found the break.

K: (固定! Fixate object – Sword!)

Katachi placed a Word of Power on the sword's underside, effectively sealing the sword low on the ground. With that, she would not be able to see the sigil and decipher its limitations.

R: (-!! My sword's suddenly way heavier than it should be!? What the- What just happened? What did he do?!)

K: "I'll take my leave."

R: "Wait, you- !?"

Before she could even look up to get a good view of Katachi, he had long snagged his belongings and sprinted off quickly, his wooden sabots clacking loudly as he ran away.

*** ***

Twenty minutes elapsed since Roberia fruitlessly attempted to move the sword.

R: "Curses! Forget it!"

Roberia kicked her comfortable boots against the sword's grip and placed her knuckles on her hips in frustration.

R: (Today's attack is an utter failure. Instead of earning more coin I'm stuck with this unmoving sword! Did he curse my sword or something? I've never heard of a spell that freezes a sword in place like this.)

She had been shockingly close to the answer despite her ignorance – There was indeed a Curse Word applied onto the sword which secured it in place.

R: (Maybe I'm looking at it wrongly. He could be using magic that requires the sword to be at a certain height or position. Assuming that he somehow made the sword heavy to the point where it can't be moved... I'll need a new weapon that renders the magic ineffective. Getting one that can use the increased weight against him would be preferable.)

She turned around and picked up the deflated knapsack she hid under a heap of rocks.

R: (To think that I would lose my weapon this early even when I've maintained it so well... How exciting. I have never fought someone the likes of him. At the very least, I now have a target to work towards rather than wandering about and fighting random strangers.)

Roberia stormed off toward Rulid in pursuit of the black-haired boy who wanted little to do with her.

CHAPTER 27

Katachi narrowly escaped a rather dangerous encounter. A few hours ago he had been struck in the shin by a pebble and a red-haired lady who appeared about sixteen swung a large, heavy sword at him. It gave Katachi a severe affliction of paranoia.

K: (What... What in the good woods was that? I could have sworn she wanted me dead with those crazy attacks of hers. Has word of me collecting the Words of Power spread out this quickly that people are hiring bandits and marauders to attack me now?! I don't even look rich to begin with! Why else would anyone attack a child wearing such worn-down clothes and noisy sabots!?)

Katachi continued his slow cautious walk towards Rulid with a great sense of insecurity in his mind. He couldn't help but peek and glance furtively the whole time he remained on the winding trail.

*** ***

Rulid was a small town about three quarters of an acre with some mountainous regions about so most of the houses were hillside terraces surrounded by pines, canes and many ornamental plants. It was a town ideal for the seniors and the considerably aged to purchase retirement homes.

K: (They look like they're ready to welcome spring. It's the Month of the Axe already and most of the snow melted mid-Halberd.)

Though they bear great beauty, the plants were mostly cosmetic in nature and scarcely profitable. So it was unfortunate that only small trades came by a rarely visited town like Rulid. Katachi slowly clacked his noisy sabots on the stone path and came upon a grocer that sold pickled vegetables and some caged birds.

"Hello, little boy. What would you like today?"

The old lady behind the stand peered through the sagging flesh on her face and earnestly looked at the boy.

K: (They have corn already? Must be the work of a magus. What spell is that, though? It seems really useful.)

Katachi chose a brine-covered corn cob that was slightly smaller than the others, dropped three pieces of copper and prompted a question.

K: (Seeing how she's a grocer she might know quite a bit about the town's happenings and events. Even if it's hearsay, the slightest peep of a Word of Power is more than enough.) "Have you heard any interesting rumours about town?"

The old lady smiled slightly, but her limp cheeks made that almost unnoticeable.

"Oh no, no rumours for me, young man. I'm too old for it. Far too old."

K: (Nothing, huh.) "It's okay, thank you. I'll ask around elsewhere."

Katachi thanked her and headed deeper into the town.

*** ***

K: (From what I can gather, the town is quiet. There's nothing major going on and there's little I can do here except rest for the night. Though... I do get a rather creepy feeling somewhere.)

Katachi took out the rope from his bag and began tying it between two trees. He was worried that mildew might gather on the new clothes so he used the rope as a makeshift clothes line to air them briefly. He also attached his wooden sabots onto a wooden hook he made along his journey and dangled the pair on the rope. When the sabots were secured properly, he withdrew the ear of corn he bought and started peeling off the silk on the cob.

K: (These string things are a little hard to pluck... Maybe I can use the Word of Power to make my job easier. 解除! Remove exteriors – Corn!)

A dry whisper echoed in the back of his head as a golden 解 was placed onto the cob. The silk peeled off cleanly as expected and fell to the ground. However, the kernels attached to the brined corn also began falling out and what remained on his hand was the bare cob. The expunging was almost instantaneous so he couldn't stop the process in time.

K: "Ahh! The corn!..."

Corn kernels of three copper's worth lay on the ground.

K: (I'll need to clean them now. It's a pity the brine is going to get washed off.)

Beggars can't be choosers. Katachi picked up the small pieces of corn kernels with delicacy, cupped them in his hands and placed them onto a stone counter left outside one of the terrace houses. He withdrew the pebble with Urdythari's rune engraved onto it and recited the tale.

K: "An unending stream flowed."

The pebble became damp and water started to form on its pores. He washed the kernels briefly and dribbled the water from the pebble gently into his mouth. It wasn't as though he could actually quench his thirst with the illusory water, but it was enough to get by for the moment.

K: (I can't exactly stop here to do jobs for coin since there is no reason worthy of spending a while in this town. Expenditure on meals should be controlled... I'll have to get my own food the usual way.)

Katachi surveyed about and saw only Melkwood pines and Sugarpelt canes around the town. He couldn't find any fruit-bearing trees anywhere, and was starting to get a bit nervous. So the child began walking around town in search of anything that resembled edible food. Just as he turned the corner of a terrace house, the vibrant green and orange patch in the corner of his eyes caught his attention immediately.

K: (An orange? I've never seen one in real life before. Quite literal to the name, I see. As far as I know those take about a decade to mature and bear fully ripened fruits. It's probably going to be very sour but it's better than nothing.)

Katachi walked toward the orange tree and rested his foot against the soft, smooth bark. One bare foot upon its trunk and anyone could tell the significant difference from most trees with a coarse blistering bark – This was the bark of a tree none would be able to afford as a form of commerce because of its ridiculous ripening time.

He slowly extended his arms and grabbed at the branches. It took him some effort before he reached the fruits of the tree given his size, but he did it after a risky leap. Katachi plucked one off and sat on the branch of the tree to relax himself for the meal. He dug his thumbs into the soft, fragrant skin of the fruit. As he pried apart its smooth skin a sweet fragrance entered his nose and he saw the mysterious insides of the orange for the first time in his life.

It seemed as though the fruit's flesh had been divided into eight separate segments that detached individually into bite-sized chunks. It was a big change from sweet fruits like the papayas or mangoes with their wholesome fleshed-out insides he used to eat. The fruit had a tangy taste to it – A sweetness tinged with a hint of sour flooded his entire mouth and the fragrance of the juices seeped into his nostrils more concentrated than ever.

It took a single slice to have him nod his head in solid approval of the fruit's wondrous taste and thirst-quenching capabilities. He chewed on the delicious fruit for a couple of minutes, completely indulged in the exotic taste.

K: (This... This is an orange? It feels like a mellow mango mixed with a bit of lemon, but it's so good! I can't believe an orange actually tastes this great! I was expecting an overwhelming vinegary taste since the book often says that it is sour when it isn't ripe, but this only bars a hint of sour!)

He stopped himself when he derived at a startling answer.

K: (Wait, then... Are these oranges fully ripe?!)

Katachi tensed up in reflex.

K: (For at least ten years counting the maturity rate and the ripening process this tree has probably been tended to frequently. Taking the unripe oranges to eat is one thing, but this... I feel kind-of bad for taking the hard work and efforts of the person who planted this tree.)

He glanced around the tree and saw an abandoned, demolished house behind the thicket of leaves.

K: (The house is abandoned... There seems to be quite a bit of neglect for this house since I can see some cobwebs on the windows, but... Finding the fruit outside of an abandoned house does not pardon me from the sin of theft. To the owner of the orange tree, forgive me. I was unaware of my wrongdoings.)

Katachi leapt down, securely wrapping his forearm around the skin and slices while walking back to the stone counter where the corn kernels lay.

K: (It's still a waste leaving the orange behind though, since I already plucked it – Might as well eat the rest of this.)

*** ***

Roberia arrived at Rulid just as the sun cut into the horizon. It would normally be nightfall by the time she reached. But, Roberia lost her sword to a peculiar curse which comprised the majority of her luggage. She jogged her way back at a pace much faster than the hike out.

R: (I didn't think I'd make it. That's great.)

She set the leather strap of the flattened bag down and reached her hands out toward a tree, scaling up its side quickly. She sat down on a sturdy branch, plucked an orange from the tree, broke its skin and slowly enjoyed the flesh within. When the flesh was gone she tore a piece of orange skin and tossed it into her mouth.

R: (Good to the last bit. I should head to the blacksmith for another weapon, and then rest for today. I feel sleepier than usual.)

She thought about her lodging for the night, but there was only the run-down and miserable excuse of an inn located at the south of Rulid. The occasional traveller or official would visit the town from time to time, and even they chose the house of their relatives. With limited feedback from their patrons, the accommodation at the inn was subpar at best.

R: (I guess this will do. There's an abandoned house I can sleep in.)

Roberia landed on the soft ground with a thud and walked towards the blacksmith's house.

*** ***

Katachi originally planned to sleep on a bench outside a watering hole.

K: (The rumble of thunder?)

But as the sun set more and more the dark clouds above seemed to impose upon Katachi, almost taunting him.

K: (It's about to rain. I have to look for shelter... But I have no intentions of spending coin so liberally. Where should I go?)

Somewhere in the deep recesses of his mind, a familiar location surfaced; the abandoned house at where the orange tree was.

K: (There's an abandoned house near that orange tree. It's okay if there's a lot of dust and dirt, but I'm more worried about spiders crawling on me in my sleep... I guess I can use the groundsheet to cover my body for protection, and use the blanket only when the night becomes too cold and harsh.)

Katachi kept his clothes line and packed his stuff before the rain and storm could claim them.

*** ***

R: "Yes, just like that. Just attach these onto an existing one with a slightly more durable handle, please."

"Okay. It's just cutting and welding so it should be ready in a few hours. Why don't you come and pick it up tomorrow morning, little missy?"

R: "That would be great. Thank you."

Roberia left the blacksmith's abode and walked towards the old, abandoned house.

R: (That child is probably sleeping inside the inn... That may be the reason why I haven't seen him yet. But now, it's far too dark for me to see even my own hands clearly. I'll worry about his route tomorrow.)

A rumble echoed and the dim moonlight obfuscated by rolling clouds impaired her vision. Roberia hurried into the abandoned house.

R: (It's raining soon... That makes the night air harsher, but it gives away any thieves that may come in the middle of the night. It's not primarily a bad thing.)

Roberia dropped her belongings, walked to a corner of the room farther away from the windows and lied down. She curled up to preserve what little warmth was available in her body.

R: (The ground is more comfortable than I thought... Or maybe that's just me.)

Roberia rested quietly on the floor and slept the night away.

*** ***

R: "Mmmhh..."

Roberia slowly opened her eyes to the cries of the birds outside the abandoned house. And to her shock, before her was the serene face of Katachi sleeping peacefully right beside her. She gasped and retracted her head a little.

R: (No, wait! I shouldn't make any noise at all. I don't want to wake him up.)

She slowly rolled off the groundsheet and backed away from Katachi. However...

R: (He's beneath the groundsheet? I... I slept on his groundsheet. So he didn't make any moves on me?)

Roberia shook her head a little bit to energize and compose herself.

R: (The storm last night made the room so dark I didn't even see him right there. Not noticing him was actually my mistake. I actually thought he was enjoying himself at the inn when his situation is not that far off from mine... At least I've established the fact that he is poor to the point that he sleeps out here.)

She picked her stuff up and slowly made her way towards the doorway, looking back at Katachi once more before leaving.

R: (He's not a rich target. But he's definitely strong – A foe trickier than most I've met thus far. That's more important than simply attacking the rich for resources just to survive.)

Her resolve was not one to wane so easily.

R: (If I can beat him, that shows my physical and mental growth. This victory would surely serve me well to prove Rugnud's might to other countries. But I should retrieve the weapon first.)

CHAPTER 28

As he fastened a strip of fabric over the cloth, a red string lay mangled on the groundsheet.

K: (There's a strand of red hair on this?)

Katachi didn't seem to understand how the strand of red hair got onto his sheet. Had he been awake fifteen minutes ago, he would have caught sight of the girl's sleeping face on the groundsheet he was under.

K: (Did this get here somewhere from the scuffle yesterday? That can't be. Maybe it belongs to the people who made the groundsheet?)

If only he knew that the lady he fought yesterday spent the night right next to him, the misunderstandings to come would not be as awkward.

K: (It doesn't really matter. Time is wasting away, I ought to start out soon.)

Katachi placed the rolled sheet above his bag and strapped it on firmly.

*** ***

Before venturing out, however, Katachi climbed the orange tree once more. He reached for a smaller orange on the branch, plucked the fruit and cupped it in his hands.

K: (恒定! Constant status – Orange!)

Katachi placed the delicate fruit into his pocket, though why he chose to be careful with it despite the sigil's presence was a mystery. A little rough handling did little against an orange meant to remain constant and resist change.

K: (I know it's bad of me to take another when I've already had one, but I'm going to give this to Mother Rin when I get there. It's not for me so I really hope the owner of this tree wouldn't mind too much.)

Katachi made his way to the north east of Rulid facing Mielfeud. But, just to be sure he's walking in the right direction he approached a sentry.

K: "Excuse me, which way is it to Mielfeud?"

"Oh, that way. Walk straight along the path and the road over yonder splits. The left leads to Fereport, so take the right to reach Mielfeud."

K: "Thanks."

Katachi's wooden sabots clacked loudly against the sandy path and he hoisted his bag under his arm.

K: (Go down this road, and don't take the left...)

He glanced at the road ahead briefly to gauge how much distance he had to cover. But, as he tiptoed on his sabots to view the road over the horizon, a metallic sound of something being dragged along by chains could be heard. Katachi spun around to see a lady running and swinging the grey blur at him without warning.

K: (!! I have to dodge!)

Katachi leaned backwards and pressed his hands against the ground before rolling away further in the direction away from the attacker. A crunching, clashing sound was heard and he quaked to think that his head would have been on the receiving end of that strike. As he looked up, the slender lady with a ponytail entered his vision. She was holding something new this time; to be specific, it was a flail with a long handle and three weights tethered onto it.

K: "!! It's you again!"

*** ***

Roberia wasn't concerned with greeting him back.

R: "Haaah!"

She did not bother with his unfocused rambling and mauled the flail at him hard. The balls of steel attached to the chains swung through the air and Katachi evaded the attack by a few inches. He sprawled his body out and withdrew that peculiar wooden dagger once more.

K: (I can't fight like this...)

Katachi stood hesitant with his body leaned backwards, indicating his choice of flight as opposed to the stance he adopted yesterday. He seriously did not want to fight her as things stood – But Roberia didn't take heed at all. On the contrary, she became a lot more aggressive than before, now that she wielded a weapon she could freely manipulate without having to use her whole body to control it.

She proceeded to draw out ferocious attacks that would maim him on his limbs, forcing Katachi towards the trees by the roadside. She tried pressuring him to a restrictive place where he had no freedom to run and no choice but to fight back. As expected, he was cornered easily since he was rendered incapable of any offensive action.

K: (Gh! I can't risk her damaging any of my stuff! I need to find an opportunity to get away from her and put the bag down!)

Roberia mercilessly brandished the flail about, disregarding her opponent's handicap completely. The tethered weights made full revolutions around its handle and crashed against the trunks of the trees with no signs of restraint.

K: (I-! Can't-! Find an opening! 固定! Fixate object – Weight!)

A hoarse whisper rang in the back of his head and a 定 formed on one of the metal eggs. Roberia suddenly felt the limitations of her weapon as the chain between the handle and the fixated weight was stretched to its maximum allowed length.

R: "! What the-!" (The weight is fixed in mid-air?! Wait a minute, it's just as immovable as my sword! Then- !!)

Katachi took advantage of the confusion to leap back and placed his bag down gently. With the dagger in hand he stood firm and finally prepared to retaliate.

K: (恒定! Constant status – Self! Constant status – Dagger!)

定 formed on his chest and the dagger's blade. With the shade of the trees blocking out the sunlight above Roberia could finally see the Word of Power on the dagger properly for the first time.

R: (It's not a hex on my sword that made it too heavy to move. He sealed my weapon in that space, that position, so it won't be able to move! And that Word... I recognize that magic anywhere!!) "That's a Word of Power!"

K: (What... What did she mean? Did she not attack me because I had the Word of Power in the first place?) "Who are you? Who sent you?"

Katachi failed to recognize that she was buried in deep thought.

R: (This is great. Excellent! Defeating him and getting his Word of Power for my own is worthy of securing Rugnud's strength!) "Looks like my choice of targets isn't as bad as I thought!"

Roberia fished out something he did not expect – A tough pair of shears sashed on her back. She wedged the chain close to the fixated weight between the scissor blades and snipped it off cleanly with the flattened clamp base.

K: "!!" (She snipped it off... That is going to be problematic. If the weapon can be broken down and segmented like that, then stopping it won't be as easy as I thought.)

With a combat craze yet unseen Roberia swiped the weapon at Katachi once more.

*** ***

R: (As expected of a Scholar... He's real tough!)

The lady repeatedly whipped him with no intent on letting up. Yet, neither did he flinch from the pain nor stagger from the blows. It was as though he was one of those wooden dummies that Anikans used to practice their techniques on.

R: (It figures that I can't get him to crack easily. I have to target something important to him. I need to force a fight out of him if I want a chance at his Word of Power!)

Roberia continually swung the flail at regions where it would hurt badly – At the waist, at the neck and larynx, the calf muscles and even at the genitals, but Katachi may as well be part of the unmoving background. She relented on her flurry of attacks for a while and backed off to reconsider her strategy.

R: (Come to think of it, he didn't defend like this when he had his stuff on. Maybe there's something important in his belongings? Would he start attacking me actively if I aimed for his stuff, then?)

Roberia threw glances briefly at his bag and Katachi, for some reason, reacted to that by shifting between her and the bag.

R: (! Oh? So his bag is valuable to him.) "What's so important in the bag that you have to guard it so strictly?"

K: "... It was given to me for free."

The answer was so out-of-place that Roberia couldn't help but cringe a little.

R: (What? 'Given to him for free' is a reason to protect it? That's so cheap! What a miser!) "Really? That's the reason you'd place yourself between me and that?"

K: "Yes. I also have a gift to deliver, so I cannot let any harm come to it."

R: (Maybe it's fragile.) "Hoho, a gift! That's more like it. What could be so valuable that you have to protect it like this?"

Roberia stormed forward, swinging the flail in circles and warming up for a powerful swing carried by momentum. She changed her stride suddenly and rushed at the bag, swinging the flail down at it. Katachi had to sacrifice his left arm in response and snagged the flail onto his wrist to stop the attack.

R: "It wouldn't happen to be something you bought in town like flasks of dried goods, would it?"

She pulled back and the two locked eyes with each other fiercely.

R: (I had thought of him a poor bloke, but if he's simply the miserly and stingy type to put value above all else then I don't feel as bad for attacking him!)

K: (I can't have her ruining the free stuff blessed to me by their goodwill. I should just end this quickly. 固定! Fixate object – Weight!)

The remaining two weights on the flail were fixated in the air, but Roberia simply snipped them off again. Two weights now floated next to her and the third metal egg to Katachi's far left.

R: "I figured you would use that technique again. Did you think I wouldn't expect this outcome?" (I didn't expect this outcome at all... But this is good too. It gives my weapon speed which seems to fare better than power.)

But if it irked her opponent to disarray, it was an acceptable strategy regardless.

R: "You played right into my trap."

K: (So this is her trap... It was one thing with the weights that slowed down when she whacked me, but her chains can swivel so quickly that I cannot place my 定 on any of the segments. It's all a blur and I can't imagine the 定 on the chain clearly enough.)

Roberia began spinning the three loose chains at very high speeds. It was not synchronized at first, but she spun it so rapidly that the three chains united into a whip-like fashion. She ran towards Katachi and whacked him clean in the head, the chains wrapping around his neck from the momentum. She grabbed at the chains with her free hand and pulled at it from separate ends.

R: (I'll choke him out if I have to!) "I got you!- ... !!"

But Katachi grabbed the handle of the flail with his left hand while ignoring the attack altogether and plunged the wooden dagger at her face, forcing the warrior to step back. When he unhanded the weapon to retreat a 定 was engraved on the handle.

K: "No more. Please."

He then pulled the chains off his neck, kept his dagger, turned around to pick his stuff up and continued on his way-

R: "Don't turn your back on an opponent, you miserable skinflint!"

-and Roberia revealed a hidden steel dagger behind her, jabbing it into his back. Or so she envisioned, but the simple knife skidded off his body like stabbing a brick wall with a twig.

K: "Please go away. I really don't want to fight you."

That plea fell upon deaf ears. Roberia continued to violently swipe her blade at Katachi, but as he side-stepped to avoid a lunge...

R: "! Guh!"

K: "!!"

... Roberia accidentally brushed her side against a sharp branch. She clutched her gut in agony and a shiny, sticky red liquid as brilliant as her hair glimmered on her hand.

K: "By the gods... Lie down!"

R: "Aahhh..."

It was only in moments such as these that the boy took a proactive role.

K: "Lie down, and don't move!"

Katachi ran towards his bag and returned with a corked bottle.

R: "I... You're smaller than me... I should have... Seen that branch..."

K: (What kind of nonsense is she spewing?! Injured people shouldn't exert themselves!) "Stop talking! Don't worsen the wound any further!"

He removed the wooden cork and rubbed the ointment-like substance against the gashing wound. It was not much, but he did the best he could to ease her pain and stimulate the recovery. When he was done applying his salve on the wound Katachi laid her body completely flat and cast a Word of Power on her.

K: (固定! Fixate position – Red-haired girl!)

Roberia's body stopped moving completely and she remained stiff as a board. He tied two straps of fabric to a long branch, bound her limbs with much care and rotated the makeshift stretcher so she would face the sky with her back against the branch. He dragged the rotting plant matter back to Rulid carefully while holding her under the arms.

"Wha- Hey, what happened to her?"

K: "She needs treatment! Her waist got stabbed by a branch! Please tend to her immediately!"

"Understood! Leave it to us."

*** ***

Katachi rested Roberia on the cold floor of the abandoned house which he- Or rather, they spent the night in.

K: (She will get better in a couple of days. Looks like I'm going to spend another day in Rulid after all... I have to ensure she's fine before I go. I also need to stock up on Mestiel now.)

Mestiel comprised a major component of the ointment he made along with some Curamel and Dolosseia to sterilize and sedate the wound. If he were to prepare more of the ointment the healing agent was imperative. It was unfortunate that Mestiel was uncommon around the Month of the Halberd as it was harvested in the Month of the Reeds, but with any amount of luck he would find some. Katachi spread his groundsheet on the floor and laid Roberia on it gently.

K: (She received proper treatment from the sentry, so everything should be okay now.)

Katachi couldn't help but blush and redden at the slender waist while the sentry patched her up. The strange and almost elegant red mail beneath her shirt had to be removed so her injury could be tended to. As such, it was natural for him to shy away upon the sight of Roberia's navel.

K: (At least the sentries didn't violate her body or anything... !! What was I thinking!? Mother will punish me for this!)

Katachi rid his head of the embarrassing emotions and walked out of the abandoned house's awkward atmosphere he conjured in his own mind. He took out the bottle of healing salve and swivelled the fluid within a little to measure how much he had left.

K: (I should have a look around town, hopefully there'll be an apothecary here. But Mestiel won't be cheap this time of the year... I should consider my options carefully.)

Katachi headed towards the south of Rulid with high hopes of finding what he needed.

CHAPTER 29

If only it were truly that simple to locate the herbs.

K: (This much should have been expected... The majority here are elderly too, so the demand for medicine is much lower than towns with healthier folk.)

Katachi's head drooped a little as he walked back towards the orange tree. Earlier that morning, he thoroughly scoured the south end of Rulid in search of Mestiel in the district. However, Rulid was a small town with minimal forms of prospering commerce, therefore the chances of an open apothecary was marginal to begin with. As a result he ended up wasting most of his time searching around pointlessly.

K: (I'm hungry, I'm tired, my dry rations are running out and the medicine shortage's dog-piling on... Good grief, I got this disoriented over a lady whose name I don't even know. What am I doing with my precious time? At least my shirt isn't that dirty because I rolled backwards with the bag strapped on so I can wear this for a few more days. As for the bag, dusting the sand off should suffice... ?)

The abandoned house was vacated. He wasn't expecting the slender lady's absence, certainly not when she was unwell. His groundsheet and bag were still laying in the corner. However, her belongings were still inside the house, which suggested that she would return. But that was only true if she was not the ditzy type to forget her own luggage.

K: (She's not here? If she's already awake and able to walk away then she should be capable of handling herself. Maybe she's the type to recover fast like that- Oh no. Oh dear me. That's not good at all.)

Katachi carefully walked towards his bag and took out a wooden hook along with a net of sorts.

*** ***

Roberia leaned against a bench in central Rulid with her left hand pressing against the wound on her side. Her headstrong personality would not allow the numbing pain to hinder her pride, certainly not when she was imposing on him with her presence. As she struggled away she continuously held nothing but spite towards the child.

R: (Being saved by the likes of him... This goes far beyond damaging my pride. He doesn't even see me as a threat. What kind of powerful leader am I supposed to be if I can't make a fearful impact on my enemies?)

Her bandage was coming apart but she pressed against it with her forearm to keep it in place.

R: (I don't want to rely upon that kind of power Father's using to protect Rugnud. Using magic to enhance the physical self does not befit the image Rugnud should bear. Luck will run out just as the gold in mines, the water in wells and the trees in a forest.)

She slowly made her way into the old blacksmith's shop.

R: (I have to become stronger.)

The wooden chime at the top of the door clacked together melodiously as the door was opened.

"Hello again miss, how'd you like the flail?"

Roberia's eyes darted off to a side in disappointment. She didn't want to disappoint the blacksmith by saying his craft failed to perform ideally in the situation, but she could use his valuable consultation.

R: "It's a nice weapon. I really like it, you see, but I need something with more power and weight to it."

"You certainly don't sound pleased. Is there something wrong?"

R: "I thought the enemy was using a magic that increased the weight of my weapon, which would make the flail that much deadlier. But it turns out that the magus used a magic that can lock a weapon in place, making it completely immovable."

"I see. And what would you like, then?"

R: "I want a weapon with many separable parts. Ideally it should be one with a good weight that can render that magic useless at the same time, the kind that can break down and chip off bit by bit, so even if he tries to seal the weapon I can simply remove the immobile part from the body."

"A weapon that chips off deliberately, hmm? It sounds a little tricky, but I'll give it a shot. Give me a day or so and I'll see what I can fix up for you."

R: "Here's payment."

Roberia emptied the pouch of gold onto the table top. What fell out easily dwarfed gold pieces or ores of silver that most merchants held – Fifteen rare, high-grade Regal coins manufactured a long time ago, back when Rugnud barely started thriving on ores and minerals. Those precious coins, with only 1307 of them left intact, was supposed to be a form of saving grace should the situation turn too bleak to resolve with one's might alone. Each individual coin held immense value both in the historical and monetary sense.

"Whoa-ho-ho! That's way too much even for the weapon, miss!"

R: "Keep it. Consider it as a form of gratitude for your immeasurable service."

"In that case, I shall accept only five. Times are hard enough, miss. Just a few of these Adamantiff and Brusetellian coins like these can grace my grandchildren with unbound wealth. Besides, there's only so much I can do with the minimal ores I have anyway."

R: "I understand."

Roberia picked up the coins and dropped them back into the pouch.

"Good luck defeating that magus, Your Highness."

The blacksmith winked at her as he prepared the furnace. The coins may as well be a dead give-away to her actual identity. Roberia exited the house of Pybuit, the retired blacksmith who once held the title of Rugnud's Pride.

*** ***

Katachi laid out his items over the floor and began sorting out his inventory.

K: (First things first, let's clear the bag of anything that might be trapped within.)

He turned the bag upside down and a few grains of sand and dust fell from the bag with a 'puff' sound. To his relief nothing else was inside. There was no need to fear or worry about injuring or killing anything by accident.

K: (Good. Right then, clothes in first, the new shoes next and then the pebble inside the shoe. The water pouches are clean so I can stuff them inside as well. After that, the rope- ?)

A rustling came from outside the house. Katachi turned his head and greeted the red-haired girl with a brief wave of his hand. To his chagrin she clicked her tongue and snapped at him.

R: "... Tch. You're here?"

K: (The first sight of me and she's already aggressive?) "You could at least thank me for letting you use the groundsheet."

For some reason, Katachi didn't feel shy at all when talking to her compared to Bael – But looking back, her monstrous strength probably blew away the illusion of a delicate woman in his eyes. It was apparent that he tried to reason with her by treating her as an equal.

R: "... Thank you for the- ! Where's my bag?"

K: "Oh, that? I hung it on the wall there."

Katachi stuck out his thumb and pointed at the general direction behind him. Her belongings were dangling upon a thin net latched onto a hook wedged in a crack running along the wall.

K: "There were ants about the floor and you probably wouldn't like them crawling about, so I kept it off the ground."

R: (He touched my stuff!? It's a good thing that I kept the regal coins with me.) "Gh..."

K: "They crawled into mine too. I had to flap out every shirt to make sure they weren't in them because I went to hang your bag first-"

R: "Don't touch my bag."

Katachi's eyes widened at the cold, monotonous and malicious response.

R: (He's strangely bubbly today. Why would he care if ants went into my bag?)

K: (She seems really unhappy. Her bag must be precious to her as well. I need to restrain myself.) "... Sorry."

Katachi had gotten overexcited for a moment there over having small talk with someone in two weeks – So much that he was actually getting friendly with her and neglecting the danger that came with her presence. Though, for those who knew better that exchange between them could scarcely be called a proper conversation.

R: (Now that I think about it, I don't know how he's holding out. He's trying to save resources for his family but I don't know if he's starving himself for them. It's not ethical to pick on him when he's struggling, and I'm being bothersome wasting his time and resource. To exhaust and starve an enemy before beating them is cowardly.) "... Hey."

K: "Yes?"

R: (His head's turning naturally. He's not even the slightest bit wary of me? That is somewhat vexing.) "Have you any food?"

K: "No, I was about to go get something once I repack everything here."

R: (So he'll be fine, huh? Good.) "I see."

Roberia walked towards her bag and placed the pouch dangling on her side into the bag. She undid the net, saddled the knapsack on her back and walked out of the house.

*** ***

It was truly a strange sight to see a child apologise so earnestly to a tree. Katachi picked yet another orange to eat.

K: "I am sorry. I am truly, truly sorry. I've searched for alternate sources of food as much as I could but nothing else turned up. Please bear with me."

Apologies lost effectiveness the more they were used, but it was all he could give. He quietly uttered his prayers and indulged in the round fruit once more.

*** ***

Roberia went to a watering hole and ordered some food and ale.

R: (He didn't even tense up in fear of me being there. Am I not terrifying in his eyes? Am I just a bully who picks on the slow and gullible, foolish enough to believe that I am worthy of ruling Rugnud simply by being the strongest among the weak?)

Yet the child, if anything, showed her a world beyond.

R: (But I can't blame him for this misfortune. He's put into perspective the possible trials I will have to face from here on, and this won't be the only time I'm stumped. I should take this chance to plan my next steps carefully.)

Roberia gulped and chugged the ale down to wash away her sorrows.

*** ***

As the two carried out their activities for the day, twilight had long since faded. After an arduous day of fruitless searching, inventory reorganization and scavenging, Katachi tucked himself under the groundsheet once again and made sure his arms and legs were snugly fit and warm.

Before he could fall into light slumber something was heard outside the abandoned house. Someone was coughing and in suffocating pain. Katachi looked out through the door and saw a silhouette of someone with familiar hair vomiting on the orange tree roots.

K: (Is it food poisoning?!) "! Wha- Where have you been?"

R: "I could have another mug, and another!"

She gagged and puked once again on the previously vomited patch of grass next to the orange tree.

K: (She's been out drinking?) "Segus bless you..."

Katachi held her by her biceps and dragged her into the house. Of course, this was not without resistance.

R: "Another round, another round! I want to drink!!"

Roberia struggled and twisted about in her unsightly stupor. The act made Katachi's attempt to help her significantly harder considering his size.

K: "Just... Come inside first, please!" (Good lord, her breath smells like ale! How much did she down?!)

He laid her across the groundsheet and checked her face for pain.

K: (Her face is red probably from drinking, other than that she looks fine. Her temperature's a bit high... An orange should help.) "Wait for me, I'll get an orange."

Katachi picked a fourth orange from the tree outside and peeled it carefully before placing a slice into her mouth.

R: "Nnngh... I don't want any..."

Katachi made sure she chewed the flesh and swallowed, took another slice-

R: "I said, I don't want any!"

Roberia smacked the orange out of his hands in annoyance. It was slight and subtle, but he heard Roberia's stomach growl just seconds after – She vomited out her food before it even got a chance to digest so she must have been hungry even when she insisted otherwise.

R: "Don't give me fruits soaked in ale! Pass me a barrel instead!"

Roberia clutched her stomach with her forearms to suppress the growl. Her persistence to drink was appalling to the young boy.

K: "Don't be so stubborn. You're hungry. Even if you don't like me, you should at least take care of yourself. Your body will weaken if you avoid proper meals."

Roberia groaned a bit out of discomfort. Katachi laid her flat onto the plain ground and picked up the orange that rolled off.

R: "Shut up... I can't... I can't afford to be weak..."

The slender girl continued her protest until she passed out from the pent-up lethargy. Katachi rested her head on his lap and fed her orange slices one by one. The alcohol fumes coming from her mouth were unbearable, but she finally ate five slices of orange before Katachi left to fetch his blanket for her.

K: (Can't afford to be weak? She probably has it tough. Maybe she has a family to feed, being the eldest of her siblings or something. I'm just a solitary traveller on a pilgrimage hunting the Words of Power, while a farmer's daughter has to become strong enough to protect her family from harm.)

There was something truly admirable about her indomitable spirit.

K: (I'm simply doing it for my own selfish reason, whereas she has probably been forced into this out of survival. May the gods guide her in her journey... And may the gods grant me the strength to help the unborn avert these cruel fates.)

Katachi carried her in his arms with much effort and gently placed her atop the groundsheet, trying his best not to stagger. The blanket was then pulled over her gently, forming a proper setup for her to rest her weary body.

K: "Good night. Segus bless you."

Katachi bid the red-haired lady a good night's rest without expecting a response.

*** ***

K: (... I can't sleep.)

He tossed about and turned to look at Roberia's peaceful sleeping face devoid of her inexplicable hatred.

K: (I really can't sleep with her here. I feel so... So uncomfortable, knowing that someone's next to me in this room. I really want to leave now, but she has my blanket and groundsheet...)

It wasn't much of a surprise – Katachi was not accustomed to sleeping around strangers. Naturally, this was a new experience for him which he was completely unprepared for. And so Katachi hesitantly hugged his bag for the whole night with his eyes wide open.

CHAPTER 30

P: "Here you go, little missy."

Pybuit presented the object covered in a sheet to the girl.

R: "What's with the cloth?"

It was a surprisingly large object, about 1.7m in length. It was shaped similar to a long keg barrel with a hollow shaft that could fill multiple beer mugs at once, a broad and cylindrical blade accompanied by a thick grip. At least, if the cane-looking object could be considered a blade.

P: "What do ya think?"

R: "What is that?"

The blacksmith pulled the draped cloth backwards and revealed a baffling marvel – A huge sword. Or, from its appearance of a crumbling pillar solidly bound together...

R: "You can't be serious. This is a weapon?"

... It looked like a stone pillar with a stick for a handle.

P: "Don't be shy now, try it out!"

It had been a while since Roberia was injured by a branch stabbing through her side. She inconvenienced her target by using his groundsheet to rest for three days in a row, and even had a comfortable blanket for the most recent night. The humiliation was too much for her to bear and she quietly slipped away while Katachi was asleep.

She did not realize that the child was awake the whole night resting his strained eyes and weary legs due to her presence in the room. Katachi wasn't the type of person to sleep soundly knowing there were others around, his natural distrust given form after receiving innumerable scars. When she left, he packed his belongings and quickly headed off on his journey.

R: "This... How is this thing supposed to help me fight against the magus? It looks ridiculous! It looks like it's in shambles! How heavy is it anyway?" (It looks so stupid. Is this really the work of Rugnud's Pride?)

P: "Little missy, I wouldn't underestimate this weapon. It's been tailored to your needs so you could at least give it a shot. You'd be delighted at what it's capable of."

Pybuit turned his back to Roberia and continued tending to the whetstone and shears.

R: (I can't believe tying a weird and cracked column to a rod can even be called a weapon... Whatever. I trust Pybuit enough to know that this... Thing, must be good in its own way.)

P: "Oh, a word of warning, little missy."

Pybuit honed the edge of the shears against the whetstone over and over again, its screeching sounds masking their conversation quite thoroughly.

P: "Care not to take any iron on you."

R: (Iron- ! Magnetism?) "... I see."

That small hint gave Roberia everything she needed to know about the weapon.

*** ***

The lack of apothecaries in Rulid delayed Katachi's journey in more ways than one. He spent unnecessary time on his search for herbs fruitlessly. He wasted valuable daylight tending to a wounded lady that for some unclear reason, wished to fight and kill him. The impediment in his progression was becoming more and more severe.

Katachi closely observed his surroundings for any useful medicine to grind into pulp. He took detours of all sorts – Climbing up ledges by the sides, walking full circles around countless trees and rocks all to look for the coincidental miracle. No such luck befell him and so he continued his journey searching high and low.

What he didn't expect to find was Jaanthro growing behind a mossy rock. Though the medicinal herb was commonplace around the south side of Findel, it was a rarity in the northern regions where the air was more humid.

K: (It's just Jaanthro. That won't help a lot, I still have plenty with me. I have to look for Mestiel-)

R: "There you are!!"

Something choked up his throat and churned the moment he heard that nostalgic voice.

K: (That voice... It's her again. I don't want to turn around, but she's going to attack my bag if I don't so I might as well be prepared to fight her.)

With repetition came experience. Katachi set his luggage down next to a mossy tree. He reluctantly turned around to face the familiar, slender figure of the lady with something new in her hands once again.

K: (What... What's that supposed to be? Is that... Is that a broken marble column tied to a rod with a handle? Where does she even get these weapons? Where does she even get the coin for the- No, more importantly, why would she even pay gold for that? Did she make them herself or something? And why is she still following me?)

R: (I should make sure that he's fighting me seriously.) "I won't hold back, and if you so much as loosen up on me I won't forgive you!"

K: (Is she... Trying to, to scare me or something? What purpose does that serve? She wants me to fight her, but she also wants me to be afraid and run from her?) "... Okay?"

Katachi wasn't old enough to understand the purpose of intimidation. He understood the pain of being bullied but such treatment only placed him in an inferior role. To have him come to terms with a psychological tactic like intimidation, which raised the opponent's guard when he was of an equal role, was far too early for the immature child. Such was the nature of his darkness stirring deep within, a misery that honed his perception and cynicism at the cost of his own growth.

R: (No response from him. His eyes aren't looking at me, but at this, this... Stupid-looking thing. He doesn't even have his dagger out.)

Roberia elevated the large, heavy weapon up vertically to a striking position and Katachi's eyes followed suit just as she predicted.

K: (All things aside, that looks like it'd hurt a lot... Maybe I should prepare myself? 恒定! Constant status – Self! Constant status – Dagger!)

R: (He's like a dumb animal. Just looking at him staring at my weapon and not watching the opponent carefully makes this really awkward.)

Roberia readied the blunt object on her right shoulder and prepared to swing it in a diagonal. She planted her foot against the ground and shot forward at Katachi with celerity that kicked up the leaves.

*** ***

K: (Fast!)

Katachi quickly swung the dagger to the front, intercepting the pillar's attack. A powerful grinding slam struck him from above and tiny pieces of rocks attached to the weapon came off and showered him. He felt the huge strength behind the swing from both the sword's weight and the girl's arms pressing down on him.

K: (It's a type of weapon that deliberately chunks off to bypass the opponent's defence? I can see how viable it is for those dust-like pieces to enter the opponent's eyes or nostrils when they lock blades... That's pretty troublesome. I'll have to stop it in place.)

Katachi pushed the pillar sword away and a golden word formed on the huge weapon. But in response Roberia forcefully pulled her weapon backwards, leaving a piece of the pillar the 定 was placed on suspended in the air.

K: (The stone piece has 定 on it instead? In a sense, I guess that is a way to overcome the fixation since that rock is counted as a detachable part of the weapon. If the weapon breaks apart like this, even I can't lock it and just walk away from her. I need to attack the core somehow.)

R: (He must have noticed that his magic is useless against me. How will he react now?)

Roberia ran forward and spun her body about, swinging the pillar in a wide arc and forcing Katachi to dodge towards her left. She slid on the grass with the rotational force and advanced her positioning to a strong and assertive stance, her back unexposed. He ran toward the suspended rock with the momentum of his dodge and pushed against it as a support to charge at her.

K: (A battle of strength won't work in my favour. I've seen how strong she is so I need to end it with speed. Take advantage of the fact that her weapon is heavy and bulky.)

Roberia, whom was already prepared to offset the weapon's weakness, swung the pillar sword at him hard. There was no advantage for Katachi to use at all. He held his hands up to cushion the impact and was sent flying backwards – Into the rock fixated in mid-air.

K: (!! My shoulder!) "Guhkgh- !"

He collided his left shoulder onto the fixated pillar fragment.

R: (His face changed! He definitely felt that!!)

K: (This pain... I'm pretty sure I was sent flying towards that rock I fixated. I remember taking attacks far more severe than this, like the time I fell from the scaffolding- !! Wait... It can't be... !)

Katachi wore a gobsmacked look upon his face.

K: (Two objects with the same precedence level, like the fixated rock and the constant me, function as normal... She's using that against me? I was wondering how I managed to feel the rock on my palm when I pressed against it to lunge at her, but this...)

Naturally, the most obvious result would be the Word of Power with a higher precedence level overcoming the inferior, but there were cases where the Words of Power with equal precedence levels clashed against each other. It boiled down to two possibilities – One, when the two Words of Power had inept users with the scarce knowledge they had about them.

R: (It's a window!)

K: (A diagonal swing!)

And the other, when the Word of Power was used against itself. Katachi held up the dagger into the trajectory of her attack and received the earth-shaking blow of the pillar. Once again the realization painfully paralysed his arm. The dagger he wielded had, too, been grinding against his body the whole time. He was simply ignorant of the fact that he could 'feel' the dagger in his hand because it was natural to hold an object and feel its presence in his own hands.

R: "Kh!" (He's still strong enough to block and his mobility is higher than mine. I should avoid close range fights when I have a bulky weapon or he will lunge at my face again.)

K: (This dagger is redundant!? No, maybe I can use the dagger somehow – Just not in this situation. She's the careful type – I should confuse her first to stall for time.)

As Roberia leapt backwards to distance herself he quickly sheathed his dagger and readied his bare hands.

R: (He sheathed his dagger? And he wants to fight me bare-handed? What is he thinking? It may not differ much from the wooden dagger, but I won't go easy on him just because he is unarmed!)

Roberia lunged forward with the pillar sword leaning on her shoulder and swung it down on his hand. The magnetic stones on the sword cracked and a loud, deafening sound of the stone smashing against something tougher was heard.

R: (He splintered the pillar with his fist!? Does he have some sort of magic that exponentially increases his power when the odds are against him?!)

K: (I didn't even feel my fist punching that! The dagger has indeed been hindering me. How did I not realize that?)

Katachi stumbled backwards on the mossy earth and knocked his body against the fixated rock again.

K: (Ah, what- Oh, this is still here. I should undo the bind.)

The 定 on the pillar fragment faded off. But, while Katachi turned towards Roberia's direction the rock suddenly retaliated. It sprung to life and knocked against the back of his knee, causing Katachi to stumble slightly. It then 'flew' back to the pillar sword and simply attached itself to the pillar sword's surface without refilling the small hole it made. For the child who knew not of magnetism, it was a true shock.

*** ***

K: (That rock can fly?! It flew, didn't it!? It definitely hit my leg there! Then, all those rocks are alive!?)

It was the first time Katachi witnessed a mysterious flying rock like that. The rocks on the pillar sword all looked like they were made from the same substance so it wasn't an understatement to assume that all the rocks could glide like that.

R: (If he has magic that makes him stronger the more unfavourable the battle is, then I have to beat him at an equal level? But, that blow just now... That's the first time I've seen his face show pain. I can't believe it, but as stupid as this weapon looks it's actually effective.)

K: (Those rocks look pretty menacing... What kind of spell do they possess? Is it derived from the true history of another country? What should I do, then? I won't have the luck of disarming her like the first two times – Her reach is much longer than mine and she should have already prepared against that by now.)

R: (No, wait! Think! What he's trying to do is to force me to his level to make me throw this weapon away. That's his goal – He must be trying to make me remove this weapon which is actually effective against him. He's not strong or fast enough to beat me, but I'm not powerful enough to break that defence of his neither. I need to trap him somehow and make him draw his dagger!)

K: (That tree to her left seems like a good place to take cover behind. If she smashes through that, maybe I can get to her back? Then... Get her tangled in the branches of the tree and fixate the whole tree, perhaps?)

R: (He's looking about. Is he trying to use the surroundings to his advantage? I can't give him time to think about that. I'll taunt him if I have to!) "Are you so confident that you can take me bare-handed!? Don't underestimate me!"

Roberia lunged forward and thrust her pillar sword at Katachi. He dodged it just barely, forcing him to ram against a tree.

R: (I can't give him time to think. I have to choke him out. He'll have no way to hurt me from my reach and he'll be forced to cut the tree behind him!) "Dodging?! What, is that the only thing you're capable of!?"

K: (! Only thing... Capable of? Wait a minute, I'm not restricted to 定 alone. I have 解, 安 and 信 as well! I only know 安心 for 安, and I know 相信 for 信. But I know ample about 解, don't I? 解释, 解决, 解脱, 解开, there's a lot of options available.)

She heaved her whole body weight towards her right, sandwiching Katachi's neck between the tree and the blade. For some reason his flesh itself felt like the face of a mountain and the rugged surface of the pillar sword did not seem to affect his skin. She slowly shifted the pillar sword by twisting it in alternate revolutions towards the tip so the distance between them was the greatest, but oddly enough his neck was unscathed from the friction.

R: "Dodge your way out of this!!" (What is this nonsense!? He's tougher than a boulder! It's as though he turned the pillar into waxed cobble, or soap or something!)

K: (I feel... Strangely moved. My neck is being pressed against, but it doesn't hurt like my hands or my back. This inability to feel anything... So this is what using the Word of Power properly feels like.)

She continued to clamp Katachi and inclined her body weight against the tip of the pillar. The tree briefly shook at the pressure from the hold.

R: (What's he planning? Isn't he going to use his dagger to cut his way out? Come on, take the dagger out already!)

K: (The most appropriate words to release the rocks from its core would be... Ah, I got it. 解散! Disband objects – Rocks on the pillar!)

The rocks on the pillar sword explosively bolted out in directions away from the weapon's core.

R: "!" (What the-)

All Katachi needed was a single glance at the dull black rod within.

CHAPTER 31

R: "Come... On!"

Roberia tugged, yanked, pulled and struggled with all her might at the pillar sword. But all her strength couldn't move the weapon fixated in space.

K: (Maybe now's a good time to dissuade her from attacking me any further.) "Why are you attacking me anyway? Won't the sentries at Rulid make for a better sparring opponent?"

The look on Katachi's eyes indicated that he was beginning to grow weary of her tireless pursuit.

R: "And let your Word of Power slip from my fingers? I don't think so. I'll take that sigil of yours and bring glory to my family."

K: (So she was after my 定 after all...) "I suggest against that. Surely there are better ways of bringing said glory to your-"

R: "Enough of your cheap excuses!!"

The roar was accompanied with a silence of the forest.

R: "Do you still not understand why I am doing this? I must best you in combat."

K: "Why?"

The lack of cultural knowledge coupled with the opponent's disfavour of combat made Roberia relax herself unconsciously – Something she would never do had Katachi attacked her proactively in the previous skirmishes. Roberia leaned against the pommel of the now immobile sword to recover her stamina.

R: "Seeing how you're a strange Findeli with an Ohdean descent, I suppose you don't know of our traditions."

K: "What kind of tradition requires you to kill others like that?"

R: "It's not necessary to kill your opponents. I simply have to defeat you to show that I have improved."

K: "Improved from what?"

R: "From when I lost to you."

Katachi had a brief glint of light in his eyes as he came to a simple realization.

K: (That's easy, isn't it? Just beat someone that is stronger than me, someone that has defeated me before.) "Then... Go beat someone else that has defeated me. That should suffice."

R: "It doesn't work like that! It's the experience and growth factor from defeating you that is important! The point is to overcome your tricks and defeat you, not to rely on someone else's convenient strength!"

K: (How troublesome... Isn't it sort of bad that she's out here with her life on the line like that? Won't her family worry for her safety? It would be better if she returned home and worked as a farmer instead of joining the knights in Rugnud.) "Then why don't you just give up on being a warrior?"

R: "Is that supposed to be an insult?"

K: (That doesn't sound good.) "No, I-"

R: "You want me to give up on being a warrior?"

K: "Well, uh, no, uh... Yeah."

R: (What a way to say it in my face. I thought he would have been more tactful at least, but I hate inconsiderate people like him who don't pause to consider the hardships others have been through.) "The next time we meet, you best ready yourself."

With a brief warning and a gesture of running her thumb over her neck, Roberia picked up her light bag and hurried off.

K: (Was it something I said?)

*** ***

"Halt! State your business!"

Roberia cut through the forest toward the neighbouring town Fereport because it was the shortest route to a large town with much commerce. However, her emergence from the woods instead of the cobblestone road was highly suspicious so the sentries held her back.

R: (Tight security... Is there a big event or an important official present?) "I came to purchase goods."

"The search warrant issued by the Findel Magus Association requires all magi to cooperate. Men! Search her thoroughly for- !"

An intimidating stare from Roberia made the sentry reconsider his standard procedural checks.

R: (Lecherous bastard, you've seen me before when I was en route to Rulid. How dare you try to cop a feel!)

"... Never mind that! Let her pass."

*** ***

The daunting task for Mestiel was never-ending. The futile search eventually brought him to a small run-down shack.

K: (A hut... Maybe I can find someone that knows where I can get some Mestiel?)

The shack was of a small, rather shabby structure. The log walls with stones attached were rotten and its condition was sub-par. There was nothing that remotely resembled furniture and the windows mere holes in the wall. The roof of the hut was covered with flayed and disorganised stones and hay which reflected on the oversights of the carpenter.

As he walked in, a child younger than Katachi was tending to an adult woman lying on the gaudy slipshod bed. The two blankly exchanged glances with each other.

"Who are you?"

K: (Oh my. This was someone's house after all. I invaded their privacy...) "I am sorry for walking in like that. My name is Katachi."

"I don't really mind that you walked in. But could you do me a favour and help look for some water or herbs for me?"

K: (! He mentioned herbs? Then, maybe he's knowledgeable in herbs too. I suppose I should help him.) "What do you need?"

"My sister's suffering from a fever, so something like tea to clean her stomach would be good. Also, maybe something that can soothe her throat like Intundia would be great."

K: (! Intundia!? That's a high-grade herb! How am I supposed to find a high-grade herb around here-... Unless, they grew some? Did they grow any?) "Have you planted any Intundia of your own?"

"Uh... No, but I heard from some adults that Intundia can soothe a person's throat, stomach and intestines."

Katachi's sigh after that over-enthusiastic response was almost tragic.

K: (So he learnt it from hearsay... It makes sense, I can't possibly find something as valuable as wild Intundia about this region anyway. It may be worth helping him though, he knows this area more than I do. Maybe I can find Mestiel around here and his advice, however tiny, will definitely hasten the search.)

That optimism was bound to delude him time and again.

K: "Well, we can't use Intundia, that's for sure. But I'll see what I can do."

"Please do."

K: (Okay, soothing a person's throat and a cleansing effect... Molwed nectar and Pixle tea should do nicely.) "Wait here. I'll be back soon."

*** ***

Roberia had a deadly, frightening look on her face as she withdrew the pouch of regal coins from her satchel. The atmosphere of the armoury turned ominous when she punted the door open.

R: (Looks like I've been approaching it from the wrong angle all the long. The point of consistency in these three skirmishes would be that all my attacks are physical in nature.)

She had a horrifying expression that was a mix between an epiphany and teeming rage.

R: (But the pillar weapon was technically a weapon that uses magnetism, which can be associated with earth. It's possible the child reinforced the pillar fragment with a spell of sorts when he pressed against it to rush at me. Maybe his sigil prevents blunt force, but not magic.)

An imposing walk toward the blacksmith, hinting at her intolerance for those who obstructed her, made the two other customers give way to her stride. She pinched a coin between her fingers and emptied the contents of the coarse pouch onto the table.

R: (It's a disgrace for a Knight to use a weapon that is not reliant on the wielder's skill... But if this is what it takes to turn the odds, then so be it.) "Magical or not, pricey or otherwise, I don't care how crazy, obscure or weird it is. Get me your most powerful weapon."

The shopkeeper could only nod timidly and oblige to her demands.

*** ***

Katachi nipped a bit of salt and sprinkled it gently over the roots and stem of the Molwed. It seemed to screech just a little, perceiving Katachi's presence as a threat, but the plant quickly gave way to its dehydration.

K: (That should be enough salt... I think?)

Katachi placed an empty vial beneath the spongy portion and gently squeezed the Molwed flower. The lucrative juices seeped from its pores and filled up the vial at the bottom to its brim easily.

K: (Still no Mestiel around... There are clumps of Curamel and Tinjengel growing about the riverbed, though.)

He capped the glass vial and secured the cork well.

K: (I hope the nectar isn't too salty. I should dilute it a bit before serving it to her.)

Katachi grabbed whatever else he needed and headed back to the hut.

First, he opened a vial containing a crushed pink herb and left it out onto the windowsill-Or rather, the rim of the hole in the wall. A mild bitter odour gradually filled the room. Next, he took out another vial of Pixle leaves and placed a few in a ceramic pot with water simmering over a small fire. While the tea was being heated, Katachi opened the vial of Molwed nectar, sniffed at it to ensure he retrieved the correct vial and poured a bit of water within.

Then, Katachi slowly shifted the lady's posture to an upright position before having her down the vial of Molwed nectar. With a cleared throat the irritation from within could finally be relieved. The lady coughed violently and laid back on the uncomfortable hay pillow. After that he poured the tea into a cup carefully, preventing the Pixle leaves from leaving the pot. The lady sat upright by herself and slowly drank the tea.

A soothing, lukewarm burst of heat dispersed from her gullet throughout her body and she finally relaxed. The itch on her throat was removed, her body loosened considerably, and her face let up with a peaceful smile. The lady gave a brief bow and some hand gestures Katachi didn't understand before returning to sleep.

"Thank you! Thank you so much!"

K: (The lady seems to be deaf... It's sad that I can't ask her about it.) "If you want to thank me, I'd like to ask you a question."

"Sure! Anything!"

K: (Let's hope he knows what Mestiel is.) "Have you seen any Mestiel about? I'm in need of some."

"Mestiel? I... I don't know what Mestiel is."

K: "It's fine. Thank you for your honesty."

It could not be helped that he knew little of the plants when the child did not find the herbs himself despite their residence near the abode. Katachi exited the hut with down feelings.

K: (What a big shame. I thought I'd have a shot at that herb- Herb?! Wait, my Jaanthro! I forgot to take it back!)

Katachi hurried to the windowsill and corked the vial of crushed pink herbs before placing it into his bag.

*** ***

R: (I've placed everything on this gamble. I won't hold back this time. With this... I will have my victory, or I will go back a shamed princess who can't even beat an Ohdean miser. There is nothing but my pride to lose now.)

K: (I feel so insecure without the ingredients for the salve. I'm low on Mestiel so I have to find some fast. I don't have a mortar and pestle, though I can always use the one at home if nothing else.)

The two gradually approached an encounter neither could afford to back away from.

CHAPTER 32

As Katachi trudged onward through the forest area, a familiar scent in the air prompted him slowly toward higher ground. He eventually arrived at a flight of smooth stones laid out like stairs.

K: (It's been a while.)

He took off his bag and placed it on the ground gently. The smooth stone wasn't as slippery as it appeared to be, but a little caution wouldn't hurt a child wearing sabots not meant for vertical travel. After a few minutes of climbing the stone steps, Katachi reached the top.

He leaned against a familiar tree and glanced down at the small, haven-like meadow from the vantage point – The meadow where he would watch the Plaincoat Sheep graze. The lookout where he would longingly stare at the children of Mielfeud play with each other and tease the sheep merrily. His gaze wandered to the nostalgic root ladder.

K: (I used to climb that a lot, didn't I?)

Katachi often used the ladder repeatedly in the past but that ceased completely when Mother Rinnesfeld claimed it was too dangerous. A strong, reminiscent urge overcame him and he was compelled to scale the roots once more. He slowly made his way down and landed on the soft fragrant grass.

K: (I'm back.)

The place where he was found by Mother Rinnesfeld. The herb ledge – His very first, and perhaps his fondest memory of Mielfeud. Katachi took off his sabots and felt the warmth of the earth beneath his feet.

K: (The soft moss between my toes... It's so welcoming.)

Usually Katachi would have reached the ledge via a sandy path. But, having taken the root ladder his old habits kicked in and he sat upon the strange rock instead of the stump. The neglect on the rock caused moss to grow over it thinly while the stump now had a pansy sprouting from it.

K: (These curves, this shape... It feels good to be back. How long have I been away for? I hope Mother does not have too hard a time managing the church. I miss her.)

A red Grovelark chirped merrily and flew onto a vine, pecking at the little aphids on the trees.

K: (That red-haired lady... Does her family miss her? She's fighting to become stronger, likely to protect her family and home. Even if she didn't want to, she probably doesn't have much of a choice.)

Katachi stared at the little bird as it took off in search of more food.

K: (That virtuous personality ought to be sung of. She's ambitious, righteous, strong and devoted. She is a great fortune for anyone whom would befriend or ally with her.)

He frowned briefly at the pain that everyone had to endure. Should the day come where all of the world's descendants would be free from the darkness of these sigils, a world where Mother Rinnesfeld's role would be unnecessary...

K: (I should head back while the sun hasn't reached its peak.)

... And yet, no matter how bright and hopeful that wish was, it was also a future where he would never belong.

*** Achievement: The Child Who Never Smiles ***

Katachi finally arrived at the town he grew up in. And, as predicted the red-haired lady was waiting for him at the entrance.

K: (It's her.)

Roberia unfolded her crossed arms and pushed herself forward from a leaning pose to a dueling stance, withdrawing the sword with a curved blade. Katachi put down his bag to a side and faced her with grieving, headstrong determination.

R: (Losing to someone like him, a commoner like him nobody recognizes... It is the ultimate humiliation especially with a weapon like this.) "I will make this painless. Brace yourself, Kotsuba Katachi."

K: "Do we really have to do this? Where did you get all these weapons anyway?"

R: "This will be the last one you will see, I assure you." (Because everything I have is now on the line. This battle will make me... Or break me.)

K: "Is there really no alternative to this?"

R: "Enough talk! I will end you right here!"

Roberia primed her new weapon towards Katachi's body.

K: (Does she not see...)

With a silver glow and a howl, a powerful gust of wind lashed forth from the sword with such ferocity that the dust kicked up and distorted the air around the blade.

K: (... How much her family misses her? 恒定. Constant status – Self.)

A golden word formed on Katachi, this time in plain view without being concealed underneath his ragged shirt... Since there was no real need to hide the 定 in the town that branded him a heretic for it. The wind roared past the child yet he remained unmoved.

R: (What? He didn't get hurt by that?! Does that sigil defend more than just physical attacks?!)

Katachi slowly walked forward towards Roberia.

K: (This is different from the last weapon. There's nothing that takes advantage of my limitations, all she's using is a sword carved with excerpts from Byrh's legends. But, the winds are distorting the image of the blade so I can't place my 定 from here. I need to get closer.)

R: (He's going to do it again...) "No! Don't... Don't come any closer!"

She knew what it meant for him to approach her. The routine was about to happen all over again – He would close the gap, fixate her weapon and disarm her entirely. Even before the actual battle began Roberia foresaw what was to come. She swung wild blasts of air and continuous streaming gales towards Katachi to little effect.

The house behind him eroded and chipped off from the howling winds, yet as powerful as the enchanted blade was it proved ineffective against Katachi's 定. Such was the nature of the accursed sigils known as the Words of Power, for Man to indiscriminately hate and wish harm upon the Scholars. A Segus follower in possession of a sigil was no different from heresy in many ways.

R: (This is far less useful than the pillar sword Pybuit sold me!)

Roberia tried leaping backwards and moving away from Katachi by using the winds circling the blade to bolster her mobility. She threw herself about everywhere but she didn't have ample time or training to be accustomed with such a bizarre and curious form of mobility. As such, Katachi quickly caught up after a few attempts.

K: (She's done plenty against a Scholar like myself. So, for the family that misses her so, for the village welcoming her return, I will stop her here. 'All of danger upon my flesh, for the incapable deserve a reprieve.')

Katachi was now less than a metre away from Roberia. The uncontrollable winds which were supposed to lift her off and increase their distance steered the sword diagonally at his body only for the blade to be stuck on his shoulder.

R: "Wha-..."

K: "Please, give up."

A 定 formed on the wind blade and Roberia was forced into a state where she must face her opponent unarmed. Though he was a passive child who harboured no malice, that was tantamount to defeat as knights should always expect their foes to strike with the intent to kill.

R: "No!!"

Roberia's face twisted into one of pain and anguish over the routine that, once more, could not be prevented. She knelt on her knees and clutched her torso tightly.

R: (I'm sorry, father, brother, everyone... I have failed. I can't even beat a miserly Scholar.) "I can't go home like this... I have failed."

K: (She's worrying for her family... Perhaps her family is under some sort of threat? Maybe she hasn't reached a point where she can repel the threats to her family and farm?)

The end was nigh.

R: (Living on is useless now. I lost. It's a complete, utter failure. I got in over my head and thought that I could handle him myself, but this... This dirtbag defeated me.) "Put an end to my misery. Kill me."

K: "I wouldn't do that even if you paid me to. Segus forbids killing."

That quote in itself amplified her pain tenfold.

R: (Segus, he says? This... This is the ultimate smack of disgrace. The worst. I lost to a peace-loving Segus follower. A passive, weak Segus follower younger than me who doesn't even train himself strictly, one who advocates peace and dismisses conflict.) "You're a follower of Segus?"

K: (She looks even sadder than before! Why?!) "Yes... I am... ?"

She could barely believe her ears.

R: (My life is over. Utterly, utterly over. It would be something else if I was forced into servitude, but this...) "I lost to a Segus follower... My worst nightmare brought to life."

K: (She seems pretty down... What... What do I do? Should I...)

THE MOMENT THAT DEFINED FATE

What should Kotsuba Katachi do in this situation?

Herald) Persuade her to go back to her family.

Messiah) Work out her problem and give her advice.

Of Bad Ends And Bloopers) Put an end to her misery.

Endus Reignum) Put an end to her nightmare.

Printed in the United States
By Bookmasters